FALL
OF THE
KINGS

A. J. WALKER

Fall of the Kings by A. J. Walker

KARTANIA
NORTHLAND
RIDGEBACK MTNS
GRANDWOOD MTNS
HIGHBORN BAY
MT. SWIFTCURRENT
MT PARSIGHT
MT BLOODTOOTH
WESTLAND
EVERLIGHT KINGDOM
NAGANO
GRANDWOOD
SHARP STONE MTNS
FROZEN-TIP MTNS
EASTLAND MTNS
EAST-LAND
BROOKSIDE
THE RIVER LANDS
GLACIAL MELT BAYS
MT DREND
ARGON
ROLLO ISLANDS
BAREBACK PLAINS
MARAUDER'S SEA
BLACK WATER BAY
AQUINA
BAREBACK PENINSULA
STARVE TO DEATH PLATEAU
ROUGH WATER BAY
HIGHSIDE PLAINS
N
W
E
S
PELAGIC OCEAN
HIGHLAND PEAKS
KINGSTON
SPLIT MTN
GOBLIN'S GROVE
YELLOW SANDS DESERT
RAMHORN
SOUTHLAND
CRESCENT ISLAND
KEWIAN ISLANDS
DRAKESHEAD

CHAPTER ONE

Hope

ax cast a troubled glance at the others. Seeing similar lines of concern etched across their faces brought him little comfort. Thomas looked the worse for wear, his pale complexion a ghostly white against the dark night. His bright blue eyes dulled, and his normally smooth sandy blond hair was ragged and dirt-brown from the rough escape through the Grandwood Forest. Max felt for his companion, Thomas' pain was nearly palpable as he knelt near the fire, holding Kirsten's limp body in his fatigued state. Max's gaze focused on the streaks in her arms, the red darkening in the light of the fire. He followed the streaks to their source, the palm-sized chunk of flesh missing from her left shoulder. If it weren't for the injury, she would mirror her brother's appearance. Kirsten's bloody wound had been left exposed when they tore apart her sleeve. Despite how hard each of them tried, the blue-hued crystal's mystical powers eluded them.

A groan from inside the tent brought Max's attention back to the man who'd met them in the woods and was now speaking to someone in the nearby tent. Max pushed his grimy hand through his black hair, its length two months longer and his appearance more rugged than before. Traveling cross-continent and battling creatures he'd previously only heard rumor of had brought more muscle and definition to his slender form. Keeping his eyes fixed on the tent, he wondered if an ordinary man would know how to help them with something that clearly began with magic. Max heard fumbling and then cursing before a second man stumbled out into the night. Seeing that the middle-aged man was still half-asleep, Max hoped he could truly be of some use to their unique situation. He was pale-skinned and brown-haired like most Westlanders, but stood taller than his countrymen. His build was lean yet defined, letting Max know he didn't sit idle for long.

Finding his footing, the man pulled up the collar on his wool coat and stepped closer into the light of the fire. Before Max or any of his group could offer an explanation of what had happened to them, the man snapped out of his drowsiness and moved quickly to kneel beside Thomas who continued to hold Kirsten in his arms. He watched as the man examined her overall appearance, muttering to himself.

"What do you make of it Rune?" his bearded companion asked in a gravelly voice. The burly lookout had spotted Max and the others as they passed below their camp.

"She's been bitten," Rune said in a soft voice, one that didn't match his outward appearance. He passed the back of his hand over Kirsten's face. "Still breathing," he added as his hand continued down to her wrist, "weak and thready pulse."

Max moved around to get a closer look at the man's examination process. Standing behind Thomas, he watched as Rune reached into his right coat pocket, pulled out a pair of spectacles and slid them onto his narrow face. Taking Kirsten's infected arm, Rune held it close, studying it intently. His gaze hovered over the bite as he mumbled under his breath.

Raising his hazel eyes from the wound, Rune found his companion and said, "Saaja, bring me my clean cloths and a bowl of water." Rune turned his gaze back to Kirsten and asked, "How long ago was she bitten?"

Thomas was first to speak, "The goblin. She um… It was…" he said in a trembling voice, the words falling flat as he attempted to answer the simple question.

"It's been at least four hours. Maybe six," Britt said, her tone commanding authority and drawing Rune's attention. He did a subtle double-take upon realizing there was a Rollo Islander among the small group. Her self-assuredness told him that she was a leader among her people. How she came to be traveling with these desperate Westlanders was another story, he was sure.

Turning back to Kirsten and placing the back of his hand on her forehead, Rune shook his head saying, "No. That's not possible. This is a goblin bite and when a goblin chooses to release its venom," he shrugged, "let's just say we humans don't last very long. Once the venom is injected, you have less than an hour to remove the affected area before it spreads."

"She's not lying," Thomas said, finding his voice again.

"The bite happened earlier this evening just outside Grandwood. We've been walking for hours since then," Max said, feeling the need to defend them.

Saaja interrupted Rune's attention with the retrieval of his requested items, pushing them onto the man.

Taking the bowl of water from his broad-shouldered companion, Rune held it in his hand as he dabbed a white cloth and began to clean Kirsten's mangled shoulder. After several passes, dabbing and wiping around the bite, Rune said, "The amount of dried blood in this wound does seem to confirm the timeline you claim. Judging by our proximity to Grandwood, it's nothing short of impressive that you managed to come this far so quickly." Rune paused, pointing a bony finger to the edge of the wound. "You can see that the blood has crusted suggesting there's been at least an hour or more since the wound was inflicted. When I remove the newly hardened scabbing, the blood begins to seep, suggesting the wound is fresh, but, as I said, I would say it's at least an hour."

Max watched as Rune pondered the situation, rubbing his forehead in thought. Before anyone could ask him his opinion of Kirsten's status, Rune continued, "The red streaking extending from the bite and moving into the veins is consistent with a goblin's bite, as are the markings around the bite's edges. I've been practicing army medicine for decades and I've never seen anyone with this type of wound survive for more than an hour, unless the limb is removed before the infection spreads." Rune's gaze fell to Max, "Goblins are magical beings and when they deliver a venomous bite, there's no stopping it. How is it possible that she's survived for four or even six hours?"

Britt's dark-eyed look told Max that she wondered the same thing, but feared telling him about the sapphire's power. Max heard all too often of the things some Westlanders would do to someone who claimed to have magical powers. *He's helping us now, but if he found out that the sapphire had powers, we might need to make another escape,* Max thought to himself as he broke away from Britt's charcoal face.

Hearing him say the words before Max could stop him, Thomas stammered, "She has this special necklace. It, um, started glowing." Folding back the collar of Kirsten's shirt, Thomas exposed the pink-hued sapphire clasped around his sister's neck. In that moment, Max noticed the stone shown more dimly than it had before, but its appearance was enough to cause a gasp from Rune.

"So the rumors are true," Rune whispered. "The crystals do exist."

Max held his breath, stiffening as he waited for Rune's next course of action.

Rune leaned in closer, pulling back more of Kirsten's shirt, exposing the streaks spreading down her chest and fading around her heart. Bo reached his tanned hand out and stopped Rune from revealing any more of Kirsten's chest. Max could tell by the look his brother gave the doctor that he didn't appreciate Rune's searching eyes. Exhaling through his nostrils and giving Bo a stern look, Rune flexed his narrow jaw and said, clearly irritated, "I'm a professional, if you want my expert opinion, I need to see her," he paused, "symptoms," and he motioned to the streaking across her chest.

Bo relented, withdrawing his muscular arm and Max could see his brother's well-defined cheeks flushing despite the dim light. Still keeping their eyes fixed on him, anticipating that the doctor might snatch the sapphire necklace, Max and Britt remained poised and ready to pounce.

Rune pulled Kirsten's shirt back, exposing her and showing the effects of the crystal. "Remarkable," he murmured.

"That's a poudrettite!" Saaja gasped. The man's sudden exclamation made Max keenly aware of the lookout's presence over their shoulders.

Thomas hastily moved Kirsten's shirt; he, too, was caught off guard, now realizing that the strange man was still observing them.

"What's a poudrettite?" Rune asked.

"It's a type of rare stone," Saaja explained. "My granddad used to collect rare things, he did. He used to show us his precious finds when we came to visit him, and I remember that one. It's unique because of its pink color." Max could hear the pride in his voice for contributing to the conversation.

"Will it cure her?" Thomas asked. Max now heard hope in his voice as Thomas perked up, a hint of color returning to his face.

Rune carefully peeled open one of Kirsten's eyelids and Max wondered what kind of information the man would gain by covering her open eye with one of his hands and pulling it back, examining her eye carefully. After repeatedly covering and uncovering her open eye, Rune answered, "I'm not sure. The use of magical items isn't anything I've ever dealt with before. I'm trained to treat mortal beings with modern medicine. The fact that this girl isn't dead already is astonishing. Clearly this poudrettite crystal is staving off the effects of the goblin venom and is most likely a host to some kind of magical force."

Max started to relax slightly, feeling that the doctor

didn't have a desire to take the sapphire for himself or harm them for having a magical crystal. Rune returned his focus to the bite, wetting the cloth and dabbing at the sore.

"Well," Britt said, frustration in her voice. "Can you help her?"

Rune wrung out the cloth, expunging the blood. He sighed, "The good news is she's stable."

"That's not what she asked," Max said, wondering if there was hope for Kirsten.

"If you want me to help her any further, I will need to remove the affected area," Rune said, pulling the wire-rimmed glasses from his face and placing them neatly into his pocket.

"You mean cut off her arm?" Thomas asked in alarm.

Rune nodded.

"The whole thing?" he asked.

Rune sighed shortly, "In my experience, the only way to prevent death from a venomous goblin bite is to cut the limb off before the infection reaches the rest of the body. Even then, I've only had success with those in whom the venom hasn't spread beyond the injured limb. The veins in her shoulder and chest on the left side of her body are already infected. At this stage, even if I were to take the limb, I'm afraid the infection would continue to spread."

"Then what are you telling us? She's a lost cause?" Thomas asked, his breathing increasing rapidly.

"What I'm saying is that the only thing keeping her alive right now is that necklace," Rune said, pointing at the pink sapphire. "The venom could continue to spread, but as long as she's wearing the necklace, she should remain stable."

"So, that's it?" Bo interjected. "Just keep the necklace on and send us on our way?"

Rune stood. Rising slightly taller than Bo, he met Bo's gaze, which vacillated between angry and terrified, "I'm afraid I can't help her. The level of surgery required to remove all of the infection is beyond my skill level. Even if surgery worked, out here on the run it's almost sure there would be infection. The possibility of her surviving such a procedure in these conditions is marginal at best."

"No!" Thomas shouted. The outburst caught the whole group off guard. Tears welled in Thomas' eyes. "I can't lose her. She's all I have left. Please, you can't let her die!"

Rune shrugged, "I'm sorry, but that's all I can tell you from a medical standpoint."

"Is there anyone you know who might be qualified to help in our current situation?" Max asked calmly, trying to keep a positive vibe among the group.

Rune pondered the question and looked to Saaja, "With the current state of activity in Brookside and the Riverlands, I'm not sure anyone's available. Even if they were…"

Max cut him off at the mention of his hometown, "What's happened in Brookside?"

Rune raised an eyebrow, "You haven't heard? I assumed being in Grandwood you would've heard by now. The entire nation of Westland is being taken by force. It started with the coastal towns. Grandwood followed by Brookside nearly three weeks later. Ever since then there have been waves of occupation by foreign soldiers. They fly the black and red banners of the King's Army from

Southland," Max watched Rune eye Bo in the officer's uniform he'd taken as a disguise from a soldier in Grandwood. "Brookside and the villages continuing up the valley are swarmed with supporters of this new Emperor who's been backing the insurgence. Last I heard, the governor of Mergwood, as they're calling it now, was named warden of Westland."

Max asked, "And the people? What's become of the people in Brookside?"

"Anyone who opposes the army is quickly snuffed out," Rune replied.

"This can't be happening," Max said, shaking his head. "How has no one stood up against them?"

"There is a resistance," Rune continued. "They have a large encampment in the Riverlands. It's the only place where the locals can outsmart the insurgents and keep their location secret. There are more doctors and healers in their company."

"How do you know this?" Bo asked.

"It's where we've come from," Rune replied.

"How would we find the camp? The Riverlands are vast and we don't have that kind of time," Max said.

Rune narrowed his eyes, "By the way, what was it you five were doing near Grandwood that got you mixed up in a goblin attack? It's not very common to see a warrior of the Rollo Islands in these parts, traveling cross country in possession of a magic crystal, no less."

Max motioned to Thomas to remain silent this time. He didn't want them giving Rune and Saaja too much information, even if they were possible allies.

Britt responded, "We're crewmen of a merchant ship

that was commandeered in Grandwood's port. The governor and his armed militia took our goods and sent us away. As we were preparing to leave, the town was attacked by a horde of goblins. We barely escaped with our lives and she was bitten in the process."

Rune nodded, though Max saw from his expression that he didn't put too much trust into what Britt told him. "Merchants would explain why you're not armed. Though I doubt any of you have ever worked a single day as a trader, you're no enemy to us. We're on our way to Merg, er, Grandwood rather, on a recruiting mission for the Resistance."

"You'll have a hard time getting anyone in or out of there, I'm afraid," Max said.

"The whole town's been overrun. There's a magical force there, a powerful one. It keeps those who enter through its portals trapped behind a barrier. But after the goblins attacked, who knows if it's still up," Britt said.

"How'd you escape if there's a force keeping everyone inside?" Rune asked and Max could tell he was fishing for more information about who they really were.

Max shrugged. "Could've been her necklace for all we know," he lied.

"Yeah," Rune said his gaze flickering between Britt and Max.

"You think anyone survived?" Saaja interrupted.

"Hard to say for sure," Max said, looking this time to the broad man. "I'd bet anyone safely locked inside their homes made it through alright. But if the barrier keeping everyone trapped inside is still operational, the goblins might be stuck there, too."

"True, but goblins are magical creatures and crafty in that. If they found a way inside, they could find a way out. You found a way, so they could too," Rune said.

"What about my sister?" Thomas said, trying to draw the conversation back onto what mattered most. Max saw the pain in his face again as Thomas asked, "What are we going to do?"

Rune snapped his fingers. The sudden movement startled Max into nearly attacking the man. "I've never met him, but there's rumor of an old wise man who lives just outside Brookside. I believe he's called Slamoran or something," Rune said.

"Solomon!" Bo blurted out.

"Yeah, that's it," Rune said. "Maybe he can help you? I've heard rumors he has a wealth of knowledge about magic and the like."

"Why didn't I think of that before?" Max said, cursing himself.

"So you know him?" Rune asked.

"Yeah, I know him," Max said, then stopped himself from revealing any more about his backstory.

"But old Sol lives at least four days' walk from here," Bo said. "And that's on rested legs and without the extra weight of someone to carry."

"It's closer than the Riverlands and at least we know where it is," Max said.

"Do you think Kirsten can make it that long?" Bo asked.

Thomas nodded, "She's tough and stubborn as all get out. Kirsten will hang in there as long as she knows there's a chance." Thomas bent over and whispered into his sister's ear. His words were gentle, but Max could still make them out over the sounds of the crackling fire. "We're taking you to someone who can help us, okay? Kirsten, listen to me, you have to hold on as long as you can. I can't lose you. We're going to get help, you just need to hold on."

Max turned, recalling the horses they'd passed when approaching the camp. "If we took one of your horses we'd get there in a day," he said.

"There're four others in our group. Our mission is of great importance to the cause and we'll be needing those horses for our journey. I'm sorry you've been dealt this difficult hand, but there could be people we can help in light of what's happened in Grandwood. We can't let you take the horses; they're essential for the greater good of the Resistance," Rune declared.

"We don't need to keep them," Britt argued. "We can bring them back after we get help."

Rune considered it briefly, but shook his head, "How would you find us? That would be at least three days. We'll be gone from here and getting the horses back to us would be too difficult."

"What if you came with us?" Bo asked.

"No," Rune said. "I'm sorry, I truly am, but I can't help you."

"Wait," Max said. "Bo's got a point. What if you came with us? Not as our doctor, but as our transporter. You could escort us, with the horses to Solomon's, about a day's ride. Drop us off there, then turn around and lead your horses back here. If you're planning to go to Grandwood in its current state, you'll need to spend at least a day scouting it out before entering. You can meet back up with your group in a planned location."

Rune grew quiet for several long moments, "But if my group needs my medical expertise while I'm gone, they could suffer."

"Maybe not," Saaja said. "Ophelia is getting a solid handle on things. You even said so yourself."

Rune's glare told Max he knew Saaja's comment held weight. Sighing, Rune said, "If I help you, I'll be needing compensation."

"Done," Bo said. "Name your price?"

Rune leveled his gaze on them, "If I help you, you'll need to tell me why you were really in Grandwood. And if it's for the reason I suspect, and after this goblin bite issue is resolved, you'll volunteer your services to our cause by joining our forces in the Riverlands."

Looking to his brother, Max already knew his answer. He nodded to Bo and leaned toward Britt to consult their captain. After a hushed discussion of their options, Britt came to her conclusion. Glancing at Kirsten, who lay limply in her brother's arms, Max offered his hand in agreement to Rune's terms and said, "I can't vouch for Thomas, or Kirsten, if she makes it through this alive, but for my brother and me, we'll join your cause."

Rune nodded, moving his gaze to Britt, "And you? Will you join the revolution to save your friend?"

Max saw Britt flare her black nostrils before replying, "I don't agree with the tactics you're using to drag us into this mess, but since we're already fighting for the same cause, I don't see why we wouldn't join forces. I won't guarantee that I'll remain in Westland, but I can guarantee that I'll oppose anyone who sides with the imperial forces trying to consume the free nations of Kartania."

Rune's cheeks plumped slightly as he grinned, "Good. Then you can have our horses. I'll ride with you to the Brookside area, but will have to turn around and rendezvous with my companions again. I'm sorry I can't be of more help to you."

Bo started to help Thomas as they lifted Kirsten in preparation to leave.

Rune wrapped his coat closed by crossing his arms again and started toward the tents. "You're welcome to the warmth of our fire and a meal before we leave in the light of day."

"We're not leaving now?" Thomas asked, halfway through lifting his sister.

Rune stopped just outside the tent and faced his guests, "You are tired from your escape. It's clear you're all exhausted. A little rest will do you good and we can leave in the morning. The trail will be more easily navigated in daylight."

"But she might die," Max said.

"Your friend is stable. Yes, it's true she's in grave peril, but I'm willing to wager the sapphire she has is imbued with a potent magic. If it's held for this long, it will hold until we get to Brookside."

"Do you treat all of your patients this way?" Max said, trying to encourage Rune to agree to a more hasty departure.

"Those are my terms. You're welcome to walk if you won't wait, but if you want the horses, then you'll wait until morning," Rune said as he disappeared through the tent door.

"Who does this guy think he is?" Bo growled, helping

Thomas gently lower Kirsten back down onto the ground near the fire.

"We could just take the horses now," Britt suggested.

Saaja stepped in closer, and Max became keenly aware of the long broadsword he held as he raised it, resting the flat of the blade on his shoulder. "I wouldn't do that if I were you," he said sternly, in offering fair warning.

"Well, it doesn't make any sense to walk. We'll get there way faster if we just wait," Thomas reluctantly agreed as he let go of Kirsten for the first time since they'd arrived. He sat on the ground, carefully propping Kirsten's head on his lap.

Max could tell Thomas was exhausted from the trek they'd made thus far; they all were. Letting the radiating warmth of the fire lull him in, he glanced to Britt and Bo, "If we're gonna wait, we might as well get some rest next to this warm fire." Squatting, Max plopped his rear-end on the ground next to Thomas and leaned back, crossing his hands behind his head. He watched as Britt and Bo reluctantly joined him. Before Saaja sheathed his sword again, Max asked the lookout, "Saaja, could we bother you for some water?"

Saaja put down his blade and pulled the log he'd been perched on closer to them, reached into his coat and pulled out a leather flask. Max accepted it gladly.

Taking the full tear-shaped leather bladder, Max uncorked it and took a long pull. The moisture eased his drying throat. He pulled the flask from his lips, swallowing hard. He offered the waterskin to Britt, who was quick to accept. Thomas and Bo drank next. Thomas poured a small amount onto the corner of his shirt and held it against Kirsten's lips.

As he lay next to the fire, Max took some comfort in the fact that they'd be arriving at Solomon's home the next day, much faster than if they had to walk. He just hoped Kirsten could hold on long enough for the old wise man to help. Closing his eyes, Max passed into a dream state with ease.

***

Waking, Max was pulled from his slumber when the first bird alerted them to the rising sun. Its call tweeted continually until others joined in. Within minutes, the trees were erupting with the chatter of winged creatures. Lying on his back with eyes open, Max peered at the rough outlines of the trees slowly becoming more clearly defined.

The fire burned with fresh logs. Max knew it to be the work of their lookout. He sat up and turned to see that the shift had changed during the night and a much smaller person had replaced the broad-shouldered man. For all Max knew, the shift had changed several times and multiple strangers had been sitting nearby while he slept. The thought of someone he'd never met watching over them while they slept sent a chill down Max's spine. At least with Saaja, they'd had time to speak a little before he'd gone lights out.

Bo, Britt and Thomas were quick to stir after Max. He sat up and warmed his body by the fire. The other members of Rune's group emerged from their tents. Max stared at each one as they realized there were five people who they didn't know sitting at their fire. Before conversation between them began, Rune walked up from behind.

Slapping his hands together and rubbing them, he said, "Ready?"

Max jumped slightly by the sudden clap that came from behind them. He heard Bo offer to carry Kirsten, giving Thomas a well-deserved break. As they left the fire, Max turned to see all of Rune's fellow travelers gathering around the fire. He counted four men and two women and wondered what would happen to them when they came across the wreckage in Grandwood.

Reaching the saddled horses, Rune helped each of them climb onto their steeds. He loaded Kirsten and Bo last. Being the most experienced rider, Bo took Kirsten in his saddle. Max knew he and Thomas could ride, but doubted Britt knew how to ride at all. When they were settling into their saddles, he noted that Britt appeared pleased with the idea of riding her own horse, but once they'd mounted, she changed her mind. When Max offered to ride double with her, she quickly joined him.

Saddled and eager to get going, Rune led the way south, away from camp and toward the trails that would lead them to Brookside. Dividing Grandwood and Brookside lay two mountain ranges with a valley in the middle. Both the Grandwood Mountains and the Sharpstone Mountains ran northeast by southwest. Max recounted the last time he'd traveled this way and hoped they wouldn't run into any more goblins.

Riding as fast as they dared, Rune led the group. With the changing seasons, autumn's chill nipped at their cheeks as they rode. Max wasn't sure if the horses moved any faster in the cooler temperature, but the peace of mind in knowing their horses wouldn't die from heatstroke gave him comfort as they rode.

Passing the location where he and Anders had

encountered goblins in the fog while in pursuit of Thargon's ships to Eastland, Max thought about how much his life had changed. He hoped the next time he passed through this area it would be under ordinary circumstances.

The group stopped twice to let the horses drink water. Kirsten's condition didn't worsen, so they continued at their constant pace after stopping both times. Approaching Brookside near evening, Max took the lead since he knew better how to reach Solomon's place while bypassing the town proper. The veil of darkness soon aided their skirting of Brookside and the horses allowed them to move through the wooded area more quickly.

Although the darkness made it more difficult to identify, Max and Bo eventually came upon the treehouse belonging to the old wise man. While they all dismounted, Thomas and Bo hastened to get Kirsten inside. Max stayed with Britt, helping to string the horses together for Rune's return journey. Gripping Rune's hand in a gesture of gratitude, Max thanked the doctor for all he had done to get them there safely.

"If it benefits the cause, it's worth the risk," Rune said as he gripped the reins. "When you find the Resistance in the Riverlands, tell them Rune sent you."

Max nodded and Rune spurred his horse into motion, the train of horses pulled along behind him disappearing into the night.

By the time Britt and Max caught up with Thomas and Bo, they'd just reached Solomon's front door. Bo pounded, his fist hammering against the wooden face. The pounding echoed into the treehouse as they waited for Solomon's answer. Max had been here many times and the old man had never turned away a guest. He was reliable to a fault, never venturing far from his home. This time, however, they heard no sounds of shuffling feet or muttering under his beard. For the first time in all of his visits, Max knew the home to be empty. Cursing, he pushed his brother out of the way and shouted, "Sol! If you are in there, we're coming in! We really could use your help!"

He burst through the door, the rush of wind from its sudden opening sent parchment on the nearby chairs and shelves flying. The group pushed their way inside the small home, into a living room cluttered with books, papers and maps. The darkness of Solomon's home reflected its welcome, absent of warmth and light.

"Sol!" Max called again as he hustled to the bedroom door. He pushed it open. The room was empty. Max cursed and rushed back into the main room where the others were laying Kirsten on the couch. Looking down at her pale complexion, Max shook his head, "Guys, he's not here. Solomon's gone."

CHAPTER TWO

Nagano

aija tingled with excitement, the thrill of what she was doing sent chills down her spine. Trying to control her body's response to the dragon's calling, she filled her lungs with the cool Eastland Mountain air, exhaling with a shiver. She had never made such an impulsive decision in her life, to leave her companions in search of a dragon. Her desire to follow the scarlet dragon thrummed through her like an instinctual passion she couldn't ignore; the call urged her to find him. Stepping forward, she aimed toward Nagano and broke into a run. Feeling the wind in her flowing brown hair, Maija let her elven legs carry her. Her recent discovery of her heritage as an elf brought with it more than learning that she haled from a dragonrider family; it also gave her the elf's gift of inhuman speed.

The uneven ground rushed beneath her as she rapidly gained speed. The adrenaline pulsing through her veins carried her into a higher state of being, and she let out a cry, unable to contain the animal she was becoming. She had never felt so alive. Not fully understanding where she was going, Maija let her instincts guide her. She could feel the scarlet dragon's pull drawing her toward it and willing her to run free with him. Her desire to know where she was going and why was overridden with the sensation the dragon gave her. Maija passed into a trance-like state, the rocks and forest washing by in a blur. No longer caring about the choice she'd just made to part from her first love, Anders, and her recently found sister, Maija let her mind become consumed by the animal inside her and allowed the dragon to guide it.

Suddenly she halted, skidding over loose rocks as they clicked, scattering atop a cliff-lined ridge. A wave of clarity washed over her as she snapped into reality. Looking down at her feet, she realized she stood at the edge of a precipice. Panting, she turned her gaze out toward the open expanse of green fields and lush hills sprawling into the distance below. An arc of jagged mountain peaks spanned the horizon, creating a spine of rock protruding from the far off hills. Winged creatures soared over the peaks, their familiar silhouettes hardly recognizable from such a distance. Those dragons told her where she was, on the edge of Eastland with the entirety of Nagano spread out before her. Somewhere in this great place the wild, red-scaled dragon was calling to her. Maija had touched the dragon and he imparted something to her in return. From that moment she could feel the dragon's desire to be with her again, to share a bond.

It'll be dark soon, she thought, noticing the changing light across the sky. Maija could still feel the dragon calling, but she suppressed it and retained her self-control. *I should find shelter. I'll need my legs to be well rested if I give in to this sensation every time I start to run.* She walked along the edge of the ridge, searching for a place to descend into the lush valley below. *There has to be some way down,* she thought.

Maija broke into a jog, careful not to let herself run wild again. She trotted along the edge hoping to see a ridgeline extending north and dropping down into Nagano, but the sun was setting rapidly and the wall of Eastland Mountains continued with no end in sight. As darkness approached, she abandoned hope of reaching the fertile land below and instead dropped south into the tree line, hoping to find some refuge from the evening elements.

Happening upon a large boulder jutting out from the slope, she thought, *It doesn't get much better than this.* Quickly gathering several armfuls of dead, low-hanging branches, she prepared to make a fire. Pulling her flint and steel from her pocket, she thought, *Good thing I didn't put this in Zahara's saddlebags.* Realizing now all that she had left in Zahara's saddlebags, she cursed herself for not thinking to load a pack with supplies before she'd left. All she had with her were the travel clothes she was wearing when she intended to return with Anders to the elf capital of Cedarbridge. She felt at her belt, checking to see whether her knife was still holstered in its sheath. She fingered at the empty leather flap and groaned. *It must have fallen out when I was running; stupid,* she thought. Not only had she left Anders and Natalia, the most important people in her life, she'd done it on a whim and without anything to aid her, save for her trusted flint and steel fire starter.

Striking the flint into the dry bits of debris she'd collected, Maija reviewed her impulsive decision to leave her comfortable life as a rider in training. Why had she decided to run off into the mountains? Hadn't Anders, Natalia, and Ivan needed her help in confronting Lageena? She could've helped bring justice to Nadir. She was, after all, a dragonrider in training, even if she hadn't bonded with a dragon yet. That thought, though, confirmed her decision; the potential for just such a bond was why she had left them. It was the one thing in this world so difficult to obtain that only a select number of elves, humans and dwarfs throughout history had managed to experience it. A wild dragon of Nagano had found her, and they had shared a connection; it had to be something. That connection was what Anders described when he first met Zahara. She longed to feel that sensation of being with the dragon again, the warmth it brought to her soul. She needed to find the scarlet dragon.

The sparks caught, smoking in the dry strips of bark and needle cast. Blowing gently, Maija saw the embers ignite, flames rising from the debris. Quickly she added more fuel to the fire until she felt comfortable that it wasn't going to blow out. Lying next to the fire, she propped herself up with her elbow in the soft dirt. The welcome warmth of the fire soothed her into relaxation. From the ever-increasing evening chill, Maija could feel that summer was coming to an end. As she watched the fire dance among the small logs she'd added to her fire, Maija thought to the many days she'd spend with Anders in the Everlight Kingdom.

The warming flames lulled her to sleep. When she awoke, darkness had settled in, consuming her surroundings. She shivered and saw that her fire had turned to embers. Rolling onto her side and reaching for the stack of wood she'd gathered, she placed several small sticks on before another set of larger logs. Luckily the rock radiated the fire's heat back at her and she warmed up quickly.

With the fire roaring again, Maija laid back, nodding off once more. She was awakened when she heard the clacking of a rock rolling downslope across the exposed ridge above. The click-clacking of the rock got her attention, but she knew many animals lived in the Eastland Mountains, most of them small and docile. When several more rocks slid and began to roll downslope toward her, Maija forced herself awake and sat up in the dirt.

Sliding back and pushing herself up against the overhanging boulder, she held her breath and listened for movement. She wondered momentarily if her heightened sense of hearing had returned. Heavy, hollow-sounding thuds slowly walked their way along the ridge above and she knew from how close whatever was up there was that her elven ears had not regained their former powers. Her eyes widened and she quickly kicked dirt onto the fire, attempting to snuff it out before being discovered. She watched the smoke swirl and carry itself downslope with the slight evening breeze. At least the wind was moving in the right direction to help her remain unnoticed. Then the wind shifted. An unexpected gust rushed up through the trees carrying the smoke toward the ridgeline. Maija cursed under her breath.

The heavy steps came to a stop, kicking more loose rocks down off the ridge. Noise carried well across the chill evening air and Maija's pointed ears could hear the creature sniffing. Suddenly a thought crossed Maija's mind, *What if it's the dragon? What if he's come looking for me?* She rolled on her hip coming onto her hands and knees. Inching toward the edge of the boulder, she stopped. The sniffing she'd heard also stopped. After a moment of silence, the steps continued, this time lighter than before. *But what if it's not the red dragon and it's a different dragon? Wild dragons will eat humans, elves or dwarfs, won't they?*

The fear of being discovered by another wild dragon, one that she hadn't shared a connection with, terrified her. The wind shifted again, returning to a gentle downslope breeze. The steps stopped again. Red dragon or not, whatever was above her would find her soon. She decided to catch a glimpse of it, so she would know how to react.

Crawling on her hands and knees, she edged herself to the brink of the large boulder. Slowly she leaned forward. Trees came into view and she could see the rock ridge silhouetted against the darkness. Straining to focus, Maija couldn't see the creature between the ridge and her hiding place. Moving her hand forward, she leaned farther out beyond the edge of the boulder, then stopped. A dark mass stood, two-legged halfway between the ridge and her boulder. It moved slowly, shifting to one side, then the other. Maija held perfectly still, not wanting to move an inch in case the creature saw her.

That's not a dragon, she thought. *What is that?* The dark mass was much larger than any elf or human she'd ever seen, but it stood on two legs as a human or elf does. Its limbs were thick, its torso wide, and its stature rising to three times that of her own judging by its outline next to the trees. The thing didn't appear to be holding a weapon. It sniffed the air between them, then stalked forward, stepping carefully into the wooded area where Maija crouched.

Maija glanced to the side, feeling the urge to run. *I could outrun it, couldn't I?* she thought. Guessing by the size of it, she didn't think it could move very fast, but she wasn't in a very good position to find out. *What if it is fast, its legs are long, and maybe it could cover some ground quickly.* Watching warily as the large creature approached, Maija decided to stay put. *There's only one of them and as it comes close, I can move around the boulder, staying on the opposite side where it can't see or reach me.* Sticking with her plan, Maija stayed against the boulder waiting for whatever the creature was to come closer.

As the oversized, two-legged creature came into view, Maija could make out some of its features in greater detail. Its bare legs moved like a humans; however, its proportions were much larger. Each of the giant's legs was nearly as round as the high elevation trees' trunks. Short, gray fur covered its core and chest, leaving its bulking arms bare, much the same as its legs. Maija gaped at the enormity of the creature's head. It would've easily matched the size of most elf and human bodies. Its dome showed more skin, as if the creature were balding like many human males do with age. She could see two enormous ears perched on either side of its head, two bulging eyes and a rounded nose between them. This enormous human-like being walked carefully, stepping lightly as it made its way around to the opposite side of the boulder. Maija shifted, rounding the rock and remaining out of view. It was difficult to stay completely hidden from the curious creature, purely due to its looming size. Relying on the darkness and her stealth to remain hidden, Maija attempted to blend into the rock.

As the furry giant came to stand alongside the boulder, Maija could see its hairy torso wasn't natural fur at all; rather it was wearing fur from another creature, like a vest.

It's intelligent, she thought as she maneuvered herself

again into a more hidden position.

The creature placed its hulking hand on the boulder, bending down to peer under the overhang. Maija took the opportunity to step quietly away from the rock, upslope, tucking herself behind a nearby tree. If she stood profile, the tree did a better job at keeping her hidden than the opposite side of the boulder.

The massive thing sniffed the area under the rock, running its hand under the overhang and feeling the dirt. As its bare skin brushed over her smoldering fire, the creature reeled in its arm with alarming speed. Leaping away and shaking its hand, the creature's human-like eyes bulged and frantically searched its surroundings, the expression on its face fearful. Maija had seen this expression many times since she'd been captured in Grandwood. She watched with interest as the grayish creature backed away, scared for its life. Suddenly, it whirled around and broke into a run, lumbering through the forest.

How strange, Maija thought as she stepped out from behind the tree and watched the dark mass disappear quickly into the night. *I guess that thing is fast after all,* she told herself. The gray, human-like thing moved out of sight much more quickly than she would've thought possible given its size.

Maija returned to her spot under the overhang. Grabbing the unburned ends of the smoldering logs, she picked up the firewood, shaking off the dirt. Using a stick from her dwindling stockpile of wood, she stirred the embers, bringing more oxygen to them and clearing any leftover dirt to the ground. Piling the remainder of her wood onto the coals, she brought the flames to a crackling roar once more.

Staring into the orange flames, Maija considered the strange encounter with the giant human-like animal. *Whatever that thing was, it really didn't like fire.* Gathering another armload of wood before settling back down by the fire, Maija felt sure that the creature wouldn't return as long as she had a flame going. With the comfort and safety of her warm fire, Maija lay down on the dry patch under the boulder and let the heat lull her back to sleep.

***

When Maija awoke she quickly scanned her surroundings, to make sure that the creature who visited during the night hadn't returned. Relaxing slightly, she felt her stomach turn and heard it groan. She hadn't eaten since before leaving Hardstone and hadn't brought any food with her. She swallowed, finding her dry mouth aching for water.

I need to find a way down to that valley. There are plenty of rivers and streams to drink from down there, and hopefully I'll find something to eat.

Deciding to leave the safety of her campsite, Maija brushed the dust from her clothes after sleeping in dirt all night, extinguished the fire, and then made sure her flint and steel were in her pocket before setting out for the day. The forest opened, exposing the stone ridge top. She stepped to the precipice again, looking out over Nagano. Dragons had already taken to the skies, soaring in the distance. She searched the cliff face that dropped abruptly to the valley floor, looking for waterfalls or seepage from its cracks. Scanning the wall, she spotted a vertical slot, slightly wider than others, where water trickled out from its base. With a hint of hope, she set out to the east along the wall, jogging toward the general area where the slot rose to the ridge top.

As Maija approached, the crag came into view. The small canyon extended to her right, inland from the cliff's edge. The canyon narrowed as it retreated inward toward the tree line just downslope to the south. Following the canyon's edge she dropped again into the woods, glancing for any sight of the gray giant she'd seen running this direction. The slot canyon closed just inside the tree line and she stepped closer to the horseshoe-shaped cliff marking the backend of the crag. Maija stared down the steep canyon's walls. One look at the vertical descent told her she wouldn't be climbing down from here. The canyon bottom stair-stepped its way north and Maija thought it looked navigable if she could somehow get down to it.

Seeing the water flowing at the base of the horseshoe to the crag, she thought, *That water's coming from somewhere.*

Squinting into the shadowed canyon bottom, Maija thought she could see an absence of rock near the bottom of the back wall. Looking closer she saw a cave. Recalling how far the Eastland wall extended without a way down, she thought attempting to find the other end of the cave, where the water originated was worth investigating. She smacked her dry lips together, hoping to find the water's origin soon, and continued walking south, downslope into the forest.

After several minutes, Maija came across a flattened area. Stepping onto it, her feet squished into a swampy wallow. Bending, she pushed the backside of her tanned hand into the soft ground, water filling her cupped palm. She drank the muddy water, not caring if twigs and debris came with it. The cold groundwater soothed her dry mouth. She repeated the process three more times before continuing her search. Walking the perimeter of the flattened area,

Maija discovered water trickling down a small relief to the west. She followed the trickle, and within a few yards from the edge of the wallow a small creek began to form. Shortly after the creek began it ended, disappearing into a hole in the ground. Maija grinned, knowing she'd found the canyon's water source. Now she hoped this hole was an entrance to the cave she'd seen at the slot canyon's back wall.

Crouching, Maija drank several more handfuls of water before lowering her ear to the ground near the head-sized hole. She could hear the water falling into a cavernous opening. If she was going to explore where the water went, she would have to excavate. Reaching inside the hole, Maija grabbed a rock along its edge and pulled. The rock wiggled loose. She was able to pull it out on the second tug. She reached in and yanked on another, the second rock coming free more easily than the first. She rose to her feet and stomped at the edge of the widening hole. The ground around the hole bent. She stomped again and the ground she was standing on gave way. Gasping, she dropped into the hole. Her feet touched down almost instantly and she realized she'd only dropped into the hole up to her waist. Gathering her confidence again Maija felt at the spacious opening with her feet.

Sitting, she found herself in a human-sized tunnel. She maneuvered her body to be face-forward and inched on her stomach through the dark opening. The little creek flowed under her belly as she crawled, the sound of water falling off a drop in the near distance. Not yet able to see the drop, she imagined it to be much larger than she had hoped. *Maybe I'll be crawling back out shortly,* she thought as she felt for the edge of the drop-off. Finding the sharp rock edge where the water fell, Maija pulled herself forward and pushed her head out over the edge.

Her body blocked the light from above and she could just barely see light from the canyon far below. Taking a minute to think through the situation and let her eyes adjust to the faint light, she scanned for the next chamber. To her surprise, she thought she saw the water splashing just a few feet below. She chuckled at the image she'd conjured up from the deceivingly loud-sounding drop. Carefully continuing headfirst over the edge, Maija used the large jutting rocks to keep from sliding head over heels down onto the next level. Once her legs were past the edge, Maija pushed up and out on her handholds, bringing her feet under herself as she dropped the short distance to the cave floor.

Now that she was beyond the entrance tunnel, she found that this next chamber was fairly well illuminated and she could see the best route down. The small creek cascaded through a boulder field as it dropped deeper into the expanding cave, eventually leading to the steep canyon walls she had seen from above. Shivering from the cold water saturating her clothes, Maija continued her down climb through the cave toward the bright light below. She stopped at the mouth of the cave, the place where she had seen the absence of rock from above and admired the beauty of the slot canyon before her. She had made it to the canyon bottom and hoped the rest of the way into Nagano would be as easy to navigate.

Descending through the canyon's stair-stepping configuration was, at times, extremely dangerous. Maija didn't consider herself an experienced canyon explorer, so she continued cautiously. After the initial descent through the cave and into the canyon bottom, she found that each drop wasn't as steep as she'd anticipated, but the topography quickly changed the farther down the canyon she ventured. In several locations she was forced to contour and down-climb the canyon walls to continue. Fortunately, the rock had naturally large holds for her hands and feet, which gave her some comfort whenever she was forced to maneuver through steep sections.

As she worked her way down the slot canyon, she tried not to focus on the idea that one false move or misstep could send her falling. A mistake here could be the end of her journey. Even if she survived a significant fall, her injuries would most likely cripple her. With water, but no food in the canyon, she would slowly starve. Solving the puzzle of how to safely make it to the bottom of the Eastland wall became a game, a dangerous game she couldn't afford to lose, but thinking of it as a game distracted her from her fear.

With most of the day spent navigating the canyon, Maija finally reached its end. She stopped to drink from the pooling water at its base and looked back up at the slot she'd come through. The canyon opening where she'd started her descent far above was no longer visible. Stepping out from the cliff, Maija grinned when she saw the lush fields of grass, speckled with leafy trees. Her next priority was finding food, then she would allow herself to feel for the dragon's lure.

Physically drained from the down-climb, her stomach cramping with hunger, Maija set out through the shin-tall grass. As she walked, she took comfort in the notion that she could see if any creature was coming from a long way off.

She wouldn't be startled by a dragon suddenly popping up from seemingly nowhere. If something large was coming toward her, she'd have time to react, much more than last night. Seeing nothing but a few small patches of short trees to hide her presence in the open fields, Maija understood why the predators of the sky claimed this place as their home. A dragon could locate its next meal with ease.

She walked up a shallow rise for a better vantage point. A herd of four-legged beasts stood with their heads buried in the grass, grazing in the lush expanse. Their brown fur stood out starkly against the green backdrop. The thick-bodied animals massed in the thousands, alarming Maija at the size this one herd. She'd never seen these animals before, though they reminded her of cattle. The shape of their heads was much larger than a cow and a pronounced hump rose from their backs over their front shoulders. Gauging their size was difficult at this distance, but since this animal was likely the current prey of wild dragons, they had to be large. Knowing she wouldn't be able to take down or eat such a large animal, Maija eyed a grove of small trees along the creek that wound out from the canyon she'd descended. She started out for the trees, hoping they were fruit-bearing.

Reaching the grove of stunted trees, Maija was grateful to see many oblong-shaped brown shells hanging from their branches. She plucked one and examined it. The oval husk-like shell had a hard exterior, rough to the touch. Holding the sizable pod with both hands, she struck it against the tree trunk, attempting to break it open. The hard fruit, however, bounced off on impact. Instead of cracking the rough shell, the oblong husk had gouged a deep scrape into the tree's bark. The scarified tree trunk oozed a turquoise liquid.

Surprised by the vibrantly colored sap seeping from the light-colored tree trunk, Maija scooped a finger of the sap, then sniffed it. The sap's fragrance made her mouth water. It smelled like the butterscotch pudding her grandmother, or caretaker rather, would often make. She tasted the turquoise goo, sticking to her tongue as she licked her finger. Swishing the substance around in her mouth, Maija's eyes widened at the flavor. It was delicious, much better than her grandmother's pudding. She scooped another finger full of the sap, more generous than the first.

Sitting down at the base of the tree Maija continued to scoop the oozing sap from the tree's base. Its sugars quickly gave her renewed energy and she began to wonder what the fruit tasted like. Searching the immediate area, she found a stone sticking partway out of the ground. Finding the stone too large to dig out, Maija repeated the process she'd tried earlier using both hands to bring the oblong shell down hard against the exposed rock. A chunk of the shell fragmented away on her third strike. She looked at the brown casing and saw a crack form, splitting the shell. Rolling the shell in her hand, she saw where the rock had chipped away a portion of the hard exterior. Just under the rough outer layer was a light tan fibrous husk. She pressed her finger into the exposed soft spot and more turquoise sap oozed out.

Lightly hitting the fruit along the hairline fracture, she carefully worked her way around the fruit. Once the crack was larger and more defined, Maija pulled the shell apart and ripped it in two. The sap spilled as she fumbled to hold each half upright. Using the oblong shell as a cup, she slurped down the sap, draining it in several minutes. The tan husk's innards flaked off at the lightest touch and Maija scratched away at it until there was enough to take a mouthful. The husk wasn't as sweet as the sap inside, but eating something more solid was welcomed. She repeated the process with the other half of the fruit and again on several lower-hanging shells. Once she'd had her fill of butterscotch sap, Maija felt energized and eager to set out in search of the dragon. It was late in the day, but her need to continue this search overrode making camp in daylight.

Maija could still feel the pull of the dragon, though the sensation had faded after she'd ignored it for so long. Closing her eyes and focusing all of her mental energy on the dragon's call, she was able to locate it again. She started out, running through the grass, the thrilling sensation of elven speed and agility arising again. She welcomed it as it urged her faster. Losing sight of any specific destination, she began to allow the draw from the dragon to take over. The grazing animals scattered as she ran by. Within a mile, an enormous shadow distracted her, pulling her out of her trance. She looked toward the figure. The thrill turned to fear when she realized she was running past an enormous dragon feasting on several smoldering hump-backed cattle carcasses. She had to dodge the burning grass. If she hadn't noticed the dragon's shadow, she would've run directly into the burning grass. For a moment she wondered if the fire would burn across the entire grassland, but the lush greenery quickly snuffed out the flickering flames.

Maija didn't slow her pace as she ran past the feasting dragon, its dark purple scales reminiscent of a raven's feathers shimmering in the afternoon sun. She kept her eyes on the beast and felt it watching her as she sped by at an inhuman pace. Once she'd made it beyond the dragon, she glanced back, hoping she wouldn't see the winged predator choosing to pursue her. To her relief, the raven- scaled dragon remained in place, devouring its meal.

Once more returning to her focus on the call, Maija allowed the thrilling sensation that drove her toward the scarlet dragon to envelope her mind, this time resisting its trance just enough to allow her to be aware of her surroundings and recognize whether a dragon was hunting her. She didn't want to be blind to Nagano's predators but needed to maintain the animalistic connection if she wanted to follow it. She held back on sprinting headlong and settled into a more desirable pace for long-distance running. As night approached, Maija noticed the absence of dragons from the sky as they returned to their lairs to rest. Though she was worn out from the day's events, Maija determined it would be safer for her to run across the open expanse at night. Continuing her pursuit through the darkness, she searched for the scarlet dragon by the light of the stars and moon.

In the coming days, Maija spent her evenings and most of the night searching for the red dragon. With the variety of fruit-bearing trees in Nagano, her food source was plentiful. Clean, flowing water also was easy to come by. Aside from other dragons hunting during the day, Maija perceived Nagano to be a utopia and found it hard to imagine that the Dragon Wars had occurred here. Hiding among the trees, she spent the daylight hours napping and resting before the next evening's search. She found the dragon's position had changed each night, bringing her to the conclusion that this dragon didn't have a nest it frequented like the dragons in her homeland, the Everlight

Kingdom. These wild dragons of Nagano lived as predators do, nomadic and always hunting for their next meal.

After following the dragon's lure for several nights, Maija became aware of its absence. As hard as she tried, the dragon's draw that had pulled her before had disappeared. She began to panic, wondering if she'd come all this way and spent all this time only to have the dragon disappear from her forever. Days passed with no sign or pull from the dragon; Maija struggled to maintain her faith in its call. She longed to return to the elves and Anders, knowing they would understand if she came home empty-handed.

One afternoon she was napping in a butterscotch sap tree when the dragon's sensation woke her. Her heart sprang to life and pounded rapidly, sending the familiar tingling sensation through her limbs. The scarlet dragon had returned. Not wanting to risk losing the dragon's pull again she dropped to the ground and started running in plain sight of numerous hunting dragons. To her surprise, the predators flying overhead paid her little attention. She wasn't going to let the red dragon elude her any longer; she would run all day and all night if she had to. It had been ten long days since she'd left the comfort of family and friends and she'd searched relentlessly, hoping to find the dragon. She had nearly given up.

There was something different about the dragon's call with this renewed search, though. It grew much stronger as she followed it. She could sense the connection deepening in her consciousness. The sensation led her to the shore of a large lake that extended along the base of the Ridgeback Mountains. The thrill she felt became overwhelming, like a bright light blinding her. Coming to a halt, she frantically combed the lakeshore. The draw from the dragon had never been so strong before; it pounded through her body with force. She knew the dragon was here, he had to be.

A shadow swept over her and Maija craned her neck to search the sky. A giant red dragon glided low overhead, circling and then landing gently in the shallows of the lake just a few hundred yards away. Maija's heart skipped a beat when she saw him. The dragon she'd been searching for was standing right in front of her. She watched intently as it lapped up water with its large forked tongue.

Maija stepped hesitantly toward the enormous creature as she'd done before on Mount Orena. She walked gently, careful not to spook the wild beast. She wanted so badly to call out to him, but she didn't know his name or if that would startle him and scare him away. Closing in on the dragon she came within fifty yards of the winged creature. The dragon stopped drinking and swept his head around in a wide arc to stare her. Maija stopped dead in her tracks, wide-eyed and wondering what the dragon might do.

The scarlet dragon shifted its weight, letting its hind legs bear the brunt of its bulk while he ruffled his wings. Maija almost shouted for him to stay, but managed to hold her tongue as he folded them tightly against his body once more. He walked toward her, splashing through the shallow water as the he neared. She remained perfectly still, scared, but thrilled to have him choosing to come closer at last. He stopped directly in front of her. The dragon lowered his vast head to observe her at eye level. Flaring his nostrils slightly as he exhaled, the scarlet dragon snorted, washing Maija in a blast of sulfuric heat before he started sniffing at her. Maija shook uncontrollably; she had no idea if the dragon was deciding whether he wanted to befriend her or devour her.

The scarlet dragon pulled his head back, lifted it high, and then turned his side toward her. Standing broadside in the shallows, he lowered his shoulder and beckoned her to climb on. Maija's eyes bulged as she realized what he wanted her to do. Shaking with fear and excitement, she approached him. First, she touched him by resting her trembling hand on his shoulder. Instantly, she felt a warm electric energy shoot through her body, tingling her senses. Next, she gripped one of the many spiked protrusions sprouting along his back and hoisted herself up. She had to climb several steps, while grasping the spikes to get on top of the enormous creature.

Searching for a place to sit, Maija wondered, *How does Anders sit on Zahara?* She cringed at the sharp bone spurs poking up from of the dragon's back. She tried to recall whether Zahara, Anders' dragon, had any spikes along her back. She didn't think she did. Maija stood on the scarlet dragon's shoulders gripping its neck as it rose to all fours again. When the dragon shifted, Maija was nearly thrown off his back, but luckily, she held tight around his bony protrusions.

I need to sit down, but there isn't anywhere without spikes, she thought.

Suddenly the spikes along the dragon's back where it met his neck retracted and flattened as if responding to her thoughts. She sat down with her legs straddling the large dragon. She found his scales were hard, but warm and surprisingly comfortable. Suddenly, the dragon crouched. Caught off balance, Maija grabbed a bone spur protruding from the dragon's neck with each hand. The red dragon readied its wings and leapt into the air, flapping hard to lift its large body off the ground. Soon they were climbing into the sky, the dragon spiraling, letting its wings catch the thermal rise along the mountain front. Maija shouted with joy. With the wind in her amber hair and the sky all around her, she felt truly alive.

From her perch, Maija surveyed the land. She could see the enormous cliff wall stretching across the Eastland Mountain front. She saw dragons flying at varying heights around them and the herds of hump-backed cattle roaming the grassy expanse below. She could see everything from up here and she realized that together they could go anywhere.

In the distance Maija saw a bright flash, an orb of white light appearing and vanishing in an instant. She squinted, focusing on where it occurred. A dark mass lay on the ground in place of the flashing orb. The dragon had seen it, too. They rocketed toward the disturbance. As they flew closer, Maija's heart skipped a beat and she felt a sinking sensation in the pit of her stomach. Where the orb of light had flashed lay an iridescent dragon and on its back a hunched and ragged rider.

Anders!

CHAPTER THREE

Kirsten

hat do we do now?" Thomas asked, his frightened tone telling Max what he couldn't see through the darkness.

Max could feel everyone's eyes fall on him. Racking his brain, he attempted to conjure up a solution to their predicament. *Damn it, why isn't he here the one time we really need him,* Max thought. Aloud, he attempted to calm their collective fears, "Um, I think, I mean I know Solomon has books about magic and magical creatures. Maybe we should start there?"

"Let's get some light in here," Britt said and Max could hear her rummaging for a candle.

Finding a candelabra tipped over on the table, Max grabbed it and walked to the chair where old Solomon always took his pipe. Further touring the house built into the trunk of a tree based on his memory of prior visits, Max stumbled over obstacles he didn't recall being in his way. When he reached the chair, he felt for the side table and discovered that it had been knocked over. Rummaging through the mess, he found Solomon's flint and steel and hurried to the fireplace built into the wall separating the living room from the kitchen. Tossing kindling into it, he struck a spark, igniting the dry grass Solomon kept on hand for kindling. Taking one of the burning straws, he used it to light the candelabra.

Rising with the candlelight in his hand, Max saw the wreckage in Solomon's home. The living room was a mess, more so than usual. The stacks of books and maps had toppled and were strewn across the floor. With the chairs and table knocked over, only the couch remained in its natural place near the door. Someone had turned over almost everything in the room, clearly searching for something.

"There's got to be something in here that can help us," Bo said as he grabbed books from the floor.

Max pushed past his worry for what could've happened to Solomon. He needed to focus on Kirsten right now. Joining his brother, he lent light on the scene as they searched through the mess. Slowly Britt added wood to the fire and lit more candles so Max could see the room more clearly.

"How do I know which books are about magic?" Britt asked, joining them on the floor.

"Look for the ones that have this insignia on the side," Max said, showing her the golden ampersand stamped on the spine of one of the books he clutched.

"So what exactly are we're looking for in these?" she asked.

"Anything to do with goblins," Max said. He saw Britt thumbing through the pages of a thick text and shaking her head.

"Bo," Max said. "You go to the table and start scanning

these while Britt and I find you books, papers or anything relating to magic or healing." As he spoke, he made eye contact with Britt and she nodded.

"I'll make sure she doesn't get any worse," Thomas said while attending to Kirsten on the couch.

"Excellent," Max said.

As they gathered the contents of Solomon's library from the living room floor, Max and Britt organized the collection by piling any book bearing the magical symbol in front of Bo. In a separate pile, Max placed anything that appeared to deal with medicine or healing. In short order, Max and Britt had cleared the floor of books, stacking those that did not fit either category along the walls. They joined Bo in his search through the stack of those focused on supernatural literature.

"Check the 'G's' in the index and thumb through for any drawings or depictions of goblins," Max said to Britt.

"I know; it's not the first time I've opened a book," Britt responded tartly.

Max felt a warmth creep into his cheeks as he realized he'd embarrassed himself by assuming she would need help. "Sorry, it's just that Landish is your second language and…"

Britt cut him off, "All captains must keep logs and, therefore, have to learn to read and write."

Max refocused on his own search, opening a book that was written in a language he didn't know. After what he'd said to Britt, he realized it was foolish of him to assume Solomon only had books written in their native language. Struggling to make sense of it, he flipped through the pages searching for anything with a drawing. After reaching the end of the book and starting on the next, Max continued to scour the pages for any mention of goblins or goblin venom. Time passed and as the candles burned to stubs, Max closed the last of the books.

"Nothing in these," he said, picking up the stack and carrying it to the bookshelf that had been ransacked. As he placed them back on the shelf, he noticed a book that hadn't been on the floor. Seeing that there was no title on the spine, he pulled it off the shelf. Opening the unmarked book, he found it to be a sort of recipe book. "What kind of recipe calls for hen's blood?" he muttered under his breath.

"What's that?" Britt asked, carrying another stack of books to the shelf.

"Oh, some kind of recipe book," Max said, closing it.

"Did you say hen's blood?" Britt asked, setting her stack down.

"Yeah, I wonder what kind of dish that would be?" Max asked.

"Can I see that?" Britt asked.

"Yeah," Max said handing her the book. "Are you going to tell me that you're a professional cook now?" he joked.

Shaking her head, Britt took the book from him. Max watched as she flipped through the pages, a look of realization crossing her face.

Max asked, "What is it? Did you find something?"

"This book," she said. "It's a recipe book."

Max eyed her curiously, "Yeah. That's right."

"A recipe book for potions," she said.

Max's eyes widened.

"Solomon used to make potions, didn't he?" Bo asked, rising from the table.

"Can I see that again?" Max asked, taking the book from Britt. He flipped through its pages, looking at the recipes and seeing the detailed notes Solomon had written in the margins. "Bo, are you finding anything over there?" he asked, suddenly snapping the book shut and eyeing his brother.

Bo looked up from his stack of books and replied, "No. This is the second pass through them, just to make sure. But so far I've only found sections about goblins' desire for objects of wealth. Could explain why they were attracted to Grandwood, but I've found nothing about their venom or bites."

Placing the potions book in front of his brother, Max said, "I want you to start looking through these for any potions relating to healing or curing infections."

Bo set aside the book he was reading and opened the potions book, "How will I know which are healing potions?" he asked.

"I was hoping you could figure that out," Max said. "I have a very distinct memory of Solomon hastily putting away bottles." Max turned and walked toward the kitchen, "Perhaps Solomon still has some potions lying around."

Max pulled open cabinet door after cabinet door, peeking into them and then running his hands around the back corners as he searched. Britt handed him a candle to light his endeavor and he thanked her for the help. She grabbed another lit candle and assisted him in the search.

"So you're looking for bottles?" Britt asked.

"Yeah, anything in a bottle, marked or unmarked," Max said.

"Is this place always this messy?" Britt asked, tiptoeing

around the mess in the kitchen.

"No," Max said, his voice echoing inside an empty cupboard. "Sol isn't tidy by any means, but this place looks like it's been turned over."

"Like someone was searching for something," Britt added.

"Yeah," Max said. "It's kind of troubling. I hope Solomon's okay and didn't get himself arrested or worse."

"Maybe he's joined the revolution?" Britt suggested.

"He's not a fighter," Max said. "I mean he isn't one to be violent."

"Nothing here," she said, stepping back from the open cupboards.

"Nothing here either," Max said, taking his candle back into the living room. Looking around the small space, he spotted a little cabinet alongside the bookshelf. It was tucked neatly behind the shelf in a corner of the room that would be easy to miss if someone was in a hurry. Max crouched to look through the frosted glass panes on its front doors. He smiled and said, "Over here! I found them."

Reaching into the cabinet, Max began pulling out bottles. The unlabeled bottles varied in size, color and quantity. Consequently, he had little idea of how to identify which might be helpful. He tried to recall more memories of Solomon's potions from his childhood, but struggled to produce anything useful. The only helpful thing he could remember was Solomon warning him not to play with them, as they were very dangerous. He hoped the potions book would give them clues about which were healing or harmful. Britt joined Max as he pulled the bottles out and placed them carefully onto the table where Bo continued to read.

The bottles were coated in years of dust, suggesting Solomon hadn't used them or added to the collection in a very long time. Max wondered if potions left unused would turn sour or unstable. Choosing to focus on lining up all of the bottles so they could scrutinize them, Max pushed any negative thoughts from his mind.

"How do these work?" Britt asked, placing two clear bottles of different colored mixtures on the table.

"I'm not sure," Max answered while making sure the bottles were placed on the table in the order in which they'd been removed from the little cabinet. "But I'm guessing one of them treats poisons or toxins of some kind."

"And what if we can't find one? What do we do then?" Bo asked, looking up from the book.

Max shrugged, "I'm open to suggestions."

Bo thought for a moment, then shook his head and focused back on the book in hand, "There's got to be something in here."

"How do we know these are still good?" Britt asked blowing at the dust collected on the bottles.

"I think, if we find a healing potion or one that treats poison, we should test it first. Pour it onto the table and touch it or something," Max suggested.

"You want me to touch a random potion? What if it blows up?" Britt asked.

"Well, maybe not touch it, but we should test it somehow," Max said.

"And if we think we got it right and accidentally give her something that does her more harm?" Britt asked.

"Like I said, if you have any better ideas?" Max said.

"If we give her something from these bottles, we need

to be sure it won't harm her," Thomas chimed in from the couch and Max realized how small the room really was.

"I promise to only give her something if we know for sure it won't do more harm," Bo said.

Max looked to Thomas and saw him nod, the pain still present in his expression. "Okay, let's get on it," Max said, turning back to the cabinet and feeling more confident that they would find a way to treat her. As he pulled even more small bottles from the cabinet and handed them to Britt, he said, "Keep track of the order their coming out. I know Solomon wasn't the most organized person, but I've got a feeling that with this, he had them arranged a certain way. If nothing else tells us what the potions are, perhaps we'll be able to decipher how he's arranged them and why."

Britt nodded and continued to line them up in the order they'd been filed in the cabinet. Bo held the book of potions close as he read in the candlelight. Often, he would look up to check a bottle, then set it down and continue reading. When they had removed all of the bottles from the cabinet, Max managed to find two towels from the mess in the kitchen. Handing one to Britt, the two began wiping the bottles clean of dirt and debris.

"How's the identification coming along?" Max asked his brother as he continually looked from the book to the bottles before him.

Selecting a long-necked bottle from the group and holding it up to the candlelight, he said, "Not very clear. The descriptions of each potion can vary in color depending on the ingredients used. Some are simple and easy to decipher, but others aren't so easy. There are also a lot that have a green shade to them, but the purposes for them ranges from wart removal to pest removal. It's almost impossible to tell them apart."

"What about any notes Sol scribbled down on the recipes?" Max asked, looking over Bo's shoulder at the book.

Bo angled the book so Max could see clearly. Together they worked to find identifiable qualities in each potion, while Britt continued to clean the bottles. "Maybe we should start with those that are very different from the others. Pick out the bottles that are a drastically darker or lighter shade than most and then try to correlate them to a recipe," Max suggested.

"Yeah," Bo agreed. "That could make things go faster."

Assisting in picking the more unique potions, Britt helped Bo and Max to pull five potions from the bunch, all of which were drastically different from the others. One, in a vial-like bottle, tubular in shape, was a deep purple and had flecks of reflective particles floating through the solution. Another, a bright yellow, and a third, a crisp white. Britt found a coal-black bottle and separated it from the bunch. The fifth potion varying greatly from the others was in a teardrop-shaped bottle and held a thick, deep red liquid, almost resembling blood.

When Max pulled it out of the bunch, Bo groaned.

"What? It's probably not real blood," Max said. Swirling the thick liquid, he shrugged, "Well, maybe it is."

The brothers started searching through the book, arguing about whether one description matched better than another. As they bickered through their process of elimination, Britt realized something about each of the bottles they'd pulled. Connecting the order of their retrieval from the cabinet and associating them with the shelves in the cabinet, Britt said, "Did either of you notice that each of these bottles came from a different row on the shelf?" She waited for a response, but the two brothers were deeply engrossed in their argument regarding whether the yellow bottle was the hunger potion or a diluted warrior's potion.

Sighing, Britt grabbed a bottle from the bunch and began to wipe it down with the cloth. As she cleaned it off, she watched the liquid swirl, causing the whites and streaks of black that had settled at the bottom to mix in the solution. The colors didn't blend as she would've expected, but stayed separate, like oil and water, bubbling and streaking separately through the mixture. Britt flipped the bottle upside down to see if the colors would shift. When she did, a shimmer caught her eye and she noticed a glint of light reflecting from the base of the bottle. She looked up from the bottle to see if Max or Bo had seen it too, but they were still consumed by their argument. She flipped the bottle again, and, again, she saw the shimmer at its base. She turned it back and forth until the glimmer could be seen clearly. To her surprise, on the underside of the bottle a bright label shone and she let out a gasp.

Max heard Britt's exhalation and noticed she was flipping a potion in her hand. Finally abandoning his insistence on being right in his debate with Bo, he asked, "What are you doing?"

"I'm trying to explain to you," Bo began, but Max waved a dismissive hand in his face.

"Not you, Bo. Britt?" he asked as she looked at him with a stunned expression.

Britt stepped up to the table and held the bottle's underside toward them. "Look at this," she said, turning the bottle's underside back and forth.

The shining glint of a label flashed in his eyes and Max leaned forward. Grabbing the bottle from Britt's hand, he asked, "How did you find this?"

"What is it?" Bo asked, leaning over to see the bottom of the bottle.

"Can it help you figure out which potions are which?" Britt asked.

Max tilted the bottle to reveal the hidden label and recognized the insignia. Taking the book from Bo, he flipped through the pages, stopping at the one he was searching for. Pointing at it on the page, he showed it to Bo, "I knew I recognized that symbol."

"Helianthus," Bo said pointing to the description. "So that's why it's yellow."

"And the black streaks in it," Max said pointing to the bottle.

"What's Helianthus?" Britt asked.

"Sunflower," Max said not looking up from the book. "I'm not sure what it's got to do with the potion, but in horticulture, Helianthus is the genus of sunflowers and the like."

"How in the five nations did you know that?" Britt asked.

"Our stepmom," Max said as he felt Britt's gaze lingering on him. Looking up from the book, he added, "She was really into flowers." Britt shook her head in disbelief. Shrugging, he added, "I don't remember what they were all called, but that one I always liked, so it stuck."

"Okay. It's good to know your knowledge of the obscure is wide-ranging," she said with a grin.

"And I thought you were the funny one?" Bo said under his breath.

Max elbowed his brother and returned his focus to the book, "The Helianthus Papaver potion. It's used in tinctures as a powerful numbing agent. Solomon's commented on the side here that one drop of this will turn anyone into a bumbling fool and render them useless in any physical endeavor for hours."

"Not exactly what we're looking for," Britt said.

"Which row did you get this one from?" Max asked.

Britt pointed to the third row down from the far end of the table. Max grabbed two potions from the row, one greenish-hued and the other a turquoise blue. He flipped them over until the reflective symbols on the base could be seen clearly. He pointed them toward Bo, asking if he could find them in the text.

A short time later Bo answered, "They're both potions used to treat physical and mental pain."

"That must mean this third row is pain treatment," Max suggested. "Didn't you say each one of these five we selected came from a different row?" Max asked Britt.

"I didn't think you heard me," Britt said.

Using the labels on the base of each row's bottles, they determined which rows could help them, identifying the fifth row as healing potions.

"What did that say it was used for?" Max asked pointing to the blood-red one, wanting to make sure he heard his brother correctly.

"Healing of a broken heart," Bo repeated.

"Wow, I didn't know old Sol was in the business of love potions," Max said, picking up the red potion he hoped wasn't actually made with blood.

"Anyway, that must be the healing potions row," Bo said enthusiastically.

Together Britt and Max sorted through the fifth row, narrowing their selection to three potions that might actually help heal Kirsten. A mud-brown bottle was described as healing infected stings and sores, but the recipe included nothing regarding goblin venom. The second of their selected potions was designed to drive foreign substances from the body. The recipe didn't specify whether this related to physical objects or something in the bloodstream like venom. The third potion was a simple generic healing potion that evidently covered a wide variety of things. Its description offered nothing specific like a goblin bite or poison.

"How do we test them?" Thomas asked as he rose from the couch.

Max had become so enthralled with their task that he'd forgotten to ask for Thomas' opinion on the matter. Taking the brown bottle and sliding it to the edge of the table, Max bent down and rolled up his pant leg, exposing a cut he'd received in their escape from Grandwood. The cut wasn't deep, but the scratch running the length of his calf appeared puffy and on the verge of infection.

Uncorking the bottle, Max first poured a drop onto the table, just to see if it was safe to touch. He'd almost put his finger into the bottle when the drop on the table started smoking. The burning liquid emitted a putrid smell. Max froze, his eyes wide at the reaction the liquid had with the wooden tabletop. The small drop of brown goo had actually burned through the table and dropped in a sizzling froth onto the floor. It continued to smolder and eat away at the organic tissue of the wood floor.

Shaking his head, Thomas said, "I don't think that's a good one."

"Maybe it only does that with wood and would be fine on skin?" Britt suggested.

Max cringed at the potion, "I'm not going to touch it. Thomas is right; that one's gone bad or something." Quickly corking the bottle, he placed it back in the lineup on the table. Shrugging, he grabbed the second bottle and popped the cork. Once again pouring a small amount onto the table, Max stared at the turquoise liquid. After a long minute with no reaction, Max exhaled and said, "Here goes nothing." He placed his finger into the bottle coating it in the residue. He winced as he pulled it out and held it away from his body like it might spring to life and attack him. When nothing happened, Max brought his covered finger to his nose, sniffing the liquid. The potent smell burned his nostrils as he reared his head back, bringing his clean hand up to his nose and rubbing at his nostrils.

"What was that?" Bo asked. Max could hear the concern in his voice.

Snorting, Max answered, "It's fine. It just smells strong is all. I think it's okay." He brought the potion covering his finger up to his lips, this time pinching his nose shut to keep from smelling it. He stuck his tongue out and carefully licked a dab of the turquoise liquid off his finger. Moving it around in his mouth and tasting it, he swallowed carefully. Waiting, Max didn't move for another long minute before he said, "I don't feel anything."

"Maybe you need to consume more?" Britt suggested.

Max dipped his finger into the bottle again, making sure he coated it in the liquid, then stuck it directly into his mouth, sucking it clean and swallowing. He stood motionless, with his eyes closed for several minutes before shrugging, "Nothing."

"That one expelled something that's supposed to attack your body, right?" Thomas asked.

Max nodded.

"Well you're probably healthy. It wouldn't work on someone who's healthy, would it?"

"Good point," Max said pointing his dirty finger toward Thomas.

"Should we try it on her now?" Bo asked, nodding at Kirsten who remained motionless on the couch.

"What about the other potion?" Britt said. "We should see if that one works before giving this one to her, just in case. You never know, maybe it won't work and she'll need this other one to reverse the effect? It's a general healing one, right? So, it would heal the effects of a bad reaction?"

Max shrugged while they looked to Bo, flipping through the book to find the potion's description again. "That sounds right to me," Max said, opening the bottle and pouring a drop onto the table for the third time. With no reaction to the table, Max fingered the bottle, collecting a dab on his fingertip. The substance acted in the same way as the second potion, no reaction. He stuck his potion-coated finger into this mouth and swabbed it against his cheeks. A moment later he said, "See, nothing," then he cut off as he collapsed onto the floor.

"Max!" Bo and Britt shouted together as he crashed back first onto the ground. They were just coming to his side when his leg began to glow. A bright orange light flashed, lighting up the darkened room in a burst before flickering out.

Britt, Bo and Thomas shielded their eyes from the flash. Max suddenly bolted upright, sitting on the ground and wondering how he'd gotten there. He looked to Bo as his brother lowered his arm and asked, "What just happened to me?"

"Your leg," Bo and Britt said simultaneously.

Max looked down at where he'd rolled up his pant leg. The puffy pink line scratched into his calf was gone. Rising to his feet, he said, "It worked. At least in healing my minor injuries."

"Will it work for Kirsten, though?" Thomas asked.

"I don't think either of these will hurt her," Max said, examining himself again. "I mean, I feel fine."

Thomas grabbed the generic healing potion and walked toward Kirsten.

"Wait," Britt said, grabbing the second potion Max tried from the table. "Shouldn't we try this one on her first? It's designed to expel toxins. The goblin's venom is essentially a toxin."

Thomas hesitated.

"She's right. We should try the toxin remover first. If anything goes wrong, at least we know the second one works," Max said, agreeing with Britt.

"Okay, let's try that one first," Thomas said.

Max joined Britt at Kirsten's side, carefully holding the vial of turquoise liquid. When she uncorked it, Max covered his nose and saw her reaction as she failed to do the same. Shaking her head, she quickly corked the bottle again. Max almost said something clever, but held his tongue as he realized this wasn't the time to poke fun. He watched intently as she tilted Kirsten's head back to allow her to pour the liquid into her mouth more easily. Pulling the cork again, Britt pinched her nose while gingerly placing the bottle at Kirsten's lips.

Britt poured a small amount at a time, and the group silently watched as Kirsten unknowingly drank the potion. Britt then moved the bottle away. Max understood why – in case Kirsten reacted violently. They wouldn't want to spill the remainder of the contents. When Kirsten showed no initial reaction, Britt resumed pouring until Kirsten had consumed the rest of the potion.

Max kept his eyes fixed on the dark red streaks spreading from the goblin's infected bite. Suddenly he saw them begin to pulse. He shouted, "They're moving!" He looked to Britt, who instantly pulled the bottle away from Kirsten's lips.

"Look," Thomas said, pointing to her chest.

Max could see the red starting to recede. He stepped back as Kirsten began to move, stretching and moving as the potion did its work. The potion pushed the goblin venom out, back into the bite. The small group stood in awe watching the red streaks retreat from her heart and back toward her shoulder. After a few moments, Kirsten stopped wriggling uncontrollably and lay motionless on the couch. Max's heart sank as he waited for another reaction. Then, Kirsten opened her eyes.

She stretched her arms up past her head and arched her back as she lay on the couch. Max and the others continued to hold their breath as she let out a long yawn. Sitting more upright on the couch, she looked around the room, her eyebrows pinched together in confusion. Max exhaled, his sigh of relief matching the others' upon seeing her gain consciousness.

"Kirsten!" Thomas shouted, throwing himself on her. "I thought we were going to lose you!"

"You really had us worried," Bo said with a smile, a mix of worry and relief.

Max could see her confusion grow in response to these comments as she rubbed her eyes. "Where am I?" she asked, reaching her hand around her neck and unclasping the necklace.

"No, Kirsten, don't," Thomas said.

Max watched helplessly as her brother attempted to catch the necklace as it bounced from the couch onto the floor.

Kirsten yawned again and asked, "Why are you all watching me sleep?" as Thomas scrambled for the necklace on the floor. As the words escaped, Max saw the red streaks from the goblin's bite extend out in all directions, filling her veins once again.

"The necklace, get it on her now!" he shouted.

In an instant Kirsten was seizing, jaws clenched, and eyes rolling back, just as she'd reacted when the goblin bit her. Thomas fumbled with the clasp as he and the others clambered to get the sapphire against her chest. The dark red venom continued to extend out and down Kirsten's arm. Thomas wrapped the necklace around his sister as the tracking venom reached her chest. Just as it had done before, the crystal began to glow and the goblin's poison was driven back away from Kirsten's heart. She stopped seizing and lay unresponsive on the couch again.

"What the hell!" Thomas shouted. "Why did you take off the necklace?!" he shouted at his sister, tears welling in his eyes.

"That nearly worked," Britt said in frustration.

"Is there any more potion left?" Max asked.

Britt held up the bottle, "Not enough to have as strong of an effect."

Max cursed.

"That's why we saved this?" Bo said picking up the second bottle. "We can use it, but this time make sure she doesn't remove the necklace." He handed the potion to Britt.

Opening the bottle, she said, "Here goes, it's everything we've got."

She put the rim of the bottle to Kirsten's lips once more, ensuring Kirsten would drink the liquid at a steady rate. When more than half the bottle had gone down, the bright orange glow they'd seen in Max began to show. Britt pulled the bottle away from Kirsten's lips and corked it, not knowing if Kirsten would thrash like Max had. The orange light erupted from her skin and her shoulder shone bright, the blinding light lasting much longer than it had for Max. When the light faded, Max and the others instantly saw that the red streaks still wrapped Kirsten's left arm and chest, but the chunk of flesh missing where the goblin had bitten her was healed. Max watched again as Kirsten opened her eyes, waking up for the second time.

Looking at them with wide eyes, she asked, "Why are you all looking at me like that?"

Max felt himself relax for a moment. He noticed that

Thomas held the sapphire firmly against her chest.

When she looked down at his arm, he pleaded, "Don't ever take off this necklace, do you understand? Never take this off again." She nodded and Thomas flung himself around her letting his emotions take over.

Kirsten reciprocated the hug, "I think you better fill me in on what's happened."

Chapter Four

William's Return

nable to raise his arm, Ivan instinctively closed his eyes to protect himself against the bright flash. He knew that flash and what it meant. They were about to transport. Feeling every ounce of energy leave his body, Ivan broke off his mental struggle with Merglan and allowed the white light burning through his eyelids to take him. He felt a hand grip him, too tired to open his eyes, Ivan thought, *Anders has found a way. We're leaving now.*

The light vanished, followed by a deafening crack that echoed into a hollow space. He slumped on his knees, wavering to keep his body from falling. With his eyes still clamped shut, Ivan inhaled through his nostrils, trying to smell the new surroundings where Anders had taken them. As he sniffed, he found the strength to crack open his eyelids. The light in the space around him was dim, what little there was seeping in through stained-glass windows. *No!* he thought, realizing where he was. He felt the hand that gripped his arm let go and then smelled the familiar scent of dragon fire on charred stone.

Ivan felt the last of his iron will shatter as he toppled to the stone floor. He lay trembling from the exertion, having given all of his energy to helping Anders and Zahara find an opening. He heard Killdoor's terrible roar and felt the dragon's hot breath over his body. His ears screamed from the deafening roar so close to his head as the fierce dragon's crow ended.

The ringing in his ears blocked out the clicking of heels as they circled around him. Ivan saw Merglan's boots, but his eyelids felt too heavy to keep his eyes open for long. He blinked slowly, resting his eyes for short intervals. He could see his enemy moving from standing to kneeling in a few choppy blinks. He saw Merglan shake his head. In a blink, Merglan was standing over him again. Then Ivan felt something hard push against his shoulder and he rolled onto his back, now looking up at the high ceiling.

"I didn't think you had that in you," Ivan heard Merglan say through his fog.

Ivan tried to move, but his quivering muscles didn't respond. His verbal response came out as a low groan.

"Careful now," Merglan said again, this time sounding closer. Merglan's hand was on his chest. "Don't overdo it. It's over, Will. For you. Your little son might've escaped me this time, but if you recall, so did you once." Merglan's words cut through the fog. Ivan understood that his efforts weren't for nothing. He had allowed his son the time he needed to escape.

Ivan attempted to summon magic, his last-ditch attempt to take Merglan down once and for all. If he could sneak in one well-placed shot to an artery, Ivan might have enough left in him to take the dark sorcerer out for good. His body seized as he attempted to summon the energy and Ivan knew he was likely going to overexert himself with this last attempt. The energy required to kill Merglan would, in turn, kill him, too, but based on how he felt, he was already dead. Better to die now in taking out the greatest threat to Kartania, than to die in a cell where Merglan was likely to place him.

"Oh, Will," Ivan heard Merglan say as he struggled to force the magic to come to him. "You can't possibly think that will work; you're practically broken."

Ivan didn't give in, instead trying harder and feeling the tingling of magic starting to well in his skin. *This is it, how I die, how I was always meant to go,* he thought.

Unfortunately for you, Merglan said, his voice now penetrating Ivan's mind. *I can't let you kill yourself, not yet anyway.*

Ivan's eyes snapped open. Just as he was attempting to force his last act of magic, Merglan's hand covered his face. A red spark shot from his palm and all went pitch black.

***

When he awoke, Ivan's head swirled with pain. He tried to move, but his body felt like stone and every muscle burned. Cringing as he attempted to move, Ivan's head spiked with pain as if Killdoor's massive claws were crushing his skull. When he mustered the courage and energy to open his eyes, he found his surroundings cloaked in darkness. The searing pain in his head made him dizzy as he stared blankly into the dark. Gagging from the intolerable pain, he rolled to his side. Every muscle in his abdomen cramped and locked in place as he dry-heaved in the billowing bedsheets. As his abdomen continued to tighten, he became aware of the bed he was lying in.

The sheets were soft, much softer than any wool

blanket he'd used on the trail. He could feel the ends of feathers poking through the case covering the fluffy pillows as he curled into the fetal position. Gasping for air, he felt the weight of a heavy down comforter on his body.

Wishing the physical and mental pain would end, Ivan wondered angrily, *Why am I in such luxury?* It didn't make any sense to him. A moment ago, he was trying to take out Merglan with one final spell, one that would've undoubtedly killed him at the same time. Now he lay in the most luxurious bed he'd lain in since he was a young man; since he was a prince in the capital of Southland.

As the cramping subsided, he straightened, once again able to lie still and ease the relentless aching in his mind. Light glowed through a window, somewhat dimmed by thickly woven drapes. He couldn't see the window without turning his head, but if he looked straight ahead and focused on the outer edges of his peripheral vision, he could see the ambient glow of daylight outlining the curtains. The bed's frame came into view, its dark wooden footboard arched with two pinnacles rising on either side, the canopy blanketed in dark cloth overhead. With the familiar bedframe, elegant bedding, and location of the window to his right old memories flashed into his mind.

Is this where I think it is? No, it can't be. But if it is, why? he wondered while gathering the courage and strength to stand. Moving slowly, he moved the bedcovers aside and planted his feet on the stone floor. Balancing with the aid of the stone wall backing the headboard, Ivan shuffled to the window. He recognized the curtains as those his father used to decorate the castle. Ivan felt the thick fabric with his fingers, then drew them back, allowing sunlight to fill the room. Squinting and blinking to clear his watering eyes, Ivan turned and confirmed where he was.

He was standing in his childhood bedroom; the room he'd grown up in, back before he was known as Ivan, back when he was William, Prince of Southland and heir to the kingdom of humankind. It was exactly as he remembered it the day he'd left, the day when he and Hannah set out on a journey and never returned. The memories of his time in this room came flooding back, but he didn't have the time to linger. He saw that he was alone in the room, his captors likely thinking he was still unconscious. This would be his opportunity to escape. Looking to the door, the only entrance or exit from the room apart from the widow, he began limping toward it.

He cracked it open and carefully glanced into the hallway. Wall-mounted torches lit the castle's stone interior hallway. Opening the door farther, Ivan realized that no one stood watch, he could attempt an escape.

Grasping the wooden doorframe, he hobbled out into the hallway, except he didn't move into the hallway. Ivan stopped, his breathing quickening at the strangeness of what had happened. While he continued to cling to the doorframe for balance, he was now looking into his bedroom as if he was just entering. Looking over his shoulder, Ivan saw the glow of torchlight in the hallway.

Confused, he shuffled on stiff legs to again face the open doorway. Cringing as he forced his body to move quickly, he stepped awkwardly through the doorway. This time his momentum carried him through the doorframe, yet he stumbled back into his bedroom. He reached out for something to hold onto and cried out in frustration as he found himself entering the room he'd attempted to exit. He fell to the floor, landing on an ornate rug in the center of the room. Using the marble table at its center and the nearer of two wing chairs, he pushed himself back to his feet.

This is some twisted trick only a madman could come up with, he thought, cursing the sorcerer he knew was responsible. *There's got to be a way out of here,* he thought, searching the room.

As he looked around the room in search of another exit, he noticed that nothing had changed since he left this room all those years ago. The bed remained in the same place with the same bedding. All of his old trunks lined the far wall, presumably filled with clothes and other trinkets any young prince would've desired. His expansive closet was filled with suits and rich silk shirts hanging from wooden hangers to keep from wrinkling.

Everything is exactly the same, except for that, he thought, his gaze landing on the small wooden box on the seat of one of the chairs. Simple in design and the size of his palm, Ivan stood staring at the box. He could feel something familiar about it, though he didn't recognize the box and wondered why it was placed so deliberately in that chair. Ivan scratched at his head, the memories of how he'd gotten here started to blur. He blinked, the pain from this thinking squeezing his mind.

This doesn't make any sense! Why am I here?

He limped around the small table to the large-paned window on the opposite wall. Flipping open the latch, Ivan pushed the window open. Fresh air blew past him as he looked out over the courtyard. His room was three stories up, too far to jump safely. He'd die trying from this height.

Looking down the stone castle wall, he thought, *I could climb down. I did it before when I was younger.*

Ivan pulled up his pants and sat down on the window frame. His stumbling about the room had actually loosened his muscles slightly. Raising one of his tired legs, he now straddled the window frame. Looking out the window, he cursed.

The right side of his body, the one that had been facing outside, was now also facing inside his room. He looked left into his room and then he looked right into his room. Just to confirm that this wasn't an illusion, he dropped his right side into the room. His foot landed firmly on the floor. He pulled himself through the aperture and back into the room. Turning around to look out the open window once again, he could see the courtyard below and feel the breeze gently blowing on his face. Ivan spat at the magically altered opening in frustration.

Stepping away from the window and toward the table, Ivan said aloud, "Why am I here?"

As if in response to his question, Merglan appeared in the doorway, spreading his arms in a welcoming gesture.

"You," Ivan growled through gritted teeth. "What have you done to me?!" he shouted lunging at the man despite his feeble state.

Merglan easily sidestepped Ivan's assault, allowing him to stumble past through the doorway and boomerang back into the room again, tripping on the rug as he fell to the floor.

Merglan brushed his hands together and said, "My dear friend, I thought you'd appreciate being put up in your old room."

Ivan sat up and glared at the sorcerer. He wanted to kill this man with every inch of his being. Merglan had destroyed his life several times over and Ivan wanted revenge. He called upon the magic within him, but there wasn't anything there. For the first time in his life since he'd bonded with his dragon, Jazzmaryth, he reached for magic that wasn't there. He tried to feel for any dwindling powers he might have retained after his latest battle with Merglan, but he couldn't sense them. His eyes darted back and forth, and he began to panic. Straining, he tried desperately through his aching mind to sense something, anything. He thought he might at least feel Merglan's presence as he stood directly in front of him, but he couldn't; there was nothing. Ivan looked down at his hands in horror, the realization hitting him in the gut like a steel fist.

Merglan stepped closer and knelt to Ivan's level.

Ivan glanced at him, hatred for Merglan welling inside him. "What have you done to me?" he asked through trembling cheeks.

Merglan laced his fingers together, resting his forearms around his knees as he squatted, "I haven't done anything to harm you, my dear old friend. On the contrary, actually. I plan to restore you."

Ivan narrowed his eyes, "What are you talking about?"

Rising, Merglan said, "Ivan, you were trying to kill us. You would've succeeded in killing yourself if I hadn't stopped you." Merglan stepped past Ivan to the window and peered out at the courtyard. "That spell you were trying to conjure up was far beyond your capabilities, but you already knew that, didn't you? You were exhausted from our mental struggle, which was truly impressive by the way, the fact that you were even able to accomplish that without Jazz and all. I'm surprised you could still perform any magic at all."

Ivan slammed his fist against the ground, drawing Merglan's attention, "Damn it, Merg! What did you do to me?"

"You always did have a short fuse," Merglan replied as he folded his arms across his chest and sat down on the open windowsill.

Ivan stood, turning to face his enemy, jaw clenched and ready to assault him.

Ivan saw Merglan raise an eyebrow at him, then return his gaze to the courtyard below, "I saved you from yourself, Ivan. You were dying. I almost let you, but at the last moment when you were slipping into the void, I broke into your mind and stopped the spell you were about to finish." He turned to face Ivan and continued, "Luckily, you hadn't gotten very far in casting the spell because you were so weak." Rising to his feet again, Merglan stepped closer to Ivan, "You were broken. Basically worthless. Killdoor and I repaired you. We brought your body back. I thought you would feel more comfortable waking here in your old room. I even left you a little gift." Merglan nodded toward the chair directly behind Ivan.

Ivan knew what he was referring to without having to look. The box. "What is it?"

Merglan stepped around him, letting his stare linger longer. "Why don't you open it and find out," he said, pulling the chairs out from the table with a snap of his fingers. Merglan sat down. Ivan glared suspiciously at him as he gestured to Ivan to take the other seat. Ivan hated that he was in the same room with his nemesis and didn't have a way to attack him.

At every other breath, Ivan searched for his magic, but it really was gone. His mind simply drew on blank space and emptiness. Fingering for the sword that had been at his waist when they'd come to the castle from the battle, he felt nothing at his side. Of course Merglan had taken that, too. He was unarmed and his mind was broken. He should've been dead, but Merglan even stopped that from happening. Ivan thought about trying to strangle Merglan, but the sorcerer would only have to wave his finger and Ivan would be rendered useless.

Ivan stepped warily around to the chair, lifted the box from its leather upholstery and sat. He set the box on the table between them.

"Don't you want to know what's inside?" Merglan asked with a slight, almost snarling smile.

Ivan leaned back in the chair, shaking his head.

Merglan glanced at the box, then leaned forward, eyeing the chessboard on the table. "No? Okay. I thought it was worth a try. How about a game instead?" Merglan said, moving a pawn forward.

"What's wrong with you?" Ivan asked, shaking his head.

Merglan frowned, "You used to love this game."

"Can't you have a real conversation with me for once?" Ivan asked irritated, leaning forward. "Why do you always have to do things through games and metaphors? Why can't you just talk to me straight?"

Merglan didn't lift his eyes from the table, "It's your move."

Ivan slumped back into the chair, "Merg, I really don't

want to play right now."

Merglan narrowed his eyes, "Don't you miss this, Will? We were pals, best buds. We were going to rule the kingdom together. What happened to us?"

Ivan's forehead creased, he couldn't believe Merglan would ask such a thing. "What do you mean, what happened? You came after me and Hannah with magic. You killed her and my oldest child! You took Jazz, my father, my brother-in-law and so many bonded riders. Do you even feel anything anymore?!" Ivan studied Merglan's blank expression, then continued, "And you ask me what happened? You killed your own father!"

"Oh, that was ages ago. Can't we just let bygones be bygones," Merglan said. "I was a different person back then. And you weren't in the right headspace to see things clearly either. Let's just start over, shall we? We can start by playing this friendly little game," Merglan leaned down over his white chess pieces.

Ivan grabbed the table and tossed it aside, sending the wooden box and chess pieces flying. Merglan bolted from his chair, waving his arm and freezing the mess in midair. The room grew dark and a strong wind began to blow in through the window. Merglan's eyes glowed with an anger Ivan had never seen before.

As abruptly as he'd started to unravel, Merglan regained control over himself. The wind stilled and the bright light of day returned in the window. He calmly returned the table to its original place and arranged the box and pieces as they had been. Straightening his shirt and pants, Merglan cleared his throat and said calmly, "I know it may take time for us to become reacquainted, but I believe we'll get there. It seems as though you don't wish to be with me at present, which is understandable given that we've just experienced a traumatic event together, so I'll leave you to your thoughts." Merglan strode from the room, exiting successfully through the door that had sent Ivan back into the room.

Ivan's nostrils flared in frustration. He tried to summon energy, anything from his decreased magical abilities, but nothing came. Shouting, he flipped the table over watching the chess pieces crash onto the floor. He pushed himself from the chair and hobbled angrily to the window trying to discern his invisible prison bars.

***

Merglan exited Ivan's room, breaking through the magical barriers he'd installed. He strode down the torch-lit hall. Descending the stairs, he walked out onto the main floor and turned sharply, entering the throne room. Striding confidently to the iconic chair, he recalled the day he'd first taken the throne, the day he'd killed the king. With a flick of his wrist, the crown came whirling onto his head as he sat.

Not a moment passed from the instant he leaned back into the throne to when the doors swung inward and an orc entered. Clad in armor and grimy from battle, the creature came into the room alone.

Merglan's jaw dropped. Irritated at the orcs' overall refusal to follow orders and use the chain of command, Merglan rose from the throne to ensure that his voice sounded full and more authoritative. He commanded, "What are you doing here? Have you no respect for your Commanding Officer?"

The orc began to speak in Grog, a wormy language full of hard clicks and sharp grunts. Merglan could speak it well enough, but the language sounded so awful. He hated it. He cut the orc off by pinching his fingers together, magically closing its mouth.

"Speak Landish, or die," Merglan said, stepping toward the orc and raising his hands as if to throw a spell on the creature. The orc stepped back, its lower lip quivered, exposing the lower tusks.

Speaking slowly and in a thick accent, the orc began to explain, "Forgiveness, my Lord. I bring news of the battle."

Merglan returned to his seat on the throne, deciding he wouldn't kill this creature, yet. "Why are you reporting this to me and not your commander?" he demanded.

"Our battle chief has been slain, your Excellency," the orc said in a higher-pitched tone.

Merglan shifted. Surely this creature wasn't telling him that his battle was lost and his appointed leader killed. There had been thousands of orcs massing on the eastern coast. "The death of your orc chief doesn't deserve my consult, that's why I have Lageena in charge of you filth. And you can address me as your Imperial Highness now."

"Sorry, my Imperial Highness, but you misunderstood my meaning. Lageena is dead. She was killed in one-on-one combat with the elf prince."

Merglan flung himself from the throne and onto the orc, who now crouched in fear. He kicked the creature in the shoulder guard and sent it skidding across the throne room floor. He sprung, leaping high into the air with inhuman skill and drew his knife from his belt. As he crashed onto the orc, Merglan held the sharpened steel against the creature's face. Lowering himself to inches above the orc, he snarled, "If you're lying to me, I'll gut you."

The orc, a female Merglan now realized having come close enough to see her defining cheek markings, stammered in her native language.

Merglan roared at her, "Landish, you insolent grunt, speak Landish!" he pressed the knife blade against her cheek, drawing the orc's dark blood.

"I swear it, Imperial Highness. I saw it with my own eyes. She's dead. A dwarf stabbed her through the heart with a burning blade."

Merglan narrowed his eyes, lifting the blade slightly, "By a dwarf? I thought you said it was the elf prince?"

She mumbled, "It was a dwarf that killed her."

Merglan pulled back and punched the orc in the face, knocking her to the ground, her head bouncing off the stone floor. "Get your story straight! If you and your orc friends think you can pull one over on me by telling me that Lageena's been killed, then you're wrong. Did you come here to coax me out so your orc friends could try to take me on? Is that your plan!?" he shouted, lifting the orc by her armor and shaking her furiously.

"Honest!" she cried out. "Lageena's dead. In one-on-one combat with the elf, but sneakily killed by the dwarf!"

Merglan stopped shaking the orc and released her. "Are there more of you outside?" he asked.

She nodded.

He marched from the throne room and into the entrance hall, dragging her along by the armor. Throwing open the heavy castle door, he stood in the entrance and stared out at a group of messenger orcs. They had carted

Lageena's dead body from the battle site. Merglan spotted it at once. Releasing the orc, Merglan stared at them, breathing heavily. He watched Killdoor circle in and land on the castle's outer wall, eyeing the orcs in the courtyard.

Merglan turned to the nervous orcs and shouted, "This is what happens to anyone who enters my throne room unannounced!" With that he pulled back and thrust his knife into the female orc's temple, letting her drop heavily to her knees. He turned his attention to Killdoor and commanded, "Devour her," as he kicked the orc messenger down the steps.

Her body rolled onto the courtyard. In an instant, Killdoor leapt off the wall and glided down to the castle's front steps. After charring the body with dragon fire, he lowered his head and crunched into the steel-plated armor. He then took the orc into his mouth and flew up to his roost on the outer wall. The other orcs gawked until Merglan shouted at them, "Gather your forces and bring them to the city gates! You'll be needing a new commander."

Merglan spun on his heels, the crown on his head nearly tumbling off. He entered the keep and slammed the doors behind him. Swelling with rage, he stomped to the throne and took his perch, pondering on how the death of Lageena would affect his plans.

CHAPTER FIVE

Disbanded

unning deeper into the bramble, Nadir barreled through the forest's undergrowth as he snapped and tore a new path away from the orcs swarming Ryedale. Suddenly, Nadir passed into a small clearing, striding midway across before skidding to a halt, his feet cutting into the soft dirt as he stopped. Looking warily, his gaze darted in all directions in search of friend or foe. The sounds of elves collectively crashing through the forest filled the air, as his army fled from the fairnheir. He'd seen their orc masters following steadily behind them as they climbed the canyon slopes after the retreating elf, dwarf and Lumbapi forces.

Sweat seeped into his eyes as he searched the clearing, the sweat stinging his eyes and blurring his vision a bit. Trying to make sense of where the Lumbapi were taking their fleeing troops, Nadir called out to the last Lumbapi he'd seen before entering the forest, "Inama! Where are you!?" With the roar of crashing branches and stomping feet, he thought his shout might go unheard. Waiting for a response, Nadir recalled the Lumbapis' head start on their retreat. He ordered his soldiers to follow them, but the natives seemed to disappear upon entering the forest. He knew the Southland natives were attuned to the network of trails in this dense forest, but his people and the dwarfs were not. With the enemy on their scent, Nadir worried that his soldiers, with their elven ability to run at high speeds, would outpace the locals leading them to safety, and possibly miss their directions entirely.

After taking several deep breaths to slow his heart, Nadir prepared to call Inama once more. During this pause, he heard a series of screeching whistles piercing their way through the crashing in the forest. His instincts told him that only a native Lumbapi could produce such a unique sound. Orcs communicated in a guttural monotone and the fairnheir were too hound-like to produce such a high-pitched, bird-like sound.

Launching into a sprint toward the sound, the newly succeeded Elf King barreled through the undergrowth. Nearly crashing into his fellow elven soldiers, Nadir gathered followers as he ran, shouting, "With me!" in hopes that more elves would join them.

Slowing as he neared the origin of the whistle, Nadir stumbled trying to avoid running into the group of humans who suddenly came into view. Though he and his elves arrived in the Lumbapis' midst startled and half-crazed, Nadir felt a sense of relief at seeing their allies.

"Where's Inama?" Nadir asked, backing away slightly from the surprised humans he'd nearly overrun. His elven speed, though slowed, was still much faster than what the humans were capable of.

Princess Inama pushed her way through the cluster of Lumbapi soldiers to address the elf. She leaned heavily on her staff and her waist was saturated in blood. Nadir admired Inama's determination to continue. He wondered how much Natalia and Solomon had been able to help. Inama's breathing quickened from their flight as she addressed the elf king, "We must act fast if we're going to sneak our armies back into camp. If we take too long, the orcs will learn where we've gone and hunt us relentlessly."

"Leaderless," Nadir nodded, also panting with exhaustion. "We can use it to our advantage now, if we lose them in the forest. They'll not work together long without a strong leader."

"Can you gather your people and the dwarfs in all of this confusion?" she asked, straightening slightly.

Nadir glanced to the soldiers behind him and searched their familiar faces; Natalia wasn't among them. Nadir knew she could communicate mentally, sending direction to all those lost in the forest. He needed to find her if their armies were going to have a chance at making it out of this forest alive. Thoughts of hungry fairnheir sniffing out dwarfs wandering through the forest furthered his sense of urgency. "I can manage it once I've located Natalia. Just leave a few of your crew here with us, so they can help us navigate our way back to the camp."

Inama nodded, pointing quickly to several of her peers and speaking to them in native Lumbapi. Before disappearing into the forest, the princess said, "Good luck, elf. I do hope to see you again," and she vanished with her people into the greenery.

With the three remaining natives now looking to him for direction, Nadir couldn't help but feel lost at Inama's absence. A moment of panic caused his heart to flutter a bit, resulting in a slight cough. Clenching his fists, Nadir forced himself to calm down and carry on as any noble leader would. He was in charge now and he had to get his people's attention.

Possible solutions began to occur to him. He and those elves with him now could circle in different directions until they'd gathered all of their fleeing soldiers. Or, he could quickly climb a tree to gain a better vantage point and see in what directions his fleeing troops had headed. He could then use the soldiers close by to chase after them. Or, he could start shouting, which had worked when he sought to find Inama, but after hearing the native's shrill, bird-like call, he was forced to consider the repercussions of this option. Shouting would alert the orcs to his presence and possibly location. His best option was his first thought — he had to find Natalia. If he found her, she could lead all of his wayward troops by way of telepathy.

Why hasn't she contacted me already? Doesn't she fear the idea of becoming lost forever in the forest, spread out with no direction? Nadir asked himself.

The elves and selected Lumbapi clustered around Nadir watched as he played out the different scenarios in his mind. Their impatient and frightened expressions forced him to make a decision. Suddenly, he found his answer. He didn't know if it would work, but it would be the fastest way to communicate with Natalia. The elf king closed his eyes, pushed out all other distractions, and focused on finding Natalia with his mind. He had to create a link with her. He'd practiced the art of telepathy during his training to be a prince and, with hope, a dragonrider. His father believed he would one day be bonded to a dragon and saw fit to begin the mental training he would need. Recently, however, he had only communicated with others who formed a link with his mind first. It had been decades since Nadir practiced the art of controlling his mind, but now more than ever he was determined to have it work for him.

His soldiers' worried questions faded from hearing and Nadir passed into the trance his instructor had taught him years ago. Feeling for any mental presence, Nadir broadcast his thoughts over the forest. After a moment of doubt, Nadir heard Natalia's voice in his mind.

Nadir, she said, her tone heavy with worry. *Where are you? The elves and dwarfs are running blind. We're going to lose them to the forest if we can't find the Lumbapi.*

Nadir opened his eyes in surprise nearly losing the connection. He'd done it! Fumbling to hold the connection, he closed his eyes, focused and felt the link strengthen again. *Natalia, I'm here with several Lumbapi, but we're going to need your help in directing everyone to follow us back to camp. How can I find you?*

As he spoke, he felt a presence sweep over him like a slight breeze. *Stay there, I'm coming to you now,* Natalia said, and immediately the telepathic link weakened.

Nadir asked whether she had the strength to call everyone at once, but when he posed the question in his thoughts, there was no reply. He tried again, but Natalia had severed the connection. Grunting at the missed attempt, Nadir pounded his fist against his armor, the plate metal clanging. Realizing he'd had the conversation internally without sharing a word with those around him, Nadir felt the group's collective stares. He could see their concerns about his mental state written across their faces.

Clearing his throat and straightening his shoulders to address them as their leader, Nadir said, "I've communicated with Natalia just now. She knows where we are and is coming this way. She'll communicate to everyone with mindspeak and help lead them back to camp." Seeing a collective look of relief among the group, Nadir added, "Look lively while we wait. A fairnheir could find its way into our midst at any moment."

Within minutes, Natalia, Solomon, and several dwarfs stumbled into the group. Limping, Natalia leaned on a dwarf soldier and winced before speaking to Nadir. "I'm weak, but if we pool our strength, I could broadcast a message to the others, emitting a beacon signal for them to follow. I can't guarantee that it will work as quickly as we need it to, but I can get everyone headed in the right direction."

"What about you, Solomon?" Nadir said pointing to the little old wise man. "Can't you help with the beacon?"

Solomon shook his head in somber silence and Natalia answered for him, "Sol's tapped out; most of his powers came from the lizards."

"What happened to the," Nadir asked, but Natalia's signal halted him mid-question. Following a brief hesitation, Nadir continued, "Um… the, ah, rest of the elves?" he managed to ask.

"I'll explain later," Natalia said, motioning for the elves to gather around. "If I'm going to broadcast this message, I'll need to draw on our combined energy. I'm almost done, so this might be it for me."

Nadir nodded. He and the others gathered in a circle close to Natalia as she reached for the elf next to her. Nadir recalled from his lessons on magic that linking physically required less power to pull energy from another individual. Once they had clasped onto one another, Natalia summoned the strength of the group and sent a message into the minds of elves and dwarfs alike. Nadir instantly felt the pull of energy from his body. He experienced a chill as Natalia drew on their collective strength. He began to shiver, as did others in the circle, and then Natalia broke the link.

"It's done," Natalia said, again seeking support from the dwarf who'd been assisting her earlier. "We can continue to the camp."

"Now?" Nadir asked. "But the elves aren't here yet," he protested.

"I managed to place the tracker on one of the Lumbapi here," Natalia said, pointing to one of Inama's guides.

Nadir saw the Lumbapi soldier begin to search his body, looking for something stuck to him.

"Don't worry, my friend. The tracker is only a signal, it's nothing physical that you can see. It will last as long as my strength does," Natalia said, addressing the worried man.

"Astonishing," Nadir remarked.

"Well," Solomon said, and Nadir heard the irritation in his voice. "Let's go."

Looking to the Lumbapi soldiers, Nadir said, "Lead the way. The faster we're away from here the better."

Breaking trail through the dense forest, the three Lumbapi soldiers led the small group of elves, dwarfs, and the old wise man as they hurried away from danger. Soon the roar of elves and dwarfs fleeing into the forest faded to soft footsteps slipping away from fairnheir and orcs. Each time Nadir looked back, he could see that their group had grown, others finding them as they moved toward camp.

Their march continued through the night. Nadir walked at a mind-numbing pace, his eyes drifting closed and snapping open as he followed the set of feet in front of him. The darkness faded and a new day brought clarity to their surroundings as they marched. Drawing near in the early morning light, Nadir noticed the tents indicating they'd reached their camp. The shrouding magical barrier that had once concealed their tents from any outside viewer had long since disappeared.

Nadir walked into the camp, his body and mind worn from their campaign. Lumbapi soldiers hurriedly packed their belongings, readying to leave at a moment's notice. Elves and dwarfs filed into camp, more trickling in after the initial wave arrived. Nadir stood near the camp entrance watching the soldiers return. He knew from his own weariness that they might be inspired upon seeing their leader watching over them as they reached camp safely. Elves and dwarfs alike took rest after entering the camp, dropping their shields and weapons as each found an empty patch of dirt to collapse onto. The battle had been grim and as the last of the soldiers trickled in, Nadir greeted them respectfully. Their numbers had dwindled into the hundreds. They'd lost many to the orcs; a reality Nadir did not want to face. In addition to losing well-trained soldiers, Nadir's campaign had cost them three of the most valuable allies they had: a bonded rider pair and their mentor, taken by a sorceress, had failed to return to battle.

Nadir pushed the thought from his mind when he saw

Remli, the dwarf king, bringing up the rear. Grizzled from action and appearing to be more beast than dwarf from the grime and branches protruding from his hair and beard, Remli managed to smile when he saw Nadir.

Walking up to the elf king, Remli said in a full voice, "Might've been lost without the witch's help. So, what happens now?"

Nadir wondered at how the dwarf could continue to exude so much energy after such a grueling ordeal. He wasn't in the mood to discuss strategy, but knew the topic couldn't be avoided. Nadir stared blankly at Remli. He came to Southland for revenge and achieved it in the elimination of Lageena, the traitorous elf queen, but after the overall defeat in battle left Nadir worried about the fate of their world.

"What say you, elf?" Remli said, stepping closer.

Shaking away any defeatist thoughts, Nadir answered, "A council with Inama. I'll gather those of my leaders who've survived and we'll meet back here in an hour to discuss a strategy."

"Make it a half-hour," Remli said sternly. "Those orcs lost our trail during the night, but that doesn't mean they won't pick it back up again. Besides, it wouldn't take Merglan and his dragon very long to dispatch us now that this camp's been exposed."

Nadir nodded and began searching for the commanding officers who survived the battle.

Locating next-in-command proved to be even more difficult than he anticipated given that so many high-ranking officers had fallen during the fighting. Nadir felt the burden of loss hang heavily on his soul each time he learned of a loyal elf's death. Somberly promoting those next in line, Nadir took no joy in rewarding elves on this day. It had been decades since the elven army had suffered such a defeat and it had happened under his command. The hasty assault fueled by his father's murder had cost the lives of so many of his nation's proudest elves.

After gathering and promoting nearly half of his commanding officers, Nadir took the most senior three to council with the Lumbapi and dwarfs. Walking stiffly to where he'd last seen Remli, Nadir found the dwarf king accompanied by a select four dwarfs as well as his daughter, Maylox, who had recently saved his life in battle. Inama and two other Lumbapi stood next to the dwarfs. Nadir nodded to them as he joined the group.

"What do your people intend to do next?" Remli asked, directing the question to Inama.

"We can't stay here," Inama said, leaning hard on her staff. "What our people do is move quickly after an attack. It's how we've stayed so effective in this war. We can't remain in the same place for long. When Merglan learns of his commander's death, he'll come searching for our camp. If he doesn't, the orcs will, and they'll find it eventually. We will retreat to the Ramhorn and join my father's tribe."

"You're going to abandon this ground?" Remli said in protest.

"We don't have an option now. Merglan and his dragon could come at any moment and, without the concealment spell, we're at his disposal."

"They could always come at any moment!" Remli growled. "He has had that damned dragon for nearly thirty years. We just forgot about him when he disappeared last, growing comfortable in their absence, but the threat has never gone away."

"We've been effective thus far in the fight because we've been able to strike quickly and get away unseen. After seeing the size of his army in Southland, I doubt he even noticed us before. Now that we've gotten so big, though, we'll surely attract his full attention," Inama said

"Damn it all. This ground is good for an ambush. We shouldn't just abandon it. So we suffered a defeat. We'll find a new place to hide, here on the Drakeshead, and we'll send for reinforcements," Remli urged.

"No, it's too late for that. We're going to join our other tribes, and we'll hold ground there. I've dedicated myself to my people's preservation. We thought that we could defeat the orc army by combining our forces, but now, after seeing what they've brought to the fight, there's no way we can compete with their numbers in open combat."

"Not with that attitude!" Remli bellowed.

"What about you, Nadir? What are your thoughts in all of this?" Inama asked, motioning toward Nadir.

"Don't forget what I risked in order to save you back there," Remli growled, his face reddening.

"Remli!" Nadir warned. "I don't want to back down from this fight, just as Remli you don't."

With a snort, Remli nodded curtly and Inama opened her mouth in protest.

Before she could interrupt, Nadir quickly added, "But that doesn't mean I want to drag out the fighting here in the Drakeshead." Addressing Remli, Nadir said, "You have to acknowledge the massive loss we've suffered from this battle. If we continue to fight with dwindling numbers, we'll only be delaying the inevitable. Eventually we'll be caught outnumbered and out-ranked."

"That's why I say we send for reinforcements," Remli said. "I have an army of dwarfs in reserve at Hardstone. We can send your ships to bring them here. And this elven force you've brought, Nadir, isn't even half the full might of the Everlight soldiers at your command. You could bring them in full force and together we could crush this orc army."

"This is not our battle," one of Nadir's officers interrupted.

Nadir turned to face the voice that came from behind him, "How do you mean?" he asked. "Did we not come here to fight in the name of Kartania?"

"No," the elf responded, firm in his stance. "With all due respect to you and King Remli, we came here with you to avenge the death of our leader. Lageena's dead and the tie to Merglan has been severed. We can now return to the safety of our Enlightened Forest where the sorcerer can't touch us."

Nadir stepped back, slighted by his soldier's opinion. "Are you suggesting we abandon the world to Merglan's control?"

"Not at all, my King. I am suggesting that we survive his wrath. From the protection behind Cedarbridge's walls we can replenish the dragonriders and hold out until we're in a position to pose a real threat to the sorcerer."

Nadir searched the officer's hardened expression. "You'd be condemning entire nations to slaughter. By holding back in our protective bubble, we'd be allowing evil to destroy free will in Kartania."

"I stand firm in my belief, Commander, as do many of

our race. We're done fighting here and need to return home. The fate of the world depends on our ability to produce more dragonriders. You saw for yourself that we can't rely on a single rider pair," Nadir's officer continued, his words an offense to the level of trust he'd held in Anders and Zahara.

Before Nadir could respond, Remli shouted, "And what about us!? When you leave, would you at least bring us home? Or will you just leave us behind because we're all dead anyway?"

The elf's face reddened and he responded with a frown, "I'm sorry, my King. Your army has spoken. We're returning to the Everlight Kingdom. Our people need a ruler now more than ever. Bring us together and we might fight another day. Divide us and we'll descend into chaos like the realm of humans."

"And what of Anders, Zahara and Ivan? I will not abandon them here," Nadir said.

"They have a dragon. If they survive, they can fly away. We don't have that luxury. We need to move before Merglan can make a plan."

"I am your King," Nadir said.

"And we want you to continue to be our king," the elf said. "But if you stay with the Lumbapi and we return home, the High Council will vote in our favor, for the preservation of life on this earth, and they'll choose a new king."

"I don't have time for this," Inama said. "You do what you want, elf. I'm leading my people to the Ramhorn. We're moving out within the hour." Inama waved her fellow Lumbapi to follow her and she limped away.

The elf officer addressed Nadir again, "We'll begin

loading the ships and wait for your decision before leaving. But we, too, need to leave this place."

Nadir watched silently as his senior officers turned away. The Elf King turned to Remli and said, "What about Anders and Ivan? I can't abandon them."

"What happened to them?" Remli's daughter asked before Remli could give Nadir a piece of his mind.

"Lageena, she used the crystal to transport them from the battle," he felt at his side where he'd placed that crystal, forgetting he had taken it from her corpse.

"Lageena came back, but Anders, Zahara and Ivan didn't," Maylox said, looking toward Nadir's feet.

"We can't just give up hope for them," Nadir said. "I refuse to leave them with no way of knowing what's happened."

Remli's face turned a paler complexion as he heard the elf king's grief, "We're clearly outnumbered and now the Lumbapi are moving west. They don't fight like we do and, with or without us, they'll be effective with their guerilla warfare. We have hardened soldiers at Hardstone who will fight for the fate of the world. I don't want to lose my good faith with the elves at such a critical time. We're going to need to fight together if we want to win this war."

"But you've seen what just happened. I've lost control. They won't follow me anymore," Nadir said.

"Being a leader is not about ordering your people to obey, it's about making compromises, just like I'm about to do now," Remli said. "Your people want you to lead. They need you to lead them, but they can't have you lead them from here. We're just sitting ducks for Merglan if we stay put, despite what I said about the good ground. Sure, if we had enough forces, we could put up a good fight and maybe win, but no one else seems to agree. So, I propose you go with your people and take us back to Eastland along the way. That way I can rally my army and lead a strike force against Merglan. You'll need to convince your people that together we can defeat Merglan."

"What about Anders and Ivan?" Nadir asked.

"From what I learned in my time spent around Ivan and Natalia, she won't be going with you, not even if you ordered her. She'll stay here with the Lumbapi until she learns more about what's happened to them. And, at this point, a smaller extraction team led by some fierce dwarfs, Lumbapi guerillas and an elf or two would be the best way to get them out of trouble if Merglan's found them."

"You don't think he'd kill them on the spot?" Nadir asked.

Remli shrugged, "He might. I would. But I'd be willing to bet he thinks he can control or convert them. That's why he hasn't just ridden in and killed them already. He's obviously got a plan for them, so if Lageena somehow tricked them into getting close to Merglan and they got caught, I bet he's going to hold onto them for awhile."

Nadir nodded thinking over Remli's theory.

"At the very least, I'll want to leave a few people here with the Lumbapi. We'll need to know where to strike when we return," Remli said.

"I'll stay," Maylox offered.

"No," Remli commanded, shaking his head. "You're needed with me."

"You didn't want me with you when you came here, but now you need me to join you when you're leaving?" she asked. "You've guaranteed me a position in the dwarf army; let me start here with this mission. I won't let you down."

Remli swelled with pride, "Well, no one will ever accuse you of not being like your old man."

Maylox chuckled.

Remli nodded, "Yes, I need to let you go, don't I? If this is what you truly desire, then you can stay."

"I'll task Natalia with staying, even though she would regardless. Solomon will follow the Lumbapi, as he did before, so that leaves us with some allies here among the Lumbapi."

"Very well," Remli said. "I'll order my dwarfs to the ships. 'Tuck tail and sail' as I used to say to those Rollo Islanders."

Nadir grinned, chuckling at the slight. He found Natalia resting against a tree, eyeing the Lumbapi soldiers. Kneeling next to her, Nadir handed her a small pouch.

"What's this?" she asked, taking it.

"Keep it on you at all times for communication," he said as she opened the pouch.

"Your father's communication mirrors," she said, sounding confused.

"Our people need convincing to stay in this fight. I need to lead them to make the right choice," he paused, shaking his head. "I should be staying to help you seek out Anders and Ivan, but I can't. The council will usurp my reign if I don't follow our army home. That's why you need to stay and keep me updated. Follow the Lumbapi and keep me in the loop. I'll return with the full strength of the elven army and the dwarf army."

Nadir rose to his feet once Natalia had nodded. "Serve

me well, Natalia. Our rider's fate may very well depend on it." As Nadir walked back to the ships, he hoped Anders, Zahara and Ivan would be waiting for them at the Everlight Kingdom.

Chapter Six

Anders

nders awoke with a gasp, his eyes peering into the vast emptiness before him. The darkness encased him as he lay on his back, his body damp with feverish sweat. Rising to a seated position, he winced with pain. His muscles taut with days' of overuse; he also felt a burning sensation across his back. Groaning, he attempted to control his rapid breathing and slow his heart rate while trying to make sense of the darkness. Confusion hung over him like an early morning fog, blanketing his memory.

Where are we? Where's Zahara? he questioned, the thoughts making his head feel pressed as if a vice squeezed on his brain.

Fighting physical fatigue, Anders again squinted into the darkness, hoping to discern even the outline of something that would give him an idea of where he was and whether Zahara was still with him. Twisting to expand his search, he felt the skin on his back crack and then a wet trickle from the crack. It stung. He gritted his teeth to fight off the pain. He didn't want to risk crying out in this strange place for fear Merglan and Killdoor might still be after him. As he tried to settle back into a more comfortable posture,

Anders recalled a fleeting glimpse of a dragon; the brilliant red of the dragon shining against an opal sky. The image seemed like something from a dream, but stood out so clearly that Anders knew it to be real. The fog clouding his memory broke in patches, bringing to mind a glimpse of their hasty escape. Ivan had been locked with Merglan in a mental struggle when Anders had broken free from Merglan's grip. He recalled diving toward Ivan on Zahara's back and somehow summoning the will to transport them. Then a bright flash.

As his mind continued to clear, Anders grew nearly frantic to find them, so he opened his mind, attempting to search for Ivan and Zahara's presence. Calling upon his mental power, Anders was hit by a tidal wave of pain that again robbed him of his focus. Grunting, he put his fingers to his temples and applied pressure. He closed his link and retreated within, quickly giving up on using magic to locate his companions. He would have to rely on his other senses to find them.

Reaching straight ahead, Anders felt into the empty black space. Slowly moving out to his sides, he was careful to avoid further cracking the burning patch of skin on his back. Feeling nothing but open to either side, he began to panic. A fear of complete loneliness and isolation crept into his thoughts and he felt his pulse increase. Attempting to control his emotions, he tried to push through the worry and focus on where they might have been transported.

He closed his eyes to gain some self-control and saw a bright flash. Suddenly he recalled sliding across the stone floor with Zahara and grabbing Ivan as they skidded past. He could almost feel the release of the tainted energy from

Lazuran, his empowered sword, as he sent it from his body. The sphere of light grew around them, ever so briefly turning Merglan's own energy against him to allow for their escape. Visualizing the enclosing sphere gave Anders a sense of safety, allowing him to calm down for a moment. Then he remembered a hand shooting into the white orb, gripping Ivan and yanking him out of sight an instant before they were transported. The heartache he'd felt in this fog was now explained. He planted his hands at his sides, clutching at the wool blanket beneath him.

His sudden awareness of the blanket knocked him from the horror of leaving Ivan behind. How did this wool blanket come to be underneath him? He carried two in his saddlebag, but now he could clearly recall the moment of transport. The sight of his mentor and friend being ripped from his life as the energy from casting the transport spell took its toll on him. Following the flash came the red dragon, approaching, then darkness.

Fighting through the memory of the hand ripping Ivan away, Anders returned to his search. He knew he didn't arrive wherever this was alone. And the sight of the red dragon confused him all the more. Was he back in the Everlight Kingdom? The sensation of not knowing where he was or whether anyone else was nearby sent him further into a state of panic. Shuffling ninety degrees, Anders sought to feel at the space behind him. He swept his hand freely to the side expecting to feel open air when the side of his hand slapped into something hard. Shaking his hand, Anders whimpered a solemn, "Ouch!"

He reached, slower and more gently this time. The feeling of dragon scales was unmistakable, even in the dark.

Anders knew Zahara slept at his head as she so often did when they were traveling. Turning onto his hip, Anders fought through the physical pain searing in his back and gently stroked the dragon. Despite his heartache for Ivan, he felt great relief and a sense of wholeness at knowing he hadn't left entirely alone. Zahara was here with him. Now he just needed to figure out where 'here' was.

Did Zahara set me on this wool blanket? Has she made sure that we were safe before choosing to sleep here? And what of that red dragon?

Anders abruptly stopped petting Zahara. Doubt entered his mind when he heard the deep rumbling exhale of a dragon; a dragon that wasn't Zahara.

Clamping his hand over his mouth, Anders stilled his breathing and remained motionless. The deep grumbling of the unknown dragon drew fear Anders thought he'd escaped. Quivering, he breathed unsteadily into his cupped hands as he tried to decide what to do. He again tried to open his mental link with Zahara, but the pain was too excruciating. Because of his fatigue, his magic proved inaccessible.

Deciding he had to move, Anders weighted his palms and shifted silently in the darkness. As he pressed down and bent to pull his legs up under him, he felt the tight patch of skin on his back crack open again. Biting down to avoid crying out, Anders flexed every muscle in his body. Moving silently though carefully, he rested momentarily on hands and knees. Slowly, he lifted his right hand and began to crawl. As he moved off of the wool blanket, he paused, feeling the ground beneath him. His hands touched bare grass, damp with early morning dew. The grass suggested that he wasn't in the dense forest of the Everlight Kingdom. So where then? He continued crawling, knees on the grass dampening his riding pants.

Clear of the blanket and the dragon, Anders rose to his feet. His stiff muscles urged him to lie back down and the throbbing pain in his back nearly forced him to, but the fear regarding their current situation kept him moving.

How did I come to be in this predicament? Anders asked himself. *And why is it so dark?*

On his third step, Anders' foot landed on an unfamiliar surface. He tried to stop, but his momentum carried him forward. In his attempt to hop around the object, he wound up stepping even farther into the uneven mass. Metal clanged as he weighted his feet onto a loose bulge. The pile he stepped into shifted and sent him toppling to the ground. Unable to help himself, Anders cried out as he landed on his back. If the clattering of the metal wasn't enough to wake the dragon, his screaming did the job.

The sleeping dragon went on alert, scales clicking as it leapt to all fours. Spraying the air above with fire, the dragon illuminated their surroundings. Anders quickly assessed his whereabouts. He was sprawled in the pile of Zahara's saddle and his riding armor. Zahara was to his left, her head perked up in alarm as a red dragon expelled another arch of fire overhead. The wool blanket he woke up on was spread out in the grass next to him and a ring of rocks marked a campfire that obviously had been burning earlier in the night. Across the fire ring, close to where Anders had been sleeping, he saw a girl with brown hair rise onto her elbows, a look of shock on her half-asleep face. The dragon's fire extinguished and Anders' world plunged back into darkness.

All thoughts of his pain vanished as he recognized the girl in the fleeting light. He tried to untangle himself from the saddle's many straps and get out of the pile.

Awkwardly moving to his feet, he spoke into the void, "Maija, is that you?" Now that the darkness had returned, he wasn't sure if it was Maija. He waited for a response.

"Anders?" Maija's voice floated across to him, soothing his fear. "What's wrong?"

"Maija!?" Anders said, more loudly and in disbelief. "It's you, but how?"

"Yes, it's me. Hold on, don't move. I'll come to you," she said, her voice moving closer as she spoke.

Anders heard wood clack together as she tossed a few small logs into the fire ring and muttered something he didn't hear clearly. A narrow stream of flame poured out of the red dragon's mouth, dripping flames onto the wood. The orange and red glow from the dragon's mouth lit the space between them. Anders could see Maija lock eyes on him from several arms' lengths away. The glow lessened as the dragon's fire cut off and the flames began to burn the logs, but the small fire provided more than enough light to see.

All of Anders' worries melted away as he stepped hurriedly into Maija's embrace. They held each other tight for several long breaths and Anders allowed himself to become lost in her familiar touch. Pulling back, he could see the wrinkles of worry on her face as she asked, "Anders, is everything all right?"

Anders glanced to Zahara as he saw her move closer to the enormous red dragon, sniffing the air carefully as she leaned her head in his direction. Anders shook his head, the throbbing stab returning to his mind. He asked, "What's happening? Where are we?"

Maija's jaw clenched and she glanced down, obviously considering where to begin, "Let's get you back onto the blanket; it's sort of a long story. You and Zahara have clearly been through some trauma and you're exhausted." Ushering Anders back to the blanket, she helped him sit back down. She gasped as she glanced at his back, "Anders, you're bleeding again!" He felt her chilled hands touching his bare skin. "And I had finally gotten it to stop."

Anders smiled as she moved swiftly to the other side of the fire. Grabbing the other blanket and a small satchel that he recognized from his riding saddle, she returned, setting them down at his side. Reaching inside, Maija pulled out a cloth and dabbed it on his back. He flinched as she prodded the wound, "You're going to have to be more careful now that you're awake." She placed the cloth across his back and said, "Don't move."

She then hefted Zahara's saddle around the fire, setting it behind him. Touching him on the shoulder she said, "Okay, now lie back, but carefully."

He did as she asked and gently leaned against the leather. Maija spread her wool blanket out next to him and leaned back, sharing the saddle. He couldn't help but grin when she leaned into him and wrapped her arms around him, pulling their bodies closer together. He kept an eye on Zahara, who continued to circle the red dragon, sniffing at him as he lay on his belly, stretched out behind them again. Seeing the dragon settle in, Anders realized he must have been stroking the dragon's hind leg when he thought it was Zahara. Glad to be in safe company and looked after, Anders desperately needed some answers, "Alright, now that you've sorted me out, will you fill me in on some details? Like how you all of a sudden are traveling with a dragon and how we got here?" As Anders spoke, Zahara shifted her focus and laid down near Anders' feet, exhaling with a snort as she relaxed. But she kept her eyes fixed on the red dragon. Her actions had Anders wondering whether she had known the dragon was there or if she, too, had just become aware of his presence.

Maija inhaled, turning to meet Anders' eyes, "I think you're going to have to fill me in a little bit, too. I only found you and Zahara by chance."

"I'll try, but I'm a little foggy on the details still," Anders said, rubbing his temple again. "My memory is coming back in waves."

"You two were in pretty rough shape. I thought you were going to die a few times, based on your breathing patterns."

"Really?" Anders asked surprised.

Maija nodded, tightening her grip around his arm, "But you didn't. Anyway, how I found you, it was so strange. You and Zahara just appeared out of nowhere. We saw a bright flash of light and then, poof, the two of you showed up. By the time we reached you, both you and Zahara were out cold. Your armor and her scales were coated in blood and charred as though you'd walked through fire. She had some deep gashes and your riding armor was torn across the back. Raffagaun and I had only just become acquainted."

"Raffagaun?" Anders interrupted, nodding toward the scarlet dragon.

"Yes, he's the dragon we saw on Mount Orena. It took me over a week, but I found him," she said, swelling with pride.

"Of course you did," Anders said.

"So, we'd just met, and I was riding him for the first time when we saw you two pop up." Anders wanted so badly to interrupt and ask her more about Raffagaun, but he held his tongue. "Our communication wasn't perfect at first, but with a little trial and error, I told Raffa that we needed to get you two somewhere safe, which wasn't easy, by the way. Not so much for you, but Zahara; she isn't exactly light, you know."

Anders eyed Zahara, her gaze still fixed on Raffagaun, "That's incredible. So, we're at Mount Orena? Maybe we can arrange for the dwarfs to…"

Maija cut him off, "Not exactly."

"But King Remli is our ally," Anders said. "He helped us on our campaign in Southland."

"No, not about the dwarfs," Maija interjected. "About being at Mount Orena."

"But I thought…" Anders began and trailed off.

"I said it took me a while to find him," Maija said. "That's because he didn't stay in Eastland. Anders, we're in Nagano."

Anders' eyes widened, "As in, the land of dragons, Nagano?"

Maija nodded.

"Are we safe here?" Anders asked, unsure how wild dragons would react to the rider's presence. He knew from his studies that the last time riders came to Nagano was during The War of the Magicians, and Merglan had caused a civil war between young and old dragons. He hoped those affected by the war wouldn't associate that king of devastation with all riders.

Maija nodded, "We're safe here, at least we will be during the night. Raffa's provided us with a comfortable hiding place, so hopefully during the daylight the other dragons won't take much notice of us."

"How long have Zahara and I been here?" Anders asked.

"Since yesterday afternoon. It must be near dawn now," Maija replied.

Anders shifted slightly and stared into the flames. He didn't like it when he lost track of time, no matter how long it had been.

"I was beginning to get worried you weren't going to come out of it. Your breathing at times was not normal. What happened to you two? There was a campaign to Southland with the dwarfs? And you transported?" Maija asked hesitantly.

Anders continued to stare into the flames, recalling the battle at Ryedale and the confrontation with Merglan and Killdoor. Flashes from the battle danced among the flames before them. Orcs falling one by one at the hands of Lumbapi soldiers. Elves flooding into the streets in the riverside town. Zahara and Anders battling Lageena. The chaos of slaughter, the explosion, Lageena transporting them directly to Merglan. That's when things became patchy for him. He could clearly recall transporting and Ivan being pulled away. He recalled the mental struggle with Merglan and the sensation of Killdoor's claw cutting through to his flesh.

Maija nudged Anders back to reality. "It's okay. Whatever it was that happened, you're here with me now."

Anders shook his head. He was glad to be with Maija, but what had happened to the others? What had he done by leaving them behind? Somehow, amidst the chaos of what was happening in Merglan's lair, Anders had used the somewhat tainted power of Lazuran to will himself and Zahara to Maija.

"I know whatever it was, was awful and involved a lot of bloodshed," Maija said.

Anders turned to meet her deep brown eyes, glinting in the firelight. Taking in her stunning features as if he'd never see her again, he said, "I did things, terrible things in the name of vengeance. And the others, we left them behind."

He wanted to say more, but Anders couldn't bring himself to describe what had happened, not yet anyway. Maybe he would tell her more in the morning, but for now, he rested his head against the saddle and felt the heartache and pain again. Maija placed her head against his chest and wrapped her arms around him in an embrace. Anders closed his eyes, letting the memories of the encounter with Merglan seep back into his consciousness.

***

Waking hours later in the early morning, Maija slowly lifted Anders' arm up and over her head and carefully stepped away from the wool blanket she'd taken from Anders' saddlebag. He didn't have much in the small side pouch compared to the larger bags Zahara had carried on their way to Mount Orena. This time Zahara's saddle had been outfitted for combat; she only carried two small bags holding a few essentials for survival.

Maija added several logs to the smoldering fire that Raffa had started for them earlier. She heard the now-familiar movement of his clacking scales as he woke. Maija turned to face the dragon as he raised his head from the grass. She placed her index finger over her lips, shushing him. He immediately obeyed her command.

Stretching his leathery wings out and folding them back in, the red dragon spoke in Maija's head. She almost jumped at the sudden presence of his deep mental voice, *When will the human and she-dragon be well enough to ride?*

Stepping toward Raffa, Maija replied with mindspeak, *I'm not sure. They're still weak from their fight. They're going to need food when they wake. I can't say for sure when their last meal was, but sometimes Anders will go days without eating if he's too focused on his task.*

Is that a long time for humans to go without food? Raffa asked.

Yes, Maija replied. *Without fuel for the body, they'll grow weaker with each passing day. Usually humans eat three times a day.*

Raffa groaned in surprise.

How long can dragons go without food? she asked.

I have gone months without meals, he said triumphantly.

Months? Maija asked skeptically.

It depends on how big the catch is, Raffa explained. *When I hunt in the land to the north, I can take down a real dragon-sized meal. The sustenance will last me two to four months with the right use of energy.*

Seriously!? Maija exclaimed. *I had no idea. I've seen Zahara go without meals for a few days, but I guess I've never seen her eat anything larger than a deer.*

What is, deer? Raffa asked.

Raffa was new to communicating by way a mental link with anyone other than a fellow dragon, so when he converted his thoughts to Maija, each of them struggled with some unfamiliar language or terms. She sent him an image of a deer.

Yes, the deer is a small meal and doesn't last long as energy, Raffa confirmed.

I think we'll need to feed Zahara then, too, when she wakes. Can you catch an extra something or other when you go out for your morning hunt? Maija asked.

Raffagaun agreed and quietly stepped away from the camp before spreading his wings and taking flight.

Maija had been preparing for Anders to regain consciousness for more than a day. She and Raffa had scouted out their hiding place among a widespread grove of trees bordering an open field. Staying beneath the low-hanging canopy, they were concealed to aerial hunters while still able to keep an eye on the open valley. This way they could see anything or anyone approaching from a great distance. Water ponded in several low-lying locations within the grove and many of the trees bore the fruit that had sustained Maija during her time in Nagano. While she waited for Anders and Zahara to wake, she harvested fruit and placing the pods in a pile near the fire ring. With several of the hollowed-out shells from her past meals, Maija reused them as water carriers. Their camp was well stocked with drinkable water, food from the trees, and wood for fire, all gathered from this small area. Maija didn't like sitting still so she took every opportunity she could to update or improve the camp.

When Anders finally awoke, Maija was sitting next to him on the wool blanket using her hand to scoop out the innards of one of the pods she'd broken open. Spooning the turquoise goop into her mouth, she mumbled, "Goo morn'n," and quickly swallowed as Anders pushed himself upright. "I mean, good morning," she repeated more clearly.

"What's that?" Anders asked, nodding toward the gourd.

Maija shrugged, "I call it Nan's butterscotch. Nan's because it tastes just like my Grandma Nan's or whoever she actually was. It provides lots of energy. Want to try some?" she asked, offering him the open half of the gourd.

She watched him eye the fruit skeptically. He leaned forward to smell it. "That really is just like butterscotch," he agreed.

Maija nodded and motioned for him to try it.

"I like butterscotch," he said dipping his fingers into the shell as Maija had. She smiled at his reaction upon tasting the fruit.

"It's good, right?" she nodded.

Anders nodded back as he smacked the goo in his mouth. Swallowing, he said, "Yeah, it's really good. How did you find this?"

"By accident," she said dipping a finger in and licking it clean. "The sap from the tree tastes similar. I tried breaking one of the shells open on a tree and accidentally tore the tree's bark. The sap's turquoise, just like this fruit, and smells strongly of butterscotch. Later I found a rock and broke open the shell."

Anders scooped more of the super goo into his mouth. "That's amazing," he said.

Zahara rolled onto her back, lying with her arms and legs pointing up into the air and flopping down at the joints. She bent her neck so she could see Anders and Maija and sniffed the air between them. Maija raised an eyebrow at her and asked, "Does she do that often?"

"Lie like that, all upside down? It's the first I've seen," Anders replied.

"She's probably hungry," Maija said

Rolling back onto her side, Zahara swept her head around the camp and asked Maija, using their mental connection, *Where's the red male?*

"I sent him out to collect something for you to eat," she said aloud, handing the shell to Anders.

Zahara smacked her lips together and asked, *Water?*

Maija pointed into the trees behind her, "There's surface water over there in that depression."

Zahara nodded, rose to her feet and went to get a drink.

Realizing Anders would want a drink, too, Maija walked to the pile of gourds and grabbed a hollowed-out shell full of water. She handed it to Anders and asked, "How do you feel now?"

"Pretty good, actually. Much better than last night. I had a terrible headache, but it's starting to go away now."

"Good. Maybe after you've had some more food you could try to heal yourself and Zahara," she suggested.

Anders nodded, "I might have to build up more strength for that. I'd never used up all of my energy before. Normally a full days' rest should be enough, but every time I try to use my senses," he winced, shaking his head. "Yeah, not ready yet."

"I've got a lot to learn about that kind of thing," Maija

said, looking toward the sky, hoping Raffa would return soon with their food.

"You found him just a few days ago then?" Anders asked.

Maija nodded and proceeded to fill him in on the path she'd taken after they parted ways. Anders devoured butterscotch shell after shell while she finished her story. As she reached the point where she met Raffagaun along the lakeside, the great red dragon landed just beyond the tree line, carrying a fat hump-backed cow in his jaws.

Coming into camp, Raffa presented the meal to Zahara, bowing low and backing away as he laid the animal before her. She bowed, keeping her eyes locked on the dragon. Raffa rose from his bow and trotted into the trees to get a drink while Zahara began consuming her meal.

"You ate more than I thought you would," Maija said, looking at the empty shells surrounding Anders.

She grinned as he lay back against the saddle, "A few days without a proper meal will do that to a person."

"Maybe now that you're feeling better, you can tell me what happened after we parted ways?" she asked.

Anders looked away; she could tell he was troubled by the thought. Slowly, he recounted the details of their quest, taking a few short intermissions to drink more water and snack on the husked fruit. From the moment they left Hardstone, to their arrival in Cedarbridge, Asmond's murder, Nadir's escape from prison and calling his soldiers into action. He touched on the divide among the elves' High Council as to whether to pursue Lageena. Anders told her of his and Zahara's journey to the Rollo Islands and his difficulties with Red. He spoke of their exhausting flight to

Southland. She saw some pain in his eyes as he skipped again to their arrival. Meeting the Lumbapi and their plans for attack, then Anders stopped. "The rest is violent. Battle with the orcs and…" he trailed off.

"And how you faced Merglan?" Maija asked.

She saw a look of surprise come over him, "How did you?"

"Well, your injuries pretty obviously reflect a dragon attack and I can only think of one person who could cause so much damage to you and Zahara and exhaust you to the point of draining you of your energy," she said.

"Yeah," Anders said quietly. "Ivan was there, too. He didn't make it," he said and Maija saw his pain as he remembered the battle.

Placing her hand on his, she said, "Take your time. You can tell me more when you're ready."

He met her gaze and nodded. Maija could imagine how awful it must've been to endure such a struggle and then to flee; having all those who fought so valiantly vanish in a blink of an eye as Anders and Zahara were forced to run for their lives, and then waking up here, half a world away.

Chapter Seven

Encounter with the C.F.D.D.

hy don't you try it again?" Maija asked.

"I don't have enough to heal both of us," Anders said.

"But you were so eager to get moving after Zahara finished eating, I thought you were well-rested."

Anders pointed to a glimmering surface in the grass about a mile ahead, "Let's get water there, my gourd is running low and it doesn't seem like it's going to get any cooler today. The dragons will want more water, too." He looked skyward. Raffagaun flew over them, circling to stay with their footpace while Zahara walked behind them.

"We could travel much faster if we were both able to fly," Maija said.

Looking at her, he said, "Maybe I'll try again after more water. There's a technique I could try that I didn't earlier this morning."

Maija nodded.

Anders knew she was right; he needed to return to Southland in a hurry. He wasn't, however, anywhere close to fit for combat with Merglan and Killdoor and he knew he'd most likely have to face them if he was going to rescue

Ivan. Although Anders felt well rested despite the short recuperation period, his and Zahara's wounds needed healing. After exhausting his magical energy to transport himself and Zahara out of Merglan's lair, Anders was hesitant to try healing them with magic. The fifteen hours of deep sleep combined with the heaps of butterscotch pudding he'd eaten earlier this morning should've replenished some of his stores, but if he wanted to heal them properly, he needed more time. Following the battle in Eastland, Anders had used magic to heal Rollo Island warriors in the field, but that simple task had nearly drained him then and that was when his magic was fresh.

You lacked the experience and control back then, Anders heard Zahara's voice enter his mind.

Cringing from the sudden intrusion into his thoughts, Anders put a finger to his temple and began massaging his stinging headache. *I still don't feel right in the head. Merglan's power did something to me that we never learned about. Even Ivan couldn't explain how the crystals work. How do I know if my own magic is still pure? What if Merglan's tainted my powers forever?*

We'll have to use them eventually, Zahara said as trailed behind Anders and Maija.

I know. I'm just worried that if I lose control again, I won't be able to stop the healing spell and I'll die trying to heal us. I'm rested physically, but my magic hasn't been restored. If something were to go horribly wrong, we don't have anyone to help. We're a long way from help.

I could ask Raffagaun to assist us, Zahara suggested. *He could provide the extra power source we'd need to complete the healing process.*

Anders looked to the sky again, impressed by the vast wingspan of Maija's dragon friend soaring over them. As he contemplated the idea of tapping another dragon's magic to fuel their own, he thought to the times he had used the power of Lazuran. His empowered sword, Lazuran, had triggered a potent desire to drink in the crystal's energy until it was exhausted, filling his body with an exuberant amount of strength. Exuberant, but dangerous. Suddenly Anders felt Lazuran's hilt in his hand. He quickly released his grip on the handle that included the tainted crystal. Merglan's desired effect had done its work on Anders; he longed for the power from the sword's crystal and found himself cursing that he'd used it all and yet it hadn't saved them all. Ivan was still in Merglan's possession and, for all Anders knew, had been killed moments after he and Zahara had escaped.

When are you going to tell her? Zahara asked, still feeling his thoughts and emotions.

Anders looked to Maija, studying her as she walked, *You think she should know?*

I think it's important for you to tell someone, about who you really are and what significance it bears, she said.

With Merglan in control, it means nothing of significance, Anders said.

It doesn't change your birthright, Zahara said.

Letting her sense his emotions on the matter, Anders neglected to address the topic any further. Reaching the rushing stream, Anders stepped into the flooded grass near the bank's edge, dipping the hollowed-out gourd Maija had given him in the clear water. As he sat in the tall grass surrounding the stream, he watched Raffagaun and Zahara lap up water with their forked tongues.

"He said yes," Maija said, breaking the silence.

Anders jaw slackened for a moment, thinking he'd missed something, then asked, "What do you mean?"

"Raffa," Maija nodded toward the dragon. "He wants to help you and Zahara, give you some of his energy."

"Oh," Anders said raising his eyebrows. "But I shouldn't. It's just that, I wouldn't feel right if I took too much."

I'll keep you from taking more than we need, Zahara said in both their minds, joining them in the grass.

"There you have it," Maija said.

Anders looked to Raffa and shrugged, "Let's give it a go." Speaking to Zahara as he stood, Anders said, *I'll need some help reciting the healing words, and one other thing.*

Of course, what is it?

I really don't want to drain Maija's dragon of all his power.

And neither does he want you to. He won't let it come to that and I won't either. You need to create a physical connection to do this, remember? If you're feeling anything similar to what happened with Lazuran the first time, just pull your hand away from him. If you can't, I will do it for you.

Anders nodded, approaching Raffagaun. Standing between the two dragons, he took a deep breath, trying to calm down and assure all of them that everything was going to work out fine. He wouldn't take too much energy and, if he wanted to, he would just step away. Looking to Zahara, Anders nodded, signaling he was ready to begin.

Raffagaun leaned into Anders so he could place his hand on Raffa's enormous foreleg. Helping him recite the healing words that Ivan had taught them to work on large gashes in dragon flesh, Zahara spoke them in Anders' mind, keeping his focus and accuracy on track. As the last of the words left his tongue, Anders felt an influx of magical force pass into him from the red dragon. The energy he pulled from Maija's dragon felt as pure as it had when Anders first drew on Zahara. The electric thrumming of magic warmed his body as he sourced his own powers. Sending the tingling sensation out to his hand extended over Zahara, he began healing her wounds. He watched Zahara's open gashes close through the haze of light glowing from his palm. Working on her back legs and rounding to her front, Anders and Raffa stitched together her most severe injuries inflicted when Killdoor had attacked.

Having healed his dragon, Anders turned the healing on himself, mentally focusing on closing the torn flesh across his back. As the stiffness left his back, Anders slowed the pull of magic from Raffagaun. Zahara's voice in his head coached him through the easing out of the connection with Raffa. As he slowly lifted his hand from Raffa's scales, Anders' other hand shot to his hip and all coaching from Zahara was silenced. Anders looked down and saw his hand wrapped around Lazuran's hilt, tightening his grip. A low whisper entered his mind, pulling his attention further into the blade. Anders flexed, trembling as he fought the urge to listen to this new, awful voice. He didn't understand what it said, but felt what it wanted. Lazuran wanted out. Suddenly, a second voice cut through the intruding whisper and broke his attention. Anders stood in the tall grass with his hand still gripping the sword, but he no longer felt the overwhelming pull from the blade.

"Anders!" Maija shouted. Her voice brought him back into the moment. Seeing her pointed glare, Anders realized she'd been the one shouting over the whisper. Anders focused on Maija's face and blinked as he returned to a more calm state of mind. His hand loosened and he drew it away from Lazuran's hilt, looking around for the dragons.

Both Zahara and Raffa stared at him. He felt his head spike with a sharp pain when Zahara's voice returned to his thoughts, *What's happened, Anders? Why did Maija shout at you?*

Anders realized Zahara and Raffa hadn't seen what Maija had and they'd somehow been blocked from his thoughts. When he took his hand off Raffagaun, they'd assumed he was finished, but Maija must've seen his posture and watched his hand fly to Lazuran.

I, um, don't know, Anders lied. *Did it work?* he asked, trying to change the subject.

Wonderfully, she said, spreading her wings. *Anders, are you okay? Nothing like the first time happened right?* she asked. Anders could tell that she sensed his lie.

Um, no, I'm alright now; nothing like the first time happened.

Okay, she said. *I'm going to stretch my wings. Raffa will join me,* she said, turning to take flight.

From the corner of his eye, Anders saw Maija approaching warily, "What was that?"

Anders rubbed the back of his neck, trying to think of an explanation, but he couldn't. Shrugging, he said, "I don't know how to explain it. It's this sword." Anders pointed to the hilt. "It's got a presence about it that draws me somehow. It should've ended when I used all the energy from the crystal."

"What do you mean, it should've ended?" she asked.

"When I transported us, I used all the corrupted energy inside it, but just now," he paused. "Did you hear the whisper?"

Maija shook her head, "Anders, you're not making any sense right now. You're scaring me."

Anders ran his hands through his hair, "I think it's Merglan still working against me through this sword."

"He's always working against us. Just tell me what happened to you," Maija said, stepping closer and taking his hand.

Anders nodded as he met her gaze. At last he was able to recount the events as they had unfolded from the beginning of the battle at Ryedale to waking up in the dark in Nagano. He told her everything except that Ivan was actually the true king and that he was his son and heir to the throne. Nearing the end of his story, he wondered if he should tell her about the first time he'd used Lazuran's energy against the orcs, but decided against it. She might not look at him the same way if he told her of the evil energy that had overtaken him. By the time he'd finished talking, Zahara and Raffagaun were landing nearby.

"Get rid of it," Maija said.

"What if I need to defend myself?" Anders asked.

"Zahara and Raffa will do that for us," she countered.

Anders frowned. He didn't want to give up the rider's blade that Nadir had gifted him. After a moment's consideration, he said, "What if I just try to remove the crystal? That's the part that's affecting me anyway."

Maija nodded, "Just do whatever you need to in order

to make sure Merglan can't control you."

Anders nodded, "I will."

He strolled to a nearby rock on the water's edge. Holding Lazuran by the scabbard, Anders whipped the handle down toward it. With the intensity of a wood splitting maul, he knocked the hilt onto the stone and heard a loud crack. Anders felt the freshly healed soar on his back begin to crack again, distracting him from the action. When he looked at the handle, the sapphire stood fast in its place. The crystal had broken the rock he tried to use as an anvil. Cursing he tried again. Six times Anders broke through the stones, each time nothing so much as a scratch showing on the pommel. With each swing, however, the wound continued to reform.

Giving up, he said, "The sapphire only speaks to me when I use magic, right?"

Maija shrugged, "I don't know what it does to you, you've only just told me."

"Well it does, only when I try to use magic. I don't want to leave the sword here in case I need to use it, so I have a compromise. I'll remove the blade and place it far enough away when I do attempt to use magic that its effects can't reach me. Once we arrive in Cedarbridge, I'll get a smith to remove it properly."

Maija nodded, "If you think that will work?"

Anders thought over what he'd just said. He had no idea if the distance from the crystal was enough to dampen its influence on him, but he couldn't leave the sword behind. He felt connected to it like it was a part of his body. Anders didn't know if Maija would understand that, so he spoke his next words with confidence, "It will work."

"Alright," Maija said and cocked her head to the side to see Raffa and Zahara coming in to land.

Joining them, Zahara sensed the scene and asked, *You told her?*

Everything except about Ivan and the orcs, he replied, leaving out the fact he'd tried to dismember the elven sword.

Anders, she should know.

I just need more time to process it, he said. *Then I'll tell her.* When Zahara gave him a questioning look, he added, *I promise.* She accepted his word and shook out her wings.

I think I'm ready to try carrying you again, she said. *How's your back?*

Anders felt at his back, the freshly opened gash wetting his shirt again.

"Oh, Anders I didn't even offer to check," Maija said, seeing him feel at his back. "Allow me," she said, lifting his shirt.

"Well," he asked. "How'd I do?" He heard Maija groan as she lowered his shirt.

"Not your best work. It's bleeding again. You shouldn't have swung your blade so many times," she said. "We're all out of bandages. Your shirt will have to do."

Anders shrugged, "Maybe I'll try to heal it again on my own when I feel better."

She placed her hand on his shoulder and said quietly, "Anders, I'm sorry for what happened to you. It must be really difficult not knowing what's happened to Ivan." Anders forehead creased, wondering how she suddenly knew about Ivan? Then she added, "I can't imagine what that would feel like, watching your mentor being ripped from your grip like that."

"Thanks," Anders said. "And I'm sorry I worried you earlier. It's probably just some residual effects left over or something. I'll get better with time." He returned the smile she gave him. "So, you think you're ready to fly?" Anders asked Zahara out loud so Maija could hear, too.

Zahara purred her response.

Adjusting the saddle, Anders heard her voice in his mind, *I know you're still craving Lazuran's power.*

What makes you say that? Anders asked.

Don't try to deny it. I saw you reach for him when you broke away from Raffa. Anders, you can't rely on that crystal anymore. I know using that amount of magic tired you, but you're going to have to get used to replenishing yourself as we used to, with time, food and rest.

Maija thinks I should remove the crystal or get rid of the sword but I worry physical distance won't cure it. I think whatever happened might have taken hold within me, why else would I still feel drawn to it when there's nothing left inside? Anders asked.

If you're going to beat Merglan, you must become better than him in every sense, with or without that sword.

Anders cinched down the strap around Zahara's core, looking to the sword at his hip. *It's going to be hard for me at first. I just want the cravings to go away.*

I have a feeling they won't on their own. You're going to have to face them, she paused. *I can help you. We'll beat them together. And remember, you're not in this alone.*

Anders gently stroked her neck, reaffirming their bond. *What would I do without you?* he asked.

You'd be dead, many times over for sure, she said.

Anders' gaze passed over her, checking the freshly

healed tissue on her scales. The only evidence of Killdoor's gashes and bites were patches of raw under-skin bare of scales.

Zahara shook like a wet dog, testing the saddle's security before letting Anders climb on.

We shouldn't push ourselves. Once we get back to the Everlight Kingdom, the elves will need us to go directly into action, he said feeling the residual draining effects from their healing efforts.

I know, but I feel alive again. It's been too long since we've flown.

Is one day without flight a long time for you? Anders asked.

Yes, it feels like ages since I last tasted the rushing wind in my jaws, she said.

Feels like it's been awhile to me too, actually, Anders said.

"Everyone ready?" Maija asked, approaching Raffa. Anders watched her grab the dragon's spikey bone protrusions as handles to climb up onto Raffa's back. Even though he crouched low to the ground, she still had a bit of a climb to get to his back.

She's going to need a saddle, Anders thought as Zahara crouched for him. Anders reached up, grabbed hold of the saddle horn and fitted his foot into the stirrup. Pushing down with sore muscles, he hoisted himself up into the seat, grunting as he swung his leg over her back. Rising to her full height, Anders felt Zahara's legs quiver, a feeling Anders had never felt on her before.

Anders looked to Maija as she sat straight-backed on Raffagaun, gripping two of the spikes for stability. Anders thought the whole of Raffa's back had been covered in spiny bones protruding through the scales, but clearly he was wrong because Maija sat on a flat-scaled space between his neck and his shoulder blades. Anders nodded, letting her know they were ready. Maija leaned forward and Raffa leapt into flight. Anders realized that the red dragon's wingspan practically doubled that of Zahara's.

Here we go, Zahara said, starting with a run before jumping into the air.

For a moment Anders forgot all of his worries as she lifted into the sky. Nothing was as freeing as soaring into the open air on the back of a dragon. After three flaps, Zahara cried out in pain, her roar shrill and high-pitched. She listed hard to the right and careened down toward the grass below. Anders tried to correct her course, but she couldn't stop her momentum and she collapsed as she hit the ground chest first, sending Anders' face directly into the back of her neck. The impact would've sent him flying except the magic embedded into his saddle had been designed to keep him in his seat.

Zahara skidded to a halt on her stomach and then used her wing claws to hoist her legs up under her. Dazed from the impact, Anders hunched over in the saddle. He glanced down at the front of his shirt, fresh blood spread across it. Thinking at first it was coming from Zahara, he searched her neck, but quickly saw the steady stream pouring from the tip of his nose. Surprised that so much blood could come from his nose, he quickly pinched his nostrils together and shouted from the instant pain. Letting go almost as quickly as he touched it, he realized he'd broken his nose.

Zahara, are you alright? he asked, slowly bringing his shirt to his nose in an attempt to stem the flow of blood.

My wings, she said with a gasp. *I think I tore something. What about you?*

Just a broken nose, I think, Anders said as he felt gingerly at the bridge of his nose. It's normal straight ramp down from his brow had an abrupt zag to the right. He placed his hands on either side of his nose, took a deep breath in through his mouth and pushed on it to the left, bringing it into alignment again. When it fell into place the flow of blood increased. Pinching his nostrils together, he climbed down from Zahara's saddle.

Maija landed as Anders inspected Zahara's underside for any obvious injury. One of her freshly healed wounds had cracked open slightly, blood beading along her exposed flesh.

"Are you two okay?" Maija called out, jumping down from Raffagaun and rushing over.

Still pinching his nostrils tightly together, Anders responded in a nasally voice, "I think we'd better stick to walking for a while. Zahara might've overdone it with her earlier flight and she thinks she tore something in her wings."

"Ouch," Maija said when Anders turned to address her. Blood continued to drip off his hand as he pinched his nose.

"Yeah, it sounded like it hurt. I'm going to heal her," he said still holding his nose shut. "I might pass out from the amount of energy it will take."

You could use Raffa again, Zahara suggested.

No, Anders said firmly, thinking of the whispering from Lazuran. *Like you said, I need to learn to do this on my own.*

Anders, I'll be fine, she said, trying to spread her wings and folding them back as quickly as she'd started to spread them while cringing with pain.

You aren't fit to fly. Let me see if I can repair the muscle tissue.

Zahara didn't reply and Anders sensed she knew he was right if they were going to continue to venture across Nagano.

He warily summoned the energy within him and found the torn pectoral muscles. With his magic running dangerously low, he used the last remaining ounces he'd managed to build up to heal Zahara's injuries. As he felt the warmth of the electric energy pass from his body, he ended the magic session. Stepping out from under her, he fell over backward, plunging into darkness.

Blinking when he finally opened his eyes, his view was limited to the ground passing beneath Zahara's body. As she walked at a steady pace, he became aware that he was slung over her back. He attempted to push himself up, but when he tried to move his arms, they didn't budge. He felt ties holding them together. Anders tugged with his legs and realized they were also bound. When he wiggled against the restraints, Zahara halted.

You're awake, Zahara's voice came into his mind.

Why can't I move? he asked.

You wouldn't stay put, so we had to tie you down. Hold on; I'm going to tell Maija.

Anders waited patiently as Maija's feet came into view. Crouching down to make eye contact, she said, "Brace yourself, you're going to fall. I'll try to catch you." She walked a ways out of view and Anders felt the rope holding him break. He slid forward. Bringing his clasped hands out, he braced for impact.

Stopping just before he hit the darkened earth, he let out a, "huh," as the rope around his legs tightened. Looking underneath Zahara, Anders could see Maija standing on the opposite side holding onto a rope as she lowered him to the ground. He rolled onto his back, summersaulting his legs back underneath him as Maija let go of her grip. Sitting on the ground he untied the restraints around his ankles. Maija rounded Zahara and assisted him with the rope around his wrists. Once free, he felt a tickle in his nostril and lightly touched at his nose. Two tufts of cloth stuck out from his nostrils. He pulled them out, and found that his nose was no longer bleeding.

Maija extended a hand and he took it. As she hoisted him from the ground, he asked, "Why did you tie me to the saddle? If you would've seated me, the magic in the saddle would've held me fast."

"We tried that," Maija said. "You kept falling around all over the place, bumping your head on her neck and bobbing back and forth as though your spine was going to snap if Zahara moved too fast. It was easier for us to continue at a steady pace if you were stretched out. I thought your saddle would hold you if you were lying on it, but that didn't work either. You kind of took a header to the ground."

"That probably didn't help my cause," Anders said, rubbing a tender spot on his head.

"After a few more tries, we figured out a good way to keep you up there."

"A couple more tries?" Anders asked in surprise. "How many times did you let me fall off?"

Maija chuckled, then cut herself off by clearing her throat, "We took care of it, okay? Luckily you had some rope in your saddlebags. Otherwise it could've been a lot worse."

"Well, thanks," Anders said looking around in the dark.

"You're welcome. And we stopped your nose bleed, although we can't do much about those black eyes," she said.

"Where are we now?" Anders asked.

Anders could see enough of Maija's darkened silhouette to know she shrugged, "Somewhere in Nagano."

"Why didn't we stop to make camp?" he asked.

"As evening approached, we noticed several dragons in the sky that didn't return to their nests for the evening,"

"You think they're watching us?" Anders asked.

"It was hard to tell from such a distance. They could've been hunting late, but I thought they were coming closer."

"These dragons wouldn't attack us, would they? With Zahara and Raffagaun here?" Anders asked.

You'd be surprised how aggressive some male dragons can be, Zahara said. *It's not always about food either. Males can become hostile over their territory, if they've established one. And females will attack anything that comes too close to their nest if they've got little ones.*

I doubt a mother would leave her nest to follow us and if a male were being territorial, why would he have a companion? Wouldn't the male attack the other dragon if that were the case? Anders asked.

That's why we're continuing through the night. We don't really know. Hopefully we'll lose them while it's dark out, Zahara replied.

Anders helped Maija pack the cut rope into Zahara's

saddlebags and joined them as they walked into the darkened landscape. After several hours of near complacency, Anders stopped when he heard an unfamiliar voice breach his thoughts. Seeing the others stop as well, Anders understood the command to halt must have been heard by all.

Before he could take another breath, Anders shot his hand to Lazuran and brandished his weapon, falling instinctively into a fighting stance. He saw Maija move in closer toward him and felt her jerk free the knife he kept on his backside.

"Who said that?" she whispered as Raffagaun and Zahara snarled, sniffing the air for the intruder.

Just as Anders shook his head to indicate he couldn't sense where the source of the voice had come from, a shadow against the dark sky swooped overhead. Anders saw a dragon angle down toward them. Coming in to land, the unfamiliar dragon folded its wings and bared his teeth.

Keep away, Anders heard Zahara say with a snarl. Zahara opened her communicative link to Anders and Maija so they could hear the new dragon's thoughts as it spoke to her.

We have no issue with dragons in these parts, the dragon said, his voice slightly soothing but obviously holding back anger. *That is unless you've bonded,* he continued, eyeing the saddle Zahara was wearing.

What do you mean, 'we'? Zahara asked. Anders could sense she was searching for other dragons nearby.

Why the Collective of Free Dragons for Dragons, of course, the dragon said as if this were common knowledge. Anders could sense his pride for their cause.

We're just passing through. We'll be gone from Nagano soon enough, Zahara replied, keeping her eyes keenly fixated on the dragon in front of them.

That's not the point, the dragon said. *We, as a race, have been held back by those who seek to force us into bondage. Our belief at the C.F.D.D. is that all dragons should be free from bonds. For too long, elves, dwarfs and humans have sought to hold us back, forcing us to bend our wills to their desires. Our goal is to irradiate all bonded pairs, freeing dragons everywhere to live the lives they were born to live.*

Anders shot a wide-eyed glance to Maija, not sure if she was privy to what the dragon was saying.

"What should we do?" Maija whispered to Anders.

Anders shrugged, trying to decide if this matter could be dealt with peacefully. He hoped Zahara would tell him they weren't bonded, so the lone dragon would let them pass.

May I ask why you're traveling with the human and elf? Anders heard the dragon question. While he could sense that Zahara was searching for an explanation, Raffagaun was quick to answer for them.

Leaning forward and crouching as if to pounce, the red dragon growled, *What we're doing is none of your concern, Kodoulen.*

Kodoulen flared a fanlike set of leather spikes out around his face and hissed. *Raffagaun. I should've known it was you. If you defend these intruders, I'll be forced to report you.*

Raffa unleashed a deafening roar and sprang forward snapping at the dragon. Kodoulen leapt back, dodging the red dragon's snapping jaws.

So be it, the dragon snapped, lunging at Raffa before Anders or Zahara could react.

Raffagaun reared back and slashed out at Kodoulen's advance. With two pounding strikes from his front paws, Raffa swatted his attacker, driving his head into the ground. Anders could see the shimmer of blood from the other dragon's snout in the dim light.

Stepping forward with Lazuran in hand, Anders prepared to join the fighting, but Maija grabbed him while Zahara said, *Don't be foolish. We need our strength. Raffa can handle him.*

Watching the two large dragons square off again, Anders listened to her advice and allowed Maija to pull him back.

Raffa burst forward in a thundering charge. Snapping down, he caught the dragon's neck in his jaws as he plowed into him. Thrashing to escape Raffa's tight grip, they tumbled into the river with a monstrous splash. Raffagaun never let loose his grip as they crashed into the water. Regaining his footing, Raffa pulled himself out from the water, dragging the other dragon in his mouth. Letting go, Raffa positioned himself between Kodoulen and his companions. Breathing heavily from the sudden burst of energy, Raffa said to the other dragon, *Leave now and I'll spare you your life.*

Kodoulen rose, rattling his scales as he shook off the water. Snarling, he pulled back, rearing slightly and Anders could see his chest beginning to glow in the darkness.

"Cover!" Anders shouted to Maija as he recognized that deadly source of fire.

As the dragon released his fire, Raffagaun met the

dragon's jet of fire with his own. The dragon flames exploded as they collided halfway between the two. The fireball ballooned out to either side as the streams of fire met. After the initial explosion, Anders saw Kodoulen's flames driven back and soon Raffa's flow bathed him in a plume of fire.

Screeching in pain, the dragon bolted upward, taking flight. Anders could see his leathery wings smoldering as he flew away. *You'll pay for this Raffagaun,* the fleeing dragon called back.

Returning to them, Raffa said, *We're going to need to move much more quickly than before. He'll be back with more dragons.*

In that moment, Anders realized this was the first time he'd heard the scarlet dragon's voice. Its depth was much richer than anything he would've imagined, and he was impressed with how the dragon handled himself in the fight.

Zahara can't fly, Anders noted.

She can without your weight, Raffa responded. *The girl can run almost as fast as we fly, especially over this flat ground. I'm not the fastest because of my size, but I will fly faster by only carrying one of you.*

Are you suggesting leaving me behind? Anders asked.

No, human, you will fly with me, Raffa said shortly.

Anders shook himself, the idea of being left for the dragons quickly vanishing from his mind. He looked to Maija and asked, "Can you keep up if I go with him."

"Yes, I can probably run faster than Zahara can fly right now with her injuries. Just go and we'll look for a place to hide," she said.

Anders nodded, sheathing Lazuran and running to

Raffa's side. The red dragon bent and Anders used his spiny protrusions to climb onto his back the way he'd seen Maija climb up earlier. Anders paused, trying to remember where Maija had been sitting to avoid more spikes. In the shadowy darkness, Anders saw the spines retract into scales, creating a comfortable seating area. Filling the gap with his rear, Anders gripped the bony protrusions as Maija had and held on as Raffagaun jolted into flight. The massive dragon overwhelmed Anders; he felt minuscule compared to the creature. How had Maija come to befriend this magnificent creature? Admiring the red dragon, Anders felt Zahara's shared interest in the dragon and looked to see her flying at his side.

Are you feeling okay to continue? Anders asked her.

For a short while. We're going to need to find a place to hide soon, though. I won't be able to stay in the air for long. My wings still don't feel fully healed.

Anders searched the darkened landscape for anything they could use to their advantage. He saw Maija moving with elven speed under them and wondered how long she could keep up the pace. As he searched for a place to hide, Anders saw only flattened valley bottom and realized they were more than likely going to have to face the dragons when they came searching. He swallowed hard knowing he wasn't rested enough to use magic effectively. He'd never attempted to fight a dragon with just his sword. Focusing on the task of finding a hiding place, Anders scanned the evening shade of Nagano's landscape.

CHAPTER EIGHT

Keep the Necklace On

A h!" Kirsten yelped as she caught a glimpse of the markings on her arm for the first time. Turning her left hand palm up, she used her right hand to slowly peel back her sleeve, following her dark red veins as they tracked the length of her arm up through her shoulder. "What is that?" she gasped, lifting the collar of her shirt and peering down at the venom as it tapered near her heart.

"Don't take the necklace off!" Thomas exclaimed, raising a hand to block her if she tried. "Kirsten, please, whatever you do, do not take that necklace off!"

"What happened?" she asked holding her arm up, twisting her inflamed arm toward them and searching their faces for an explanation.

"Don't you remember?" Britt asked, narrowing her eyes. Kirsten's gaze fell on her and Britt added, "You don't remember the goblins?"

Kirsten's eyes widened. Instantly, she reached for her left shoulder where the goblin had bitten her. Her shirt was torn where they'd ripped her sleeve to expose the injury. Kirsten pushed her shoulder forward, trying to get a better look at the bite. All that remained from the once gruesome sight were goblin teeth marks etched in a serrated oval outline on her shoulder. The patch of skin taken by the goblin had been healed with Solomon's potion, filling in with pale new flesh. Feeling at the scar while also looking around Solomon's living room, she asked, "How long have I been out?"

"Almost two full days?" Bo said, taking the open seat between Thomas and Kirsten.

"But this scar, it's healed; and why are my veins like this?" she asked, holding her arm out where she could again see the streaking.

Thomas leaned forward to look past Bo and said, "The goblin poisoned you and it spread through your arm in seconds. We thought you were going to die, but suddenly that crystal of mother's started glowing and you, you started breathing again. The poison appeared to recede from your heart and we got you here."

"The crystal," Kirsten said, remembering the one she'd taken from the governor. "What happened to the other crystal that I took from Rankstine?"

Thomas gasped, slapping his hand against the couch, "What the hell, Kirsten, you almost died! All you can think about is the crystal you stole? Have some respect for the people who've been worried that you weren't coming back."

Kirsten cringed slightly, "I'm sorry, Thomas. I'm so grateful to you for taking care of me. It must've been terrifying seeing me like that." She looked down at her necklace and clutched it against her chest, "Family is everything to me."

Thomas swiped at the tears that had started to roll down his cheeks. Pushing Bo back, he threw himself around his sister again, hugging her tightly, "Don't you ever take that necklace off. I can't imagine doing this without you."

As Kirsten returned Thomas' embrace, she looked over his shoulder at the others surrounding them. Britt held up the crystal from Rankstine, wagging it to show her that they still had the magical stone. Kirsten grinned and saw Bo scooting out from under Thomas' lower half on the couch. Max and Britt smiled, drawing Kirsten's attention back to them. The bags under their eyes and their grimy faces told her they'd gone to great lengths to save her life. She knew she was lucky to have such loyal friends.

Releasing Thomas, Kirsten asked, "So, why can't I take this off?" Kirsten put her fingers around the pink sapphire and lifted it off her chest slightly to glance at it.

"No!" they shouted in unison, reaching for her as though she was a glass vase about to fall. Instantly, she let the crystal drop to her chest and dropped her arms to her sides.

"We used one of Solomon's potions to push the venom out of your veins," Max started to explain. "You woke up when it worked and, well," he hesitated.

"And you took off the necklace," Thomas said angrily.

Max nodded, "And you took the necklace off," he finished. "The venom instantly began to attack your system again. Luckily, we got the necklace back on before the venom reached your heart."

Kirsten examined the red streaking in her veins again. "So, that's when the crystal started working again and I woke up? But how did the bite heal?" she asked, fingering the scar again.

"Well, we had another healing potion that we used.

This time Thomas made sure you didn't take the necklace off when you woke up. The second healing potion didn't push the venom out the way the first one did, but it did heal the bite wound," Max explained.

"And brought you out of your coma," Bo said, sitting where Thomas had been on the couch before his emotions took over.

"And where are we?" Kirsten asked, looking around the room.

"Solomon's," Max said.

"He's an old friend from Brookside," Bo added.

"We're in Brookside?" Kirsten asked surprised. "In two days?"

"Yeah, it's sort of a long story," Thomas said.

Bo and Thomas took over explaining all that had transpired since Kirsten first fell unconscious. When they had finally finished, Kirsten shook her head in disbelief, "Wow, that's nuts. So, you met some people who said there's a resistance?"

Thomas threw up his hands, "That's what you took away from the story. No, 'wow, I can't believe my brother would lug my heavy limp body up a mountainside'? That really speaks to our strong relationship!"

Kirsten nudged him lovingly, "Hey, I'm not that heavy."

Thomas chuckled, "When you're running up a hill, trying to escape from an angry goblin horde in the middle of the night, yeah, you're that heavy."

Kirsten slung her arm around her brother, pulling him in, "Thank you, Thomas. Thank you for hauling my heavy limp body up a mountain in the middle of the night."

"Thank you and you're welcome sis," he said with a grin.

"Where's the water? I'm parched. And is there anything to eat around here?" Kirsten asked scooting to the edge of the couch.

"Yeah," Max said. "Hold on."

Kirsten watched him step carefully toward the back room, maneuvering through the mess. The place looked somewhat torn apart, furniture was turned over and papers scattered about. As he disappeared into the kitchen, Kirsten placed her hands on the edge of the couch and rose. Her legs wobbled and then buckled under her own weight.

She felt firm sets of hands grab her on either side and lift her back onto the couch. "Are you okay?" Bo asked as he and Thomas crouched beside her.

Kirsten rubbed her head, looking to Bo, "That was weird."

"Your body is probably weakened from fighting off the venom," Max suggested, walking back into the room with a pitcher of water.

"I don't think I've ever felt this weak from just two days of rest," Kirsten said, reaching for the water.

"I wouldn't call what you went through 'rest,'" Max said, handing her the pitcher.

"You'd better take it easy until your body adjusts to the venom," Britt said, stepping closer. "Your system might act differently now that it's been affected."

Kirsten nodded as she sipped from the pitcher.

"How about that food?" Thomas asked. Kirsten could see he was rubbing his stomach.

As Max and Bo went into Solomon's kitchen, Kirsten

continued to drink from the pitcher, downing half of it within a minute. Both Britt and Thomas didn't take their eyes off her, not saying a word.

"Why are you staring at me? I feel fine, other than my legs feeling like jelly," Kirsten said, feeling like a caged animal.

"Sorry," Britt said. She unfolded her arms and looked around the room. Kirsten watched as she made herself busy returning bottles of various shapes and colors to a cabinet across the room. Kirsten noticed that she was placing them in a particular order and assumed they were the potions Max mentioned.

"I can't believe you found a potion that worked," Kirsten said, tracing the red streaks in her veins with her finger.

Thomas shifted on the couch, "I didn't help much with that part; everyone else really pitched in. I was too upset to do much other than make sure you were still breathing. You're the only family I've got left, you know."

"What about Anders?" Kirsten asked.

"He's close, but you're my sister. Besides, Anders is half a world away, training in magic and flying on that glorious dragon. Who knows if we'll ever be close again?"

"I wonder how that's going?" Kirsten asked, directing the question at no one in particular as she imagined what it would be like to fly on the back of a dragon.

"Clearly not as well as they intended," Thomas replied. Kirsten shot him a glare to which he responded, "If Merglan's forces are allowed to invade Westland unchallenged, that's definitely not a sign that things are going our way."

Kirsten didn't let the silence after his statement linger

before she redirected the conversation, "How did you all know that there would be something here that could help me?"

"When we were talking to that doctor, Rune, I believe his name was, he suggested that we seek out Solomon's help. I'm not sure who that is, because when we showed up, Solomon wasn't here, but Max and Bo said they have known him for years. Apparently, Max, Ivan and Anders stopped here to gain some information when they were trying to rescue us," Thomas said while folding his legs crossways onto the couch.

"Really? So, Anders got to meet this miracle worker and we didn't? That's funny."

"What's funny about it?" Thomas asked.

"That this Solomon probably indirectly saved my life more than once now, and I've never met the guy."

Thomas snorted, "Yeah. Well if that's the case, then I guess I owe him some thanks, too, if he had anything to do with helping Anders out."

"So, how did they find a potion that worked? I mean, you said Solomon wasn't here, so did Max or Bo know things about them?" Kirsten asked, glancing to Britt as she continued to restock the cabinet.

"Max got everyone to search through Solomon's books, looking for anything about goblins and poison," Thomas began.

"Yeah, you mentioned that earlier, right after you all realized he wasn't here," Kirsten interrupted.

Thomas nodded, "Anyway, Max found a book about potions and Britt saw those bottles," he pointed at Britt and the cabinet.

"It was all Max, really," Britt said, pausing with several bottles in her hands. "He had Bo looking up potions while we searched through these bottles and vials trying to identify which ones were which."

"Britt found the tags linking them to recipes in the book!" Max shouted from the kitchen.

Kirsten watched Britt's dark cheeks flush slightly. She shrugged, "But Max and Bo decided which ones were going to be useful. And Max tested them to make sure they were still good."

"He tested them?" Kirsten asked. "How?"

"Max poured a drop from each on the table. If the table looked okay, he would place a dab on his finger. And If nothing bad happened to his finger, then he would taste some of the potions himself, making sure they wouldn't hurt you," Thomas said.

Kirsten glanced toward the kitchen, shocked that Max risked his life for her in this way. She couldn't help but wonder why Bo hadn't volunteered to do the testing. She was so sure he was the one pining for her affection. She'd wanted him to kiss her on the Bareback Plains, but he hadn't. Perhaps she was after the wrong brother.

"It was a bit nerve-racking, but it ended up all right," Britt said, returning to her cleanup efforts.

"That's amazing," Kirsten said, eyeing Max as he and Bo stepped out of the kitchen.

Bo carried a plate of bread and jam while Max righted a side table that obviously had been knocked aside. He moved it in front of the couch. Kirsten locked eyes with him as he set the table down and, for a moment, he held her gaze before turning away. She watched him as he went to help

Britt restock the potions, keeping her eyes fixed on him until Bo obstructed her view. Setting the plate of bread and jam down in front of her, Bo took the chair where Britt had been sitting.

Kirsten noticed he was grinning at her, "It's called a poudrettite you know." When she responded with a look of confusion, he continued, "That type of sapphire. Apparently, it's quite rare, I mean besides the whole lifesaving properties and all."

Kirsten returned the smile, "Thanks Bo, that's good to know." She spooned the red jam onto a slice of bread and took a healthy bite. The flavorful sweet jam made her pucker and salivate instantly. She hadn't realized how hungry she really was. Taking the bread in large chunks and spreading the jam over it in gobs, she ate like a gluttonous pig. She didn't care about manners or looking respectable, she was famished. Through a mouthful of bread, she asked, "Do you really think there's a group of people forming an army in the Riverlands?"

"That's what Rune said," Bo answered, but Kirsten had hoped the question would raise Max's interest.

"Is that where we're going next?" she asked.

The question got Max to look up from his work. They were nearly finished putting the bottles back. He glanced at Bo before answering, "Bo and I gave our word to Rune that we'd go in exchange for his help. We'll have to honor that."

"Just you two, or can we come?" Kirsten asked.

Max shrugged, "He said they're always looking for able fighters. I don't see why you couldn't join."

"Well, there isn't much for us to go back home to now," Kirsten said, turning a raised eyebrow to Thomas.

"What about your arm?" Thomas asked. "We should find a cure, shouldn't we?"

Kirsten took a bite from the ever-smaller loaf of bread and held out her arm, "I think we already did."

Bo chuckled.

Kirsten smiled, her cheeks full of bread, and saw him flush as he stared at her with his deep brown eyes.

"You realize that the necklace is the only thing keeping you alive, don't you?" Thomas said.

Kirsten nodded, "Yeah. And you realize that we would be dead already if we'd spent any more time in that fortress with Merglan. We need to take risks, Thomas. Besides, those brave men and women who've managed to gather a force of people who are willing to fight will need our help."

"What are we going to offer them that they don't already have?" Thomas asked.

"The crystal," Kirsten said. "We'll offer them the power inside that stone Britt has in her pocket." She saw Britt's hand feel at her side, where she'd pocketed the sapphire.

"You're welcome to come with us," Bo said, looking to Max for his approval.

Max nodded hesitantly.

"What about you, Britt?" Kirsten asked.

Kirsten saw Britt glance down. She could see worry etched across her face. That look told Kirsten that she was thinking of her crew. Would they return to Grandwood for them, finding it overrun with goblins instead?

"Come on, don't make me be the only girl in the group," Kirsten said, trying to draw her out of her distant stare.

Britt looked up and managed a smile, "I warned the members of my crew not to come ashore back at Highborn Bay. I told them to go back to the Rollo Islands and bring as much help as they could to fight against Rankstine. What will happen to them when they come back if I'm not there?"

"What will happen if you go back alone and your ships have sailed on because they saw the destruction of the town from a distance?" Max countered. "They're not stupid, Britt. You've trained them well. When they come back, they'll scout the town out before they land. When they see that Grandwood's been overrun with goblins, orc or kurr, whichever survived, your crew will move on."

"Exactly, they'll come back looking for me," Britt responded.

"Would they risk coming ashore to find you if they knew the place has been overrun?" Kirsten asked.

"I guess it would depend on how many ships they have and how many warriors they brought," Britt said. Kirsten could hear the hesitation in her voice. "I want to continue on with all of you, but I'm their Captain, which means I have an obligation to them."

"The Chief of your people, Red, let the whole warrior clan abandon you in Grandwood! You don't owe your loyalty to him anymore. Red wanted you out, so he left you marooned under Merglan's rule," Max pleaded.

"I may not owe my allegiance to my leader, but I owe more than that to my crew. I can't just let them fall into the trap at Grandwood or continue searching for me without any word."

"But surely they wouldn't go ashore if they saw the destruction that has occurred?" Max said.

"I don't know what they'd do. Like I said, it depends on whether they have enough ships."

"Think about it, Britt," Max urged. "Red's in charge. The other clan leaders were okay with him following in his father's footsteps. Do you think he would allow a force large enough to take on the orcs, kurr and goblins depart the Islands if he knew they were coming to rescue you?"

Kirsten saw Britt clench her jaw as Max spoke. "No!" the Rollo woman shouted. "He won't! He and the other clan leaders hate me for being a woman and challenging their beliefs. But that doesn't mean my men won't come back for me. I have to warn them." Kirsten had to remind herself she wasn't strong enough to chase after her as Britt stormed across the room and out the front door, slamming it behind her.

"Britt!" Max called after her. "Britt, wait!" he shouted and Kirsten felt a touch of jealousy at how passionately he called after her.

Thomas sat up straight, looking to Bo and Kirsten as Max closed the door behind him. "Should we be going after them?" he asked.

Bo shook his head, "No. I think this is something they need to figure out."

Kirsten put the empty plate down on the side table, "I hope she comes back. I don't want that to be our final goodbye."

***

Max stepped off the front porch of Solomon's tree house, ducked under a low branch, and located Britt as she broke into a run. "Britt, wait up! Britt!" he called after her as he ran to catch up. "Hold on! Can we just talk about this?!"

He saw her speed increase when she realized he was chasing her. Max grunted in frustration as she disappeared up a small hill and into the trees. The evening darkness didn't help him keep an eye on her. He slowed as he reached the top of the rise. Looking in all directions for any sign of movement, Max cursed at himself for driving her away.

He cupped his hands around his mouth and shouted, "Britt!" He waited several moments for a response before trying again. "Britt!" he shouted even more loudly. Five times he called her name with no response. Britt had disappeared, running toward a town full of enemies, unarmed and alone. Max groaned and kicked at the base of a nearby tree. His groan turned to a moan as he bashed his toe. As he hunched gripping at his throbbing foot, he thought he could hear a faint sob to his left. His heart leapt, *Britt.*

Max rushed toward the sound, knocking and thrashing through the brushy undergrowth. He came to a halt several moments later. Looking at the base of a large oak tree, several yards ahead, he saw Britt sitting against the base of the tree. Her midnight hands cupped her face. Max slowed as he approached her.

He sat down next to her, wrapping his forearms around his knees and gripping his wrists, then said in low, quiet voice, "I'm sorry, Britt. I didn't mean what I said about your people."

Lowering her hands, she sniffled and wrapped her arms around her knees as Max had. She turned, looking away from Max as she spoke, "Don't lie to me. You meant what you said, and I know it's true." She cleared her throat, trying to force herself to stop crying.

"Britt, I," Max started, but she cut him off.

"You're right. Red wouldn't allow my crew to bring anyone to my cause. Hell, he probably wouldn't even let my crew return to the islands after coming back for me." Britt turned to look at Max, her dark checks shimmering with tears. "I'm just worried that I'm going to get my crew killed trying to find me in that place."

Max let go of his wrist and put his right arm around her, pulling her into him. "I know," he said. "But they're smart and you've trained them better than that. When they return to the waters near Grandwood, they're going to spend days observing activities onshore because you warned them how dangerous it was there. They won't just storm the shores blind."

"But if they come to shore and that barrier is still up, they'll be trapped."

"Once they see the enemy patrolling, they'll keep their distance. They might even sail south, thinking we've moved on," Max said hopefully.

"How can I warn them that we're not there?" Britt asked, palms up.

"What about a falcon?" Max said, remembering the last time he was in Brookside.

"To carry a message?" Britt asked, sounding more hopeful.

Max nodded, leaning away so they could look at each other face-to-face, "Yeah, Red and his cronies did that when we were here last time. That's how they got word to the ships coming from the islands that our ship had sunk and we were traveling on foot." Max spoke faster as he saw the hope in her eyes.

"Yes," Britt said, sitting up straight now. "That could work. I'll send a falcon and if it doesn't reach them sailing across the ocean to Grandwood, it will reach the Rollo Islands. That way someone will know what's happened here in Westland. If the other leaders find out, then Red will have no choice but to come to our aid."

Max smiled. He loved seeing her confidence, she was so determined and full of drive. As he stared into her eyes, he barely noticed how close they'd become until she kissed him. Her lips met his as they had once before on that night atop Highborn Bay. In that moment, all of his thoughts melted away.

She pulled back and said, "Come on; I've got to find a falcon."

Max sat half-dazed from their kiss. He shook himself back to reality and stood up, hustling to join Britt, who was already headed back toward the trail. Catching up to her, he heard her ask, "Which way to town?"

Max reached out, grabbed her by the hand, and said, "Hold on, you're going the wrong way."

Britt stopped, turning into Max.

"We need to tell Bo and the others about what we're going to do. We shouldn't just walk into an occupied town without a backup plan," Max said, staring into Britt's brown eyes.

"You're right," she said stepping into Max, placing her hand on his chest. "We should come up with a plan."

Max moved his arm around the small of her back, holding her close. His eyes searched hers, taking in their radiance. He didn't have to lean far before Britt met him with another kiss, this one lasting longer than before. They stood locked in each other's embrace until Britt leaned away and he could stare at her with dreamy eyes.

Laughing, Britt continued to let him hold her close.

"What?" he asked.

"You're easily distracted," she replied.

"And you're quick to change your mood," Max said, wishing he hadn't phrased it quite that way.

"Careful, Max, you don't want to say something you'll regret," Britt teased.

Max blushed, "I only meant," he started.

"What?" Britt asked.

"That you sure seem happier all of a sudden," he said.

"Can't I be happy now that my friend isn't going to die from goblin venom and I'll get to warn my crew of the dangers here in Westland?" she asked, turning on her heel and walking away once again. Over her shoulder, she asked, "Aren't you coming?"

Max nodded, allowing his eyes to linger on her form before joining her on the trail to Solomon's house.

When Max and Britt came back to the house, the mood hadn't changed. Max saw their attention shoot to the door as they walked in. Despite her fatigue, Kirsten bolted up off the couch, only to sit down as soon as she'd risen. Thomas helped her stand up again and they stared at Britt and Max with eager expressions.

"Well, did you?" Bo asked, meeting his brother's gaze.

Max blushed, thinking of their kiss, "Did we what?"

Bo shook his head and asked, "Did you convince her to stay?"

Max exhaled and looked to Britt, seeing the relief on her face as well, "You could say that."

Max watched their stares lock onto Britt, waiting for her confirmation. "Well, Kirsten, it looks like you're not going to be the only woman going on this next adventure," she said. Max saw their postures relax with the news.

Kirsten grinned, "Now you can show me more of your fighting moves," and she pretended to recreate one of the warrior stances she practiced, pulling Thomas off balance as he struggled to keep her upright.

Britt chuckled, "I'll show you a lot more than that." Max noticed her hands move to her waist, and she said, "Which reminds me, we need to get some weapons. I can't believe I almost went into a town full of enemies without so much as a butter knife to protect me."

"Good luck finding any weapons here," Bo said.

"Yeah, Solomon didn't believe in using weapons for fighting," Max said.

From her expression, Max could tell this way of thinking was new to her. She asked, "How did he think people should fight without weapons?"

"I don't think he thought anyone should fight," Max said. "But I know he used to tell me about some magic tricks he could do to render an opponent useless."

Britt frowned, "That helps us a lot."

"If there are any weapons here, they'll be down in the cellar," Max said.

"He's got a cellar?" Bo asked.

"Yeah," Max replied. "Mostly to store his produce from the garden, but he's got a few chests down there that might have things from his younger days."

"If he ever had younger days," Bo said.

Max chuckled, but quickly stopped as he realized that

nobody else in the room understood what that meant. They hadn't ever met the old wise man so how would they know how old he was. "I'll show you," Max said. "Then we should come up with a strategy of what to do next, including finding you a falcon." He saw Kirsten and Thomas' reaction at the comment, but didn't explain further as he moved to show them the cellar.

Encased in the wall on the far side of the living room was the outline of a door, which looked like tree bark. If you weren't looking for it or didn't know it was there, the cleverly hidden cellar door would be easy to miss. Max kicked at the base of the door and the top corner popped out slightly, enough so he could pull it out. Once the door was out of the way, a small person-sized opening revealed a set of stairs descending steeply into a darkened room. Bo handed him a lit candle sitting atop the nearby potions cabinet. Max took it and led them into the cellar.

The dark dirt walls under the tree were damp. The air was thick and dank. Handmade shelves lining the walls were crammed with canned goods and potatoes. Several trunks lay at the foot of the shelves.

"Score!" Bo said, eyeing the food. The bread and jam had been the only edible things in the kitchen. Max set the candle on a shelf as his brother began to gather the canned goods.

"Might be something in here?" Max said, bending down to open one of the trunks.

The trunk was full of totems from Solomon's past. Drawings, maps, elegant robes and jewelry, no doubt gifted to him from a person of exceeding wealth, but, just as he had suspected, no weapons. Another trunk held spare kitchen utensils, but no such luck with anything that could do a person harm. Ending their search, Max and Britt helped Bo carry food from the cellar up to the kitchen. They got to work outlining a plan to sneak their way into Brookside, break into the aviary, retrieve a carrier falcon, and send Britt's crew a message. After accomplishing Britt's task and giving Kirsten time to recover, their small band would seek out the Resistance Rune told them about.

CHAPTER NINE

Natalia

atalia stopped to catch her breath, watching the blackened figure as it flew outlined against the blue sky. Her battered and bruised ribs still throbbed from the orc's war hammer. Keeping her gaze fixed on the now-distant dragon, she was reminded of the last time she'd seen the rider pair. The loss of her dragon and their bond cut deeper than any physical injury ever could.

One day, I'll get back at them for what they did to me, she thought as Killdoor flew from view, continuing to burn the forested areas along the Drakeshead.

A touch to her shoulder startled her from her memories of that night over two months ago when she faced Merglan over the Eastland Mountains. Spinning around, Natalia's brilliant green eyes found the old wise man's wrinkled face.

"Natalia, are you okay?" Solomon asked as she continued to stare at him in surprise for too long. "We can rest if you need more time to heal."

Natalia saw him searching her face, trying to read what she was thinking. Touching the side of her body where the hammer had struck hardest, she said, "I'll make do. I can keep going."

Stepping around him, Natalia joined the line of Lumbapi hurrying through the forest. The Southland natives followed trails little known to anyone on the island; only a random hunter might stumble his way across the interior network of lightly traveled paths the Lumbapi used in secrecy. She continued on, pushing through her pain, using her magical talents sparingly now that she was the only one among them who could wield the energy. Natalia knew she was weakened physically as well as in magical strength from the battle they'd just fought.

That night, Natalia sat with her back against a tree trunk thinking through countless possible scenarios of what might've happened to Anders and Ivan. She couldn't explain it, but something inside her told her that Merglan was holding them prisoner. The Lumbapi Princess Inama's voice cut through her thoughts. The Lumbapi accent in Inama's voice felt light and calming to Natalia, not startling her as Solomon's touch had earlier.

"I must thank you, elf, for your efforts in saving my life. If it weren't for you and your unworldly powers, I'd be septic by now and beyond the healing forces of our medicines," Inama said.

Natalia opened her eyes to see the sinewy young woman sinking into a squat and settling on the ground at the base of a tree directly across from her. Keeping her head against the tree as she spoke, Natalia said, "You can direct your thanks to Solomon for that. His lizards gave me the strength after the dwarfs rescued us; all I did was channel the energy for them."

"You are a proud woman and I admire your strength. I can find more reasons than healing me to thank you. Your skills with the blade helped us to escape the orc horde," the Lumbapi princess continued.

Natalia stared at the quaking leaves rustling in the evening air overhead. "How is it healing up since the magic effort?" Natalia asked. She lowered her gaze and watched as the short-haired young woman exposed her tanned torso and looked to the pink mark where a serious gash had been.

"No infection or weeping. I expect it to leave only a slight scar," Inama said, running her finger over the recently-healed skin.

"How about yours?" the princess asked.

Natalia arched slightly as she pulled her shirttails out from her waistline. She showed Inama the black and blue bruising fringed in yellow that covered a majority of her side.

Inama flinched at the sight, "Can't you heal it more?"

Letting her shirt drop and shrugging, Natalia said, "Well, with only three days and considering my situation," she paused, trying to force down thoughts of her dead dragon. "I'm doing a little more each day. I used most of my stored energy during the battle and I don't want to overwork myself. I need my strength to travel."

"Can't Solomon help you?" Inama asked with a frown.

Natalia shook her head, "Those lizards were his channel for magic. Now that he's sent them to mislead Killdoor and Merglan, he doesn't have any power." She gave a half chuckle, adding, "I'd only heard rumors that the razor-backed lizards were still in existence. Fitting that they should end up in the hands of a man who doesn't believe in wielding a blade."

"How long do you expect Merglan will chase them

before they find out we aren't with the lizards?" Inama asked scratching at her head through her short black hair.

"If they're clever enough, they could make him think he's already dealt with all of us," Natalia said closing her eyes again.

"How so?" the princess asked.

"The dragon's fire consumes all," she replied. "If the lizards followed Solomon's instructions, Merglan and Killdoor will think they've located us in the dense forest. Assuming our location and sensing we're trapped," Natalia said spreading her hands. "The dragon's fire consumes all. Trusting that Killdoor's deadly fire would claim our camp, they'll think the Lumbapi in the Drakeshead have been taken care of.

"Would it really work?" Inama asked wrapping her tattooed arms around to hug her knees and nervously tongued at her septum piercing.

"Solomon used those two little creatures' magical abilities to shield us from Merglan's mind's eye. From what I saw today, Merglan returned to destroy us after learning of Lageena's fate. The lizards' concealing presence should have done the trick. To Merglan, the space created by their concealment spell would appear to be a large group hiding in the forest. That's what would make him think he's trapped us. If the lizards end their spell, he'll be encouraged to think that the fire consumed us. If I were him and had more pressing matters to deal with, like controlling the entire world, I would assign my army of orcs to hunt out any survivors and trust that the matter will be resolved. With luck, Merglan will think the Lumbapi have been disbanded and defeated; his gaze will turn elsewhere."

"Your magic is like that of the other riders, but you don't ride a dragon. Did you also lose your bonded partner?" Inama asked.

Natalia bit the inside of her lip. She nodded as she opened her eyes to look at the blurred canopy through the tears welling up in her eyes.

"Like Ivan," Inama said. "I'm sorry for this pain you must carry. It has to be difficult."

Natalia forced herself to respond in a steady voice, "I've lost both my parents and thought I lost my sister for over a decade, yet I can tell you that there's nothing that cuts deeper than the loss of your dragon. It's a part of you, a part of your soul. Once you've bonded, that's it. You'd do anything for your dragon."

"How long until," Inama began, but the question faded from her lips.

"It could be years or months," she said.

"But Ivan," the princess started, only to have Natalia speak over her.

"Ivan's different, he's one of a kind, a king among men. I'm not sure how he's retained his powers for so long. I can already feel the effects of my loss and it's been almost two-and-a-half months." Natalia closed her eyes again, searching for her slowly depleting powers.

"That's why you can't risk healing yourself? You don't have the power?" Inama asked.

"A year ago, I would've had no problem. Now I'm tapped and it feels like it's taking longer to regenerate more energy."

"You're good to keep going, though? Solomon told me that he's worried about you," Inama said.

Looking sideways toward the other Southland natives gathered nearby, she said, "The bones are healed, he was able to do that much before we left. I should be better by the time we get to the Ramhorn, unless we come across some unforeseen difficulties."

Inama nodded, "It won't be long. If we keep moving quickly and the evil dragonrider doesn't find us, we'll be reunited with the bulk of our people in a week."

"Maybe by then I'll know for certain whether Ivan and Anders are in Kingston," Natalia said.

"And if they are?" Inama asked.

"I'll go to them," Natalia said.

Inama nodded, "I can't force the others to attack, but as for me, I'll go with you. I owe them that much."

"For a mission like that, a smaller group is better. Merglan won't expect it, so we'll have the surprise to our advantage."

"If there is an army in Kingston, it will be hard to sneak in unnoticed."

"That's where your army would come in handy. The army could draw out or distract Merglan's forces while we complete our mission. That's what Nadir wanted."

"My people will do what is best for their country. If going to battle outright is best, then they will do so, but if they decide we can win the war by slowly pushing the invaders out, then that's what they'll do. Like I said, I owe a debt to Ivan and Anders, and to you, so I will help you in your mission."

"Thank you," Natalia said with genuine appreciation. "With surprise in our favor, we might be able to extract them unharmed; if they're still alive."

"Let's hope so," Inama said, rising and leaving Natalia to her thoughts.

Natalia remained distant from the bulk of the Lumbapi. Gripping the mirror Nadir had given her, she fell asleep waiting for his call.

***

The trek from the Drakeshead to the Ramhorn took the battle-worn Lumbapi longer than they had anticipated. Inama had told Natalia that it would take one week to reach the bulk force of her people, yet the seventh day passed with no sign of the others. They'd lost a fair number during the fighting in the Ryedale canyon and Inama gave her tired soldiers more time to rest in the mornings than Natalia desired. Though she blamed her frustration on their slower pace, she was angrier with herself for not knowing the way to Kingston. She could've led Maylox there if she knew where they were, but the dense forest and her lack of familiarity with the area left her at the pace of the Lumbapi. Knowing she needed to heal and store more energy before venturing into the capital, Natalia struggled with her current frustration.

Each night she waited for Nadir to call via the magic mirror he'd given her. They each had one but could only talk when each was listening. Nadir insisted that she should not call him, because while he was trying to win back the favor of his generals, he wanted her mission to stay private. He could not risk losing his control over his elven army. If he lost favor and was forced out as king, the elves would revert to their usual self-preservationist ways and abandon the humans to Merglan's rule. Natalia understood why the elves generally wanted to preserve their race, but she didn't understand how her people, as a whole, could be so selfish as to turn a blind eye toward Merglan and the expansion of his dangerous power. Nadir called only once during her trek to let her know that his troops had dropped off the dwarfs in Eastland and were heading toward the Everlight Kingdom. Natalia wished he'd offered news about Ivan and Anders' location, but for now, she would have to continue on her quest to find them.

By the tenth day of travel, Natalia and the Lumbapi had reached the western coast of Southland and entered the province known as the Ramhorn. Villages dotted the expansive area. The most densely populated towns were concentrated along Kingston Road, close to the coast. As they walked the short distances from village to village, Natalia became more aware of the people's firm resistance to Merglan and his invading forces. Word of the orcs' presence spread much faster than the orcs and those who were old enough to remember the last time Merglan had been in Southland fled to the southwest of the country. Natalia hoped everyone who saw their large group of battered and bloodied soldiers would look kindly on them and not set off any alarm that might alert the imposing ruler to their march. Their presence had been kept a secret as far as she knew and Natalia hoped it would continue to stay that way.

Freedom wishers passed on the word that the Lumbapi from the Drakeshead had arrived in the Ramhorn and word then came back to the group regarding the location of the sizable force of the natives' army. Inama's father sent a letter to intercept them within a few hours of their arrival. He would meet them that afternoon in a town not far from their current location. Inama shared the news with Natalia that the allied forces were gathering on the coast.

Natalia walked amid the Lumbapi soldiers, her feet sliding slightly with each muddy step as the host of fighting men and women processioned along Kingston Road. The wool traveling cloak she'd bargained for weighed heavily on her shoulders, its saturated hood drooping around her face and shielding her from a constant drizzle of rain. She glanced crossways over Maylox, who walked at her side. Maylox's short dwarf stature allowed Natalia a clear sight down the line of soldiers. The long line of Lumbapi snaked down an open hillside, entering the largest town she'd seen since leaving Cedarbridge.

"Lucky thing, you trading for that cloak and all," Maylox said as Natalia stared directly over her head.

Natalia glanced down at the dwarf, who still wore her full suit of plate armor. She hobbled along through the mud under the weight. "I asked you if you wanted me to try and get you one," Natalia replied.

"That was before it started raining," Maylox grumbled.

"I recall the Lumbapi soldier and I pointing out that the rains were bound to set in with the changing season, and what was it you said? Oh yeah, that your suit was 'watertight,'" Natalia continued with a slight grin.

Maylox shrugged, "That's what they told me anyway."

"It sounds like someone was pulling your leg," Natalia said as several Lumbapi soldiers hurried past them as they neared the town.

"No, my legs weren't touched. And what's that got to do with it?" Maylox asked, looking at Natalia as rain tinkled on her armor.

Natalia inhaled, ready to explain the idiom, but decided to let it go. The dwarf didn't have the easiest go along the trail. Natalia found her lagging far behind over their first several days in the forest. Hanging at the back of the pack because of her injuries, Natalia struggled to keep up. After seeing Maylox struggle under the weight of her armor and the short stride of her steps, Natalia suggested that Maylox join her and Solomon at the head of the army each morning. If they started in the lead, they could remain in sight of the group over the course of the day, even at their slow pace.

"What do you think about our presence being broadcasted like this?" Natalia asked.

"Inama said we're in a safe area now," Maylox said. "And, it will be nice to sleep somewhere warm and dry for a change."

"Yeah," Natalia responded slowly, catching her first glimpse of villagers.

"From the sounds of it, everyone in town is here to welcome us," Maylox said with a tinge of joy.

How safe can we really be? Natalia wondered.

Strangers lined the road as it entered the town, watching and cheering as the Lumbapi soldiers from the Drakeshead walked their streets. Hearing a roar erupt from the town's interior, Natalia wondered whether Inama and her father had just been reunited. It was all Inama could talk about over the last several days when she'd learned of their meeting place.

Once in town, Natalia grew uncomfortable. She didn't like the way people looked at her, their smiles fading at her appearance among them. The idea that so many people living so close to the capital would know their location after they'd worked to keep it a secret for so long put her further on edge. The Lumbapi thoroughly trusted the residents of Ramhorn, but she was skeptical. Besides the fact that she was an elf, walking alongside a dwarf of all things, she didn't see why the townspeople stared at her so intently.

With the hood of her dark green cloak concealing her elven ears, she didn't think anyone would recognize that she was an elf. And with her exposed tan hands and waves of brown hair cascading from under the hood, she figured she could pass as Kewian and that Southerners wouldn't take special note of her. She looked away each time she awkwardly made eye contact with those who stared at her. At first, she thought the people were staring at Maylox, but she could see that their looks rose above Maylox's head toward her.

"Are you well known around here or something?" Maylox asked as they neared the town center.

Natalia pulled the cloak tighter and replied quietly, "I've never seen them in my life. I haven't ever come this far south."

"Strange, people keep pointing at you and whispering to each other as we pass," Maylox said as she struggled to keep up with Natalia.

Natalia kept her head down for the remainder of their trek into the sprawling coastal town. She wanted to be gone from this place as soon as possible, never mind the idea of Merglan and Killdoor coming for them. She wanted the hushed words and stares to go away.

Branching off to one side of the gathering troops, Natalia joined Solomon as he stood waiting for them in the steady drizzle. "I got us a room at this fine establishment," Solomon said, motioning to the building behind them.

"Good, let's get out of this rain," Maylox said as she rushed passed Sol and Natalia toward the inn.

Stepping onto the inn's covered porch, Natalia pushed back her hooded cloak, revealing her damp brown hair and striking features. Looking back out at the people still watching the last of the soldiers walk by, she asked, "Why do these people act like they know about me or surprised to see me?"

Stroking his gray and white beard, Solomon said, "I thought I saw that reaction just now. I don't see how they could've spotted you as an elf with that hood up. You could pass for Kewian as long as you keep your hair down."

Natalia unlaced the broach and, with a fluid movement, spun the cloak off her back, holding it away from her as it dripped onto the wooden boards. She watched as the last of the soldiers continued down Kingston Road, "I'll be going to Kingston tomorrow."

She could see the old man's expression lined with concern as he asked, "You're going to try tomorrow? But don't you want to see what the Lumbapi King has to say?"

Natalia turned from the street to face Solomon, "I could hear what he has to say, but I'm going tomorrow. Anders and Ivan could still be trapped there and every second we waste is time Merglan could be using them to get some kind of upper hand over all of us."

Maylox hobbled over to them, most of her armor disassembled and removed. She reached for the ties for her chest and backplate, the last two pieces she needed to remove to be rid of the suit. "Could one of you help me out here?" she asked.

Reaching down to help her loosen the straps, Natalia said, "You're not planning on wearing that noisy suit on our mission to Kingston, are you?"

Grunting as she hoisted the remaining armor over her head, Maylox said, "No. I'll leave it in a bag at the gates."

Natalia raised an eyebrow at her and watched as Maylox's look became unsure.

"Or not? Maybe I can leave it here and come get it afterward," she tried again.

Natalia shook her head slightly.

"I'll ask the Lumbapi if we can put it on a wagon or something now that we're back in civilization," Solomon said placing a hand on Maylox's shoulder.

She grinned, her saturated underclothes sticking to her skin and her matted thick hair a fiery mess. Chuckling slightly, Natalia said, "Okay. Let's get into some dry clothes; then we'll enjoy a good meal before tomorrow."

As she led them into the inn, Solomon called out, "Inama has requested your presence tonight at the Brokencurl. It's five buildings to the right."

Natalia waved to acknowledge she'd heard him. Getting the room number and key from the attendant, Natalia and Maylox hurried to their room. Solomon must've arranged for them to have new clothing because when they opened the door, they found dry clothes folded on the bed. After starting a fire and climbing out of her damp clothes, Natalia relaxed in a chair near the flame's warmth. It was nice not having to sit on the ground for once. Her thoughts turned to Maija and wondering how her sister was faring in the North. She hoped the girl would find that dragon. The connection they shared outside Hardstone was undeniably strong.

After drying off and warming up, Natalia stood to leave for the Brokencurl. "Coming?" she asked Maylox as she moved toward the door.

Maylox grabbed one of the coats Solomon had placed in the room before their arrival and said, "Yep," as she joined Natalia in the hallway.

They ran the short distance, trying to lessen their exposure to the rain, but the five blocks to the Brokencurl Inn proved to be more than enough time to drench their clothes and hair again. After knocking the mud off her boots at the inn's doorframe, Natalia entered the establishment. Muffled street noise now turned to loud laughs and shouts within. Natalia looked around the dimly lit room for Solomon or Inama. Not seeing either near the entrance, she stepped farther into the Brokencurl.

Lumbapi crowded the room, filling each table beyond its capacity as they feasted and drank in merriment. Natalia led Maylox in search of Solomon's dreadlocked mess of gray hair. She spotted Solomon seated on a stool at the bar. She squeezed her way into a gap next to him.

Looking up from his mug, Solomon said, "Natalia! You're here! You just have to meet Puconathini."

Natalia glanced from Solomon to the mug and back again, noticing the frothy line of bubbles stuck to his mustache. "Puco who?" she asked.

Rising from the stool, Solomon said, "Puconathini. Come now, I'll introduce you."

Natalia and Maylox followed Solomon through the mingling Lumbapi toward the back of the room. Coming to a table where Inama was seated, Solomon stopped, attracting the group's attention. "This is who I was telling you about," he said, placing his hand on a bronzed man with a thick array of short black hair pricking out from his skull.

The man's muscles rippled as he rose from his seat, smiling brightly as he looked at Natalia. "So, this is the woman who will be infiltrating the castle."

Maylox came from behind Natalia and the man's smile broadened further.

"And this is the other daredevil who will be entering the city of danger," the man said in a full voice, lightly accented in the Lumbapi way.

"Natalia, Maylox, this is Puconathini, leader of the Lumbapi people," Solomon said, grinning and sipping from his mug.

She watched the large man place a hand on Solomon and say, "Please call me King Puco."

Natalia bowed slightly, "You've raised a fine warrior for a daughter, your Majesty."

Puco turned, looking at Inama and said, "She didn't tell me that she owed a debt to the veiled huntress."

Natalia shifted, that description catching her off guard. "I'm sorry. I don't know what you mean?" she asked.

"No need to apologize. Forgive my rudeness. Please sit with us," the king said, waving to three of those at his table to offer their seats.

Natalia didn't understand how the Lumbapi leader knew of the veiled huntress, a figure described from a prophecy she had put her faith behind, but accepted the seat next to Inama. Maylox and Solomon joined her with ease.

"So, tell me, elf. What is your plan to infiltrate the

castle," Puco asked, not caring if anyone overheard their talk of strategy.

Natalia described in detail how she, Inama and Maylox would enter the city disguised as farmers transporting grain from their harvest. She went on to describe their plans to climb the castle's back wall, and begin their search for Ivan and Anders. Once they were freed, the group could use their magic to locate Zahara and fly from the city."

"She is bold," Puco chuckled as he looked to Inama. When she met him with a steady expression, he looked to Natalia again. "And when will you be attempting this suicide mission?" he asked, folding his hands and leaning forward.

"Tomorrow," Natalia said straight-faced.

The king's eyebrows rose and he tongued at something stuck in his front teeth, "Will you be requiring assistance or can you pull this off on your own?"

Natalia glanced to Inama, "It was my understanding that you and your army would be launching an assault on Kingston after our arrival. I won't lie to you; my plan would be better executed with the distraction of an opposing army at the capital's gates, but I can get along just fine without it."

Puconathini didn't respond instantly, and Natalia thought he was mulling over his options before replying. "You're right in the fact that I've been planning an assault on Kingston. As we speak, most of our forces are moving into position. With the help of our friends sailing in from the north, we'll be ready for our assault tomorrow."

Natalia sat up, "Friends from the north?" she asked.

"Ships from the Rollo Islands have been landing along

our shores over the last several days. Their numbers continue to grow as they readily embrace our cause for freedom from this evil ruler."

"What's your strategy?" Natalia asked.

"Tomorrow the Rollo ships will sail just to the edge of view of the city. When their presence is known, the Kingston Navy will send out a sizable force, big enough to squash the attackers. What they won't know is that we'll be waiting for them in ambush. Once they get to the beach, we'll wipe out the force before they can set sail. Then donning their clothing as a disguise, we'll enter the city, acting as a victorious war party. Once they open their gates, we'll storm in unopposed. Catching the orcs off guard, we'll take over their city, fighting in the town's close quarters and preventing them from organizing. They'll be thrown into chaos and we'll win the day." The king sat back in his chair, grinning and exposing his teeth that appeared even whiter in contrast to his darkened skin.

Natalia nodded, "You haven't accounted for Merglan and his dragon."

"Nope. But that's where you'll come in. An elf sneaking around the castle. That will catch his attention and he'll be distracted while we carry out our plan."

Rising from the table, Natalia said, "Make sure your ships are seen." She walked swiftly through the crowded bar and back to the front door. Maylox and Solomon caught up to her at the door. Before she could leave, Solomon grabbed her by the hand and said, "Don't leave without me tomorrow."

Natalia shook her head, "You're not coming with us, Sol. We're already two people too many on this mission. I can't risk having you there, too."

"I will be of use," he pleaded.

"How? You can't use magic without the lizards."

"Just don't leave without me, okay?" he said, retreating back into the crowd.

Turning, Natalia forced the door open and rushed out into the street. She ran back to the inn, the rain consuming her again. Natalia could hear the squishing steps of the dwarf behind her. Entering the quiet inn, she walked past the rooms and took a seat at the lonely bar. Maylox joined her and they ordered drinks, sipping in silence and enjoying the peace and quiet compared to the commotion at the Brokencurl.

"What did he call you?" Maylox asked.

Natalia sipped from her mug, then replied, "That comment didn't sit well with me. He called me the veiled huntress."

Maylox shrugged, "Don't know what that means?"

Natalia stared into the froth in her mug. She didn't know how, but the Lumbapi king knew something about the Prophecy. She recalled the way the people in the streets stared at her, as if she were a threat they hadn't expected to see that day. In her gut, she knew the king's comment connected to the way the townspeople looked at her, but she didn't yet know how.

After a hot meal, Maylox and Natalia returned to their room, now warmed by the fire and their clothes hanging dry for the next day's events. Natalia went to sleep wondering if their plan to free Ivan and Anders would work and whether the two were even still being held in the capital at all. Regardless, she knew she had to try this plan to rescue them.

Luckily, warriors were going to attack the city and distract most of the orcs. King Puco was right when he said Merglan would know she was there. Natalia would have to work extra hard to hold onto her concealment spell to prevent Merglan from finding her too soon.

Chapter Ten

Entering the Everlight Kingdom

affa, you know this place better than I. Can we avoid a fight with the dragons?" Anders shouted over the rushing wind.

I know a place, Raffa said, his low voice rumbling in Anders' mind as he turned sharply, banking to the northeast.

Anders looked to make sure Zahara made the turn as well. She flew lower than Raffa and Anders knew from her slackened pace that she wouldn't last much longer in the air. Raffa must've communicated to Maija because she also turned to the northeast. "How much farther?" Anders asked, thinking of Zahara.

We're close. Tell me, human, can you see them coming after us? Raffa asked.

Anders turned and scanned the sky. He could no longer see the retreating dragon on the dark horizon. Zahara and Raffa were the only dragons flying for as far as he could see. "No," he called to Raffa. "They're not yet within sight."

Raffa dove for the ground and Anders nearly lost his grip with the sudden change in direction. Clinging to the bone protrusions on Raffa's lower neck, Anders caught his first glimpse of their destination. Directly below lay a scattering of boulders, randomly arranged in the open grassland. The rocks varied in size and bore a similar shade of red to that of Raffa's coloring. He looked from the rocks to the red dragon's neck as Raffa opened up his wings, pulling out of their dive. Raffa hit the ground at a run and came to a halt in the middle of the rocks. As Anders climbed down from Raffagaun's back, he saw Maija come into view. In a matter of moments, Zahara joined them, touching down much more gingerly than Raffa had.

With her head swiveling, Zahara asked, *Is there a cave or an alcove we can hide in?*

Anders looked to Raffa, expecting him to show them to his hiding place, but the large dragon didn't move. Instead, he opened his wings to either side and said, *If you curl yourself Zahara, I can cover you all under my body.*

"Will that work?" Maija asked. "Won't they recognize that you're not a boulder but have the mass of a dragon?"

Hurry and do as I ask; they'll soon be within sight, Raffa said desperately.

Zahara immediately lay down at Raffa's feet. Wrapping her tail and neck tightly around herself, Zahara turned into a concentrated swirl of green, purple and blue iridescence. With a nod from Raffa, Maija and Anders huddled under Zahara's shoulder, leaning closely against her bulk. Raffagaun spread his mighty wings, sat as snuggly as he could without crushing them and enveloped the three of them. The dark of night turned pitch black under Raffagaun's cover. The air was still and close. Anders listened for ensuing dragons, but only heard the steady yet nervous breathing of Zahara and Maija as they waited for this storm to pass.

Zahara, Anders said, connecting to her with his mental link. When he felt her focus, he asked, *Will Raffa tell you what's going on?* Without a reply he could tell Zahara was relaying the question to the large red dragon.

Raffa says he can see them coming. We need to remain totally still if his camouflage is to hold.

I hope they don't pick him out, Anders said.

He has cast a concealment spell. It's not much from what I can sense, but he's used it to project the overlaying texture of the rocks onto his scales and wings. As long as they don't get too close, we won't appear any different than the surrounding rocks.

I hope they don't, we've already wasted too much time if we're going to help Ivan, Anders said.

You mean William? she asked.

Yeah, Anders replied. He'd been avoiding thinking about his true identity. The man he'd known as a friend to his uncle and a leader among men and elves was his father. What Anders found most puzzling was why Ivan had kept it a secret from him, why hadn't he told Anders that he was his father? Perhaps he was afraid Anders would hate him for masking his identity and it seemed like Ivan wanted to be a part of Anders' life. But if that connection was what he sought, why hadn't he been there for Anders during his childhood? What could've been more important than family?

He loved you, Zahara said, sensing Anders' thoughts.

Why didn't he tell me sooner? It might've made a difference.

Would it have? she asked.

We might've been more sure of ourselves in the Prophecy. At least the son of a king part lines up now, even though that could refer to Ivan, too.

But if Ivan never claimed his right to the throne, does that make you a son of a king?

Anders thought about that for a moment. He didn't know how technical prophecies were. Remaining still, he said, *I'm not sure what that makes me?* After several moments of silence, he added, *We're both still the same people, aren't we? This doesn't change anything.* But deep down he knew their relationship wouldn't be the same. How could it after being lied to for nearly twenty years?

You have not changed, Zahara comforted him. *Just be grateful for the time you did get to spend with him, even if you didn't know he was your father. He offered us guidance in a time of need.*

As Anders sat in silence, thinking about how much Ivan had sacrificed to offer him and Zahara the best chance of survival and success, Zahara interrupted, *The dragons approach. Be completely silent, but ready to fight if they discover us.*

Zahara's update pulled Anders from his self-reflection. He moved his hand to Lazuran's hilt, feeling the grip fitting comfortably in his palm. He waited in the darkness, not knowing if he would need to spring forth from the grass and exhaust every last ounce of his energy to defeat the aggressive dragons. Anders heard a whisper in the silence. As the unfamiliar voice sounded, he stiffened, thinking that it came from Lazuran. As the voice grew louder, he realized that he was hearing it in his mind, yet he still wondered if Lazuran was trying to call to him. He wondered again whether the sword could do such a thing, but he swore it had done so before.

A unique mental voice that he didn't recognize came

more clearly into his mind, *He won't like hearing that we've lost them.*

When a second voice responded, Anders realized it was not Lazuran, but more likely the dragons Raffa had mentioned. *Which is why we should be looking to the forests. This isn't their natural homeland and I bet they're heading back to the elf lands. Many master-loving dragons flee there. Ever since the movement began.*

But they couldn't have made it that far in such a short time, the first dragon responded.

Precisely, but that's where they're going. If we spread ourselves out along the fringe, we'll catch them before they cross.

Clever! Shall we return to inform the others?

Yeah, there's nothing here but a pile of rocks. We'll have better luck getting ahead of them. Let them think they've outmaneuvered us for now. They can't hide forever.

The dragon voices quieted and Anders heard their wings pumping air as they took flight. He remained perfectly still, keeping a hold on Lazuran. Making sure the dragons had departed and that their conversation wasn't just a ruse to get his group to expose themselves, Anders and the others kept quiet for several hours.

When Raffa finally lifted his wings, exposing them to the night, he said, *It's time to move.*

"What if they're watching out for us?" Anders asked.

You heard them as well as I, they are setting an ambush along the elven border. They've flown away now and it's safe for us to travel, Raffa said.

"And how far is it to the elven border?" Anders asked.

I have never made this journey on foot. I do not know? Raffa said.

Anders turned to Zahara. She said, *It will take many days to venture on foot.*

Could you fly? he asked.

I can, but I'll need more healing. Raffa will have to provide the energy source.

Anders couldn't think of any other option. If Raffa used his energy to boost Zahara again, he would be left weakened as well, but they needed to leave the land of dragons with haste. Wishing he had more energy in the crystal, Anders addressed Raffa.

Without hesitation, Raffa accepted and prepared to share more of his energy with Zahara. Anders prepared himself to act as a conduit for their transfer.

Maija stopped him saying, "Anders, wait."

Frowning, he looked at her confused as to why she would protest. He realized why she'd stopped him when she reached for his blade. Taking it and running in the opposite direction, Maija distanced herself from them.

Focusing back on the task of siphoning off some of the scarlet dragon's powers, Anders began working the spell.

***

Halting on a grass-covered hill, Anders searched the moonlit landscape. In the distance he could see the tree line marking the Everlight Kingdom. Remaining still as he stood alone on the hilltop, Anders watched for any sign of movement. In the dark, he saw a dim orange glow on the forested horizon.

Dragons didn't need fire to warm themselves; they could warm up from within using their own fire. The glow would have to signify elven civilization. Anders recalled the lesson of elven culture in his broad but brief instruction on their people's history. Ivan sped through lessons on the villagers among the trees in the Everlight Kingdom. Marking the glow's location, Anders retreated down the hill to address his companions.

Zahara rustled her wings when she saw him return, giving Anders the sense that she was ready to fly again. He, too, felt more than ready to take to the sky, but now that they were so close to the dragons' trap, he knew they couldn't risk it. "We're close now. Not more than a five-hour walk to the border," Anders said as he neared his group.

"Did you see any dragons patrolling the edge?" Maija asked.

Shaking his head, Anders said, "No, but that doesn't mean they aren't there. I would say we could risk the flight, but this moon will expose us for certain, and if we're spotted, all our patience will have been for naught."

Your instincts are correct, Zahara said, her voice confirming his notion. *We would better see their positions in the daytime and know where to cross the border undetected.*

"I saw a glowing in the forest," Anders said.

"What could it be?" Maija asked.

"Most likely an elven village. It would be our best shot at finding food and water before continuing to Cedarbridge," he suggested, eyeing their empty gourds, the remnants of those Maija had picked back at their camp, two days of hard flying to the east. It had been twenty-four hours since their narrow escape from Kodoulen and his C.F.D.D. dragons. The transfer of energy into Zahara left Raffa depleted and they had to work together to take down five hump-backed cattle to restore the energy loss in the red dragon. The killing had been the only stop they'd made in their continuous flight west for the Everlight Kingdom. Anders took the opportunity to eat as much charred meat as he could stomach, knowing the sustenance would help restore his own energy stores.

The dragons at the border will not venture far into the forest if that's where they're hidden, Raffa's powerful voice boomed in Anders' mind. *We can continue under cover of this drainage and find a place to enter the forest in the morning.*

"I think we'll be good to keep going for a few more hours; then, come morning, we'll see where the dragons are, as you suggest," Anders said.

As they followed the widening drainage toward the forest, Anders asked Maija, "Did Raffa answer your questions about them?"

Maija nodded, slowing her pace and allowing them to fall out of earshot. "He didn't want to offend you, that's why he never replied yesterday day when you asked him yourself. Apparently, a sort of leader among them arrives occasionally to give them new standing orders. The dragons in the C.F.D.D claim that he's a prophet that will lead them to a new world order."

"One without dragonrider pairs," Anders said.

"Yes. The leader is careful in protecting his identity and only reveals himself to a select few dragons. They take orders and spread them among the community. Raffa said they tried to recruit him before he met me."

"I wondered if there were still tensions among the dragons in Nagano and riders, but I never thought they'd go to such an extreme as to try to exterminate all rider pairs," Anders said.

"It is a trying time for Kartania," Maija said.

Anders nodded, quickening their pace to fall in behind Zahara and Raffa again as they continued their travels in the dark until they needed rest.

When dawn arrived, Anders and the others were already in position, sprawled in the grass with their heads low to the ground, watching from the sloped drainage. Anders didn't have to wait long before he spotted a dragon rising from the trees. From their position on the grassy slope, he watched the winged figure glide out low to the trees. The dragon flew along the forested front, heading south, almost out of sight before turning back. Anders watched to see where the dragon would touch down for the day. The dragon's assigned area appeared to be wider than Anders expected. He saw the dragon fly north out of sight, returning for another pass after leaving the area for nearly an hour. This left Anders hopeful that they would have an opportunity to cross into the Everlight Kingdom sooner than they'd expected.

If he goes back out of sight, we could slip past, Zahara said.

And even if he doesn't, we could fly low, hoping to get by before he comes back, Raffa added.

How do you know it's a he? Maija asked.

You cannot tell? Raffa asked. *He projects his masculine dominance so strongly. I thought it was obvious.*

Anders caught Maija's eye with a wayward glance and shrugged.

They waited until the dragon was well out of view before mounting up. Keeping low to the ground, Raffa and Zahara flew Anders and Maija closer to the forest. Landing on the elven forest's fringe, Anders dismounted Zahara before entering the trees. He checked the skyline one last time before following his companions. He saw the outline of the dragon against the morning sky as it returned on its path back toward the area. Anders noted how much more quickly the dragon's turnaround had been compared to its prior run and hurried to hide quietly among the trees.

Anders couldn't see through the canopy but checked it continually as they headed deeper into the forest. He led the way, directing them toward where he'd seen the fire's glow the night before. The sound of each snapping twig had him flinching and instinctively reaching for Lazuran's hilt. Suddenly a wide swath of sunlight caught Anders' eye. He looked to the patch of forest that appeared to be missing leaves; it was not a meadow. Black branches shone, glistening in the sunlight. Curious, they walked toward it, eventually stopping at the edge of a burned patch.

"What caused this?" Maija asked, ankle-deep ash billowing lightly around her feet and dusting her legs as she stepped into the burned area.

"Dragon?" Anders suggested, glancing up at the exposed sky, half expecting to see the patrolling dragon overhead.

"If it were a dragon, wouldn't there more damage to the branches? It looks like this fire burned hottest on the ground," Maija said, pointing to the smoldering tree stumps.

Anders could see several leaves still clinging to the blackened branches and noted that their finer twigs were still showing, a fuel source that would've burned away in the intensity of dragon's fire from above.

And if this were a dragon's kill zone, there would be sign of a feast. I don't sense one, Raffa said, flicking his forked tongue out into the air several times.

Anders shrugged, "This must've been the area that was glowing last night."

"So, not an elven village. Well, there goes our hopes of a hearty breakfast," Maija said.

As they walked across the burned area, Anders noticed a trail exiting from the other side. Anders and Zahara walked ahead of Raffa and Maija into the dense greenery of the elven forest. The trail Anders discovered was surprisingly wide. He'd traveled on the trails to and from Cedarbridge before. Those trails were narrow and worn to bare soil. This trail was freshly formed, the plants still green and broken along the ground.

Whatever or whoever created this path did so recently, Anders thought to Zahara.

Should we keep following it or make our own? she asked, also sensing the strangeness of the path's creation.

Maybe the elves are creating some new trails? he thought.

I don't know. I just hope it's the elves and not the C.F.D.D dragons, Zahara said.

Let's hope so. I think we should keep on this trail though. Even if it was the dragons, they'll be searching the forest's edge not the interior. Besides, walking on foot will be much faster on this cleared path. It might even lead us to an elven village where we can get some real food.

As the path widened deeper in the forest, Anders joined Maija, letting Zahara and Raffa follow.

"This seems too convenient," Maija said, examining the trail. "The route we traveled from Eastland to Cedarbridge was a path worn down to dirt. And its construction didn't damage the vegetation the way this trail does."

"Yeah. The farther we go, the more I feel certain that elves did not build this trail."

"What then? This is the elven forest so it wouldn't make sense if anything else created it."

Maybe it's prey, Raffa suggested.

"You're just saying that because you're hungry," Maija answered out loud so Anders could hear.

Raffa snorted, smoke puffing from his nostrils, *This trail stinks of herd mentality. There's no reason to where it's leading.*

"How could you possibly know that?" Maija asked. Anders was curious to hear Raffa's reasoning. He thought himself to be a fairly good tracker and he'd missed this assessment of the trail's direction.

If intelligent creatures had created this trail, it would follow a path of least resistance, but it does not. We've already been through sections where it would have been easier to move around a hill or down a slope. But the moving herd is fueled by those running behind. There is an element of panic that encourages them to continue straight through. This path bulls through everything, trampling brush that could easily be avoided.

Anders continued to walk along the path, taking notice of the features Raffa had pointed out. There was no method to the trail's madness. It could've easily gone around a small stand of trees, but just rammed through, as Raffa suggested, trampling the thin trees and creating a hole through the vegetation.

Anders, Zahara said. *Something about this trail smells familiar. I can't put my claw on what it is, but something is off. I don't think we should be following it so mindlessly.*

I have a strange feeling about it now, too, Anders said as he wandered to the edge of the trail, peered into the thick forest. *If we leave this trail, we'll slow down, and we still have a two-day walk to reach or get close to Cedarbridge.*

We could camp until dark and then fly? Zahara suggested hesitantly.

The dragons searching for us could easily spot us this close to the border. I don't think they'll find us in here, but if we fly we could risk leading them to Cedarbridge, he responded.

We'll stay on the path, Raffa said in his powerful voice. *As long as we know there's something off about it, we can be ready for whatever lies ahead.*

Okay, but as soon as we find a real elf trail, we should take it, Zahara said.

They continued down the path in the forest for most of the day. Every few hours, Anders would check to make sure they were continuing in the right direction. When the sun was at its peak, this proved more difficult, but Anders had been between the Eastland Mountains and Cedarbridge several times and felt confident they were heading the right way.

Later in the afternoon, Anders noticed a slight break in the undergrowth. He glanced to see an elven trail just as he was walking past it. Hopping back, Anders grinned when he got a closer look at the truly elven-style path.

"Which way do we follow it, left or right?" Maija asked.

"Well, it looks like the path to the left kind of parallels this one at an angle. Right now, we're going southwest," he pointed to the afternoon sun arching down directly in front of the path. "This trail here to the right looks to go more directly west, which should head toward Cedarbridge."

Without hesitation, Maija took the lead, Raffa stepping in behind her. Anders followed them onto the narrow trail, Zahara close on his heels. Elven-style trails narrowed in comparison to the widely trampled trail they'd been following before, but the trees near the path had been removed to provide a wide creature, such as a dragon of Raffa's size, to move carefully through the forest.

Walking along the elven path gave Anders and the others a sense of safety that they hadn't felt in days or longer. Anders and Zahara had been unsettled in not knowing what had caused such a wide swath through the forest. If it had been a herd as Raffa suggested, Anders struggled to think of a creature that could run in a pack and also start a fire, if that's what caused the fire they'd seen earlier in the day. The more Anders thought about it, the more he confused he became, telling himself it couldn't be a herd of dragons. He decided that it was best to just let it go. They were on the real trail now and likely wouldn't be bothered by the other path again.

As evening approached, Anders saw Maija suddenly take off at a run without warning. Anders' first reaction was to look skyward, expecting to see the dragons from C.F.D.D. When he saw nothing threatening overhead, he chased after her, utterly confused. He slowed as he saw her standing near a log hut with a thatched roof. Anders could see the grin on her face as Maija walked up to the entrance. Seeing that Anders and the dragons had arrived, and realizing that there was no need for alarm, Maija entered the village dwelling.

She quickly backed out of the house with a frown, "No one is home."

"This must be the outskirts of a village. There're probably more homes nearby," Anders said, approaching her.

Maija hopped back onto the trail, eager to seek out more homes. Anders could tell from her reaction that she was excited to see other faces again after spending almost two weeks away from all social contact. He followed at a jog as Maija bounced her way down the trail and poked her head into home after home as they moved into the heart of the village. Each home they peeked into, however, proved to be abandoned. Each empty home left them increasingly anxious.

"Where is everyone? What's happened to them?" Maija asked after exiting the tenth empty hut.

Anders shrugged, "I'll try to sense to see if anyone is nearby."

Maija nodded, scratching her head.

Anders reached out to search the lay of the land with his mind. He hadn't used his senses to search for anyone since being reunited with Maija. He felt doubts about his ability to search when he felt no presence.

"So?" Maija asked, looking eager.

Anders shook his head, "I didn't feel anything."

Maija frowned, "Where is everyone?"

A sinking feeling hit Anders in the stomach. He couldn't explain how he knew something terrible had occurred. He led Maija the short distance down the trail to the center of the village. There in a heap lay the villager elves, collected en masse, clearly slaughtered. Maija stopped when she saw the pile of bodies. Anders grabbed her, pulling her away from the horrific sight.

"Who could've done this?" she asked.

As he looked away from the grim scene, Anders noticed the wide swath of trampled vegetation entering the village in the distance. He pointed toward it and said, "Whatever made that trail."

Zahara walked toward the newer path, sniffing the ground like a bloodhound. She lifted her head and said, *Anders. I know what that smell is.*

What? Anders asked.

Kurr.

CHAPTER ELEVEN

Unnecessary Risk

ax," Britt whispered, her voice breathy as she hovered over him. Seeing his eyes open, she sat back and waited for him to wake up. Carefully rising to her feet, she watched Max sit up and rub his eyes. Clearly reluctant to wake up, he eventually stood next to her and nodded, showing he was ready to go.

They tiptoed toward Solomon's front door, stepping lightly over Bo and Thomas, who remained spread out on the living room floor. As a bachelor, Solomon didn't have extra beds for everyone. Britt recalled Max offering Solomon's bed to Kirsten, but she refused, wanting to stay near the others in this strange new place. Giving in to her wishes, they all took up residence on the floor surrounding Kirsten on the couch.

Britt heard a slight rattle when Max grasped the brass doorknob. As he slowly pulled it open, she could tell he was trying to prevent it from squeaking. Midway, though, the door jerked, sounding a tremendous creaking through the house. Max paused, lifting his shoulders slightly, and Britt held her breath. Turning, they looked to see Bo and Thomas still fast asleep. Kirsten, however, was upright immediately, spotting their darkened figures at the door. For a moment Britt thought Kirsten would shout, but she didn't. Instead, she lay back down, waving at them as she did so. Britt gave her a two-fingered wave, then followed Max as he slipped out the door and into the night.

Once she'd gingerly latched the door, she smiled a double thumbs up at Max. He shivered slightly from the cool autumn air, the coldest of the day just before dawn. They knew they had only a few hours to get to Brookside's aviary and borrow a falcon, preferably one native to the Rollo Islands. She didn't think Max knew how to tell the falcons apart, but she did. Max spun away from the house and began to run at a steady jog, Britt falling in behind him. When they reached the top of a slight rise where the trail to Brookside became more clearly defined, Max slowed to let her catch up.

Puffing a bit from the run, Britt asked, "What's up?"

"You got the crystal?" Max asked.

Reaching into her pants pocket, Britt withdrew the crystal and held it up for him to see. It glowed slightly, a light blue, so light it turned white if she stared at it long enough.

"Good. You keep it. We might need to use it if we get in a jam," Max said in a normal voice now that they were well away from the others.

"I don't know how this thing works," Britt said, pocketing the crystal again.

"Me neither, but I feel better knowing you're holding it. If it were me looking after that thing, I'd be afraid I would blow myself up or something."

"It can do that?" Britt asked, her eyes bulging.

Britt saw him wince from her reaction, "Um, no. I'm

sure you'll be fine. Just try not to think about that kind of stuff."

"Right," Britt said, looking down to her side and wondering if she should even be carrying the crystal.

"Alright. Let's go. We can't waste much time if we want to be out before dawn," Max said as he jogged away, Britt following his lead toward Brookside.

Within a half-hour, the flickering orange glow of lanterns came into view. Max slowed and Britt looked into the trees, keeping a sharp eye out for any watchmen possibly posted on the fringe. They began to pass homes built along the brook that ran from within the forest and directly into town.

Nearing Brookside's formal entrance, Max moved off-trail and tucked in behind a large maple tree. Almost running past him, Britt shuffled to a stop and hopped behind the tree. Poking their heads out from the side, they examined the streets as they faded into darkness. Several shop and storefront lanterns still burned, illuminating the cobblestone in front of them.

Not sensing any movement, Max made his way quickly to the street's edge. He stepped in close against a rectangular sign at the edge of the cobblestone. Popping his head around the slab of wood, he examined the streets from the closer vantage point. Then he motioned for her to join him.

Britt slid in next to Max, mimicking him in flattening herself against the sign. As she pressed her back into the wood, a sharp point pricked her shoulder. She winced and reached around to feel at the tack. Glancing back, she saw that the board was covered in pieces of parchment. Taking a closer look, she could see that the signs included faces. She focused on one that resembled the man who'd helped them, Rune. Keeping close to the sign, she turned to gain a better look at the posters, instantly recognizing Anders and Ivan along with several others from their group. She tapped Max on the shoulder and pointed to the posters, watching his surprise in recognizing himself and Bo on their own poster. In bold lettering above their faces, she read the word 'REWARD'. Below the drawings of their faces, Britt read the brothers' names, a brief description about where they'd last been seen, and the amount in coin from the imperial chest anyone would receive if they brought in these fugitives. Britt noted the words, 'wanted dead or alive,' across the base of many posters, including Max and Bo's. She saw Max step back and scratch his head while he chewed on his lower lip.

"They got my nose wrong," he whispered, pointing to the sign.

Britt stared at him blankly. She expected anger or fear; yet, this was Max, the guy with the odd sense of humor. She shook her head as he leaned in closer to the drawing.

"See," he said, pointing to the nose. When Britt didn't chuckle, Max smiled. "Not the right time for a joke?" he asked.

She shook her head again and pointed to the drawings of Ivan and Anders.

"Of course they have the highest reward. Mine's not even a quarter of theirs." When Britt remained stoic, he added, "At least I beat Bo."

With this remark, Britt cracked a smile and pushed him slightly, "You're ridiculous."

"What's ridiculous is that you're not on here," Max whispered.

"Neither are Kirsten or Thomas," she added.

Max pointed to the drawing of Rune, the man who'd helped them get to Brookside, "What's it say about him?"

Britt leaned in close to read in the dark, "It says he's a surgeon, and that he's known to have led rebellious gatherings in protest of the imperial rule of his Lord Majesty, Merglan."

"So, he is trustworthy," Max said.

"Well, he did help us get to Solomon's."

"Speaking of whom, he should be on here," Max said, again searching the board. "Yep, here he is," as he pointed to the drawing of the old man with the thick gray beard and nappy hair.

"Does he really look that old?" she asked, staring at the drawing. When she saw Max frown, she nudged him, "What? When I do it, it's not funny?"

Max turned, placed his back to the sign, and checked to see whether the coast was still clear. Britt felt slighted that she didn't earn a laugh and heard him say, "You've got to pick your moments, my dear." Then he was off, out into the open street.

Britt shook her head, smiled slightly at his lightheartedness, then followed him into Brookside.

They slid into door wells, edged around corners and snuck through the shadows, avoiding all lanterns and often crossing the street to remain out of sight. As they ventured through town toward the beach, where the aviary was located, Britt thought there should've been more people standing watch or moving about. The complete absence of watchmen raised concern.

Reaching the last row of buildings and homes near the

dock area, Max tucked into a tight alleyway and Britt followed. The alley was so narrow that they had to walk with their shoulders at an angle to avoid scraping against the brick walls. Reaching the end, Max slowed and raised his palm to Britt, telling her to stay put.

Halting, she flattened herself against the wall and watched Max inch toward the edge of the alley. He leaned into the corner, peering out from the gap, but abruptly withdrew. He remained perfectly still, and Britt held her breath hoping no one would walk around the corner. After several long breaths, Max moved again and Britt relaxed slightly, silently cursing him for startling her. He peeked out several times, immediately retreating each time. After the sixth glance, he waved Britt forward.

Carefully edging herself up next to Max, Britt touched him lightly on the wrist. When he turned to meet her gaze, Britt widened her eyes expectantly. She wanted to know what he saw, but didn't dare speak. Placing a finger to his lips, Max motioned for quiet and quickly rolled around her, suddenly standing with his back against the wall across from her. He nodded, urging her to look for herself.

As she tiptoed to the corner, her heart began to race with excitement. She carefully ducked in and out in one fluid motion. She caught a glimpse of the group of armed men Max had seen. Dressed in uniforms, they huddled at the end of the street, less than a half a block away.

Wanting a better look, she inched around until she could see them clearly, careful not to expose herself. She counted six men standing in a half-circle facing the ocean, overlooking the shipping area where porters and merchants unloaded goods. Their uniforms were a combination of leather and plate armor, allowing these men somewhat easier mobility than the average King's soldier it would seem. With long broadswords at their sides, they looked to be a formidable group. Britt withdrew deeper into the alley and pointed the other direction.

Max shook his head and pointed out at the street where the armed men stood.

Britt narrowed her eyes and shook her head, then pointed back at the street where they'd come from.

Max firmly pointed toward the opposite way.

Britt motioned for them to swap places again. She wanted to go out the other way, not into the street where the soldiers could see them.

Max stepped back into the alley a ways and allowed Britt to scoot by. He then edged to the corner and looked out again. Britt watched Max carefully, he bobbed his head steadily, his inside hand counting one finger at a time, then balling up into a closed fist and starting over.

What's he doing? Britt wondered. After a minute, Max turned back to face Britt and grabbed her by the wrist.

She just had time to look down at his hand when Max gripped her arm and darted out into the street, pulling her along with him.

Britt stumbled to keep up as they rushed out into the open. She wanted to go back to the safety of the alleyway, but it was too late. She ran just behind Max as he arced to the right. *No,* she thought, her heart sinking. *That's where they,* she looked up to see that the armed men were no longer there. She didn't understand. The men with swords were literally standing there a moment ago. Then she understood why Max was bobbing and counting. He must've known something about their movements and timed it so that when they moved, the two of them could run out.

Letting go of her hand, he stopped momentarily at the opposite side of the street along the edge of the last building before the docks. The cobblestone path separating Brookside's port from the shoreline, extended in both directions. Britt glanced to the right. She saw the armed men turn and start down the next street over, the street that Britt had wanted to turn back to. If she had retreated to some other hiding place when they turned the corner, she would've been caught.

Max glanced up and down the shoreline and nodded. Again, they stepped out into the street running lightly along the stone path. Britt wasn't sure how much of the night watchmen's behavior Max knew of, but what he'd done just a moment ago impressed her. Stopping to glance down each cross street, Max and Britt continued to run the length of the shore until they reached the edge of town where the cobblestone path ended and the buildings began to spread thin. They rushed past the last building to a large tree just up from the beach. Britt was thankful that dense forest seemed to encircle the landside of Brookside. It provided excellent cover just outside the town's limits.

Panting as they rested against the tree trunk, Britt asked, "How did you know?"

Max smiled, leaning over his knees to catch his breath, "If we had gone back, we would've been caught, right?"

"Yes, but how did you know that?" she asked again.

"Mostly a guess," Max said.

Britt's eyes widened, not believing he would risk their lives on a guess.

"When we first reached that corner in the alley, I could hear them walking. I popped my head around to see them come to a halt. They were headed toward the docks. When they stopped to chat, I had a feeling they would stay for a moment and then head off in the same direction. That's when you caught a glimpse of them, when they had just stopped. And, well, I was right. They continued on in the same direction."

Britt shook her head, "You're gutsy, you know that?"

Max shrugged.

"So, where's this aviary?" Britt asked, rising to a full stance, ready to continue.

Max pointed away from town, "You see the metal dome poking out above the trees there?"

Britt followed his mark and saw a rounded cage sticking above the trees just inland from the shoreline.

"When we get there, you'll have to identify the bird. I don't know the difference between one falcon and another. They're all the same to me," Max said.

Britt nodded, "No problem."

"Ready?" he asked.

She nodded again.

"Let's be careful on our way up to the cage. If we wake all of the birds at once, their squawking will be like setting off an alarm."

"Right," Britt said, admiring Max's strategy in all of this. Accustomed to being in charge, she had allowed him to lead in this and, so far, she was impressed.

Max led them the short distance through the trees to the aviary. The three-story structure had a rounded and mostly wooden base. In place of the typical Westland rooftop was a massive cage-like dome covering the top, rising in height to over fifty feet. Max and Britt half expected it to be guarded, but to their luck, nobody stood watch or even napped near the base. At the door, Max carefully moved the latch and pulled the door open on rusty hinges. It creaked and scraped, but the noise didn't seem as loud out here in the woods as it had in the confines of Solomon's house. To Britt's surprise, the birds remained asleep.

Entering and closing the door behind them, Max whispered, "I don't know much about sleeping birds, but I'm guessing they're not going to be happy when we wake them up."

Britt nodded and whispered, "Careful, don't touch their perch. They might feel the movement and wake up. I know most birds don't have great night vision. If one starts flying aimlessly around in here, it's certain to start a chain reaction, and that would be bad."

Looking around the large dome, Britt sought out the familiar larger nests of the raptors. Midway up the rounded wall, near where the dome cage rose from the wooden frame, she located several large nests on platforms. She quickly canceled out two as too large to be falcon nests. Falcons were smaller than most hawks, but the Rollo Island Falcon was larger than other birds in its class. Careful to avoid touching anything that might disturb the other nests, Britt led Max under the platform she'd picked out.

Pointing up, she whispered, "I think they'll be up there."

Max pointed to a wooden ladder leaning against the wall, "You could use that to get up there."

Britt nodded. He helped her position the ladder to

reach the smaller of the large nests along one platform. Making sure to move slowly, Britt climbed the ladder to the nests. As soon as she poked her head into view, three of the seven resting birds she saw sat up and began looking around to see what was moving their perch.

Britt hesitated, trying to remain still as the birds stiffened, picking up their feet and shifting slightly. She held her breath thinking, *please don't move, please don't move.* When the bird closest to her ruffled its wings, she recognized it as an osprey. That wasn't the bird she was looking for and she knew osprey to be quite vocal. If it started to squawk, all of the birds would awaken, possibly alerting the soldiers in the street.

While waiting for the osprey to calm down, she identified her falcon. It nested two birds to the right of the ladder, just an arm's reach from where she stood. Not wanting to climb down and move the ladder, possibly shaking the nervous osprey even more, Britt decided to lean out, hoping she could reach the bird.

Britt moved smoothly, placing her left hand on the platform for balance just to the right of the ladder as she put her weight out over to the right, into space. As she reached her right hand up to grab the falcon, the ladder moved, tipping to the left. Her heart dropped into her stomach as she caught the ladder with her foot and slid it back into place. Luckily, she'd been holding onto the wooden platform, otherwise she would've fallen the fifteen feet to the aviary floor. It would have hurt and made for an irritating mistake.

Regaining her balance on the ladder, Britt quickly placed her hand under the falcon and scooped it up. Still half asleep, she carried the warm falcon against her chest. By the time the bird had fully awakened, she had it tucked away tightly and was halfway down the ladder. When she reached the ground, she nodded to Max and they quickly headed for the aviary exit.

Britt was surprised that the falcon hadn't objected more to being lifted from its nest. She chalked it up to the fact that the bird was a messenger bird and used to being taken from its nest for missions.

Just before leaving the aviary Max stopped, searching the desk near the door for parchment, quill and ink. He opened a drawer and found the materials necessary to create a message along with a strip of ribbon to secure the scroll to the bird's leg. Max handed them to Britt, but she shook her head, taking a step back. "I think you should do it," she whispered.

"Why?" he asked.

Britt shrugged, "I think your writing will be more legible."

"You can write, can't you?" he asked.

"Yes, but I'm versed mostly in nautical logs," she said.

Max spread the small piece of parchment out on the desk. He dipped the quill into the inkbottle and scratched out several lines. When he had finished, he rolled it up, ripped a piece of ribbon from the desk and fastened it securely around the falcon's leg.

Exiting the aviary, Max and Britt again entered into the night air, closing the squeaky door behind them. Walking to the edge of the tree line, Britt held the falcon up. The bird, now fully awake and sensing the fresh air and open space, flapped its wings as she held it aloft. Tossing it lightly, she sent the bird into flight.

The falcon dropped slightly, then flapped into the air, taking flight into the darkness out over the ocean. As Britt watched the message to her crew fly away over the water, she hoped it would reach her intended target. At the very least, the bird would return to its home islands and one of the members of her community would find it, read the message and know what was happening in Westland.

After watching the falcon disappear into the night, Britt turned to Max and said, "Let's get out of here!"

"There's one more thing I want to do while we're in town," Max said.

Britt raised an eyebrow, "What do you have in mind?"

"Food," he said.

"Isn't there food at Solomon's?" Britt asked.

"Yes, but you saw how much there is. We're going to need more, and soon. It's not like we're going to have many more chances to get back to town. We're going to be leaving again soon and I don't know about you, but I think being on the road without any food stinks."

Britt stiffened her jaw, weighing the risk of venturing back through the streets. "It did seem less difficult than I thought it would be to sneak all the way through town," she said.

Max grinned, "Good. I know a place where we can get all kinds of goodies. The Brookside Inn has a kitchen and their food is amazing. We'll sneak into the back and steal what we can. Then we'll head out to Solomon's, stopping by that board again so I can grab that poster of Bo and me."

"Why?" Britt asked.

"For a keepsake. It's not every day you find a wanted

poster of yourself with a price for your head."

"Fine, but we're going to have to move quickly. The sun will be coming up soon and we need to be out of here by the time the town wakes up," Britt said.

"Follow me," Max said and took off with a spring in his step toward the dimly lit cobblestone streets of Brookside.

Taking a similar route, Max led Britt back through Brookside. It appeared that the only patrol in town was the group they'd seen earlier. Stopping across the street from the Brookside Inn, Max nodded to the storefront and whispered, "There it is. There's another door around back." Britt saw that the street was empty and followed Max around to the back.

As Max worked the doorknob, Britt noted the lightening of the sky to the east. Max pulled the door open without a sound, nodding for Britt to follow him in. Stepping through the doorway into the inn's kitchen, Britt reached out to grab a white mass about to hit her in the face. Her hands punched through the cloth as she caught the white sack Max had tossed at her. Pulling it down from the air she gave Max a stern look as if to say, that wasn't funny.

Max grinned and began rummaging quietly through the cupboards. Together they filled their sacks with kitchen supplies. Leaving a noticeably diminished supply of food on the stocked shelves, Britt wondered whether Max felt any remorse for stealing from the inn's owners. She grew up in a society where raiding was a part of their culture and a right all Rollo warriors must take advantage of, but to Max, this would be theft and likely from someone he knew. Max held the door open for her. She hesitated, wanting to ask him about it, then exited the inn.

Tossing the full sack over her shoulder, she turned down the side street they'd taken into town. She froze when she caught sight of an armed man walking lazily down the cobblestone street. Max moved from the back door to join her. Britt watched helplessly as the soldier turned to see them standing in the side street behind the inn. Max crouched, then bolted, taking off in a dead sprint down a side street in the opposite direction of the guard. Britt turned on her heels and followed before the man could shout.

In an instant, she could hear the man's call, yelling in a foreign language before beginning his pursuit. She tuned out the replying voices as the pitter-patter of their feet rang through the streets. Following Max as he darted into a crack between buildings, Britt ran through the tight alley and out into the neighboring street. Max led her through a string of side alleys, angling their way to the edge of town.

In a blur of walls and cobblestone, Britt soon saw the forest. Clutching the bag of food tightly to her shoulder, she sprinted away from the streets and into the trees. She skidded to a halt as she saw Max suddenly turn back. Britt wanted to yell at him, but held her tongue, not wanting to give away their position in case the soldiers hadn't been able to follow them.

Max sprinted to the sign marking Brookside's entrance and pulled a piece of parchment from the board. Britt bounced on her toes as she watched him snatch the poster. She couldn't see the men chasing them, but she could hear them coming. Their metal-plated armor clattered against the stone walls as they tried to squeeze through the alleys where Max had led them. Their shouts alerted others in the town as the sun rose over the horizon. Max sprinted back to Britt as fast as he could. With the sack of food in one hand and the parchment poster in the other, he joined her in fleeing Brookside. Gaining a bit of distance from town, Britt turned to glare at Max but saw in his broad grin that he was truly enjoying this.

Chapter Twelve

No Return

lancing back, Britt peered through the early morning haze, seeing only the faint outline of Brookside. *No pursuing soldiers yet*, she told herself. Doubling her efforts on the trail, she surged forward, the bulk of the sack bounced against her back with every step. Max came into view out of the corner of her eye. She could see his slight smile left over from showing off at the edge of town. He still clutched the reward poster in one hand, but, upon seeing her, quickly stuffed it in his pocket.

Why did he do that? she wondered, trying to suppress her anger. Stopping to yell at him would only make things worse.

As they jogged away from town and the ensuing watchmen, the shouts of alarm gave way to sounds of nature. Expecting an attacker to lunge from the forest at any moment, Britt flinched each time squirrels chattered as they ran by. She cursed Max for the risk they'd taken in burglarizing the inn and causing her to be on edge. If she had taken control, as she should've, they wouldn't be in this mess. Britt wasn't promoted to Captain so she could let a crewman lead her into unnecessarily risky situations.

I let emotions get in the way, she thought, something she would be sure to rectify in future decisions.

The dawn's pink and red bands were turning to a golden yellow hue when Britt first heard the unnatural sound. As the steady thudding grew louder, she slowed to a halt, Max stopping beside her. She eyed him as they listened to the sound, trying to recognize its origin, both what was making it and where it was coming from. All at once they realized that it was the unmistakable sound of marching soldiers headed toward them on the road.

Without a thought, Britt turned and sped off-trail into the forest. She heard the branches breaking behind her as Max leapt into the undergrowth. Running without any idea where she was going, Britt searched for a hiding place. With the uniform marching ringing through the forest, she felt the soldiers were almost on top of them. Amid the fluster, she suddenly heard Max's voice almost next to her. Looking right, Britt found her companion kneeling beside a broad tree surrounded by thick shrubs.

Cutting in midstride, Britt rushed to Max's hiding spot and dropped the bag of food supplies as she slid in next to him. Panting, she peered around the shrubs to see movement on the trail they'd just left. Britt watched carefully as men mounted on horseback rode into view, their armor appearing in sporadic bursts through gaps in the vegetation. Britt rolled, placing her back tight against the tree trunk and closed her eyes, cursing under her breath.

"Soldiers," Max whispered, still panting heavily from their sprint. "Good thing you heard them. I would've kept running if you hadn't slowed down."

Opening her eyes, Britt glanced at him. Max rested

against the tree leaning hard on his forearm. Britt caught his gaze and he smiled at her with his dreamy eyes. For an instant, she almost thanked him, then reminded herself of the foolish risk he'd taken. She steeled her face, glared at him and shook her head, "We should've been back to Sol's by now."

A drop of sweat fell from Max's nose as he looked down, "I'm sorry, Britt, but we do need the food. Kirsten won't get any stronger without it."

Britt frowned, "I should've taken command after our mission was complete. There is food enough at Solomon's." Not allowing Max the chance to respond, she turned again toward the soldiers. Through gaps in the trees, she could just see the line of armed men stretching beyond her field of view.

"Get down," Britt said, rolling back around to the safety of the tree and pulling at Max's pant leg.

She was relieved when he listened to her, kneeling at her side. She felt she might've been a little harsh in her reprimand. Britt knew the soldiers hadn't seen them because they weren't veering off the trail. Her experience in overland strategy was limited, but she knew one rule that applied to both land and sea: If you can see your enemy, they can see you, too. Britt shifted, "This is maddening."

"Which part? The almost getting caught by soldiers in town part or the almost running right into a traveling army during our escape?" Max asked sitting down next to her.

Britt groaned, elbowing him lightly, "All of it. I can't believe you went back for that stupid poster."

Max shrugged, "I had to show Bo. I couldn't help myself."

"What if they saw you?" Britt asked.

"They did see you and me around back at the inn. Didn't think it would make a difference if they saw me again," he said.

Britt inhaled sharply through her nose and clenched her jaw in frustration, "If they had caught you because of that poster, I would've left you there."

"We were so far ahead of them," Max said. "I had plenty of time."

Britt was about to reply when she noticed the absence of marching. Seeing Max smiling childishly at her, she narrowed her eyes and rolled around the tree, staying low and looking toward the trail.

The forest's morning glow had given way to daylight and she could clearly see through to the glinting armor as it stood out against the green surroundings. Britt couldn't positively identify this army, but she could see that they had halted on the trail.

Could this be the rebel army Rune spoke of? Had they already marched on Brookside? she wondered.

Whispering, she asked Max, "Why have they stopped?"

Max replied calmly, "I don't know."

"Do you think that's the Resistance?"

Britt was met with silence as Max mulled the possibility over. After several long moments, he responded, "They're not wearing Merglan's colors like those soldiers in Grandwood, but I don't think the rebels Rune was talking about were an organized army. I imagined them more as regular folk who'd taken to the woods like a guerilla force. I wouldn't expect them to be wearing plate armor and marching in formation."

Britt wished he were wrong, but she sensed he was right. These were the soldiers who'd invaded Brookside, but why were they here and not in town? As she thought about it, a mounted soldier rode down the line, repeating a sentence over and over in a foreign language. It sounded like the same language she'd heard among the soldiers in Brookside.

Before she could ask Max what he thought was happening, Britt saw the soldiers begin to move again. It was hard to tell for sure, but she thought they were shuffling in place, not advancing to the left or right. Then all at once, the wall of soldiers started walking. At first Britt was relieved to see them start moving, thinking they were continuing toward town, but to her horror she heard branches snap and watched the brush begin to move. The line of soldiers stepped into the forest and Britt could see their faces through the patchy vegetation. Britt reached for Max and grabbed him by the shoulder; they were trapped.

***

Britt's fingers dug into his skin. She looked to see his eyes bulging as he winced in pain. Releasing him, she swiveled around to search for an escape route. If they ran now, they would be seen. They were pinned in the island of brush surrounding the large tree.

Max gripped the deeply furrowed bark of the tree and started climbing. The width of the tree hid them from the soldiers and, to Britt's surprise, he managed to make it to the lowest branch that hung well over their heads. He motioned for her to follow him and reached down for her to grip his hand. Britt hesitated, wondering if it were more soldiers hidden in the shrubs surrounding the tree's base.

She glanced at the sacks of food on the ground and imagined what would happen when the soldiers found them. The white bags would be a dead giveaway that they'd been there. All they'd have to do is glance up. Hoping what she was about to do was worth the risk, she sank into a crawl and moved out from the safety of the tree. Not chancing to look up, Britt gripped the white bags and dragged them the short distance to their hiding place. Then she stood behind the tree and hefted each food sack to Max.

Shaking his head, Britt saw Max's mouth say without words, "Leave it."

Britt shook her head pushed the bag at him again. Frustrated, he grabbed the sacks one at a time. As the soldiers approached, Britt scrambled up into the tree. Taking one of the sacks, Britt followed Max as they moved higher into the tree's thickets of leaves. Moving as carefully as she dared, Britt came to rest on a branch fifteen feet up, placing the bag in her lap. If she had her way, she would climb even higher, but they had to stop moving because the soldiers below were nearly on them.

How did they know to look for us here? Britt wondered.

The only reason she could imagine was that the soldiers from Brookside had come across these troops on the trail just after she and Max ran into the woods. Since the soldiers hadn't seen them on the trail and their pursuers hadn't caught up to them, the logical next step would be to look into the forest. Britt wondered how long they would search the forest and when she and Max would have a chance to climb down. She hoped they wouldn't be stuck in the tree for the whole day, or worse, that the soldiers would see them when they passed underneath.

Britt rubbed her thigh nervously, waiting for the soldiers to pass under them. As she moved her hand against her leg, she felt a hard lump in her side pocket. *The crystal,* she thought, reaching her hand into her pocket and gripping the sapphire. Could she use it to aid in their escape? The only thing she knew of the stone's power was that Kirsten had used it like a cannon, blasting people away with a pulse of light. If Britt managed to conjure up the same explosive burst of energy Kirsten had displayed, it would only make it easier for the soldiers to find them.

Maybe I can use it to conceal us instead, she thought. The only time she'd tried to use the magical conduit was when she attempted to push the goblin venom from Kirsten's heart, but that hadn't worked. Britt didn't know whether the crystal only worked for certain people; Kirsten, after all, was related to a dragonrider. *But Anders wasn't born with magic,* she reminded herself. Feeling the stone in her hand, she thought, *What if it did work and something went horribly wrong? I could secure our capture by trying it now.*

She slid her hand back into her pocket, letting go of her grip on the crystal. Focusing on remaining perfectly still, she forced any thought of using the magic stone from her mind. If they were going to remain hidden from the soldiers, they'd need to act like they were part of the tree.

From the corner of her eye, Britt saw soldiers coming into view under the tree. Taking slow, quiet breaths, she tried to control her racing heart. She could hear its pulsing beat in her ears. It sounded so loud that she worried the soldiers would soon hear it, too. The swath of men spread an arm's length from one another moved as a cohesive unit, like a net set to snare anything in its path.

The soldiers walked directly under the vast plumage of the tree. Britt knew she shouldn't move, but she couldn't help herself. Tilting her head, she prayed the movement wouldn't be the point of their undoing. She watched with wide eyes as the line of men broke to move around the wide tree trunk, two men peeling off to either side. Both of them kept their hands on the trunk, brushing the bark with their fingertips as they moved around it in a half-circle. Instinct told her to run, but it was experience that kept her still. Forcing down the impulse to escape, Britt waited for the soldiers to round the tree.

Reaching the backside of the tree, the two men who'd broken off fell back in line. One of them hesitated, taking a second glance at the spot where Britt and Max had hidden behind the tree. Britt held her breath, wondering if he could see any clues in the slightly disturbed ground. The soldier's head moved, from a downward look to straight ahead. He leaned toward the tree, examining the bark. Britt's heart raced and she prepared to drop from her perch. If it came down to it, she would chance an escape on foot.

Another soldier from the line called back to the one at the tree as the rest continued in their line into the forest. Britt kept her eyes fixed on the man below. He stepped back, looked to either side, then returned to the line of men advancing slowly away from the tree. Britt's heart lifted and she felt the weight in her stomach lighten. The sensation of nearly being captured left her with a slew of emotions. She was frustrated with Max for putting them in this situation, yet they might very well have been in a worse situation had they not stopped for the food. She was the one who insisted on going to town and she knew he was right about their need for food. Kirsten would need plenty to fully recover from the goblin's infection.

Waiting for the soldiers to entirely disappear, Britt let her legs dangle from the branch as she tried to get over how close they'd come to getting caught. Britt and Max shared a look, shaking their heads in disbelief.

She heard Max whisper, "We should get back to warn the others."

Britt nodded, glancing to make sure the soldiers had indeed moved on. Grabbing the bag of food she'd filled back at the Brookside Inn, Britt slowly and carefully climbed back down the tree. They hadn't made it very far up when the soldiers closed in, so she quickly maneuvered to the last branch. Before reaching the ground, she bent down, looking in all directions to ensure no one was nearby. As she looked all around, she caught sight of the sun shining on metal. Her heart skipped a beat and she nearly dropped out of the tree onto her face. Collecting her wits, she focused and saw that some soldiers had remained on the road. The men on horseback at the front of the troops hadn't gone with their footmen.

Britt cursed under her breath and straightened. She whispered to Max, "The soldiers on horseback. They're still on the trail."

Max scowled with a curt nod.

As Max struggled to come up with a new plan, Britt realized they could still descend from the tree as long as they remained on the side opposite from the road. If the foot soldiers returned and they weren't able to move, they would be seen for sure.

Deciding that she didn't want to spend the whole day

sitting in a tree and waiting around to be noticed, Britt continued her descent. As she landed on the soft forest floor, she crouched while making sure the foot soldiers had moved on. Max followed, landing lightly next to her, his sack of food still in hand. Britt leaned around the tree trunk, locating the riders stationed on the path.

"Is there another way to Solomon's?" she asked.

"We could get there by continuing through the forest?" Max suggested.

"We'll have to."

"Right then, follow me," Max said.

Britt nodded and gripped her sack, ready to move. Keeping low to the ground, they began to sneak away, at first in very short bursts. Crawling at times to remain hidden from the road, they distanced themselves from the riders. As they got more comfortable in their escape, they lengthened the distance of their movements before taking shelter behind brush or trees. With the horsemen well out of sight, Max led Britt back toward the path. He halted suddenly, dropping to his stomach. Britt hadn't yet lost her edge as a soldier and joined him in an instant. She looked through the undergrowth to see what had caused Max's reaction. Three soldiers walked down the road.

Britt looked at their surroundings. They'd dropped to the ground in an instant but didn't have thick cover; they were somewhat exposed. Unless these soldiers were blind, they would soon spot them lying in the grass next to the road. Britt's mind searched for a different solution, but at this point, there was nothing they could do. She and Max were committed to their position; their best option was to remain still.

She held her breath as the soldiers walked steadily closer. They hadn't seen them lying next to the path yet, or if they had, they weren't concerned with them at all. The men continued as if there weren't two bodies lying in broad daylight just off the trail. As the soldiers walked just a few yards from them, Britt thought they would pass without confrontation. She held perfectly still while the sounds of their trotting continued. Suddenly they stopped and Britt heard the men say something in a foreign language. She dared not move, but she knew they'd been spotted. *Should we run?* Britt thought, her eyes still peering straight ahead at Max, who didn't move a muscle.

The sound of feet shuffling across dirt started again and she knew the soldiers were nearly on top of them when they stepped into the grass. Britt could see a soldier's legs come into view. She heard one of them draw his sword, the slight ring of steel as it was removed from its sheath. Britt knew if they didn't get up and run now the soldier would soon be running them through with the point of that sword.

She prepared to bolt, her body stiffening on the ground and her legs pressing into the grass. That's when she became aware once again of the bulge in her pocket, the hard stone that pushed against her leg. *The crystal,* she thought.

Britt sprang from the ground, reaching into her pocket and pulling out the crystal. As she came into an aggressive stance before the soldiers, she pushed the lightly glowing crystal out at them, willing it to cause severe damage.

The soldiers reared in surprise at what they thought to be unresponsive subjects. The light blue sapphire's glow in Britt's hand got their attention, yet nothing powerful came from it. Britt stood with her arm outstretched near their faces, the sapphire gripped in her hand, but the intended magic did not come.

The shock of her movement passed, and the soldiers reacted, seeing she'd caused them no harm. Bobbing to the side, Britt dodged the piercing stab from the soldier whose sword had already been drawn. As he stumbled in his attack, she punched him hard in the face, his head whipping back before the others could react. Quickly she shoved another soldier as he tried to pull his sword, causing him to fall on his back.

Springing to action, Max tackled the third soldier, catching him off guard and disorienting him as he fell to the grass. The man who'd tried to stab her with his sword turned and attacked again. This time, swinging his blade. Britt dodged it twice, leaping out of the way. She still held the stone in her hand and tried again to use it, but nothing happened. She shook the glowing crystal at the soldier, giving him pause as he held the sword up over his head. Britt took advantage of the distraction she'd caused and sprang on him, dropping the crystal. Catching his two-handed grip before he could bring the broadsword down on her, Britt struggled with the man for control of the blade. With her peripheral vision, Britt saw the soldier she'd pushed to the side charge. Stomping on the man she was struggling with, Britt kicked the inside of the soldier's knee, causing him to spin into a fall. She directed the man's body between herself and the oncoming soldier. As the man fell, Britt saw the soldier recognize the change in his target, but couldn't prevent his deadly swing. The man's sword fell onto his fellow soldier, cutting deep into his neck. In an attempt to lessen the blow, the soldier must've loosened his grip on the sword, because it fell from his hands as he followed half-heartedly through his felling hew.

Hitting the ground, Britt reached for the sword from the man's dying grip. She pulled it easily from his hands as he bled out alongside the road. Seeing the soldier who'd dropped the sword fumble to pick it up, Britt jumped to her feet just in time to deflect the man's next attack. Gaining her footing, Britt blocked the man's wild swings, then launched into a series of her own. Britt's swordplay landed in a much more calculated approach than that of the soldiers, causing the remaining soldier to back up in a panic. To her surprise, the third soldier fled, running back in the direction he'd come from.

Whirling around, Britt looked to Max. He grappled with the downed soldier, rolling on the ground, their arms intertwined, each trying to prevent the other from drawing the soldier's weapon. Britt rushed over. As the soldier rolled on top of Max, she bludgeoned him over the head with the pommel of her sword. The blow knocked him limp, pinning Max. Britt helped him get out from under the heavy man's armored body.

Helping him up, Britt asked, "Are you alright?"

Max nodded, wiping the blood from his nose and looking at his hand, "Yeah, I'll be alright."

"We'd better get out of here," Britt said, moving to the dead soldier who lay bled out near the trail. Kicking him onto his back, she removed his sword belt.

"Weren't there three?" Max asked, following Britt's lead and removing the sword and belt from the unconscious soldier.

"Yeah," Britt replied. "One got away."

Max cursed, "He'll be sending those riders on us soon."

Britt belted the sword's sheath. "No. He ran back that way," she said, pointing down the trail in the opposite direction of the other troops.

"Why would he go back that way? All the others are this way," Max said, nodding as he fastened the sheathed sword around his waist.

Britt saw the conclusion come over Max's face as she realized it, too. "More soldiers are coming," they said in unison.

Cursing, Britt searched the area for the best way to run. They had soldiers behind them, and more than likely, more coming in front of them. A troop was searching both sides of the road for them and would soon be learning of the death of one of their comrades.

"I wish I could get this thing to work for me," Britt said, finding the crystal in the grass where she'd dropped it. "Maybe then we could blast our way out, like Kirsten did in Grandwood." Britt pocketed the crystal and hurried to the sack of food she'd left on the ground.

As they shouldered their bags, he said, "I think I have an idea."

Britt followed him as he jogged a short way back the way they'd come, toward the soldiers on horseback. Just off the trail he tossed his sack of food to the right, landing well within view. He instructed Britt to do the same. She did, throwing the sack in a visible line of sight from the trail.

Max then turned left and rushed across the trail, back to the side where they had originally been hiding. He then jumped into the woods, more rapidly than they had on the way there. Britt followed him as he crouched low to the ground, moving quickly into the forest where the soldiers were searching for them.

Grabbing him by the shirt to slow him down, Britt said, "Max, where are you taking us? You realize we're going right toward the line of soldiers who are searching the forest. They could be coming back this way any minute."

Max nodded and Britt shook her head in confusion. "We can't fight through them all," she said.

"Hopefully we won't have to," Max replied.

Britt frowned.

"Just come on. We need to be quick if we're going to make it," he said, resuming his lead.

Britt followed Max as they moved quickly through the forest. She glanced over her shoulder many times to ensure those on horseback hadn't seen them.

Soon Max stopped and Britt saw the relief on his face. He'd led them to the brook that followed the trail into town. She still didn't see why Max was so pleased to have found the brook.

Sliding into the water, Max lay on his back in the current, waving for Britt to follow. Without hesitation she joined him, the chill sending a shiver through her body. She floated behind him as they allowed the current to carry them downstream. The dip in the bank provided excellent cover to anyone who was just a little ways away from the stream. As long as they remained low in the water, they would be somewhat hidden from sight.

As they floated in silence, Britt wondered what they would do if they came across the soldiers who were searching for them. She hoped Max had a plan. They were moving back toward the town at a swift rate and she knew others would be searching for them there. She didn't know what Max was trying to do, but they wouldn't be returning to Solomon's anytime soon.

Although the sun was rising higher into the sky, the shadowy forest provided little direct sunlight and the chilled water began to feel colder. Above the gentle chattering of her teeth, Britt heard movement in the trees nearby. Max aimed toward the bank, sliding into the slower-moving water along the edge. Britt's heart began to race as the rustling sounds beyond the bank grew louder. She followed Max into a cluster of cattails in the shallows of the eddy. Soldiers were advancing toward them, returning toward the road. They would be crossing the water at any moment. The collective snapping of twigs, rustling of brush and sound of armor scraping against branches overwhelmed them.

Britt widened her eyes, wanting to scream at Max, what are we going to do?

Max quickly broke a cattail reed from the clump, snapped off the fuzzy brown tip and handed it to her. She looked at him in utter confusion. What did he want her to do with that? She couldn't fight off a troop of soldiers with a hollow reed.

He broke off another, creating another two-foot-long hollow reed, which he then placed in his mouth as he submerged under the muddy water. Britt understood then that she was to use the reed as a breathing tube to remain hidden underwater as the soldiers passed. She dunked, sucking on the length of hollow reed for air.

She dug her hands into the rocky bottom of the stream, holding herself down as she sat with her eyes open, looking toward the surface. She held the cattail tight in her mouth, inhaling and exhaling carefully, trying to keep her breathing under control. The dark nappy mat of her hair floated around her face, and for once, she was happy her hair wasn't long and stringy. The clump of curls held their shape under the water, not rising to the surface. She could see Max through the muddy water. He sat in a similar position, his long strands of straight dark hair rising to the surface. He caught them with one hand and held them down.

Britt heard the soldiers enter the water nearby. She could see their legs as they waded through to the other side, passing by just feet from where they were hidden. She hadn't even considered that one of them could step on her and was glad it hadn't happened. In a matter of moments, the soldiers were climbing out on the other bank.

The two stayed under the surface for longer than was comfortable, but the need to remain hidden drove them to remain in the cold water. Finally rising to the surface and keeping her body underwater, Britt quietly gasped for air. The cattail had kept her alive, but she felt a half breath short each time she breathed. Britt dared not whisper to Max as he surfaced beside her. She saw him nod and they continued to float downstream toward town.

CHAPTER THIRTEEN

Rune

une ducked as his horse passed under a low-hanging branch, scraping the nape of his neck and snagging several strands of his hair. He turned to see the string of horses behind him, lowering their heads as they hurried to keep up. His lean legs burned from posting for three days straight. He could even feel the wrinkled bags under his eyes sagging with each step. The few hours he'd attempt to rest, he rolled uncomfortably on the cold ground; he hadn't been able to pack any equipment for comfort on his speedy mission to Brookside. Rune would've continued to ride through the night, but his horses needed a break. He knew how hard he could push them, and they'd nearly hit that threshold. It wouldn't be much longer now, as he'd already ridden by the camp from days past.

Rune slowed as he and his horse worked their way sidehill across the mountains, Grandwood coming into view from behind the trees. The once-peaceful coastal town now lay in ruin, smoldering from its second major attack in a year. The salty air flowed upslope, bringing with it the stench of sunbaked flesh and burning corpses. Rune lifted his shirt to filter the smell; even though he was a surgeon and, of late, an army surgeon, the smell of death would never be familiar or tolerable. Focusing on his surroundings, he began to look for any sign of his companions. Saaja and Ophelia would be close now.

As he trotted along the well-used game trail, Rune spotted areas where the dry dirt had been disturbed. Leaning forward in his saddle, he dropped his shoulder, clinging to the saddle horn. He saw the outline of a foot, several deer tracks overlaying it. He examined the trail as he passed over it, seeing more footprints in the dirt. Sure that he was on the right track, Rune kept an eye out on either side of the game trail as it cut sidehill, switch-backing lower toward the coastal town.

As he moved into the foothills, Rune knew what signs to look for that would indicate a potential campsite. Since his companions would be scouting, they'd want to remain hidden, so he searched low-lying areas. They would need fresh water by the camp, so he passed over any that didn't include a stream. The camp had to be near enough to Grandwood that they could walk to examine the town. He found the tents pitched in just such an area, at the base of a hill and next to a running creek. Rune dismounted, unhooked the horses from their string and hobbled the lead horse. Knowing the string horses wouldn't wander far from the lead, Rune set out on foot, leaving them to graze and drink after the hard day's ride.

Coming to the top of the hill west of the tents, Rune examined the destruction below. Grandwood, or what was left of Grandwood, lay beaten and toppled at the fringe of the Grandwood Forest, its namesake. Rune compared what he saw now to the last time he'd been to the town, over a decade earlier when he was an apprentice. The place had been lively and safe; now it bore the mark of their enemy's rule. His mind returned to the words of the dark-skinned woman who'd warned him of goblins. He scanned the wreckage but didn't see any here. Rune knew better, however, than to trust what appeared harmless at first glance.

Goblins are crafty creatures, magical in ways beyond my comprehension, he thought, recalling those injured humans he'd operated on and their words before death.

As he looked over the north side of town, where a fire had done the most damage, skeletal buildings were interspersed with those left in smoldering heaps. The buildings that survived were brick and stone, or they were outliers. As he searched for movement, he examined the wall, a project abandoned while still under construction. No ships made anchor in the bay that in years past was brimming with merchants. Turning to the south, Rune noted the depressions caused by cannon fire and bludgeoned buildings, half-destroyed and also abandoned. Farther out from the town, he saw the first sign of survivors. A line of people moved in the distance, their dark outlines marching south along the coast. He stepped forward, straining to focus on the distant movement. The line of black shapes moved steadily away from the smoldering town.

Rune couldn't tell whether the figures he watched were people or the kurr the others had warned them about. According to the small group he had helped flee to Brookside, Grandwood's fate was to be the enemy's stronghold in the west. Judging from the destruction below, it seemed that plan had changed.

Rune turned his attention to his immediate surroundings. He knew Saaja and the others would be close, also observing. Not seeing them atop the hill, he started down the slope. He raked the hillside with his eyes as he moved, continuing to switchback as he'd done with the horses. Just a few minutes from the top of the hill he spotted someone in the forest. He recognized Saaja's distinct bulk perched on a downed log.

Rune knew if he startled his battle-tested companion he could be in for a deadly outcome, so he chose to make noise in his approach. Stepping hard on downed tree branches and kicking over rocks, Rune gained Saaja's attention. As Saaja turned his large head, Rune noticed others in his group popping up from behind the log.

As he drew near, Saaja rose and extended his muscular arm in greeting, "Glad to have you back, Rune. How did the transport go?"

Nodding to the others, Rune addressed Saaja, "All good. A long road and a short night's rest, but the job is done and those in the Riverlands will be better served for it."

"Did the girl live?" Rune heard his youthful apprentice, Ophelia, ask from behind Saaja. He gathered Saaja had informed the others of every detail about their unexpected guests.

Rune stepped to the side to better see the dark-haired girl when he responded, "Last I saw of her she was still breathing. Hopefully Solomon can help them now." Stepping around, Rune sat down on the log next to Saaja. Ophelia and the six others also leaned against the downed tree, all focused on him for news. Looking at the group of hardworking Westland farmers turned rebel soldiers, he asked, "What's been happening here? I saw people marching south just a moment ago."

Saaja's salt and pepper beard bent against his thick chest as he nodded, "That would be the occupying force that was here when we arrived. They formed ranks and moved out earlier today. We've kept eyes on the town for two days now."

"Goblins?" Rune asked.

Shaking his head, Saaja said, "None. They must've left before because we haven't seen any. From the looks of it, though, they prevented Grandwood from becoming a military stronghold."

"The fire," Rune commented.

"Yes. It continued until this morning. We saw civilians working to put out the various fires. Kurr and orcs forced them to work at bringing water to that chapel near the town's center," Saaja pointed. "There must have been something in there that they wanted because every time anyone tried to take water to the northern half of town, the enemy would send them right back, forcing them to work on preventing that one building from burning."

"What about the shield they told us about?" Rune asked.

"Look around," Saaja said. "You're sitting on it."

Rune looked left and noticed for the first time the sheared path, cut into the forest. Even the tree they sat on looked to have been cleaved to create a border. "Is it active?" Rune asked, wondering if it had been phased out as the occupants departed.

"I believe it was active until today. You missed

something quite special this morning," Saaja said.

"You're not going to believe this," Ophelia added, shaking her head.

Rune eyed her, a sprightly contrast to the others who'd volunteered to leave the Riverlands with Rune and Saaja. The others bobbed their heads in agreement, hardened faces of lives well lived collaborating with her assessment.

"That dark sorcerer showed up," Saaja said.

Rune's narrow jaw dropped. "Really?" he asked. "How did you know it was him?"

"Well, for starters, that big black dragon of his was a dead giveaway," Ophelia said.

"You saw the dragon?" Rune asked. He'd heard reports of it in Southland, but the black creature hadn't ventured to Westland since the first war. He saw Ophelia and the others nod, then he said, "I had hoped that the reports were only rumors and that the foul thing was gone from these lands."

"Nope. He came here just today," Saaja said. "I thought it strange, such a powerful man stopping to check in on this measly lot. We watched from the hill. He landed for a few hours, then took off again. Flew south along the coast. I'm kind of surprised you didn't see him on your way back."

Rune shook his head, "No, I didn't." Pondering it for a moment, Rune said, "That is odd for him to stop here, and for such a short time."

"Yeah. Why fly all of the way here to turn around and leave right away?" Ophelia asked.

Rune shrugged, "Have you seen any civilians since the occupants left?"

"Nah. We've just been waiting for you to get back. I

don't think many stayed though. It looked like the kurr gathered everyone up and took them off with them," Saaja said.

"I wonder who's organizing the kurr?" Rune asked. "I didn't know those creatures could follow orders."

"Maybe that's what the sorcerer was doing here? Telling them to move on," Saaja suggested.

"Maybe," Rune replied, thinking on the idea for a moment. "But that doesn't seem worth it. How many of them were here?"

"Couple hundred at the most," Saaja said.

"Exactly. That doesn't seem as though it would be a large enough force to warrant a visit from the leader. He must've wanted something else," Rune said.

"There's one last thing you should know about before we head down there," Saaja said calmly.

Rune tilted his head in curiosity, "Yeah?"

"There's been a ship."

"What do you mean, there's been a ship? Where?"

"A ship's been sailing up and down the coast for the last day and a half. They've kept their distance and weren't anywhere to be seen when the dragon was here, but we saw them again after. They stuck around."

"Is it the enemy? Possibly a transport ship?" Rune asked.

"That's what we thought," Saaja said. "But they didn't help, and we last saw them sailing north, opposite the others going south."

"Odd," Rune said.

"Yep. That's it from us," Ophelia added.

"So, you think the barrier that kept everyone trapped

inside has been deactivated?" Rune asked.

"Don't know how all those people were able to leave if it weren't," Saaja said.

"Let's test it then," Rune suggested.

Saaja turned and looked at the others, "Do we have any volunteers?"

Rune waited for a response, but when none of the ex-farmers offered, he said, "I'll do it."

"You sure?" Saaja asked.

"Yeah. This was my idea coming here. I wouldn't feel right if anyone else risked their lives over mine in this venture."

"Alright then," Saaja said. "We'll be right here if you need anything."

Rune rose from his seat on the log. Taking in a short breath he stepped forward and walked down the slope past the clear-cut line through the forest. Once he'd crossed the line about ten feet in, he turned around and looked back at his companions. They sat, leaning forward and watching intently to see if he would return. Rune gulped, hoping the barrier was down. If it wasn't, he had just committed himself to an extended stay in the desolate town. Gathering his confidence, Rune hiked back up the hill, stopping at the line in the forest. He raised his arms out in front of his body. He didn't want to run into the invisible wall face first. That would add insult to injury if he were truly stuck there.

First, Rune felt the space before him, leaning forward as he did and nearly losing his balance as his hand passed through empty air. Stepping forward to catch himself, his upper body passed the plane where the barrier had been. To his relief, the wall was no longer there. He walked back to the log, his friends letting out a collective sigh of relief.

"Well, let's get cracking. We might catch a straggler or two in this mess, and as we say, every person helps," Rune said, trying to remain calm. The truth was, he felt a tumultuous wave of emotions after having made it back through the void. His heart raced and he thought he could hear a slight quiver in his voice when he spoke. Remaining a rock on the outside, he hoped his stoic expression was enough to inspire the others.

"Good to have you back, boss," Ophelia said as she hopped off her seat and walked past him.

He grinned slightly, breaking his typical hardened middle-aged expression as he watched the lively girl lead the others downhill. Saaja was the last to walk by and he stopped two steps into his venture.

Slapping Rune on the shoulder, he said, "You can't fool me, old friend. I could smell the stink in your pants once you walked down there." He grinned and continued, "but you put on a good show for the others. Very inspiring, I must say."

Rune shook his head as the large man continued past him, joining the others on their way into Grandwood. Rune could still feel the adrenaline pulsing through him as he stepped in line after them.

Upon entering Grandwood, Saaja took their lead, shouldering his broadsword as the others withdrew their shorter swords and daggers. They weren't going to take any chances if goblins, kurr or worse were still roaming the streets. Just because the bulk of the enemy forces left earlier didn't mean none had stayed behind. Starting at the east end of town, they combed the streets, searching inside homes and buildings as they passed. The east end of town remained relatively unscathed compared to the waterfront, a nicety that quickly disappeared the farther west into town they ventured.

Making their way up and down the streets, the group saw only the remains of those who hadn't survived the recent attack. Rune noted gray-haired goblin limbs protruding from the rubble. Near the heart of the town, they came to the chapel the occupying force had been determined to save. Rune followed Saaja closely as they approached the town's tallest building. The stone walls had been scorched and the roof had collapsed. Rune wondered what could've been inside that was worth saving. As they entered through the busted down doors, he noticed dead bodies on the open floor. Seeing the swords at their sides, he wondered if falling rubble or fighting had killed them. His group searched the entrance as it opened into the large worship area, finding only more remains. Not coming across anything of value in the place of worship, they moved on.

Continuing their search outside, they found townspeople who were too injured or weak to be of use to the enemy's army. Rune and the others helped those left for dead to Grandwood's port. While Rune set to work treating the injured, Saaja and the others completed their sweep of Grandwood. In all, only twenty people were found, five of whom Rune knew wouldn't make it through the night, their burns too severe for healing. He and Ophelia provided clean bandages and tried to ease their suffering. The small medical kit Ophelia had with her wouldn't last long, so Rune ordered four others to fetch his supplies. Seeing they would need to remain with their wounded, he told them to gather up their camp and horses, and bring them down to the docks.

Rune looked up from his patient when he heard Saaja shout. He followed the man's outstretched arm as it pointed toward the horizon. Outlined against the late afternoon sky, Rune saw the silhouette of a ship's sails come into view. Daring to chance it, he ordered Saaja to signal them in.

As the ship worked its way closer, Rune was pleased to see the arrival of his medical supplies as the four from his group returned from their camp. He worked to clean and patch up the wounded, taking little notice of his companions who shouted and whistled in an attempt to gain the attention of whoever manned the ship. The only time he looked away from his patients was when Saaja mentioned that the ship had made anchor. As the sun painted the horizon in evening shades, Rune kept Ophelia busy, not bothering to watch the ship send a skiff in to the docks.

"Rune, they're landing now," Saaja said, at last drawing Rune's attention from his work. He saw the dark-haired men pushing oars through the waves as their shuttle boat skidded to shore. Rising, Rune told Ophelia to call him if she needed anything and joined Saaja to greet the ship's crewmen.

The black ink wrapping the men's tanned arms told him these were the famed warriors of the Rollo Islands. He guessed the woman he'd met on the trail was a Rollo native as well and, in that case, hoped these men would be friendly. He and Saaja approached cautiously as they watched the four crewmen heave their boat onto the shore. Because they didn't leap from the craft with weapons in hand, Rune thought they had come in peace. Rune addressed the

Islanders as they straightened and approached him.

Speaking slowly and clearly, Rune said, "Hello. We are friends." He held up his arms to show that he didn't carry a weapon. "I am doctor. Helping sick and hurt people," he continued and pointed to the people on the docks. "Are you friend?" he asked, hoping he'd conveyed his position clearly to the foreigners.

The men looked at each other, then to Saaja. Rune saw him shrug as if to say he didn't understand him either. One of the men said, "Why do you talk like that? We've not heard this slow form of Landish before. Where are you from?"

Rune's pride took a blow as he knocked himself internally for assuming they wouldn't understand him. "I'm sorry, I just assumed you would speak Rolloan." Rune waited for their expressions to sour at his insensitivity, but they nodded in understanding.

Saaja steered their attention away from Rune by saying, "We've seen your ship sailing the coast, but not getting too close. I wasn't sure if you were with the orcs until they left, and you stayed behind. What is it you're looking for?"

Rune watched as the two of the men looked past them at the group of people on the docks. "Our Captain," one of them said. "We got separated from her awhile back and she warned us it wasn't safe to come for her."

Instantly Rune's mind turned to the woman they'd met on the trail. He asked, "This captain of yours, did she have black hair and dark skin and is she stubborn to a point?"

All four of the crewmen locked in on him and responded in unison, "Yes." Then one of the warriors said, "She is fierce and does not take any orders, if that's what you mean by stubborn. She's a natural-born leader and our Captain. Have you seen her?"

Rune nodded, "I think so. She's with a small group. They ran into some trouble here a few days back and we crossed paths with them in their escape."

"How did they escape? Britt told us they were trapped here, but when we returned to see the destruction and this place crawling with orcs and kurr, we feared the worst. Our Captain told us she would be here?"

Rune nodded, "They escaped the fighting alright and I'm not sure how, but she won't be coming back here anytime soon."

The warrior narrowed his eyes and asked, "Why would you say that? Where did she go? What happened to her?"

Rune explained how he met them on the trail and what had happened to Kirsten. Saaja added some commentary to the description about how badly injured Kirsten was. Rune explained how he bartered with them to join the Resistance if he brought them to Solomon's. Rune could tell the warriors didn't fully trust him that she would abandon them in this way without any word.

"Where is this Solomon's place?" one of the men asked. "We must get there soon and be reunited with our Captain."

"You boys sure are devoted," Saaja said.

"You would be too if you knew her," one of the Rolloans said.

"Before I tell you how to get there, I have a proposition that could help us both out," Rune said with a smirk growing on his hawkish face as he looked from the warriors to Saaja.

"When we started this mission, our goal was to gather

the support of others who might be affected by the invading forces. I knew Grandwood had been under attack during the Grandwood Games and thought if I made it here before our enemy did, I could recruit the people of Grandwood to join us in the Riverlands. We were just as surprised as you to find Grandwood in such disrepair.

"I sent your captain and those she was traveling with to join our army after the girl received help. Now I know there are those among your people who fought alongside the other nations to stop the dark lord and his dragon in the first war. As I find myself at a loss for recruits in this place, I want to extend the offer to you and your crew," Rune said, watching the Rollo Islanders glance at one another, a sign they weren't completely dismissing the idea.

"From what I recall about the Rollo Island Warriors, they work together as a navy and attack in large numbers. Seeing the lone ship so far from home and without a captain makes me wonder if you all are outcasts," Saaja added after they failed to respond immediately.

"We have many wounded here with us who are not fit to travel over such rugged terrain," Rune looked to the ship. "That ship looks like it could hold quite a substantial group."

"You want us to sail you to the Bareback Plains. Then you'll show us to our Captain?" one of the warriors said, folding his arms.

Rune nodded, "If you take us to the plains, I'll show you where your captain is."

The warriors eyed each other, seeming to hold an entire conversation with their looks, then the one said, "You have a deal. We'll return with more shuttle crafts for transport."

Before they could begin hauling their skiff into the water, Rune called after them, "And when we get to the Resistance, you'll to stay and fight?"

One of them turned and said, "That is for our Captain to decide," and they pushed the boat out into the water, rowing toward the ship.

Over the next several hours, the Rolloans ferried the wounded to the ship anchored in the port. Due to the small size of the skiffs, they could only take a handful at a time. After taking the wounded and those in his group aboard the ship, Rune looked to the horses. As the shuttle landed on shore, he led his horse to the water.

The man in the boat shook his head when Rune approached, saying, "No, no. I am sorry, they cannot come with us."

Rune nodded his head saying, "This is how we'll cross the plains. We need them."

The Islander explained to Rune how there would be no way to get the steed onboard since the decks were too high. "On our ship from the Islands, we could do this thing, but with this merchant ship, it won't be possible."

"Don't you have rigging to haul up the crafts?" he asked.

The man shook his head, "Not strong enough to hold four of us; not strong enough to hold one of these," he pointed to the horse.

Rune understood his reasoning. Besides, the horses would probably get off balance in the boat rowing out to the ship and fall in. Even if they managed to train the horse to remain still in the boat, they couldn't haul it in. Rune had to decide whether to gain the possible support of these warriors and add numbers to their army with the healed wounded, or return to shore to stay with the horses. As he looked around at the foothills outside Grandwood, he knew there would be grazing and water for them here. *Maybe when next I return they'll still be here,* he thought making his decision.

Taking time to remove the horses' saddles and halters, he said goodbye to the trusted steeds he had grown fond of these last few years. As he stepped off the rowboat and climbed the rope ladder to board the ship, he turned to watch the four-legged animals wander out into the field south of town. Rune had a feeling they would fare better here than if they went back to the revolution with him and his compatriots. The warhorses would have their chance at freedom while Rune and these brave men and women fought for theirs.

CHAPTER FOURTEEN

Defiant

e could have it all, my friend. I can give you power, dominion, wealth, peace and prosperity," Merglan said, then paused. Ivan eyed the man cautiously as he spread his hands to the side, tilted his gaze and added, "and your family."

"I don't believe you," Ivan said firmly.

"What's not to believe? I've shown you nothing but kindness and good faith since you arrived, haven't I?"

If kindness is keeping me a prisoner in my childhood home, Ivan thought.

Merglan raised an eyebrow while frowning, "Will, I'm slighted by your poor opinion of our arrangement. You are my guest and you can go anywhere you like within the castle, day or night." Merglan stepped toward Ivan, then grinned. "Can't we work together and put an end to our differences?"

"You talk as if we hadn't been at war for the last twenty-odd years," Ivan said, shaking his head in exasperation. Backing away, he continued, "You speak of trust, what kind of trust is this? You've taken everything from me! My entire family, dragon and the only thing I had left, my mind," Ivan spit at Merglan. "I'll never trust you, old friend."

Merglan calmly wiped the spittle from his chest. Hating every inch of what Merglan had become, Ivan wanted to strangle him, but without magic or the use of any weapons, he was no match for the sorcerer. In the end he would only hurt himself by attacking the man. Each time he had, Merglan had taken away more of his soul. He felt like a man torn in half, as though a piece of him was being kept locked away.

Knowing the sorcerer could read his mind, Ivan sought to provoke a response by painting a mental picture of what he wanted to do to Merglan in that moment. Merglan said, "I do hope we can become friendly toward one another again. It would be in your best interest if you wanted to see your bonded ever again."

Ivan's image of Merglan's unpleasant death vanished. He gave him his full attention. "What did you say?" he asked.

"About being friends again or that last bit about seeing Jazzmaryth again?" Merglan asked mockingly.

"Impossible," Ivan said. "You killed her; I watched you take her life."

"Thargon was dead once, too," Merglan said, lifting the crystal he wore around his neck and rolling it in his fingers as he pretended to examine it.

"No," Ivan said, walking to the window. "Jazz is gone. You won't gain my trust by tempting me with false hopes."

There's nothing false about a little bit of necromancy, Merglan's mind cut freely into Ivan's.

"Get out!" Ivan shouted, pressing his hands to his head to relieve tension from the pain caused by Merglan's unobstructed intrusion.

"I have something for you," Merglan said, walking toward the open doorway. Ivan watched Merglan reach through the doorway and grab something.

Ivan looked at the sorcerer warily as he approached holding a beautifully crafted dragonrider suit. The newly stitched leather came complete with protective armor, the finest a rider could have. "Your new riding leathers, if you so choose," Merglan said, extending the suit toward Ivan.

Ivan stepped toward him, reaching out to stroke the leather. Memories of his first pair of riding leathers came back in a flash: the elven forest, with little Jazz at his side, and Selleya. As quickly as the fond memories came, so too came the memories of the deaths of loved ones, all of them taken at the hands of the man standing before him. A pulse of rage welled within him and he lunged toward Merglan, trying to grip his throat.

Ivan froze mid-lunge, his arms outstretched and hands cupped just inches from Merglan's throat. He flexed as hard as he could to force his body to move, to no avail. He tried to summon any remnants of the power he once had, but nothing came. Again he reached for the magic, refusing to give in to defeat, yet nothing came. He remained perfectly still, unable to move.

Merglan offered a false weak smile, turned and placed the leather suit on the bed, saying, "Consider it, Will. I can give you back your powers and your dragon." Merglan walked across the room and exited.

Ivan remained locked in the attack for several long breaths before Merglan released him. Stumbling forward, he shouted in frustration. His eyes shot to the leather suit on the bed. He picked it up and threw it into the closet, slamming the door shut to keep it out of sight. He walked to the window, placed his hands on the sill and looked out over the courtyard and to greater Kingston stretching beyond the castle walls.

As he stood hunched in the window, Ivan felt the dark magic working on him; Merglan was eating into his soul. He screamed, his nails digging into the wooden window frame as he felt the scraping deep within. Somehow Merglan's magic cut out a piece of him and hauled it away. As the pain subsided and he regained his faculties, Ivan felt a familiar haze cloud his mind. He felt this way after each mental attack. As he tried to shake the fog, he looked out at the glinting rooftops stretching to the coast.

How long have I been here? he asked himself, straining to remember. The days ran together in a chaotic mess of madness. Merglan would come to him, every day or was it more than once a day? Ivan couldn't remember. Merglan would tell him how they were meant to rule together, how they would usher in a golden era of leadership across Kartania. Though Ivan could feel himself being ripped apart one piece at a time, he still knew better than to trust Merglan.

Looking out once again, he focused on the section of streets he could see beyond the walls, orcs wandering about. He remembered their arrival; it happened right after Killdoor returned. But he didn't know after which time he saw the large dragon return. He could picture Killdoor landing in the courtyard below, twice with his rider and once without, but he couldn't recall which arrival also involved the arrival of the orcs? Ivan slammed his fist on the windowsill in frustration. Why couldn't he remember?

As evening approached, he watched the sun hide behind the curvature of the horizon over the ocean, giving way to the night. He sat in his chair, looking out the window as the deep blues of evening turned black. Bright white stars speckled the sky. Through the cloudless night, Ivan noticed two shapes rapidly approaching. Squinting, he could see the outline of two dragons flying toward the city. His heart skipped a beat, wondering if this would be Anders and Zahara's return. Rubbing his eyes, Ivan asked himself, *Did they recruit another dragon?*

Ivan watched, entranced by the dragons in flight as they soared down from the sky, circling over the castle, flying lower, coming in and out of view.

Why aren't they attacking? Ivan wondered.

As he watched carefully through the upper corner of his window, Ivan waited for the dragons to fly overhead where he could see them. When the dark bodies flapped over the castle, lower than they'd been before, Ivan saw the absence of iridescence in the dragon's scales. The coal-black shine of the massive dragon told Ivan that Killdoor had returned for the fourth time. Falling back into his seat, Ivan wondered at the second dragon. As the smaller dragon soared in just behind Killdoor, he could see the green hue of its scales in the darkness. He leaned forward as it flew out of sight.

Was that? he asked himself. *No, it couldn't be. She wouldn't be in that condition, not even if he had brought her back,* he told himself.

Ivan waited for them to fly around again, but after waiting an hour without their return, he gave up. He rose from the chair and walked to the bedside. He pulled back the covers and stared blankly at the bed. Curiosity overcame him as he turned to look at the open bedroom door. He walked to it and leaned his head out through the opening, looking first one way and then the other down the length of the hall. Ever-burning torches lit the passageway. With no one in sight, Ivan stepped out into the hallway and tiptoed down the length of the hall, his mind puzzling over why he'd seen a second dragon.

Whether or not that's really Jazz, I might be able to escape with a dragon's help. If its magic is strong enough, we could break the barrier and I could get out of this room, he thought as he cautiously proceeded down the hall.

Unlike the magic that no longer lived within the rightful king of humanity, the instinctual map of the castle he'd known as a princeling hadn't faded from his mind. At the end of the corridor, Ivan carefully pulled open the door. Half expecting to see guards posted at the top of the stairwell, he crouched ready to meet resistance. The opening revealed a lesser-known passageway; he was pleased to find it dark and empty. Following the narrow staircase as it descended, Ivan stepped quietly on the stones, switch-backing once before reaching the second-floor landing. The wooden door at the end of the steps was closed. Lifting the latch and pushing, Ivan opened the unlocked door. He stepped out into the expansive room where he and Anders had faced Merglan. As he walked out into the open space, he could see several pillars still in ruin from the dragon fighting, the rubble illuminated by starlight shining in through the stained glass that decorated the north wall. Walking slowly to the center of the room, Ivan used his foot to trace deep gouges in the stone floor, probably created by the dragon claws.

The large space felt so empty; his boot heels echoed against the stone floor. Metal clicking, though, caused him to stop midstride. He remained perfectly still as he heard the familiar sound of clattering scales, a sound he'd heard so often from Jazz shifting her body in the night. It reminded him of rain trickling on cobblestone streets. That unique chime brought both fear and excitement into Ivan's heart.

Slowly he turned to face the noise sounding from the shadowed back wall. Although he couldn't quite see the dragon in the shadows, he attempted to sense it. When the sensation didn't come, he grew frustrated. He'd known that his magic had an expiration date after Jazz died, but he had continued to be able to use a fraction of his old magic until his arrival at the castle. As he stood in the center of the chamber, Ivan wondered if this dragon that he couldn't see was Killdoor? If so, why hadn't Killdoor attacked him or at the least growled? Unless it wasn't Merglan's dragon?

Ivan moved cautiously toward the back of the enormous room, stopping again when he heard the dragon move. As the dragon shifted its position, its scales slid against the stone floor; he saw a flicker of movement in the darkness.

"Jazz?" Ivan asked, speaking just above a whisper. "Is that really you?" He waited several breaths, but didn't hear or feel a mental response from the dragon. Ivan again stepped lightly toward the creature, tiptoeing nearer.

Then he heard it, a low grumble reverberating off the chamber walls. Ivan stopped when he saw white fangs glinting in the darkness.

"It's me, Ivan," he said, holding his hands out as if to calm the creature from a distance. He took a step closer, moving carefully. The dragon didn't reply, so Ivan took a step closer, hoping he could reason with the creature. Ivan wished that he could use his senses to gauge the emotions of the dragon. Was it scared, angry, lonely? He couldn't tell. All he could do to satisfy his curiosity was continue to move closer in hopes that the dragon would accept him as nonthreatening.

"I can help you," Ivan said in a calm whisper. He heard the dragon shift, moving away from him as its scales scraped against the stone floor. "It's okay, you don't have to be afraid of me," he said, trying his best to exude a calming presence.

The dragon's throat hummed a low growl again and Ivan saw the flicker of fangs once more. He slowed, but noticed the dragon was shying away from him and not standing its ground. This told Ivan the dragon feared him; it was scared.

"I promise I won't harm you," Ivan said, hearing the metal clinking as the dragon moved away from him yet again. Ivan paused, *Was the metallic sound armor or chains?* he wondered. Resuming his slow advance, he added, "I can free you. I'm being held here against my will, too. We could escape."

Suddenly Ivan heard the beast spring from the ground, whooshing as its leathery wings carried it into the air. As soon as the creature left the floor, Ivan saw the welling of fire glow in its chest. Illuminating the darkness with its swell, the dragon's heart glowed, shining a brilliant green light between the gaps in its overlapping scales. With little time to react, Ivan leapt to the right, tucking behind a stone column as the room erupted in flames. In a wash of heat, the dragon bathed the space where Ivan had been standing in fire.

The flames parted around the pillar licking the air to either side. Ivan tightened into a ball as the heat burned all around him. He hadn't felt this alive since his glory days as a young rider in the dragon wars. Singeing his clothes and pinning him behind the column, the dragon released its deadly spout of flames two more times.

That's definitely not Jazz, Ivan thought as he peeked out from behind the pillar. *Even if Jazz didn't recognize me, which is unlikely, she isn't the kind of dragon to belt hellfire at anyone without trying to sense his or her aura first. She would've known my intentions were pure and let me assist her, unless,* he wondered. Staring into the sudden darkness, Ivan relied on his hearing as he tried to listen for the dragon's location.

His brain churned as he went over what he knew about a dragon's bond: *I know the bond lasts a lifetime for both recipients, but what happens if death is reversed? Surely I would feel some connection with her. Or would all memories of me and our bond be wiped clean from her mind and senses? Would she even be the same dragon if Merglan really brought her back?* Myriad questions ran through his head as he tried to think of a way to calm the dragon down. He needed the dragon to escape, even if just to break the spell that was holding him within the castle walls.

As he flattened his back against the stone pillar, Ivan could hear the dragon's anxiety as it moved continually, dragging the chains back and forth across the floor. He peeked around the pillar slowly, keeping his eyes wide to catch any flash of movement from the creature. The dragon lurched once again, flapping into the air and pulling tight against its metal chains. As the dragon's momentum came to an abrupt halt, it fluttered to regain its situational awareness. At that moment Ivan rushed across the floor, locating the chains by sound.

If I can unclasp these chains, then maybe the dragon will see me as a friend and not an enemy, Ivan thought. Finding the metal links, he followed them to their anchor, bolted into the back wall. Feeling for a pin or release mechanism, Ivan continually pulled back his hands to avoid getting caught in the ebb and flow of the chain's tension. He could not afford to risk broken or maimed hands if he wanted to escape.

When he failed to locate any release from the bolts, an idea crossed his mind. Acting on instinct, Ivan began to climb the chain. He rocked back and forth, the chain moving violently as he climbed. The sudden jerking and pulling caused him to let go, but he tightened his grip and let willpower push him higher. The closer he climbed to the dragon the more the dragon moved, flapping frantically in its attempts to escape. If he could release the chain from the dragon's harness, Ivan thought he might be able to ride the dragon away from the castle.

Thrashing back and forth, the dragon spewed fire. In the light of the flames, Ivan could see how far off the ground he'd come. Each time, Ivan gained a better idea of how the chains were secured. At the same time, he also saw how easily he could become seriously injured from the dragon's thrashing at such a height.

With his forearms pumped and struggling to hold onto the chain, Ivan reached the dragon's body. The sporadic flames guided his sight as he climbed onto the dragon's harness. The chain was clasped in several places on the back and front of the harness. Ivan used the dragon's small spines as handholds as he worked to undo the two clips attached to the rear of the harness. Excited by the possibility of an escape, Ivan managed to wrap his legs around the base of the dragon's neck. Spurring his ankles into its side, he held on for dear life as it thrashed, snapping and writhing against the two remaining chains.

In a bright burst of flame, Ivan located the two remaining clasps. Feeling the dragon duck suddenly to the right, one chain began to slacken. He grabbed it quickly, trying to undo the clasp, but the dragon turned back. Letting go just in time, he heard the chain snap tight as the dragon pulled against it once more. Poised for another chance, he released the right clip when the dragon moved again. As soon as that chain was free, the dragon felt the release in pressure and began to pull harder against the single restraint, seeming to finally realize that Ivan was trying to set it free from bondage.

"Hold still so I can get this last one," Ivan whispered. "If you calm down, I can free you." To his disappointment, the dragon didn't understand and pulled harder than before.

As the wild creature flapped and twisted, Ivan managed to undo the final clip on the chains. He held tight as the dragon flew freely in the open chamber. As he pressed his chest against the dragon's scales, Ivan felt something in the dragon calm. The creature's frantic movements settled and it lightly touched down, landing on all fours. Ivan sat upright on the dragon's back and said, "That's it. We can work together just fine."

He patted the dragon's neck lightly, admiring the green scales in the starlight. It trotted across the floor into the light near the north wall. Ivan stared at the scales in disbelief. The female's wings and other bodily features matched those of his Jazzmaryth. At a loss for words, Ivan's breaths quickened as he considered whether this could really be his bonded partner. How else could he explain her sudden change in temperament? Perhaps his sitting atop her scales jogged her memory of their connection?

Suddenly clapping broke the silence, echoing through the empty chamber. The dragon turned to face its origin. Ivan clenched his jaw when he saw the culprit. Standing in the open doors to the second-floor corridor, Merglan clapped. The slow and steady sound mocked Ivan's efforts.

"Well done, William," Merglan said, flicking his wrist to light the torches lining the pillars, the large open room suddenly awash in light.

Whispering to the dragon, Ivan said, "Come now, Jazz. Let's make our escape. Fly!" He spurred the dragon forward. To his disappointment, the dragon made no attempt to flee.

"I didn't think you would actually succeed in removing the chains," Merglan said, stepping into the room. He motioned to Ivan, "Come down and let me have a look at her."

"Jazz, come on," Ivan said, heeling the dragon in the sides once more. "Fly with me!"

Merglan continued to walk with his arm held out as if to assist Ivan down from the dragon, like a gentleman would a lady from a carriage.

With his deepest emotions and channeling all his thoughts, Ivan willed the dragon to listen to him and flee now. The dragon walked several paces, then sat back on its haunches. Ivan nearly rolled backward, catching hold of the stunted spikes along its spine just in time. As he clung to the dragon's back, he scowled at Merglan, "Was this all a ruse? Was this the same as the bedroom?" He moved, letting go and dropping to the floor, wincing as his heels tingled from the landing.

"In a way. Let me explain," Merglan said, holding his hand out to Ivan.

Ivan pushed Merglan's outstretched hand aside and stood to his full height. He turned to the dragon, seeing her in the light for the first time. She was female and green, as Jazz was, but something was different. Ivan felt foolish for thinking, even briefly, that this dragon could've been his bonded partner.

Why? Ivan asked, thinking the question before speaking it aloud.

"Because, my dear friend, I want us to be happy. With you on the back of your former champion, we'd be unstoppable," Merglan said.

Ivan frowned, "That's not my Jazz."

Merglan nodded, "Sure it is. Can't you tell?"

Ivan studied the dragon. She looked similar to Jazz, yet he couldn't help but feel that something was off. "You're controlling her?" Ivan asked, finally understanding why the dragon had calmed down.

"No," Merglan said slyly. "Well, maybe a little, but that was just so the two of you could become reacquainted after all these years. It must be strange for both of you."

Ivan hesitated to answer. Instead, he asked, "What's wrong with you? Why make me think I'm helping her escape when she's under your influence? What's in it for you?"

Merglan splayed his hands, "I wanted you to feel as

though you'd accomplished something. You did help that poor creature escape a dreadful situation. Now she owes you gratitude and you two can begin to reconnect on a more intimate level."

"Why would I need to connect on an intimate level with a dragon I've already bonded with? That is not Jazzmaryth," Ivan said.

"You're confused, Will. You haven't been thinking straight," Merglan said.

Ivan shook his head, "No. I'm thinking clearly now. You're the one messing with my head. This whole time you've been trying to make me think that the two of us can be friends again, but you are wrong. We'll never be able to work together. No matter what kind of dark magic you use on me, I'll always resist you."

Merglan tilted his head slightly and said, "I did hope you would come around to see things my way by now, but this is getting ridiculous."

Ivan heard malice return to his voice. He tried to rush Merglan before he could cast his spell. This time Ivan got his hands on Merglan's cloak and pulled before the magic stung him. Merglan's thoughts clamped down on Ivan's mind with a vice-like grip. Ivan couldn't stop the mental attack and writhed on the ground as Merglan knelt over him, pummeling his mind with overwhelming force. Grabbing Ivan by the collar and shaking him, Merglan shouted, "Look at me!"

Ivan tried to hold his eyes shut, but Merglan's will forced them open. He turned his head to the side, doing everything in his power to disobey. Merglan forced Ivan to stare directly up at him.

He could see the vein in Merglan's forehead pulsing as the sorcerer spoke, "I should've done this a long time ago." Merglan's palm spread over Ivan's face, a glowing light emanating from his palm.

Ivan felt the hot magic cut through his mind, ripping him apart. The last thing he felt was his stream of consciousness leaving his body. Still able to see, Ivan watched with eyes held open by magic as Merglan stole the last remaining pieces from his soul. As the tendrils of energy evaporated from his chest like vapor, Ivan's vision blurred and he felt himself leave his body.

***

Merglan stood alone in his old friend's bedroom, the room where he tried so hard to make Ivan see the truth. He cursed himself for being so foolish as to think that the stubborn old man would see things his way. Placing his hand over the wooden box he'd put on Ivan's table, he went to pick it up. Stopping just before touching the wood, Merglan restrained himself. He walked to the window where he'd seen his old friend standing and looking out over the castle walls. *What was he hoping for?* Merglan asked himself.

Killdoor's consciousness sounded in his mind, *You finally did the right thing.*

What, by plunging him into madness, then putting him out of his misery? Merglan asked.

By ridding your thoughts of what he could do for you. He was broken, weak and powerless.

He was my friend, once. I owed him a chance at least, a real chance to help us.

I did like feeling him being crushed in the end, making him think he was about to escape with his dead dragon brought back to life. It was genius, Killdoor chuckled.

Thank you, I did hope that illusion I put on the dragon would've convinced him she really was back. Oh well, the time she had with him, however brief, was important. And you're right, I should've done that a long time ago.

Now we can turn our attention back to what really matters, Killdoor said.

Merglan reached for the window's shutters, pulling them in and latching them shut. He turned and glanced at the ceiling above him. Encased into the stone above him, Merglan admired the collection of crystals he'd harvested from Eastland. They hung suspended in the ceiling of Ivan's old room. Drawing on their power and feeling its swelling inside him, Merglan took a deep breath, focusing on what mattered most to him and to Killdoor. Exhaling, he said aloud, "Total domination."

He cut the influx of energy off before it consumed him, sending him into a rampage as it did when he took in too much. Glancing at the box, Merglan whispered, "Goodbye my old friend," as he left the princely room.

CHAPTER FIFTEEN

Within Kingston's Walls

ingston's city walls poked out above the trees in the forest surrounding Natalia, who stood alongside the western road, her face hidden deep in the hood of her traveler's cloak. The morning air, still dank from the autumn night's heavy rain, rustled lightly through the leaves as the elf and her dwarf companion stood waiting for a passerby. Maylox stood behind Natalia, waiting for her to announce their ride into the city. From the constant shifting and sound of breaking twigs, Natalia could tell the dwarf girl was growing impatient from the lack of morning traffic. Natalia hadn't considered that the heavy rains would slow those traveling the road, but she knew it was harvest season and eventually a cart would come by on its way into the city.

Sensing the cart before seeing it, Natalia leaned out from their hiding spot to see the horse come into view and check whether her senses were correct in detecting a lone man at the reins. As the horse's head came into view, Natalia carefully tucked back into the brush. Soon the cart's wheels came splashing through puddles that pooled in the road. She gripped her elven sword by the hilt in its sheath at her side. She didn't want to cause an innocent person harm, but if that's what it would take to get past the city watch, then Natalia would do what had to be done.

Moving swiftly from her hiding place, she emerged onto the path. Planting her feet shoulder-width apart, she faced the oncoming horse with her head bowed and hood hanging low, shadowing her identity. As she watched the man rein in on the horse, she tried to exude an air of intimidation.

Stepping toward the cart, she eyed the driver carefully as he leaned forward in his seat to get a better look at her. The man straightened, then frantically began to turn the cart. Natalia had had weeks to heal and felt wholly herself, so she ran at full elven speed, catching the horse by the halter before it was halfway through its turn. The driver's startled expression belied his surprise at how quickly she'd appeared next to his horse. He shook and his wide, frightened eyes stared back at her. Panting heavily, the driver tried to back away in his seat. He shook his head and began mumbling some kind of prayer, repeating a phrase over and over as Natalia led the horse back around to face the city entrance, which was still several miles away. She thought it odd that this man, who had more than likely been directly oppressed by the invading orcs, feared a cloaked human-looking figure so dramatically. *Perhaps I'm more terrifying than I think,* she told herself.

"Get off," she commanded the driver as she stepped alongside the cart.

The man nodded, his lip quivering as he slid from his seat down into the muddy road, never once taking his eyes off her.

Natalia stepped up into the driver's seat, turned to the man, and asked, "Why do you fear me?"

Stuttering, he answered, "Y-y-you're the ve-ve-veiled huntress."

Natalia shifted on the wagon seat to face him. Before she could ask him why, the man turned and ran back the way he'd come. While she watched him, Maylox crawled out of the brush and walked around to the back of the cart.

"That really couldn't have gone any better," she said. Standing on her tiptoes, she asked, "What do we have here?" and reached for the canvas tarp covering the man's goods.

Natalia watched as the dwarf struggled to grasp the tarp. Staying the horse and placing the reins on the seat, she hopped down and assisted Maylox. Natalia saw the dwarf's determined expression turn to irritation when Natalia easily reached over and pulled back the canvas. Examining the barrels securely lashed on the bed of the cart, Natalia guessed at their contents.

"What are these for?" Maylox asked.

"Probably an alehouse," Natalia said, searching the tops for a stamp or insignia marking the barrels' contents. Not seeing one, she motioned to the cart bed, "Go on then, in you go."

Maylox hesitated, so Natalia came around to grab her. The dwarf stepped away quickly and asked, "Why can't I ride in the front with you?"

"What do you think the city watch would do if they saw a dwarf riding in on a delivery cart? You don't think they'll put together in their simple minds that their army was just attacked by dwarfs and elves? That's why we needed this cart in the first place, to hide you."

"What if they see that you're an elf?" Maylox asked, her hands on her hips.

"I'll keep my hood on. They won't think that's strange in this rain. Besides, I can pass for Kewian. I have the tan skin and brown hair. Even if they have me remove my hood, as long as my hair stays down and ears don't show, I will be fine."

Maylox snorted and folded her arms, "Alright, stuff me under the tarp. At least I'll be out of the rain."

"What rain?" Natalia asked. As she spoke, she felt the misting drizzle on the backs of her hands. "Come on then," Natalia said, helping Maylox into the cart. The dwarf girl created a gap large enough to lie down in directly behind the driver's seat. Once she'd settled into the spot, Natalia covered the cart with the canvas tarp.

Climbing back onto the driver's seat, Natalia snapped the horse into motion, lurching forward as the cart rolled through the mud. The short ride to Kingston's gates offered an anticlimactic visual of Natalia's first time to the human capital city. Rain clouds darkened the skies, hanging languidly over the clay rooftops. Natalia could see the towering castle at the city's center, its stone outline becoming visible through the patchy clouds. As they rode closer to the city wall, the wide stone entrance came into view.

Hopefully the watchmen on the wall will actually see the Rollo ships, she thought as she eyed the groups of men huddled in covered turrets spaced along the length of the protective wall. The gold and black helmeted heads crowded in the small spaces. She didn't see many of them watching.

Natalia drove her horse up to the thick wall's entrance tunnel. To her surprise, the gates to the city stood wide open. The only defense appeared to be the small group of watchmen standing with their backs against the tunnel walls, attempting to stay dry and out of the rain. Natalia slowed the horse to a halt just outside the gate. She waited for the guards to come to her, but the men waved her in, not wanting to step out in the drizzling rain.

"Here we go," she whispered to Maylox, letting her know that they were about to be stopped by the city watch.

As the cart rolled fully into the entrance, one of the men came to stand in front of the horse, bringing it to a stop in the dry space. The others took their time looking at one another to see who would conduct the search while Natalia waited patiently, listening to the rain drip steadily off the castle wall. Finally, two men pushed off the wall and approached her, one moving to inspect the cargo, while the other stopped at the step ladder up to the driver's seat. The three other watchmen returned to their conversation, their backs against the wall, not paying attention to the search. Natalia was surprised how little these watchmen cared about their jobs. The city was going to be attacked in a matter of hours and they couldn't be bothered to close the gates or step out into the rain.

The watchman at her side held out his hand expectantly. Natalia stared at it for a moment wondering if this gentleman was offering her a hand so she could climb down. She almost reached out to grab it when he said in a monotone, "Papers."

Natalia looked to either side but didn't see any papers on the seat. Just as she was about to tell the man she didn't have them, she noticed a leather satchel tucked under her seat on the floor. Reaching down, she grabbed and opened it. The only contents were three pieces of parchment. Pulling them out, she handed them over to the man whose hand remained held out expectantly. She watched him carefully as he chewed at something in his teeth while looking over the papers. Natalia saw him nod to the man at the cart's rear and heard the tarp move. She turned sharply in her seat to see the watchman examining the back end of the contents. Barrels only, no Maylox.

Covering the cart almost as quickly as he'd opened it, the man walked lazily toward the others to join in their conversation. Just as the watchman at her side was handing her the papers, she heard a man shout from outside the wall.

"Wait!" the voice called. She heard the splashing of footsteps running up to the entrance.

Natalia's heart skipped a beat as she saw the chatting watchmen suddenly take interest in what was happening. Natalia moved her hand to her side, but her sword wasn't there. She'd taken it off on their short ride and placed it under the tarp behind the barrels. *Stupid*, she thought; now she might need it.

"Wait," the voice came again. Something about it sounded oddly familiar. She turned to see Solomon jogging through the rain dripping off the tunnel's entrance. The short, bearded man slowed to a walk as he shook the wet from his wool jacket.

"What's this about?" the watchman who'd held her papers asked, looking at Solomon, then to Natalia.

Natalia stared in disbelief at the old wise man as he tried to catch his breath, resting his hand on the side of the cart and bending slightly. *That stupid old man is going to get us all killed,* Natalia thought as she watched the other four men surround the cart and bring their hands to their swords.

Through heavy breaths, Natalia heard Solomon speak, "I'm so sorry for the inconvenience, but I'm afraid my partner and I had a bit of falling out back there," he paused looking expectantly at them, then added, "Falling out. It's a pun because I literally fell out of the cart. Or pushed rather, but that's neither here nor there."

The watchman holding the parchment said, "Get on with it, old man."

"Sorry, if you check the papers, there are two people on this delivery," he said, pointing to the papers in the man's hand.

Natalia waited silently as the three men behind the cart relaxed their stance and moved back to their post against the wall. Apparently, all it took to fool them was an out-of-breath old man and a not–so-convincing lie. She could've taken them all out on her own, but that would have drawn too much attention to the gate, and there wasn't a need for such a radical move, yet.

The man still standing next to the cart looked over the papers again, this time with greater interest. Natalia swore under her breath that she was going to kill him, along with the watchmen, if he blew this opportunity for her.

Nodding, the man handed Natalia the papers and said, "You take these directly to the inns. No more funny business until you've made your rounds and left."

Natalia took the papers, stuffing them back into the leather satchel as Solomon stepped toward the ladder and said to the watchman, "My deepest apologies for the confusion, my good man. We'll direct our attention to the business at hand and be gone by midday, I assure you."

The man nodded, waving them through.

Solomon climbed onto the cart, taking a seat next to Natalia. She looked forward afraid if she looked directly at the old man, she might start shouting at him. Flicking the reins, she urged the horse to pull them through the tunnel and back out into the rain inside the castle grounds. Keeping her eyes fixed on the streets in front of them she waited until she was out of sight of the entrance before turning to Solomon and punching him firmly in the shoulder.

"Ouch!" Solomon winced, rubbing his shoulder.

"What the hell was that all about?" she said, striking him a second time. His reaction caused Maylox to peek out from under the tarp, Natalia catching a glimpse of her as she glared at Solomon.

"Okay, okay, stop hitting me! I'm sorry! I told you I wanted to come with you today, but you left without a word. How do you think I felt when I went to your room and found that you had already gone?" Solomon asked.

Natalia shook her head. She so wanted to punch the old man again, but thought twice was probably good enough. "I told you to stay back. We're a large enough group as it is." She saw Solomon look around quizzically. To address his confusion she said, "Maylox, say hello."

Maylox lifted the tarp up and said, "Hey Sol."

Solomon twisted in his seat, smiled at her and looked to Natalia again, asking, "What about Inama?"

Natalia nodded toward the wall rising above the rooftops, "I'm to send her a rope and she'll climb over with her royal guard. After seeing the lazy protection at the gates, I wish we'd planned to have them walk through like you did."

Solomon scoffed, "You're telling me that you invited a group of Lumbapi to raid the city with you, but the addition of one old man is too cumbersome?"

"It's not like that," Natalia said. "Inama and her group are backup, in case the mission goes terribly wrong. She and her soldiers will be watching, making sure their princess doesn't get herself into too much danger. They'll only make themselves known if we get into trouble."

"Typical. Once her father caught wind of the plan, he had to make sure she was protected. You didn't see anyone doing that for her back in Ryedale," Solomon commented.

Natalia steered the cart into a narrow alley between brick buildings and pulled the horse to a stop. "You'd better stay with them once we bring them over the wall," Natalia said.

"But," Solomon protested.

"This is a very dangerous mission, Sol, I'm not kidding. I don't want to see you get hurt," she said.

"You can't be serious," Solomon said, stepping down from the cart.

Natalia took her sword as Maylox handed it to her, then hoisted the dwarf from the cart, setting her down on the cobblestone street. "I am serious," she said.

"Who are you to tell me what to do? Do you know who I am?" Solomon asked.

"I didn't want you here in the first place," Natalia said angrily. She buckled the sword belt around her waist and started down the alley.

"I can help you navigate the city," Solomon said, chasing after her.

Natalia hurried along the alley and stopped at the open street at the opposite end. She looked for the rising wall marking the city's edge, but the tall, multi-storied buildings blocked it from view. She had been so distracted by Solomon on the way into the city that she hadn't paid attention to where they were going. Letting Maylox and Solomon catch her, she hesitated while considering which way to turn. Making a left, she walked out into the street. Maylox and Solomon hurried to keep up.

"Natalia, listen to me. Let me help you. I know my way around this city well. You've never been here before and neither has Maylox," Solomon pleaded.

Natalia quickened her pace, keeping her eyes on the building tops and searching for a glimpse of the city wall. Walking two more blocks, she turned right, hoping to see the wall on the horizon, but instead of the wall, she saw more clay-shingled roofs. Slowing to a stop, she spun around in search of the wall. Giving in to her frustration, she looked to Solomon and said, "Fine, you can come along as our navigator."

Solomon grinned through his white beard, rain beading down the tangled mat, "Okay. Where did you say Inama and her soldiers were supposed to meet you?"

"At the south sewer," she said shortly.

Raising his index finger, Solomon said, "Ah, it's a good thing you've got me here. You're heading exactly the opposite direction."

Natalia rolled her eyes, assuming Solomon only said that to make her feel better about accepting him as part of their mission. He could be telling the truth, but she had no way of knowing, so she kept quiet and followed the man as he wound them through the cobblestone streets and finally to the wall.

As she noticed earlier, covered turrets were spaced periodically along the top of the wall that surrounded the city. From what Natalia had seen at the gate and what she could see here, all of the soldiers manning the wall were standing under cover and out of the rain. She didn't blame them. In this weather, she wouldn't want to spend all day out in the open either.

"These are the sewers," Solomon said, pointing at vented grates along the edge of the streets. "They run out of the city in multiple locations, but this is the south wall exit."

Natalia nodded to a set of stairs zigzagging up the wall. "We'll take these," she said.

Together the three climbed to the top of the wall, Natalia continually checking to either side to make sure no soldiers had strayed out onto the wall where they could see her small team. Seeing that the coast was clear, Natalia led them toward the nearest lookout. The open doorway to the brick tower revealed four soldiers huddled inside. Natalia slowed her pace, walking through the rain on the wall toward the covered structure. She could see two of the men facing the other way, looking out the opposite open door. The other two leaned against the open window with their heads out of view.

Natalia drew her blade as she stalked closer to the covered building. She heard Maylox's light footsteps close behind. Remaining focused on the tower, she crouched low to the ground as she neared the brick structure. Just as she prepared to sneak inside the turret, two soldiers at the opposite door turned around to face her. In their hesitation to act, Natalia cleanly hewed them with two flicks of her blade. Their bodies hadn't yet hit the ground when the other two leaning in the window became aware of the intruders. As they reached for their weapons, Natalia swiped her sharp steel across their throats, felling them in one clean stroke.

She heard Solomon shudder as they pulled the bodies out of view of anyone who might be walking along the wall. She stepped to the open window and looked out from the turret, searching for Inama and her men. A whistle directed her attention to a group of trees where Inama stood half-hidden and waiting. Doublechecking with a glance that the sewer was indeed barred and sealed from any outside entries, she motioned for Inama to toss up the rope. Standing back, she heard the rock hit the wall three times before it came through the opening with one end of the rope fastened to it. Natalia tied the rope securely to the turret wall.

Once she saw the first of the Lumbapi beginning the climb, she turned to Solomon and Maylox, "Help me get these soldiers out of their uniforms."

She and Maylox got to work stripping the dead men, while Solomon leaned his head out of the door. Natalia could hear him coughing and gagging.

"Sol," she said. "Make yourself useful and keep an eye out for anyone coming this way." Based on how content the soldiers had been to remain at their posts along the wall, Natalia didn't expect to see anyone coming along the wall, but she thought it might give Solomon some focus while she struggled to loot the watchmen. She caught a glimpse of his feet as he walked through the doorway and stood just outside, letting the drizzle soak him.

By the time they'd stripped off the first soldier's

uniform, Inama had reached the top of the wall. She hurried into the tower and, upon seeing what they were doing, immediately started helping. They fitted the first four Lumbapi soldiers to climb the wall with the four dead soldiers' uniforms. When the fifth man reached the top, they'd donned their disguises and worked together to pitch the dead men over the wall, leaving their blood to wash away in the rain.

As they waited for the remaining three men to climb the wall, Solomon stepped carefully back into the guard post, whispering, "There are soldiers at the stairs."

Natalia leaned out to see four soldiers starting up the stairs, one of them already halfway up the wall. Thinking quickly, she directed the four men wearing the bloodstained uniforms to stand near the entrance, potentially blocking the others from view.

Natalia flattened herself along the inside wall and out of view. Solomon, Maylox and Inama did the same. She held her breath as the fifth Lumbapi stood behind the men blocking the door. Shortly, Natalia heard one set of boots approaching. A conversation with the men pretending to be lookouts began. She could hear the solitary soldier's voice turn from casual to serious. Before he could alert the others, the Lumbapi pulled him inside and Natalia stuck her blade through his mouth, silencing him for good. As his body fell limp to the turret floor, Natalia saw the disguised men waving down to the soldiers, indicating for them to join them. As she peered out between the gaps in the open door, Natalia watched the three soldiers climb the stairs one at a time; their heads down, they were oblivious to the danger ahead. Pulling each into the building, they quickly dispatched the men, giving the remaining Lumbapi soldiers their disguises.

Once the last of the castle soldiers had been pitched over the wall, Solomon laid out their route to the castle. Natalia listened intently as he proposed the idea of acting as prisoners to be carried to the castle. Another option would be to split up, the soldiers marching to the castle and the four of them not dressed as soldiers left to search the castle. Natalia opted to travel in smaller groups and the others agreed.

They decided that two of the Lumbapi soldiers would remain at the observation tower to protect the escape route. Another five would go to the castle walls and act as postmen, ensuring the princess' safety. The remaining four would wait outside the castle gates for the Lumbapi soldiers and then allow them to enter the city, gaining access to the castle.

Solomon led them down the stairs and they started out across the city. Natalia walked with her companions, cloaked as a commoner out for a stroll in the rain. She watched from the corner of her eye as the Lumbapi soldiers peeled away, taking the different routes Solomon had described to them. She hoped they wouldn't get as lost as she had.

As they walked through the city, Natalia wondered where the orcs were. She'd only seen men in the king's army, now Merglan's army. Once they moved closer to the castle walls, she found her answer. Orcs milled through the streets, the rain tinkling off their plate armor as they patrolled en masse. She glanced back at Maylox, hoping that the dwarf's cloak would give her the appearance of a child. In truth, she wasn't yet an adult, but much shorter than other girls her age would've been. Her thick red hair and squat features gave her away when she was out in the open, but under that cloak Natalia thought she could pass as a well-fed little girl.

They kept their heads low as they shouldered their way through the crowded streets. Orcs grunted, looking twice at them as they passed, but the orcs lacked the sense to notice it odd that no other common folk were walking around in these parts. Likely they'd all left once the large army of ugly brutes strolled in.

Natalia wanted to regroup and make a new plan. Walking in the midst of orcs wasn't the best way to get past them. She was sure there must be a better way, but Solomon continued to walk quickly through the streets. Trying to catch him, she quickened her pace. The old man navigated his way through the orcs with haste. She noticed that the orcs became more active, more attentive as they neared the castle. Each time she got close enough to Solomon to tap him on the shoulder, an orc would shove past, bumping her back.

The concentration of orcs intensified as they neared the castle and she quickly lost sight of Solomon, his gray hood disappearing somewhere beneath the mass of tusked faces. Natalia glanced back, but Inama and Maylox were no longer behind her. As she slowed her pace, the orcs pushed her along, their continual movement forcing her to shift with them. She pushed one out of the way and squeezed through a gap. Finding another opening, she darted through, pushing and forcing her way past the disgruntled orcs. Stopping against a large flat stone wall, Natalia rested and attempted to get her bearings.

Hearing the faintest whisper, Natalia looked up. There

in an archer's slotted window along the castle wall, Solomon's face peered down at her. She saw him point to her left and whisper, "Quickly, the door."

Moving left as instructed, Natalia found an indent in the stone wall. She slid inside as orcs moved in, filling the space where she'd rested briefly. The door opened and she stepped inside. As the door closed behind her, she stood still for a moment waiting for her eyes to adjust to total darkness.

"Solomon?" she whispered.

"Come," he responded, and she felt him take her by the hand.

She let him pull her blindly, turning several times before they came to a stop near a slit in the wall. The archer's window lit the darkened space enough so she could see his wrinkled, bearded face. For a moment she wondered how old he really was. This man appeared ancient yet moved with the agility of a youth. Natalia knew little of him and less about his past.

"Where are we?" she asked.

"We're inside the castle wall," Solomon said in a low tone.

Seeing his serious expression, she still couldn't help but ask, "You're sure? I didn't see it coming."

"No, it was hard to focus with all of the orcs circling the outer reaches," he acknowledged.

Natalia looked out through the slot, seeing the sea of mottled heads moving in a single direction through the streets.

"Where are the dwarf and the princess?" Solomon asked.

Natalia shrugged. "Probably still out there. I almost

lost you, too," she sighed.

"We'll go back for them," Solomon said, turning back.

Natalia grabbed him by the shoulder, "No. It's better this way. The smaller the group, the less conspicuous we are. They'll find their way out when the battle begins." She could tell Solomon didn't like the idea, but he stopped and she recognized that he was willing to go along with her approach.

"Right then, all we need to do is find Ivan, Anders and Zahara and free them without Merglan knowing," Solomon said.

"Exactly. Where do we start?" she asked.

"We should start by searching the keep."

"You know your way around the castle too?" Natalia asked.

Solomon nodded.

"How is that?" Natalia narrowed her eyes.

"I used to live here. It was a long time ago," Solomon said in a whisper as he started to move, leading Natalia through the darkened hallways inside the castle walls. "I was a person of importance at one time in my life, but felt the burden better suited another."

Natalia shushed him, hearing the echoing footfalls of people marching. They were getting closer. "Quickly, hide," she whispered, shuffling back the way they came. Turning into a side hallway, they stopped with their backs to the wall. Remaining perfectly still, Natalia watched glowing torchlight illuminate the hallway.

"They came in this way," she heard someone say. Natalia held her breath as a small group of soldiers and orcs walked just feet from where they stood, the light dimming as they passed them by. She started to relax slightly when she suddenly saw the shinning glow from her pocket come to life.

The mirror, she thought as she frantically searched for the two-way mirror she used to communicate with Nadir. As it illuminated the darkened space around them, she knew they were done for. The soldiers and orcs stopped, and she heard them reverse direction, their torch's glow cut out by the bright light emanating from the mirror.

Cursing, Natalia drew her blade and stepped out into the hallway. Steel clashed on steel as she met the orcs first. Time seemed to stop as she battled them two at a time while they forced her back down the hallway, a line of their corpses littering the stones. Shouts rang throughout the castle and Natalia knew the entire castle guard would be on them soon. Cutting her way through the orcs, she made her way into the group of soldiers. The one with the torch dashed away to call for help.

As she met the soldiers with blades in hand and worked to create an opening, Natalia heard the booming blasts of cannon fire along the distant city walls. She cut down the startled soldiers who were caught off guard by the noise. As the cannons continued to boom, she thought, *The battle for Kingston is about to begin.*

CHAPTER SIXTEEN

Kurr at the Gates

Anders," Maija cried, turning away from the heap of elven bodies.

His gaze left Zahara's and he consoled Maija, unable to hide the massacre from their memories.

"What kind of monster could do such a thing?" she asked, her voice quivering slightly.

"Kurr," Anders replied, the disdain he felt for them nearly palpable.

"How could one kurr do all this?" Maija asked, turning to face the bodies once more, tears glistening her cheeks.

Anders looked at the widened path that led into the village and said, "This wasn't the work of one kurr; this was an entire mob. We were right when we noted that the trail stunk of herd mentality and now we know what kind of creature caused it."

"Aren't these forests protected by the elves?" Maija asked.

Anders nodded, "Half of Nadir's army went with us to Southland, but the other half remained. If the High Council knew of these attacks, they would send troops to hunt them down." He paused, trying to think of a single reason why the elves would turn a blind eye to the massacre of their people. Anders shook his head, "Something isn't right in the capital. They wouldn't let elitist dragons patrol their borders so closely, much less allow kurr to run wild in their lands and kill their citizens."

"We need to do something, warn someone," Maija said, confidence and determination returning to her voice.

"We must quicken our pace to Cedarbridge and hunt down any kurr we find along the way," Anders said.

Flying would be fastest, Raffa said, his deep voice sounding in Anders' mind.

But wouldn't we risk showing the entrance to Merglan's followers? Zahara asked.

"She's right," Anders said aloud. "The other dragons could still be within sight if we fly above the trees. We'll need to get farther away from the Nagano border before taking to the skies."

And the kurr? Zahara asked.

"We hunt them on foot for now," Anders said, pointing to the freshly trampled path. "They could still be in the area, so stay on the lookout. I wouldn't be surprised to see one of those dragons leading the kurr."

No, Raffa said. *Those dragons would never help a kurr, let alone a herd of them.*

"How can you be certain?" Anders asked. "We know that they can be manipulated; Merglan already has them fooled into helping take us out."

Just because they've decided to become dragon supremacists doesn't mean your evil sorcerer had anything to do with it, this time. Scores of dragons still remember his influence from the wars. Most of the radical groups that managed to hold onto

Merglan's evil ideals have taken them and twisted their intentions into their own. Their Prophet could be any one of the many radical dragons from the wars; Killdoor wasn't the only one.

"If that's true, it still doesn't change the fact that kurr are invading lands that haven't seen conflict since The War of the Magicians. Kurr have never been able to raid the Everlight Forest unchallenged," Anders said, frustration sparking his emotions. At that moment, he suddenly had an urge to hold Lazuran in his hand. As the argument between Zahara and Raffa escalated on whether dragons were assisting the enemy forces, Anders became focused on one thing, the sapphires in his sword. Looking down at them, he moved his hand to touch the pommel.

Running his palm over the pommel-stone and down onto the shaft, Anders felt the slightness of the crystals embedded into the handle. As the voices of Raffa and Zahara fled his mind, he thought he could hear the same faint whispering he'd heard before. Longing to know how the tapped crystal managed to call to him, he closed his eyes and dove deep into the recesses of his mind, trying to create a connection with the sword.

Anders! Zahara shouted, disrupting his concentration.

Anders shook himself from the daze he'd drifted into, "Yeah?"

Do we take the elven trails to Cedarbridge or follow the kurr paths? she asked. The anger in her tone was very clear.

"The elven trails," he answered, quickly regaining his awareness. "Taking an unnecessary risk to hunt the kurr unsupported wouldn't be something Ivan would've wanted us to do. He would've said we were too important to the overall objective. Besides, finding kurr here means there must be bigger problems up the line. Right now, we need to focus on getting our allies back from Southland to face this apparent invasion that's taken place during our brief absence," he said, feeling as if the words weren't his own but arrived directly from his father.

Spoken like a true prince, Anders heard Zahara's voice say to him only.

He looked to the ground, frowning, *I don't feel like a prince.* Then he started toward the elven trail leaving the village.

"Anders," Maija called after him as she jogged to catch up. He felt her hand on his arm as she asked, "What was that?"

"What?" he asked, worried he might have accidentally spoken the final comment to her as well as Zahara.

Pulling him to a stop, she asked, "What happened to you back there? You had that look on your face again."

Anders didn't want to admit that he still felt the draw from Lazuran and had felt an especially strong surge when thinking about hunting down the kurr. A part of him wanted to let the rage take him and fly out after the kurr, repaying them for the slaughter in the village, but he couldn't allow himself to become like that, like Merglan.

His delayed reply left Maija to speak first, her words prying at him, "I saw something come over you back there. Don't try to deny it. While Raffa and Zahara were arguing, you went somewhere else. I saw it on your face, and I can tell when it's happening, just as I can tell that you don't want to share it with me. Anders, what's wrong?"

"Seeing those bodies," he lied. "It brought me back to

a dark place." He hadn't fully lied. Seeing the elven bodies piled up in the village center had shaken him. The sight brought back a number of traumatic memories.

"Oh," Maija said, eyeing him skeptically. "That's surprising, because when we first discovered them, I didn't see you react that dramatically."

Anders shook his head, "I'm just tired. Still recovering from the fight with Merglan."

"Okay," she said. "But just so you know, if there's ever anything you want to talk about that you can't or don't want to share with Zahara, I'm here."

Anders smiled, considering whether he should tell her about the withdrawal he felt from the crystal's power. He inhaled, preparing to say something, then hesitated. He looked to the side, embarrassed at being caught in his lie. "It's just," he said. "I don't want to disappoint anyone, you know. I know that sounds silly. But I've been feeling a little different since we last saw each other."

"That doesn't sound silly. I can tell that something's been bothering you. Was it something you read about in Merglan's diary?" she asked.

"Merglan's diary," he said in astonishment. He realized he hadn't shared the explanation of the diagram. The diary held the key to understanding the crystal's power. Anders starting walking again, mumbling to himself, "I think my copy is still in Cedarbridge. We need to find it."

"What do you mean your copy?" Maija asked, speeding up to keep pace with him.

Anders quickly explained how he'd discovered the new passage describing the crystal's abilities and what Nadir had told him about it. "We need to find the diagram so I can restore Lazuran's pommel. With that amount of power, imagine the things I would be capable of," Anders said, with malice in his voice.

"I thought you were going to try to have it removed?" Maija asked, pulling Anders from his daydreams of conquest.

"If we can add more energy to it, I could use the enhanced power to take control," Anders said.

"That's not what you told me a few days ago, Anders. What you're saying, it doesn't sound like you," Maija said, eyeing him warily.

"Oh," Anders flushed. "I meant, when we figure out how to work the inhabitance crystals, we can use them to bring Merglan down," he said, resting his hand on Lazuran's pommel. He suddenly felt it pulling at him again and his mind began to drift away from their conversation.

"There it is again," Maija said.

"What?" Anders asked, taking his hand off the sword.

"That look you had earlier. It's the sword, isn't it?" Maija charged.

Anders shook his head, "No. I mean, I just think we could harness some power in the sword and use it to beat Merglan."

Maija narrowed her eyes. Anders felt her staring through his denial. "Don't lie to me, Anders. You told me Merglan's control over you would pass with time. You said we would have the crystal removed, but now you're acting strange again," she said.

Anders didn't reply. He wanted a way out of the conversation, to avoid it at all costs. He wanted to pretend that she hadn't seen his desire to feel the crystal's corrupted power coursing through his veins once more. He quickened his pace to put distance between them, but felt her hand grab his arm again.

Pulling him up short, she said firmly, "Anders, stop!" Anders found himself staring directly into Maija's brown eyes, their searching stare speaking volumes. "We need to be on the same page. If you start keeping secrets like this, whether it's about the sword or something else, you put our trust in jeopardy," she paused. Anders could feel the words cutting through his urges to retreat.

"I know you're still recovering from your nearly deadly encounter with Merglan, and I know that you feel terrible about leaving Ivan and the others behind, but you need to snap out of it soon. We're almost back Cedarbridge now where you'll have to explain what happened. The High Council will want to know why you're here and their king is not. If you start drifting off and touching your sword all of the time, they're going to think you've become power-drunk and that you left Ivan, Nadir and the others behind on purpose."

He didn't want to admit it, but Anders knew she was right. He would have to explain what happened and, even if they believed him, they might still question his ability after having tasted Merglan's power. Maija stared at him. He combed her with his eyes, knowing he had to tell her about the sword's effects that continued to plague his consciousness.

"Consider what's about to happen, Anders. Think about our relationship and whether you want this to work," Maija said, pointing from herself to Anders. "You're going to have to tell me things; even the uncomfortable things. Otherwise, this mistrust will grow and become an issue. I don't want to be with someone who doesn't trust me as much as I trust him."

Anders nodded. He glanced to the side to see both dragons sitting down along the narrow elven trail, watching them intently. He returned his gaze to Maija, "You're right, I'm feeling withdrawal from the sword. I hoped the urge would go away since I used all of its power, but it hasn't. I want that power back, I crave it, and no matter how hard I try to deny that feeling, it keeps coming back. I know I said we'd try to remove the crystal from the pommel, but I don't know how else Zahara and I can defeat Merglan. If we can use the diagram and add untapped energy, in theory I should have full control. There are other smaller crystals in the sword's handle as well. If we can use them all, I might have a chance. Maija, I can't do this alone and I don't want to lose you because of my mistakes. I still need to figure out who I am before I face him again."

Maija nodded. Leaning forward, she wrapped her arms around Anders and held him in an embrace, "It's okay, Anders, you won't be alone. We're here to help you through this, you just need to be honest with us so we *can* help you."

Whispering in her ear, Anders said, "Merglan told me something about my father." He felt Maija's hug loosen as she leaned back to look at him. "Maija, I learned who my father was and I couldn't save him."

"No," she said shaking her head. "You told me you were a baby when your uncle found you. That your parents drowned in a shipwreck. There wasn't anything you could've done to help."

"My father didn't drown; he wasn't on the ship," Anders said.

"Merglan lied," Maija said. "He was just trying to get in your head, corrupt your mind."

Anders shook his head, "No, Maija, you don't understand. My father was there, too. We fought Merglan together."

"You said you fought Merglan with Ivan," Maija said.

Anders nodded, "I did and, in doing so, I learned I'm the son of William, King of Southland and rightful ruler of humankind." He saw Maija's eyes widen and he continued, "William and his wife hid from Merglan, adopting different names. During that time, they had two sons and William became bonded with a dragon. Theodor led me to believe my entire family drowned in that shipwreck, but William was never on that ship. Maija, you've met this man and spent time with him, as have I. My father is King William, but we know him better as Ivan, the unbonded."

Anders gauged her reaction as her jaw dropped. She shook her head in disbelief, "Anders. That means you're… But Ivan was your mentor?"

"He was a lot more than my mentor," Anders said, looking down.

"And he didn't make it out with you," Maija said, covering her mouth with her hands.

Tears blurred Anders' vision. He pursed his lips and shook his head, "I tried, Zahara and I tried, but Merglan pulled him back at the last second."

"Anders," Maija said, again hugging him. "Why didn't you tell me? I had no idea. If only I had known."

"It wouldn't have changed anything," Anders cut her off. "I transported us to another continent. There's nothing we could've done to get here faster even if you'd known. I didn't want to weigh you down with the added worry."

"No, Anders. You shouldn't have to carry this secret alone. I can help you."

Anders pulled away from her hug, wiping a tear from his cheek. Sniffling, he tried to wrangle in his emotions, "Thank you, Maija. If you hadn't called me out, I don't know how long Zahara and I would've kept that a secret."

"You can tell me anything, you know," Maija said.

Anders looked to the dragons. Zahara nodded approvingly. He turned and continued walking down the narrow trail with Maija at his side. "When we get to Cedarbridge," he told Maija. "I think we should keep the High Council in the dark about my identity."

"Why's that?" Maija asked.

"I don't want to give them a reason to hold Zahara and me back from any attempts to rescue Ivan," Anders said.

Maija nodded, "Okay, Anders. It will be our secret."

Anders grinned slightly. He didn't think it possible to feel relief from having told Maija about Ivan, but it did. After stopping to camp, Anders felt that a massive weight had been pulled from his body. He was glad that she was so understanding.

***

In the morning, Zahara and Raffa killed and consumed several deer before they continued on their journey toward Cedarbridge. Anders again gorged himself on some of their charred meat to bring renewed energy to his body. By late afternoon Anders thought they had walked far enough from the Nagano/elven border to chance a flight above the trees. He knew they could get a better idea of where they were if they could see their surroundings from the sky.

Raffagaun and Maija took the lead while Anders and Zahara walked along behind them. Anders wanted to make sure they had a well-formed plan of what they needed to do once they reached the city.

Are you feeling up for a flight soon? he asked her.

Yes, but are you? she asked skeptically.

In an ideal world, I would want weeks to fully recover, but as it is, I feel almost fully restored, Anders replied.

I just thought you might be feeling burned out emotionally. That was the most I've seen you two argue, Zahara said.

You were right in saying I should've told her sooner. It created the tension between us that could've caused damage had we been in a combat situation, Anders said.

You did the right thing. We don't want to lose her trust.

I told her how I'm struggling with Lazuran's residual effects.

You're still feeling it? she asked.

I felt it again in the village. I could've sworn the sword was whispering to me.

You can't let the power back in, Anders. It turns you into something else, something dark.

I know. I think you and Maija can help, keep me in check when I'm feeling its pull.

Ultimately, you're the only one who can stop it, she said.

But I'll be stronger with your support, Anders said, placing a hand on Zahara's side and petting her.

It's the difference between you, she said.

What do you mean? he asked.

The difference between you and Merglan. You've got her, she glanced at Maija and Raffa in front of them.

Anders looked to Maija, then noticed Zahara's gaze as she lingered on the red dragon's form. *And you've got him,* he said.

Zahara snorted and Anders felt a wave of embarrassment flash over her. *You don't have to be ashamed, Zahara, it's perfectly natural. I think Raffa would be lucky to attract your attention.*

He doesn't think like that, not now anyway. It's not his time, she said.

Anders wondered what she meant but didn't think he should prod her on the matter. She'd resisted sticking her nose in Maija and Anders' relationship, so he felt he should give her the same space and quickly changed the subject, *I hope we don't find Cedarbridge a bigger challenge than facing the kurr.*

You think there's something wrong in the capital? Zahara asked.

How else would you explain kurr roaming the forest unchallenged and dragon supremacists flying at will on the outskirts? If Nadir were on his throne, he wouldn't stand for it.

Maybe that's why it's happening. Many weren't happy about his decision to leave the capital. Perhaps they're allowing these horrible things to occur in hopes people will deny him his throne.

Anders thought for a moment, then said, *I hope for their people's sake that's not the case.*

If you figure out a way to recharge the crystals, will you do it? Zahara asked.

Anders had spent the night mulling over this very question, *I think I might respond differently to a freshly charged crystal.*

And if you didn't?

Then I'll be right back to square one, but at least with a charged crystal, I have a shot at beating Merglan one-on-one.

That's a dangerous path.

But one I feel myself being pulled down. Remember what Solomon told me. Follow my heart.

He also said you could be led down a path of self-destruction.

He didn't say that.

It was implied. I read between the lines, Zahara said.

Well, we don't have very many choices. Either we learn how to recharge the crystals or displace their power. That's the only way I can see us taking Merglan down.

What about them? Zahara asked, motioning toward Maija and Raffagaun. *We could train them to be riders like us and we could fight together.*

That will take too much time, something we don't have. If we did seclude ourselves and focused on honing our abilities, we'd be leaving all of Kartania unprotected for Merglan's taking. By the time we were ready to face him, his forces would be too strong for us to defeat. Right now, we still have time to stop him in Southland.

It might already be too late. He's controlling dragons in Nagano, his kurr are running wild here in the Everlight Kingdom, his orcs are flooding Southland. What's to say he hasn't invaded Westland already?

Don't say that, Anders said.

Why not? It's a rational train of thought. If he's got influence here, why wouldn't he have it in Westland, too?

Because I sent Kirsten, Thomas, Max and Bo back there assuming that they would be returning to safety, he said, feeling his heartbeat quicken.

Sorry, but I'm just stating something we might expect to learn when we reach Cedarbridge.

I know, but I hope you're wrong about this.

Anders sped up the trail to tell Maija that he and Zahara were ready to take flight. When he came alongside her, she asked, "Did you get your plans sorted out?"

"More or less. Hopefully, they'll still be receptive to us returning," he said.

"Let me guess, because you left with their new king in a hurry to kill their queen before proving to the High Council that Lageena really did do it?" Maija asked.

"That sums it up nicely," Anders nodded.

"Should be interesting," Maija said.

"Yeah," Anders said, looking through the gaps in the canopy at the sky. Clouds formed, darkening to the west. "I think we're far enough from the border with Nagano now to take a look at where we are."

Maija and Raffa waited as Anders and Zahara launched through the canopy, snapping a few tree limbs with her large wings to reach the open sky. They hadn't sensed any dragons nearby, but Anders instantly surveyed to the north and east. He thought himself well enough to trust his senses and the absence of dragons on the horizon confirmed it for him.

As he and Zahara circled slowly above the trees, looking out in each direction to pinpoint their location, Anders quickly began to identify familiar landmarks. He could see the distant blue to the south, marking the Marauder's Sea. The wash of green treetops extended far to the west until it ran abruptly into the distant Frozentip Mountains. Mount Bloodtooth hid behind a wall of dark clouds, building above the forest. A strong draft pulled in toward the ominous clouds and shook Zahara, causing her to struggle to keep her balance in flight. The thunderhead forming just above the trees blocked the remaining mountain peaks that Anders had hoped to use to gauge the location of the hidden elf city. Using his memory to envision their present location relative to Cedarbridge, Anders gathered a clear picture of the city and found it to be directly below the center of the enormous, threatening thunderhead.

Diving back down into the trees, Anders and Zahara landed abruptly. Maija and Raffa stood awaiting their report. After discussing the distance to the hidden city, he and Zahara agreed that the safest route would be to continue on foot to the city. The last thing Anders and Zahara wanted was to crash and further injure themselves by flying into the storm. Not only that, but if they weren't recognized in the darkness of the storm, they might be assumed to be enemies and, consequently, mistakenly attacked. If they entered on foot, they would have a better opportunity to show who they were, unless they didn't make it before nightfall. He gauged the position of the sun one last time and was convinced they could make it before sunset.

As they made their way through the forest, they noted several paths created by the kurr. Kurr activity this close to the elven city raised their concern for the welfare of this kingdom and their allies. Anders hoped that the elves and resident dragons hadn't suffered any attacks while they'd been away. He didn't think that was possible given that the city was hidden and protected with magic, but then again, Lageena had been able to sneak her way into the city and carry out all kinds of evil, including the murder of a respected king.

The skies darkened in the early afternoon as the towering clouds amassed further. The trees in the forest swayed and rustled violently from gusts pulling inward in the storm's updraft. Anders had watched many storms roll into Highborn Bay over the years. They arrived with updrafts followed by down-drafting winds when the storm wall hit, but this thunderhead seemed to be acting differently. It remained firmly over the elven city and didn't move regardless of the wind's direction. The storm continually drew inward, but when they passed under the storm wall, the downdraft didn't hit. Anders watched the treetops bend and sway, leaning together toward the storm.

As they neared the city, darkness fell early. Anders found he had to rely on his other senses to navigate their way along the path. The sound of rushing wind and swaying trees roared in their ears.

Maija tapped him on the shoulder, "Hey, Anders, did you hear that?"

Anders shook his head, "No, hear what?"

"The marching?"

"What, no. I didn't hear anything."

"It's coming this way."

Anders opened his senses, scanning the area around them. Suddenly he realized that they were about to be attacked. Anders could feel a group of enemies running directly toward them.

Looking to Maija, he shouted over the wind, "Kurr, they're coming this way!"

Zahara and Raffa readied themselves for a fight. Anders drew his sword, and Maija gripped the dagger Anders handed her.

"They're almost here," Maija said.

Just when Anders thought he could finally hear the stampeding over the wind, it vanished. A muffled thwacking noise replaced it.

"What's happening?" Anders asked Maija, searching his senses for them again. Anders realized he was relying on her as much as he was his magic.

"They stopped. Something else got them," she said.

Anders sensed killing, a slaughter was happening in the trees not far from where they stood.

"The kurr are being killed," he agreed.

"What could kill a group of kurr like that?!" Maija asked, shouting to be heard over the howling wind and sudden downpour.

"We could find out or make our way quickly to the city," Anders said.

Let's get to safety. Whatever's killing those kurr might come for us next. I don't want to find out if they are friend or foe, Zahara said, starting to move down the widening path.

"Come on," Anders said to Maija, who stood looking into the trees just beyond the trail.

She turned to follow them, "They sounded so close."

Anders jogged to keep up with Zahara, "Really? I couldn't hear them. I could barely sense them with my mind."

Maija didn't respond. She just kept glancing back to see if anything was now pursuing them.

Within minutes they were closing in on the gates to the city when Zahara stopped, *Something's not right.*

Anders sensed out and could feel what Zahara was talking about. The gates were fortified, locked.

"Is Cedarbridge under attack?" Anders asked.

"We need to move. Whatever killed those kurr is almost here," Maija said, rushing to Raffa and scrambling onto his back.

"But the storm!" Ander shouted. "We might not be able to fly." He searched out for whatever Maija was hearing that he couldn't identify anything. Cutting his connection off, he hopped onto Zahara.

"Whatever it is, I don't want to be here when it arrives," Maija said. Raffa jumped up into the canopy creating a hole in the trees as he left the ground.

Anders clung to Zahara as she followed, getting swept up by the storm as she took to the air.

Chapter Seventeen

Those You Love Most

ind surged into Zahara's open wings causing Anders to jolt forward as their leathery expanse caught the billowing updraft. The storm carried her higher, forcing them to climb rapidly as they were swept into the looming thunderhead. Clinging tightly to her saddle, Anders jostled as he watched Raffagaun's outline disappear into the slate-gray cloud. Freezing rain pelted Anders, leaving welts on his chest, arms and thighs. He tried to focus on creating a mental connection with Raffagaun, but the chaos of the storm made it increasingly difficult to locate them.

We need to get closer to the ground, Anders said into Zahara's mind.

She tilted her body, angling down into the wind so she could cut through the updraft's pull. Flying into the wind slowed everything around them, the rain hit with less sting and Anders wasn't pushed around so violently in the saddle. Turning back, he glanced into the storm. Behind them, he saw the shadow of Raffa's giant figure angling down after them. Together the dragons waffled as they flew against the storm, down toward the forest.

Anders squinted through the rain as it caught in the prevailing wind, obstructing his view. Because it was dark, he couldn't see the city's outer limits, so he directed Zahara as she angled lower toward the forest canopy. Anders continually searched for any sign of where they might've been swept off to, but the magical capital remained out of sight. In its place, the menacing cloud darkened. As they approached the tree line, Zahara pulled out of her dive slightly, catching the wind again as it carried her back toward the looming cloud. Anders gripped tightly as she dove, lowering them back into view of the city's forested outer wall. Working their way around the outskirts, Anders and Zahara bobbed their way through the gale-force winds to pinpoint their location outside the capital.

As Anders caught sight of the city's eastern gate, he directed Zahara to find a place where they could safely approach. Flying away from the storm front, Zahara led Maija and Raffa toward calmer skies in an attempt to land. Like exiting through a door, the wind and rain shut off once they'd ventured several miles away from the city. Anders could see the thinning strip of vegetation marking the trail to Cedarbridge's east entrance. As Zahara landed on the trail, Anders wondered if the east gate would be barred as well. They had only tried to gain entry at the main entrance along the south wall. Dismounting, Anders looked past Raffa's landing to the expanding storm cloud over the elven capital.

Why hasn't the storm moved since this afternoon? Anders asked Zahara as he marveled at its omnipotence.

Maybe it's being powered by magic? she replied.

Considering her suggestion, Anders wondered why the

magical city would conjure such a storm. If that were the case, likely all of the main gates to Cedarbridge would be barred. Anders just hoped whatever was going on inside the city wasn't a reflection of how it appeared from their point of view.

"You got a new plan?" Maija shouted as if the storm were still raging around them.

Anders jumped as he turned to see her standing just behind him. He could tell from her reaction that she didn't mean to yell. Nodding, he said, "I'll bet that the other gates are blocked as well. There is another way for us to get in, though. Ivan showed me the dragonrider's entrance near the training grounds. Only riders who've trained here can use the access. The magic won't allow anyone else to open and close it."

"Hopefully it will work for us," Maija said more quietly.

Anders nodded, "We could try the east gate, but I doubt it's open."

"Do you think this is all because of the kurr?" Maija asked.

"It could be, but I don't know why the elves wouldn't send their soldiers after them. And I don't think the city would conjure such a violent storm to thwart a few kurr," Anders said, pointing to the towering cloud.

I feel bad energy in the air, Raffagaun said in a low tone.

Anders sensed it too, but it wasn't like the other times he'd been near the enemy's army. "I think we should at least try the east gate. If we can't get in there, we'll try the riders' facilities."

Maija nodded and they climbed back up on their

dragons. Flying as close as she could to the ground to avoid the powerful winds, Zahara landed just outside the east gate. Anders shielded himself from the wind and rain with his forearm. He spoke the elven word to enter, but the gate didn't budge. He shouted over the wind but heard no reply. Anders pounded his fist against the trunk of a tree he knew to be on the gate itself but was met with no answer. He motioned for them to leave. Leaning into the wind, Anders walked alongside the dragons and Maija until they'd reached calmer skies. Mounting, they took flight and hovered over the forest, waiting for Raffa and Maija.

Zahara beat her wings and flew north, beyond the cliffs and out past the storm's headwall. Circling down below the wind, Anders wondered why the stormfront ended exactly along the cliff wall and didn't extend to encompass the rider facilities. Landing just beyond the clearing that marked the training grounds, Anders dismounted Zahara and began searching for the secret entrance. He hadn't wondered about it before, but the evergreen wall surrounding Cedarbridge did not extend out to the training grounds. Though the stretch of land between the facilities and the city was shrouded in the same magic, the training ground lacked a wall to keep it hidden from unwanted passersby.

The dragonriders' entrance differed from the other elven gates. At the others, any elf could speak a designated word to open the gate, but to gain entry with that word, those who approached first had to do so with pure intentions. This magic kept sorcerers like Merglan from opening the gates. Anders imagined Lageena would've always had others open them for her so that she could enter the city. If she'd tried it alone, the magic likely would've barred her. But being the queen, she wouldn't have traveled alone, so she wouldn't have drawn attention in declining to be the first to enter. Once a human or someone of another race, like Ivan or Anders, had been let into the city, the gates would open for them in future attempts, magically judging their intent as it did for the elves. Only elves could open the gates without ever having been let into the city before.

To access the riders' entrance, however, only bonded dragonriders and their dragons could open the gate. As Ivan explained it to Anders, only those who'd spent time training could unlock the gate, but once a rider was in the facilities, anyone in the city could access their grounds by way of the path below the cliffs. When Anders asked what would happen if all of the riders died and someone new came to the facilities, he replied, "In that case, the magic would judge them and reveal itself or not. For now, this rule is what you will follow."

Searching with his mind, Anders felt the magic emanating from the gate. He approached it with caution, trying to remember the exact phrase Ivan had taught him. Anders felt at the fortified entrance and watched as the air rippled beneath his touch. Using the ancient dialect, he spoke the words without knowing their meaning. As he spoke the last syllable, he waited for the gate to open. Holding his breath, Anders heard a click, and the gate swung open. He looked in through the gap and saw the building where his father had instructed him. He then looked again to the side of the gate and saw that where the building should've appeared, its stone walls had been replaced with forest. He knew it to be an illusion, but couldn't help but wonder at the might of whichever sorcerer created these protections.

Anders hesitated before leading them through the entrance. He could sense great tension within the city, emotions boiling up from Cedarbridge too strong to ignore. His hand at Lazuran, he stepped inside. Darkness limited their long-range vision, but Anders didn't see or sense any immediate threat as he led Zahara, Raffa and Maija inside the protected area. Gathering at the edge of the clearing alongside the training grounds, Anders heard the gate close behind them.

From inside the protected area, Anders saw the base of the storm ballooning out as the wind passed over the magic shroud. Mounting their dragons, Maija and Anders prepared to fly closer to the city.

Turning to see her grip Raffa's spines like handles, Anders called to Maija, "Zahara and I will go first. If the elves have defenses along the city limits, they might attack if they don't recognize you. They know us well enough that they shouldn't be fearful. Stay a short distance behind us until we land."

Maija nodded, brushing Raffa's scaled neck.

Flying swiftly over the valley and up the cliffside, Anders prepared to form a shield barrier around them if need be. He wasn't sure how their sudden and unannounced appearance would fare. Landing on the cliff's edge, Anders glanced around to make sure there weren't elven archers lining the cliff wall all prepped for battle as he'd imagined. He glanced up as Raffa set his wings to land next to Zahara. The storm mushroomed out into the night over their heads, wind blasting out around the city. Suddenly Anders realized how calm it actually was under the city's protective magic. Looking ahead, he saw lights glowing among the trees throughout the elven capital.

Dismounting, Anders led the way into the city, Maija, Zahara and Raffa following close on his heels. At first, the capital appeared quiet in stark contrast to the storm raging over the treetops. The farther they walked into Cedarbridge, the more elves Anders saw at their windows or standing in small groups in the streets. His small group's appearance didn't seem to startle them as much as he thought it should. Many elves scowled as they passed in silence. He'd never felt such watchful eyes from the elf community before.

Maija leaned in and whispered as they walked, "They're talking about us."

Anders glanced up at a second-story tree balcony where a small group of elves huddled. They wore red shirts. He could see them pointing down at them. Keeping an eye on them and ready to block any attack with his magic, Anders asked, "What are they saying?"

"Mostly gossip about your return and what it means. Some have said we're the cause of this storm the city's created; others are saying you're here to stop the storm."

"And what of our sudden return? Is anyone saying anything about the campaign I set out on?" Anders asked. He stopped, though, as he realized he hadn't yet asked her how her exceptional hearing had returned.

When Maija shook her head, he asked, "How did your hearing return? It started with the kurr?"

She nodded, "I don't know why I got it back, but I can hear again."

Might have something to do with this storm, Anders

thought to himself as he noticed others in the street in red shirts.

As they continued making their way toward the elven courts where the High Council met, Anders saw elves rushing past him in ones in twos. They darted by with such speed he hardly saw which direction they were going, but he sensed they were heading toward the angry mass of emotion that lay at the heart of the city. He felt Maija's fingers reaching for his and took her hand.

When she squeezed his hand, he asked, "What is it?"

"There's a crowd ahead. The mob sounds angry," she said, raising an eyebrow.

Though he couldn't hear what she could, Anders felt the wave of mixed emotions growing as they neared the heart of Cedarbridge. Anders leaned forward, trying desperately to hear what she heard, but couldn't. Gripping her hand tightly, he said, "I can't hear it, but I can feel it. There's anger in this city like I've never felt before. I had hoped the storm outside wouldn't be a reflection of the goings-on inside," he paused, looking over to see an elf step out of the entrance to a treehouse. The young male quickly pulled a red shirt over his traditional elven silks. They made eye contact as his head emerged from the scarlet cloth. The elf nodded to him, holding up his fist symbolically. In a flash, he darted out ahead of them, disappearing into low light. Anders released his grip on Maija's hand and placed it on Lazuran's hilt. "Be ready for anything," he told her and looked back to the dragons walking behind them. "I don't know what will happen when they see us arrive, but the crowd's reaction could be violent."

As they hurried through the shop-top area and closer

to the Council's headquarters, Anders could hear the shouts of the mob ahead. For a moment he wondered whether they should return to the safety of the training grounds, but so many elves had already seen him. He knew it was too late to leave undetected.

Approaching the gathering, Anders saw that elves wearing the traditional garb outnumbered those wearing red. He wondered about the significance of the red shirts. The swarming elves noisily argued among themselves. Anders couldn't make out the meaning of their conversations, but their emotions were clear. He saw pushing and shouting among them, the mass of bodies extended out of sight filling the streets. Looking down between the rows of trees, Anders couldn't see any clear path through the elves. The mob surrounded the court building, yet he had to speak with the Council.

Turning to Maija, he said, "We can fly over them to see what's going on."

Maija nodded.

Anders moved alongside Zahara and leaped onto his saddle. He nodded for Maija to follow before taking off. Zahara beat her wings several times to gain clearance over the elves and soared just above the treetops toward the heart of the crowd. Anders saw from this vantage point the swelling of elves around the courthouse steps. The elves moved and shouted over one another, but they remained so focused on their squabbles that they didn't see the dragons flying overhead. Most weren't wearing the red shirts, but looking down at them, he could see that the red shirts made up at least a third of the crowd. Flying lower, Anders felt the mass of elves turn their attention to the dragons and their riders.

Their first reaction appeared to be fear, followed by the raising of clenched fists by those wearing red. This was the reaction he had been expecting, but it wasn't as overwhelming as he'd anticipated. Not all feared the dragons circling over the courthouse. The mixed reaction confused Anders, and he grew worried at what the mob might do as their shouts turned to silence. All eyes now watched Anders, Zahara, Maija and Raffa.

At the courthouse steps where he intended to land, Anders could see elves in armor, guarding the justice building. Atop the steps, cloaked elves stood in a half-circle around a lone elf wearing plate armor. He instantly identified the elves with cloaks as the High Council, but the soldiers and the lone elf on the steps reminded him of Nadir and the elven army.

Could it be? he wondered. Deciding to hold back on using his senses, Anders circled down with Zahara, hovering to land in an opening near the courthouse steps. The crowded space offered little landing area for two dragons, especially one of Raffa's size, but the elves widened the gap for the dragons to land. Still astride Zahara, Anders grinned as he saw Nadir's shocked, wide-eyed expression upon recognizing Anders and Zahara. The elf king's gaze met Maija's; his jaw dropped further when he recognized her and realized she was riding a large dragon.

Anders quickly climbed down and ran toward the king, so happy to see that he'd survived the battle. Grinning, he caught the elf in a brotherly embrace, hugging him in front of the stunned crowd.

"Anders," Nadir said, holding him at arm's length and eyeing him up and down. "It really is you, and Maija," he said, stepping toward her as she too darted up the steps to catch him in an embrace.

"It's good to see you made it back. Anders told me about the campaign," she said.

Anders thoughts burned with questions about the battle's outcome. Just as he was about to ask a cold voice cut in over his, "This is not the time or place for emotions to run wild." Anders turned to see a tall elf clothed in High Council robes glaring angrily at them.

"You don't know the circumstances of our meeting," Nadir said defensively.

"And you don't know the state of your own kingdom," the Councilman scolded.

Anders felt the man's words cut deep at Nadir's core, the insult a blatant question of the king's authority. He realized Nadir's return wasn't a welcome one. Rather it was one met with hostile governance and a fueled mob wanting answers.

"Nadir, you will come with us to discuss the fate of our kingdom," the elf said, ushering the group of cloaked elves toward the courthouse doors.

Nadir inhaled deeply, assumed his kingly demeanor, and said, "Anders, we will do catch up after I've handled this problem. There is one thing you must do for me now, though."

Anders wanted to know the outcome of the battle and what had happened to the dwarfs. He needed to know if Ivan was okay. Struggling to hold in his objection to Nadir leaving with the High Council, he first agreed, "Yes," then blurted out, "but what of Ivan and the battle?"

Nadir clenched his jaw, narrowed his eyes and glared at

the members of the High Council. Anders knew Nadir wanted to discuss the events as badly as he did, but his glance back at the shouting elves in the streets told Anders he didn't have a choice. "I need you to go to my office, the one where we attempted to learn the secrets to the sapphires, and find that diagram you drew. I, unfortunately, need to deal with this problem first," he motioned to the mob, then continued, "before we can talk. Just find the diagram and bring it to me. Its' extremely important; Ivan's life depends on it."

Anders' objections were silenced with that one statement. He nodded and motioned for Maija to follow him. He headed back to Zahara and climbed aboard once again. Before Nadir entered the court building, he called back to Anders, "I'll wait for you here."

Anders nodded and held tightly as Zahara took flight. He turned to make sure Raffa and Maija were close on their tail before steering toward Nadir's treehouse. The building wasn't far, but they couldn't get there in a timely manner if they walked. The crowd of elves would've been too much for them to take on.

Landing not far from the edge of the mob, Anders climbed down and rushed to the door. He held it open for Maija as she ran in past him. As Anders closed the door, she asked, "What diagram are we looking for?"

They climbed the stairs to the office where Nadir, Natalia and Ivan had attempted to decipher the drawing on the piece of paper. "The one I told you about, from Merglan's journal," Anders explained.

"I thought you wanted to decipher the code for your sword? Why does Nadir think it will save Ivan's life?" Maija asked.

"Learning the workings of these crystals could be the one sure thing we can do to reduce Merglan's powers to within reason; it could level the playing field if we knew how to use them." Anders saw her skeptical look and added, "By altering Merglan's crystals, we could cast a similar spell, but on a larger scale and without all of the rage."

"What rage?" Maija asked, pausing at the door to Nadir's office.

Anders flushed, his cheeks turning a shade darker. He had told Maija everything, except about the orcs and the uncontrollable rage that consumed him when he used the corrupt power. "I didn't mention it before because, well, because I'm still struggling with it and I didn't want you to be afraid."

"Rage?" Maija asked, pinching her eyebrows together in surprise.

Anders nodded, "When I used the energy from the crystal in Lazuran's pommel, it did something to me, something far stronger than the urges I feel to use it. I already told you I did a terrible thing, but Merglan's influence, it corrupted me, and I felt what it was like to be him. I felt the rage and hatred that drives Merglan to do the things he does, and I," Anders paused, his chin quivering, "I liked it at the time."

He watched as Maija's face turned from baffled to scared, just as she'd looked when she saw that he was drawn to Lazuran. Anders thought she might run, seeing the monster growing inside him, but she didn't. He could tell she was at a loss for words, so he continued, "The sword, it whispers to my subconscious, trying to get me to use it again, but I'm afraid of what it might do to me if I answer.

I can't let the corruption tear me away from the two I love most. That's why I need you, you and Zahara are the only ones who can pull me out when I start to lean in. That's the difference between Merglan and me. You are the reason why I'm not already going insane as he did."

Anders saw something come over Maija altering her expression from fear to one of joy. She smiled. Anders eyed her in confusion as she reached out and grabbed hold of his hand. Shaking his head, he asked, "Why are you smiling? I just told you that I think Merglan is trying to make me into what he has become. That's why he fed me his rage."

"I'm not smiling because Merglan's trying to influence you, I'm smiling because you just told me," she trailed off, grinning.

Anders shook his head slightly trying to see what she was getting at, then it hit him. His mouth gaped, and he realized what words he'd chosen to describe her and Zahara. As she waited for him to speak, he turned and pulled the door to the office open, saying quickly, "Yeah, well we've got to find that diagram. Ivan's life could be at stake." Wincing at how poorly he'd handled the situation, Anders glanced awkwardly at Maija.

She'd twisted the bottom of her shirt around her finger and when Anders' eyes moved to look at what she was doing, she quickly brushed her shirt flat, and asked, "What did it look like?"

Refocusing on finding the diagram, he said, "It's a small piece of paper. It was a blank, torn from Merglan's journal. I drew the diagram on it. We were looking at it on one of these desks," he stepped toward one of the four desks in Nadir's office.

"Why didn't you just keep the journal," Maija asked, picking loose papers up by the stack and flipping through them.

"I only saw it once, and I had poured through that thing several times, so I thought maybe magic was involved. I didn't know whether it would disappear. That's why I copied it down on a blank page."

"That's what you were doing up so late that night," Maija said. Anders caught her eyeing him and shot her a quick grin.

"Here it is," Anders said, pulling the parchment from beneath several maps spread out across a desktop.

Handing it to Maija, he watched over her shoulder as she examined the sketch. After a moment, she rubbed her forehead, "Looks like gibberish to me."

When she handed it back to him, he folded it and tucked it into his side pocket. He glanced around the room to make sure there wasn't anything else he was forgetting to do, then looked at Maija. His gaze met hers, and he felt as if her amber eyes were speaking to him, telling him she would stay by his side no matter what. He felt a warmth welling inside him as their stare lingered, each waiting for the other to make the first move. In an instant, a serious look returned to Maija's eyes and Anders' mind turned to the dragons waiting outside at the edge of the angry crowd.

"What is it?" he asked.

"The mob," she said. "They've gone silent."

"It could be Nadir; let's get back to the court."

Anders led the way back down the flight of stairs and out of Nadir's home. Zahara and Raffa sat with their backs to the tree, watching the crowd. Grabbing Anders by the hand, Maija motioned for him to wait. Anders watched as she leaned her ear toward the mass of people.

"What is it?" he asked.

Shushing him with her finger, Maija observed with her remarkable hearing. "That elf from the High Council," Maija said. "He's addressing the crowd."

"Well, what are we waiting for?" Anders asked, moving toward Zahara. "We should go to the steps and hear what he has to say before we give this to Nadir."

"No," Maija said sternly, causing Anders to stop. "They aren't speaking kindly of you for leaving with the elves to fight Merglan. I think your presence there might fuel the crowd's reaction; things could become even more hostile."

"Really?" Anders asked. Maija shushed him again. He waited for several minutes while she observed and repeated important aspects of the Councilman's speech to the crowd. He gathered from what Maija told him, that the Council saw Nadir's choice to leave for battle as a rash decision. Nadir had taken nearly half the elven army with him, and now their kingdom was suffering gruesome attacks at the hands of their enemies. They blamed everything on Nadir and used the storm over the city as proof that even the magic had turned on them. The Council claimed that Nadir had acted outside his rank when he used his kingly authority before being properly crowned. Since he'd cause such grievous ramifications before his coronation, the Council was denying him the throne and withdrawing his command.

Once Maija had finished relaying the information to Anders, he heard the roar of the crowd resume. Cheers in support of the Council overpowered the "boos." Anders' heart sank when he realized his hopes for returning in full force to Southland had been squashed. With Nadir once again denied his birthright, he couldn't order the elven army into action and, from the sound of it, most of those in the street supported the Council's decision.

As the crowd began to disperse, Anders and Maija flew the short distance to the elven courthouse where members of the Council stood. Landing on the steps, Anders noted that the elves wearing red shirts lingered, holding their fists up toward him. He finally realized that they were elves loyal to Nadir. The red shirts were a show of support for their cause.

Without giving the members of the High Council a moment's notice, Anders and Maija rushed into the court building. They ran through the vast open hall, stopping to search for Nadir. Turning, Anders heard Nadir call down to them from above. Looking up, he saw his friend motioning for them to come upstairs. Anders followed Maija now, as she saw the way up the stairs to the balcony where he stood. Anders attempted to keep up at first but knew her elven speed was impossible for him to match. He caught up to them on the second-story landing. Nadir and Maija greeted each other for the second time.

"Come with me. We must talk in private," he said, walking briskly toward another room on the second floor. Closing the door after them, Anders turned to see Nadir latch it shut and look eagerly to his companions.

"Now, will you tell how the heck you ended up here without Ivan?" Nadir asked, stepping closer to Anders.

Anders then understood that Nadir had no idea that he and Ivan had faced Merglan alone. Anders explained what happened after Lageena transported them to the castle, wrapping up with his unexpected arrival with Zahara in Nagano, only to find Maija there with Raffagaun. As he hastily finished his summary, Anders asked, "But Nadir, how do you know this paper will save Ivan's life?"

Nadir described in greater detail how he led the retreat, his battle with Lageena, and her eventual death. He told them how he was forced to return with the dwarfs to gather more soldiers for their return. He told them how Natalia had stayed behind with Remli's daughter and Solomon to attempt a rescue, suspecting that Merglan was keeping Anders and Ivan prisoner in the Kingston castle. "I tried to reach her just now, but she's not responding," he said. "Last I talked to her, she was going to embark on her mission soon, but she doesn't know that you and Zahara made it out alive."

"And you think you can crack the code on this?" Anders asked, pointing to the parchment.

"I don't know the answer, but I think there's someone else here in the city who does," Nadir said, stroking his chin. "Follow me," he said as he exited the room. Both Nadir and Maija rushed ahead at superhuman speed.

Anders tried to follow. He caught up with Maija as she stood looking out the door and beyond the steps. He followed her gaze and saw Nadir, "What's he doing?"

"Informing his soldiers of his plan, those still willing to follow him that is," Maija said. "He told us to wait here."

Anders nodded, taking the opportunity to catch his breath.

When Nadir re-entered the building, Anders saw the armored elves move away from the steps, calling for the elves in red to gather around. "Nadir," he said. "Aside from the kurr and this storm building overhead, what's going on here?"

"Things changed while we were away, Anders," Nadir said. "I'm afraid my father's death and my reaction to pursue his killer caused a divide in our people's political views. I could feel it among our soldiers while we campaigned in Southland. It's why I didn't stay with Natalia, though I wanted to. Our commanding officers threatened my expulsion from the kingdom. I fear the High Council was influencing them even after they left the city. Members of my army, high-ranking officers felt their duty to the cause was complete when Lageena died. For them, vengeance drove them south with us."

"Even after seeing the effects Merglan's had over Southland?" Anders asked.

"It was that which drove them farther from it," Nadir said. "The High Council knows the ancient magic protecting our city will keep Merglan at bay, even if his kurr tear our nation apart. They want to start the draft for riders once more, forcing elves and non-bonded dragons to the task."

"Won't that weaken their magic?" Maija asked.

"Yes, it will," Nadir said. "That's why we haven't had a pairing system since the last war; the manufactured bonds will not hold against Merglan's power, but the Council thinks that with enough of them, we'll be able to outlast his storm. Whether they seek to stop him or wait out his reign by hiding in the capital until his eventual downfall, I can't say. If they force dragons to bond, their magic will indeed be weaker than if the bonding were to happen naturally like yours, Anders. Ivan was lucky in that his bonding wasn't forced. Yet even those who came out of that order of riders were slain by Merglan."

"So, we'll just rally the dragons to leave with us," Anders said. "Zahara and Raffa will make them see and they'll flee the city with us."

"Cedarbidge is under lockdown. No one in or out. I'm surprised you four got in at all," Nadir said.

"We came in through the riders' entrance," Anders said.

Nadir nodded, "I'd venture to guess that they're sealing that access as well, now that they've seen you were able to enter. I only got in because the powers sealing the place knew me as King. Now that the Council has suspended my rights, I won't have the authority on the city's magic that a king should have, which is why we need to get down to the prison cells before they change that magic as well."

"You mean we're going down there again?" Anders said, pointing to the trap door in the corner of the foyer.

Nadir nodded, "That's where we'll get the answers we need about this," tapping the diagram in his hand. "Now come on, we haven't much time."

CHAPTER EIGHTEEN

Soldiers at the Door

homas," Kirsten said, shaking her brother with her foot.

Rolling onto his side and groaning, Thomas said, "I'll be right there."

Kirsten scooted to the edge of the couch, extending her leg out to where Thomas lay on the floor. This time she jabbed him decisively in the ribs with her toe, "Thomas, get up!"

"Hey," Thomas said as he swept his elbow back, knocking Kirsten's foot away.

Kirsten met her brother's sleepy gaze with pointed intensity, "Thomas, I think there's someone outside."

Sitting up, Thomas yawned. Rubbing his eyes, he said, "It's probably Britt and Max."

"No," she warned in a hushed voice. "I can hear them talking." She slid off the couch and onto the floor, sitting next to her brother. "Listen," she hissed. Her eyes widened as the voices became more audible. The men seemed to be standing just outside the unusual treehouse. She watched her brother's expression change from sleepy and apathetic to ridged and alert.

"That's not Britt and Max," Thomas whispered.

Looking around the small living room, Kirsten asked, "Where's Bo?"

Following her search, Thomas shrugged.

Kirsten moved into a squat, her legs trembling uncontrollably, the room appeared to be moving and her head swam in a feverish daze. *Rotten goblins,* she cursed as she shuffled in a crouch toward the window, keeping one hand on the ground to maintain her balance. As she stopped under the living room window, she felt the morning sun warming her cheeks; it brought clarity to her mind. She rested for a moment, soaking up the sun's rays and feeling some strength return to her body. The strangers' voices sounded as though they were coming from behind the kitchen, an area she couldn't see from the living room window.

"Who are they?" Thomas asked as he stood, the blanket around him falling to the floor in a heap.

Pulling herself up to her full height using the windowsill, Kirsten again paused for a moment to find her balance on her weakened legs. After peering out through the glass, she turned to Thomas and shrugged, "I can't see them from here."

Leaning against the wall, Kirsten watched her brother walk lightly toward the kitchen. Along the edge of the windowpane, Kirsten could see the tree house's outer bark as it wrapped around to the kitchen wall before it rounding out of sight. Once Thomas disappeared into the kitchen, she focused on the tree's profile, hoping to catch a glimpse of whoever was out there.

After a moment, her curiosity won out, so she set out carefully from the window toward the kitchen. Placing each step with care, Kirsten moved slowly to avoid losing her balance. Her head swam from the lingering effects of the goblin's venom and she reached out to grip the table. Ever since she had awakened, her mind had remained foggy; it made her feel nauseous. Grasping the wooden surface seemed to allow her to ground her spinning mind to the fixed object. As she used her left hand to bear some of her body weight, she looked down at the table covered with books and unfolded maps. Her eyes slowly moved to her veins, raised and running like rivers of red through her arm. Her memories of the goblin attack and the pain that followed seeped back into her consciousness. She closed her eyes to concentrate on forcing them out. As she tried to calm her nerves, she glanced up to see Thomas drop down out of view of the kitchen window.

Seeing his sudden reaction, she frowned.

He explained in a whisper, "Soldiers."

"Whose?" Kirsten asked.

Thomas shrugged, "Don't know."

He rose slightly, hunching at the window to chance a look through the bottom of the glass, then quickly dropped out of sight for a second time.

Kirsten waited for an explanation.

Thomas moved toward her, crab-walking across the squeaky boards that lined the kitchen floor. "Those men out there are wearing the same armor as the soldiers who attacked Grandwood."

"Are you sure?" Kirsten asked. He nodded his response to which she added, "What are they doing here?"

"I don't know, but we'd better stay out of sight," Thomas said.

"Where's Bo?" she asked again, looking around the small home and not seeing any sign of him.

The men's voices grew louder. Kirsten could hear their metal armor clatter as they moved away from the kitchen. "They're walking to the front," she said.

"Do you think they'll come in?" Thomas asked.

Kirsten pointed to the small door that led down to the root cellar, "Down there, hurry."

Kirsten lagged behind Thomas as he quickly moved to the door and held it open. She crouched, but the sudden change in body position made her dizzy and caused her to falter. She felt Thomas' hand steady her as she stepped into the stairwell. Kirsten forced her legs to step far enough down the stairs to allow Thomas entry into the small space, and then she sat down. In a vanishing gap, the light from outside the cellar door disappeared as Thomas closed it behind them. The sudden darkness soothed her mind and she felt better until she heard the heavy footfalls at the front door and then the creaking of the door as it opened.

Kirsten sat in the dark, visualizing the ruthless soldiers entering the home. Hearing their boots sounded on the wood floor overhead, she followed them in her mind's eye as they moved into the house.

Their voices sounded clearly through the cellar door's thin paneling. It was clear that their native tongue was not Landish. From the sounds above, Kirsten could tell that the men had spread out, one on either side of the living room and a third walking through the middle of the room. Kicking through the mess on the floor and flipping over furniture in their way, Kirsten was grateful that they hadn't had time to clean Solomon's home. The ransacked state of the house made it appear as though no one was staying there. As the soldiers moved through the house, Kirsten wondered again where Bo had gone.

Hearing one of the soldier's heavy footsteps skiff to a stop on the other side of the cellar door, Kirsten covered her mouth in an attempt to silence her breathing. She pleaded to the darkness around her that the man wouldn't be curious about the cellar door and hoped that, instead, he had stopped to inspect something else. Holding her breath, she heard the handle to the cellar door clink. The door moved slightly, then rattled. She hoped Thomas was holding the door shut, but in the darkness, it was impossible to tell. Whatever was happening, it sounded like the door wasn't willing to open.

She heard the handle clink again and a breath later the click of boot heels on wood as the soldier resumed walking through the kitchen. Kirsten followed them with her imagination into the kitchen, then up the stairs and through Solomon's bedroom. Not hearing any struggle, she assumed Bo either wasn't in the house or that he, too, had found a good place to hide.

The clomping boots returned to the living room and Kirsten thought she heard two of them walk to the front door and stop. The soldiers at the door spoke to each other, or to someone else just outside. It was difficult to tell between the foreign language and their muffled voices. Then one of them raised his voice and called back into the house. Kirsten heard the third man's reply sounding from just outside the cellar door. The two other soldiers and their associate outside muttered to one another, then Kirsten heard the door to the house close leaving a lone soldier inside.

Wishing she could communicate with her brother, Kirsten sat in the darkness, waiting to hear what the soldier would do next. His feet shuffled near the wall and she could hear the tinkle of his armor as he moved. Then a hinge squeaked, followed by a sound of glass clinking glass. Her eyes widened when she heard the cork pop and a moment later the clash of the soldier's armor falling hard on the floor. The thudding shook the ground, echoing through the cellar and rattling the potion bottles in their case on the other side of the wall.

Kirsten waited several long moments to be sure she didn't hear any more movement before whispering to Thomas, "Did he just fall over?"

"Yeah," Thomas replied.

"Should we check?" she asked.

"What if he wakes up?" Thomas replied.

"I haven't heard him move yet," Kirsten said.

"Okay. I'll look."

Kirsten heard the handle to the door turn and a stream of light poured in through the crack, illuminating their stairwell. The small beam of light remained a sliver for several seconds, then grew as Thomas pushed the door open. Kirsten turned and saw her brother leaning halfway out into the room above.

He popped his head back inside and said with a smile, "He's completely out."

The wave of light made Kirsten's head start to spin again, but the idea that the soldier had just flopped onto the ground pulled her from her seat. Crawling the short way up the steep staircase, Kirsten emerged through the door cleverly hidden in the side of the wall. Seeing the soldier laying on his back with an uncorked glass bottle in his hand, she thought she knew what happened but wanted to investigate.

"Which one did he drink?" she asked as she watched Thomas crouch down next to the soldier's body. Kirsten wasn't expecting a precise response from her brother, but she couldn't help but ask. She watched as he quickly examined the man closely.

Reaching across the body, Thomas plucked the empty bottle from his hand and corked it. Standing, Thomas held out the yellow-stained bottle, "That's one of the bad ones; I'm not sure what it's called though."

Kirsten watched him place the bottle back on the rack in the cabinet and asked, "How bad?"

"I don't know. Max, Bo and Britt were the ones to figure that out, but it doesn't look like he'll be coming back from that," Thomas said, motioning to the soldier.

"Is he dead?" Kirsten asked, her head feeling slightly less clouded than it was before the soldiers entered the home. She watched her brother kneel and feel for a pulse.

"He isn't dead," Thomas said.

"Well, how long will he be like this?" Kirsten asked.

Just as she finished the question, the door flung open and Kirsten jumped in surprise. She instantly gathered her senses again when she saw Bo step into the room, breathing heavily.

Wide-eyed Kirsten leaned forward, placing her hands on her knees, her legs suddenly felt like jelly from the scare. She gasped, "Bo. It's only you."

"Where have you been? Did you see the soldiers?" Thomas asked.

"Yes," Bo said between breaths as he closed the door behind him. "I had to hide in the forest when I saw them, but after they left, I came back as soon as I could." Bo walked closer to stare down at the soldier lying unconscious on the ground. He nodded at the soldier and asked, "How did this happen?"

Kirsten straightened and pointed to the cabinet, "He took something from in there."

Eyebrows raised in surprise, Bo asked, "How did you get him to do that?"

"He did that to himself. We were in the cellar," Thomas answered. "I had to hold the door closed so they couldn't open it, but it proved to be a decent hiding spot. They were in and out pretty quickly, all except for this one."

The thought of being so close to having been taken prisoner again sent Kirsten's head spinning. The thing she feared most was being held in a cell day after day with no idea whether she would live to see her friends and family again.

"Kirsten," Bo said, stepping to her side. "Are you okay?"

Feeling Bo's strong arms catch her as she dipped backward, Kirsten worked to find her feet under her again.

"You're shaking," he said his hand resting on her back.

"I'm fine," Kirsten said. "I just need some food, I think."

Thomas moved to the kitchen and grabbed three dried apples Bo had brought up from the cellar the night before. Stuffing them into Kirsten's hand, he said, "Eat these."

As she ate, she listened to Thomas recount what transpired after they'd awakened. "Why were you outside?"

Thomas asked as Kirsten swallowed the last apple, feeling the dried fruit swelling in her stomach.

"My brother and Britt were supposed to be back at dawn," he said. "I was at the window watching for them, but didn't want to wake you, so I stepped outside. I waited near the front door as the sun rose and kept an eye on the tree line for their return. As I waited, I heard something to the effect of a large group of people marching. Like an army or something. So, I rushed to the tree line to get a better look at the trail. Keeping low and out of sight, I watched armored riders leading a troop of soldiers toward Brookside. When they'd passed, I started back to wake you two and that's when I saw the men down at the house. I was able to get back to the trees before they spotted me. Three of them went in, and one stayed outside. I wanted to rush down, but they came out of the house so quickly and left. I worried that you were being held captive or something by the one who stayed inside.

"This isn't good," Kirsten said.

"I'm sorry. Maybe there's something else from the cellar that would be better," Thomas said.

Kirsten shook her head, "No, the food was fine. I mean this situation. Bo's right, Britt and Max were supposed to be back a long time ago. What if something bad happened to them?"

"Max and Britt are more than capable of maneuvering their way around the soldiers. They're probably just waiting for the right opportunity to leave," Thomas said, sounding unsure.

"Max knows his way around the forests better than these soldiers do," Bo added. "Last night, just before we went to bed, Max told me that if anything bad were to happen and they didn't return, we were to meet at our foster parents' home. It's on the opposite end of Brookside, near the plains and just as remote. It's possible that we might be safer there."

"What about the fact that your parents hate Max?" Kirsten asked.

Bo's jaw slackened slightly, and he raised his brow as if she'd spoiled a secret.

"What, don't act like us knowing is a surprise. Max mentions it all the time," Kirsten said.

"They don't need to know Max is with us," Bo said.

"So, we should go there. Like now," Thomas suggested.

"What about her?" Bo asked.

Kirsten cleared her voice, "Excuse me. I'll decide if I'm able to go somewhere. And yes, I think we need to leave."

"But you're weak," Bo said.

"I'm feeling better now, thank you," Kirsten said, wiping the corner of her mouth. Her head still swirled, and the fog lingered, but not as thickly as before. She stepped forward and forced her legs to stop wobbling as she walked past Bo, "See, ready to go."

"What about him?" Bo nodded to the man lying on the floor.

"I have an idea," Thomas said with a grin.

As they prepared to leave the house, Kirsten grabbed one of the packs Max had brought up from Solomon's trunks in the cellar. Thomas and Bo stripped the soldier of his clothing and Thomas helped Bo put it on.

When Kirsten had finished filling the pack with what little food scraps they had left, she watched as Thomas fitted

Bo with the armor. "I guess you're our designated disguise man," she said when Thomas had finished suiting him.

"I guess that's what happens when you're the one whose body type best fits into these bulky suits," Bo said with a shrug.

Kirsten couldn't help admiring his physical appearance in the suit. He was larger than his brother and did look good as a man of action. Clearing her throat, she brought her gaze back to Bo's face, "How long will it take to us to get there?"

"That depends on how fast we can travel," he shrugged. "Could be a few hours or the whole day, depending on how well we're moving."

"Right then," Kirsten said moving toward the door. "Better get a move on."

Bo was the first to leave the house. Kirsten stood back as his armor-enhanced frame filled the space. She leapt back when she saw the group of soldiers outside making their way toward the home. Grabbing Thomas, they huddled against the wall, out of sight. "Where are these soldiers coming from?" she whispered, peeking through the gap in the open door and seeing Bo step out toward the men.

She watched as the group saw Bo come out of the house. Bo lifted an arm to them, and they turned, walking back toward the others waiting along the trail. Kirsten watched as Bo turned and circled to the backside of the house. He'd left the door open and Kirsten could see the troop begin to move again, making their way toward Brookside.

"What's going on?" Thomas asked.

"I think Bo signaled to them that the house had been searched, so the men turned around. Now it looks like they're moving on and I don't see Bo anymore," she told Thomas.

"I hope he didn't get swept up into their group," Thomas said.

They waited until the troop of soldiers moved out of sight. A few minutes later they found Bo waiting near the side of the tree. Kirsten handed the backpack to Thomas, "That was close. How many more times is this going to happen today, I wonder?"

"We'd better stick to the woods," Bo said. "The trail has been swarmed by a steady stream of soldiers all morning."

"Can we get to your folks' place easily?" Kirsten asked, eyeing the thicket of trees and heavy undergrowth in the woods surrounding the clearing where Solomon's home stood.

"I know a way," Bo nodded as he led them into the forest. Kirsten was glad to have Bo in disguise: then at least they could fake being his prisoners if need be. Bo led them down the main trail following the soldiers before cutting off into the woods. As she looked one last time at the trail to Brookside, she hoped Max and Britt really could evade such a large group of soldiers.

Chapter Nineteen

An Ugly Truth

 rabbing a fistful of grass in each hand, Max pulled himself up onto the bank. Out of the water, he rested belly down, while his legs drifted in the languid current. Lifting his head slowly, he chanced a glimpse over the brook's edge. As he looked up, Britt joined him, sliding on her stomach and remaining motionless as they stilled themselves in the lush reeds along the shore. Keeping his eyes fixed on the horizon, Max examined the best route to their next destination, the millhouse. Lurking along the bank just upstream of the watermill, they lay half in the water as Max sought to outmaneuver the soldiers.

After their near capture in Brookside, they now returned to the seaside town in hopes that the men looking for them would continue their search deeper into the surrounding forest and not back in town where all of the fuss had begun. The armed men in uniform continued to patrol the outer limits of Brookside, but luckily for Max and Britt, they were focusing their efforts on land. None of them had thought to look in the shallow brook as the two drifted past their guards.

Max slid down the bank and into the water once again,

Britt following. He signaled to her that they would keep going downstream a little farther. He admired how this captain handled the insurmountable pressure, keeping her cool in the face of their enemy, more so than he had been able to. He had almost broken off from their hiding place in the tree, giving in to his instinct to run, but Britt's steady demeanor inspired him to keep still. If she hadn't been with him, he would've run. If he had run, the three soldiers they'd met on the trail would've captured him.

With the millhouse waterwheel in sight, Max led Britt past several homes and outbuildings lining the brook's edge. They stayed low to the surface as they swam, hoping nobody within view of the brook would see them as they passed by. Max's eyes bounced between either side of the bank, trying to discover whether anyone could see them through an open window or gap in the closely developed homes. If they did, he would know when they should run.

As they approached the churning waterwheel, Max took two strokes to his left and drifted in behind the wheel. He hoped the mill's splashing would mask any noise they might make climbing out of the water. As he pulled into the disturbed water behind the wheel, Max eyed the shoreline. He could see the brook bending to the left. At the water's edge, just before it arched out of view, he noticed the profile of someone kneeling at the water's edge. As Britt came in behind him, Max decided that the woman washing clothes in the distance wasn't a threat. Most likely, she wouldn't notice them as her back angled toward them. Her head was down in concentration on her task. Max carefully crawled out of the water, checking first to see if anyone was standing nearby.

He could hear Britt close behind him, the sound of the water pouring from their clothes concealed by with the splashing wheel. Max crouched as he advanced swiftly from the shore to the back of the mill's brick building. With the flat of his back against the wall, he quickly checked to either side to make sure no one had seen him sneak between the wheel and millhouse. He felt the water collecting in his sleeves and pant legs as Britt joined him. The two stared at one another for a brief moment. They'd made it this far, yet both knew their escape from the soldiers had just begun. Max had to lead them away from town unseen and unrecognized, out to Tony's house where he and Bo planned to meet if anything were to go wrong.

Max shuffled to the left and looked out from behind the waterwheel at the far bank. The brook's size had swollen since they'd entered it in the forest, but despite the additional flow of the smaller tributaries, the channel was no more than five yards wide. With no soldier in sight along the opposite bank, Max popped his head around the corner. He could see people in the streets, walking to work and going about their business as if this was an ordinary day. Not seeing any soldiers between the two buildings and none in the street immediately in front of them, Max let Britt know with a quick tap that they needed to make their next move.

Stepping out from the corner, he stayed close to the brick wall as he walked closer to the street. His saturated pants sloshed with each step; the sound seemed to echo in his ears, mostly, he was sure, because he so desperately wished to remain unnoticed. The few people passing in the street paid no attention to him, so he continued. Following a woman and two children as they passed by the alley between the two buildings, Max noticed a gentleman on the opposite side of the road watching him. He hesitated, wondering if he should turn back. Deciding that returning to the water wasn't any less strange to the man, Max continued as if he hadn't noticed that he was being observed, hoping the man wouldn't call them out.

At the edge of the building, Max looked both ways before leading Britt around front. They drew attention as they walked in soaking wet clothes, swords hanging from their belts. They moved quickly onto the wooden decking. Max hoped that if they moved with confidence, the people who saw them wouldn't question what they were doing.

Max quickly stepped into the millhouse, Britt hurrying in and closing the door behind them. Britt instantly began searching the mill. As she walked around the millstone, he leaned against the door so they'd know if anyone was trying to enter. Though it was harvest season, Max knew people didn't bring in their grain every day. The community tried to use the mill efficiently by milling their grain in large quantities; Max hoped today wasn't a milling day.

Seeing Britt's brief search end with no result, Max pulled off his wet shirt to wring it out.

"What's the plan?" Britt asked.

Max shrugged while he twisted the water from his clothes, "I honestly didn't know if we were going to make it this far, but now that we have, well, we can't stay here all day. That guy across the street watched us come in here and if he doesn't come looking for us, someone else might." Britt frowned at this seeming lack of a plan, so he added, "The soldiers are most active right now, right?"

Britt nodded.

"They're not going to have all of their troops searching for us, that's just a waste of their time. So, I say we dry out a bit, hide in town for a few hours, then slip past the soldiers this evening and move to Tony's."

"Why not back to Solomon's?" Britt asked.

"I told Bo that if anything bad were to happen during this venture our backup plan would be to meet at our foster home."

"What if they didn't leave? Maybe they're waiting for us to come back?"

"Those soldiers were marching down the trail that led right past Solomon's house. When we didn't show up, I bet they went out looking for us, learned of the soldiers' presence and left. Bo's smart enough to avoid bringing them into town. He'd use the game trails we know of to move through the forest. They'll be there waiting for us, I'm sure of it."

Britt nodded, "Okay, but if they're not there?"

"Then we'll use the cover of the forest to get back to Sol's," Max said.

"We'll need a disguise if we're going to stay in town part of the day. I don't see any clothes in here," Britt said looking around the millhouse once more.

Max stepped into the open room, double-checking to make sure it was empty. He'd been in this building many times and knew there was a maintenance room. Locating it in the far corner, he searched through the contents inside. He remembered that on his last visit to the mill, he'd seen members in the community who were sensitive to the grain's dust wearing cloaks to cover their skin while operating the mill. Max found the milling coats hanging on the back wall.

Handing one of the long-tailed coats to Britt, he grabbed another for himself. Using the coats to cover up, Max and Britt wrung out their pants and shirts as best they could. Tying them around the detached mill shaft, they worked to dry their clothes. When Max put his clothes back on, they clung to his skin, still damp. He shrugged when Britt looked at him, then slipped the black mill coat on over his damp shirt, flopping the hood over his head as he moved toward the front door.

Cracking it open, Max looked out through the narrow gap. His eye instantly went to the older gentleman who'd been watching them before. The stranger was no longer stationed at the storefront. He instantly began to worry that the elderly man had gone to alert the soldiers. Before turning to inform Britt of this fear, a thought crossed his mind. Max pulled the door open and stepped onto the deck, walking with purpose as he led Britt out into the street. Keeping his head down and trying not to draw attention, Max angled toward the storefront where the older man had been standing. Stepping up onto the deck and opening the door, he glanced back to the street and saw that people continued to move without taking notice of them. Ushering Britt inside, he closed the door.

Max stood alongside Britt as he studied the shelves and racks lined with goods. Max hadn't been in this building before but knew it to be one of three general stores in Brookside. They carried average everyday items townspeople might need. The two stood alone in the store, confirming Max's suspicion that the owner was the man who'd been watching them and he'd likely gone to warn others of strangers lurking around the millhouse. Britt started searching and Max quickly caught on that she was looking for something to help with their disguise. They found a small selection of clothing near the back of the shop. Formal shirts and pants were neatly folded and displayed on shelving with racks of dresses hanging nearby. Rifling through the options, they decided that formal wear would only make them stand out more than their current outfits.

"Where do you suppose the shop owner is?" Britt asked.

Max's thoughts returned to the possibility that the owner might return with a handful of armed soldiers at his side. He walked to the big bay windows at the storefront to take a look and instantly dropped, nearly falling to the ground. Two soldiers now stood on the front deck facing away from him. Max crouched and quickly slid between two stools at the shop's bar top-style counter. He glanced back to be sure Britt had seen his reaction. She now crouched behind the rack of dresses, well hidden from the soldiers.

The soldiers stood side by side with the shop owner, obviously watching the millhouse. The older gentleman raised his hand, pointing at the brick building while bobbing his head. He appeared to be telling the soldiers what he'd seen. Max took the opportunity to move away from the stool while they were engaged in conversation and walked hunched over to Britt's hiding place.

"He saw us coming up from the brook. He's telling the soldiers that we're still in there," Max whispered.

"Let's get out of here," Britt said.

Max nodded and as the soldiers stepped into the street to advance on the millhouse, Britt and Max moved to the back door and slipped out just as the store owner entered.

The last Max saw of the older man, he was standing inside but looking out the windows in anticipation of witnessing an arrest.

Max and Britt jogged down the alley and emerged into another street. Keeping their heads low and walking quickly, they crossed the intersection and scooted into the opposite alleyway. Max hadn't noticed people staring at them as he had when the old man was watching, but that didn't mean no one was suspicious. Nudging Britt, Max pointed to a ladder in the alley, then to the roof above. Before she could reply, he was placing the ladder against the side of the single-story building and starting to climb.

"Wait," Britt said when she reached the flat roof. Max stopped abruptly. "Won't they see this and wonder?" she asked pointing to the ladder.

Max nodded, "Yeah, I guess they would."

"I'll knock it over," she said bending over to push the ladder down.

"No, don't," Max said walking back across the roof. "If it crashes, someone might notice that we came up here."

"Then what should we do with it?" she asked.

"Let's haul it up," Max said.

Britt considered this for a moment, then nodded.

Together they pulled the ladder up the side of the building and onto the roof. Handling the long ladder was awkward and for a moment Max thought someone in the adjacent street might notice wooden rungs sticking up into the air above the storefront's large rectangular sign. To his relief, he didn't see anyone in the street below gawking at them when they'd finished.

"Well, so much for our plan to use a disguise," Britt

said as they crouched behind the building's sign. The wooden structure stood a couple of feet taller than they did and provided good cover for them to watch those in the streets below.

"Oh well," Max frowned. "At least this is working."

"Hiding on top of a building?" Britt asked.

Max nodded, then turned his attention to the surrounding buildings. As he looked across the street and down the alley they'd just fled, he recognized the back of the general store and to the right, the millhouse. "Hey, look, you can see the top of the millhouse from here. I can just see the top of the door. It's open." With a chuckle Max said, "It looks like they didn't find what they were looking for, and there, the soldiers are walking back out."

"I've never had to hide so often in my life," Britt said. "Usually we face our enemies head-on."

"Me neither," Max replied, moving around to take cover behind the store's sign. "Usually when I climb trees, go swimming, or scale buildings it's not to hide from deadly men."

"You did this before for fun?" she asked.

"You didn't?" he responded, eyeing Britt with a grin.

Britt shook her head, "No, on my island we wrestled and fought with sticks for fun."

"What about the ocean, you never went swimming for fun?" he asked.

"We swam to hunt fish," Britt said. "Most of my happiest moments were learning to sail."

"That's a warrior's culture, I guess," Max said with a sigh.

"You could have used some warrior culture in your

upbringing, instead of having fun all the time," Britt said.

"It wasn't fun all the time," he said solemnly. "Tony wasn't exactly the best father figure for Bo or me."

"What's the deal between you two? Everything you say about him is terrible, but he took you into his family, didn't he? How bad can he really be?" Britt asked.

"He never wanted me, or Bo for that matter. It was his wife who took pity on us and brought us in."

"Why?" she asked.

Max sat down, leaning his head against the wooden sign, "Is there any chance I can convince you to drop it and never ask about it again?"

Britt grinned, shaking her head, "No way."

"Alright, but I'll give you fair warning. This story ends with me meeting you, so don't feel too bad for me, it's got a good ending."

"Oh good," Britt chuckled as she sat down next to him. "I was worried you might stop joking during this story."

"It's Merglan's fault really," Max began.

"What? How's that possible?" she asked.

"Near the end of The War of Magicians there was a power struggle over the empty throne in Southland. By this time Merglan was spending most of his time building his armies in Eastland and attacking the elves and dwarfs. Tony and Elaine, his wife, my stepmother, were, at the time, very much involved in the war effort, fighting for the free nations. Tony was in an army camp readying to participate in a raid into Kingston and take back control of the capital. It was common knowledge then that anyone still left in the castle was working for Merglan.

"When the army raided Kingston, the freedom fighters

took over the castle, killing anyone who resisted, or so Tony said. My birth parents worked in the castle. I don't know if they were working for Merglan or had been there before him and were just surviving, but when Tony and the army invaded, my parents were killed along with the others working in the castle. I was just a toddler, so I barely remember anything about it. Before my parents died, they managed to take out their killers to save Bo and me.

"During a sweep of the castle, Tony and Elaine, who at the time was nursing the wounded, found us. We were covered in blood and crying near our dead parents. Elaine wanted to spare us, but Tony refused. He nearly killed us right then and there, but her crying stopped him. He let us live and she took us in as if we were her own. I don't remember much of it and Bo doesn't recall anything from that time. Basically, that set us off to a bad start and Tony never liked us afterward either. He blamed everything on me, even the deaths of those he loved. It wasn't all bad though. Elaine loved and treated Bo and me the same way she did her own. Their oldest son, Evans, took a while to warm up to us but, eventually he accepted us, too. When Elaine had the two girls, well, Bo and I were brothers in their eyes. But Tony, he never did love us. When I took Bo with me to the Grandwood Games, Tony told us we should not bother to return, but we did at which time we stole some of his horses," Max sat in silence until Britt replied.

"That's so sad," she said.

"Yeah," Max replied quietly.

"I'm sorry."

"I'll be curious to see if he blames all of this on me, too," Max said, spreading his hands.

"How could he?" Britt asked.

Max shrugged, wiping an errant tear from his eye.

"You don't have to see him," Britt said. "We'll just meet Bo, Kirsten and Thomas, and get out of here. Tony doesn't have to know you're with us."

"Yeah. We'll see," Max said.

Max and Britt whiled away the afternoon on the rooftop, drying their clothes by sitting in the sun and waiting for those searching the streets to abandon their hunt. In the hours that followed their flight from the mill, they'd seen soldiers running in and out of stores and homes, questioning people in the surrounding area. Soldiers systematically searched the blocks surrounding the mill, but never thought to search the rooftops. Having not seen or heard a soldier for several hours, Max grew restless and ready to move. Deciding it would be better to remain on the rooftops as long as possible, Max thought up another use for the ladder.

Describing what he had in mind, Max convinced Britt to hold the end of the ladder firmly in place while he bridged the gap between buildings. Using the ladder like a plank, Max carefully walked across the rungs and onto the neighboring rooftop. Once in position, he held his end while Britt followed. They slowly made their way from one roof to the next, choosing their timing to cross when no one stood in the narrow alleys. Nearing the end of their options for rooftops to access, Max was glad to see the sun beginning to set. Wanting to stay off the ground a little longer, they decided to take a chance crossing to a two-story building that would connect them to another string of single-story roofs and bring them closer to the edge of town. Holding the ladder in place on the way down proved more difficult, but they passed the hurdle without compromising their position.

By the time they'd reached the last building on the block, the soldiers appeared to have taken their posts for the evening, greatly increasing their guard on the town's perimeter from the night before. Max and Britt watched, waiting for the most opportune moment to climb down and escape. For almost an hour Max observed the soldiers' movements, taking note of any consistencies in their behavior. The soldiers moved several times in that hour. After their third shift in position, Max knew their pattern wouldn't likely change. The soldiers walked five blocks to their right, stopped, stood to watch for twenty or so minutes, then walked again to the right, five more blocks. They circled the town, each soldier having to watch a new section before they grew tired of it. As he thought about the strategy, Max found it a clever way to keep them from getting complacent or sleeping on the job, but there was a flaw: it was predictable.

Though five blocks didn't create much of a gap in time or space for them to escape unnoticed, it was far enough to create an opportunity for the soldiers to slip up. If Max and Britt could create a distraction that caused several soldiers to rush away from their posts, they'd get the break they needed. Max just needed a diversion. He voiced his thoughts to Britt and they developed a plan. He could toss a spare brick they'd found on the roof through the window of a neighboring shop and create a disturbance loud enough that two soldiers might go to check it out. Max gauged the distance to the building across the street and thought he could throw the heavy stone that far.

Squatting on the edge of the building with a brick in his hand, Max waited for the moment when the soldiers would move to their next post. He assumed that's when they could be caught the most off-guard and susceptible in a response to a disturbance.

"They're moving," he heard Britt whisper, alerting him to act.

Taking aim, Max hefted the brick with all his might, hoping that when he released it, the stone would sail to its intended target. He watched as the brick flew down at the ground-level window. His heart sank when he saw that the brick would miss the mark. A man stood in the street just outside the building. He was bent over, evidently searching for something he'd dropped. Max hadn't seen him in the dim light before he'd thrown. He had been too focused on the window.

His eyes widened at the brick's trajectory as it arched down, dropping toward the man's back. As the brick careened into him, the man cried out with a horrific scream. The desperate cry echoed through the street, and Max winced with guilt. He hadn't intended to harm an innocent person, but once he'd tossed it, the brick was no longer in his control.

Max crouched, still cringing at the pain he'd just caused the stranger. The man's scream, though, drew three soldiers away from their posts. They rushed toward the scene with their blades drawn. Britt slid the ladder over the side and Max hopped away from the edge of the building, wanting to shout an apology to the man. He followed Britt down the ladder, lowering it to the ground before they ran off into the woods.

Max crashed through the thicket of trees, moving deep enough into the cover of the forest to remain out of sight of those in town, but close enough to the edge that they wouldn't miss the trail leading out to Tony's place.

Not stopping, Max and Britt sprinted until they reached the trail. Max slowed to a walk, then leaned against the trunk of a nearby tree. Heaving, he said, "I can't believe I did that."

Britt shook her head, "Me neither. You really hit that guy, right in the back."

Max wanted to laugh, but couldn't. He'd just pegged a man he didn't know with a brick. "I can't believe that happened. I swear I didn't mean to hit him."

"It worked," Britt said. "You got their attention. I mean you really nailed him."

Max cringed again, pushing off the tree and standing tall, "I really did just hit him, right in the back. I wanted to apologize so badly, but couldn't."

"I know. We had to leave or be caught," Britt said.

"I hope he understands," Max said looking back toward town. "But we'll never know."

"Is this the trail to Tony's?" Britt asked, pointing to the path.

Max nodded, "We should slow our pace down. We don't want to run into soldiers again."

"At least we'll have weapons this time," Britt said placing a hand on the broadsword still hanging at her side.

Max nodded and started walking toward the Bareback Plains. They walked along the edge of the trail, close to the brush in case they needed to hide at a moment's notice. As the stars grew brighter against the darkening sky, Max and Britt moved farther away from the forest's edge and closer to the rolling grasslands.

Stopping on a grass-covered hill, Max looked out over the log home where he'd grown up. Candles burned in the windows, illuminating the interior of the small country house. Max could see movement and wondered how his foster family was handling the occupation. Based on the shadows moving inside, he knew they were still alive, but he had no way of knowing if they'd undergone any hardships or raids like the rampage through Solomon's home.

As they approached the house, Max prepared himself for his encounter with Tony. He stopped on the trail just outside the yard. Britt continued past him for several steps, then turned when he didn't follow.

"What's wrong, Max?" she asked walking back to him.

Max shook his head, "I don't know that I can do this." He moved his gaze from the yellow window to Britt's face, "I don't know that I can face him again. I'm afraid of what he might do."

Britt took Max by the hand and said, "I understand if you don't want to see him, but we should check to see if Bo and the others are here."

"We could look through the windows?" Max suggested, eyeing them carefully.

"Yeah," Britt said. "If that's what you're comfortable with. We can just look to see if they're inside."

Max inhaled, gripping the sword handle at his side while gathering his courage, "Okay. Let's do this."

He walked slightly behind Britt as they approached the house, his heart racing at the thought of what Tony might do to him. Though he had protection, he knew Tony had more experience with a sword. The last thing Tony had said to him was to never return or he'd make sure Max regretted it. In this situation, though, Max felt he had no choice.

They walked carefully up the trail toward the house. Max kept his gaze fixed on the yellow glow in the window. He saw a shadow move across the windowpane and hesitated. Focusing, he thought the build of whoever it was stood broader than anyone in his family. The dark outline of the person's shoulders was too bulky to be Tony's or Bo's.

He moved faster toward the window and from a safe distance, he could see inside. He stopped, gripping Britt's wrist and bringing her to a halt as well. Max recognized the colored armor that the soldiers from town wore. His heart sank as they stared at the soldier standing in Tony's home. Max's brain worked to make sense of what he was seeing. Why would there be a soldier in their home? Maybe Tony joined their army? That didn't make sense, though, because he had devoted his earlier years to fighting for his family's freedom.

"They're in danger," Max said, turning to Britt.

Britt drew her sword from its scabbard and said, "Let's do something about it."

Max gritted his teeth and pulled the broadsword from his belt, "Follow me." He snapped into action, springing toward the house with a quick stride. He stayed ahead of Britt as he ran around to the front door, then stopped. He stared at the handle, breathing rapidly and mentally preparing for his attack on the soldier inside. Britt bobbed at his side, flexing her grip on the sword handle, ready to join the fight. Max grabbed the door and pushed it in, bolting through the doorway with his sword held out front. He shouted as they charged in, the people in the room turning and shrieking in surprise.

Max halted when he saw the frightened faces of Thomas and Kirsten looking up from the family table. His eyes moved to the armored soldier, his brother's face looking back from the metal suit. In an instant, the shouts turned to sighs and eventually to laughter as they all realized who everyone was.

"Damnation, Max!" Bo said with a wide grin while stomping across the room. "I thought you two were going to need to be rescued for sure."

"It's good to see you, too," Max said, lowering his sword and wrapping his brother in an embrace.

"What happened to you guys?" Kirsten asked, rising to give Britt and Max a hug.

"Yeah, we've been worried sick," Thomas added.

Relieved, Max and Britt offered their friends a proper greeting. "Before we get into that," Max started. "Where's the family?"

Bo shook his head with a frown, "They aren't here. They must've left when the occupation began."

Max nodded, "Tony wouldn't stand for the soldiers being here. That makes sense."

"We heard what happened between you two and your family," Kirsten said, placing her red-streaked hand on Max's shoulder.

"Kirsten," Thomas said. "You don't need to bring that up."

Max sighed, "No, it's okay. You all know now. It's ugly, but true. I just hope he's looking after Elaine and the family."

Max took a seat at the table, the others joining him and they took the opportunity to recount the events that had occurred since they'd parted ways.

CHAPTER TWENTY

Into the Storm

losing the door behind them, Anders drew Lazuran from its sheath. The dank, eerie darkness of the vaulted elven jail brought him right back to the last time he'd been there with Ivan, his father. Anders tried to recall the vocal command Ivan had used to set the torches ablaze. As Anders stepped down onto the first level below ground and investigated the black space where numerous corridors branched out away from the stairwell, he could feel his magic being suppressed, which is why he felt the need to produce Lazuran. He couldn't shake the image of a bloodthirsty fairnheir bounding through the gloom as it had on their last visit to the prison to rescue Nadir. The uneasiness he felt was obvious as he asked with a quivering voice, "Nadir, how do we light the torches?"

Repeating Nadir's words spoken in Elvish, Anders had little understanding of the words' true meaning. Despite his lack of understanding of the elves' native tongue, Anders instinctively picked up on the magical emphasis on each syllable as he spoke. Suddenly flames ignited torches, moving rapidly down each of the hallways. Anders held Lazuran in a two-handed grip, knees bent and ready to bear an attack of the hound-like creature they'd narrowly escaped before. When the light revealed that the corridors were empty, he straightened, lowering his blade.

"What is this place?" Maija asked.

"This is the most secure and tightly restricted prison in the world," Nadir said sweeping his right arm out as he headed into the left-branching hallway.

"We should be careful. This may be the most secure prison in Kartania, but if something escapes from its cell, it stays down here. Ivan and I were attacked by a fairnheir when we came for you, Nadir. If someone or something let that creature out, there could be more escapees wandering the halls," Anders said, hustling to keep up with Nadir.

"If it's so secure how were we able to just waltz in like that?" Maija asked.

"I thought the same thing before," Anders said. "There are varying levels of security inside the prison. They increase the deeper you go. The magic on each level senses the intent of whoever accesses it. In this case, Nadir accessed the first level and the magic within granted him entry."

"We keep the less dangerous criminals on this first level. How a fairnheir ended up here I'm not entirely sure. Those beasts are usually caged at least three floors down. The more logical reasoning for seeing one here would be that the magic guarding the floor saw you and Ivan as a threat and created a replica to chase you out. At any rate, the more severe the crime, the deeper the prisoner is held and the more secure the magic becomes," Nadir explained.

"If the prison did create that hound to attack us, it should've disappeared once the magic found you innocent of your crime," Anders continued. As they approached the area where Nadir had been held, Anders remembered the girl who'd stopped the creature, mid-attack, with magic. Anders could hardly use his senses to find Nadir, much less cast a spell strong enough to stop a fairnheir in midair. "Are we looking for that girl?" he asked, eyeing Nadir.

"What girl?" Maija asked.

"That woman," Nadir corrected. "The one in the cell next to mine, yes. She's Norfolk and might be our best resource for translating this diagram. She's been down here for over a century, you know, but she doesn't look it."

As they approached the ancient woman's cell, Anders could hear the slow rasp of her breathing. Slowing, he held his arm out, indicating for Maija to stay back. He and Nadir stepped into view of the Norfolk woman's jail cell. He watched, still gripping Lazuran, as he knew his magic would be of little use to him here. Last time they'd met, the woman had saved him, but he didn't trust someone with so much power who'd also been imprisoned here. Looking through the iron bars, Anders could see the small, childlike woman sitting on her hands in the corner of the sealed room. Lifting her head and shaking her stringy, blond hair from her piercing blue eyes, she stared back at Nadir and Anders.

"Hello there," Nadir said. "My name is King Nadir. Not long ago I sat next to you in that cell there." Anders followed Nadir's finger as he pointed to the empty cell. Holding the small woman's attention, he continued, "The state of our world is in chaos and we seek your help."

The woman Anders had so easily mistaken for a child, rose on spindly legs. Anders tried to see her as a haggard old woman, but couldn't; she hadn't a single wrinkle on her gangly body. She appeared to be no more than ten years old, yet Nadir had told Anders that she'd been down there longer than he'd been alive, and Nadir was almost one hundred years old. Anders wondered if the Norfolk and elves were distantly related, due to the fact they both had extended lifespans and aged much more slowly than humans or dwarfs. The woman walked swiftly to the cell door. Anders stepped back, raising his sword defensively. He'd seen what kind of power she could wield even in this magically restrictive place.

Wrapping her hands around the iron bars that caged her in, the woman spoke with a lilting childlike voice, "And what might the King of Elves need me for? Has the death of his father left him with no allies up above?"

Anders saw Nadir twitch at the mention of his recently deceased father, "Don't act like you know details about what's happening above. I know you could hear when I learned the news of my father for the first time. We need your help translating a delicate document, one that could alter the course of the war."

"Oh, but I do not pretend. I know that what you have is so important that as King, with your authority stripped and your reputation in question, you have no faith that your fellow Council members would allow you to carry out your plan," she stopped, pressing her face against the cell door. Anders' confidence that those bars were doing anything to keep her locked in began to slip.

Nadir shifted, holding the paper up to the cell bars. He showed her Anders' drawing, "I didn't come to play mind games. Can you tell us what this means?"

Anders watched as the woman's youthful eyes left Nadir and to consider the paper he was holding. Taking her time to examine the diagram, she didn't respond for several minutes.

Nadir asked again, shaking the paper impatiently, "Do you know what this means?"

She nodded slowly, "Of course I know what it means, child. I was the one who plotted this sequence out in the first place."

Anders' heart leapt and his mind raced with questions as to how this was possible, but before he could utter a word, Nadir responded, "Tell me how it works."

She wagged her finger at him, "Not just yet. I want something in return for this information."

"Name it. Name your price and whatever it is, I'll get it for you. As long as I've the power, I'll reward your knowledge," Nadir said.

The childlike woman pulled away from the cell door and said, "Release me from this prison and I'll tell you everything you need to know."

Nadir stepped forward, but Anders caught him by the forearm, "How do you know she's telling the truth?"

"Yeah," Maija said, stepping into view. Anders shot a glance at her, but she ignored him and asked the woman, "How do we know you're actually who you claim to be?"

The Norfolk woman folded her skinny arms across her chest and said, "It doesn't matter who I claim to be, child. They both know I have power beyond their understanding and the King here has run out of options."

Anders saw Maija's expression sour at the response. She turned to Anders and Nadir, "Why should we trust her? She's in prison. Obviously, she wasn't a good person if she was locked up in here."

"I was put in here," Nadir said, giving her a questioning glance.

"Yeah, but that was different," Anders said, defending Maija.

"Was it?" Nadir asked. "She was imprisoned by my father, as was I. She started out many levels down and, on good behavior, she's been moved to the top floor. What's that got to say about her character?"

"That just means she wants out and has the system figured out so she can shorten her sentence," Anders argued.

"The system doesn't let you switch floors unless you're deserving," Nadir said. "It's an ancient magic that can judge a person's character to determine if he or she is good or evil."

"I don't know," Anders said, looking to the youthful elder. "Something about this doesn't feel right."

"Your senses are suppressed, that's probably what you're feeling," Nadir said.

Anders brushed aside the suggestion and asked, "What did she mean when she said that you're out of options?"

"She means I have to free her. It's the only way we might be able to deplete Merglan's strength enough to make him vulnerable. I can't stay here in this city with the Council dictating my every move. You saw how the people reacted to the High Council's decision; they've disowned me. I've lost control of my people. If we're going to fight this war, I'll have to leave Cedarbridge, possibly for good."

"And she's the only person we know who can teach us how the crystals are manipulated," Anders said, realizing they'd been forced to make this move by the destructive political workings of the High Council.

"So, we're actually going to break her out of here?" Maija asked.

Anders shrugged and Nadir nodded.

"Before we do, I'd like to know what crime she committed. I'd like to know who we're dealing with," Maija said.

"Smart girl," the woman commented.

The pitch of her voice sent a chill down Anders' spine. He didn't like the way she kept speaking to them as if they were children. He knew she was much older than they were, but she didn't appear so.

"Nadir is correct, I was captured and kept here by his father, King Asmond. It was years before Nadir was born, back when Asmond and Nadir's mother were still together. In those days, the Order of Riders frequented Northland for my people's notorious wisdom and tutelage. The Norfolk and riders were growing closer, forming alliances outside the elf's control. Asmond saw us as a threat. It wasn't until he discovered our involvement with the true form of magic that he named us heathens. The magic borne between a dragon and its bonded rider was how elves, humans and dwarfs were able to use this energy, but we Norfolk knew the dragon's power could be harvested elsewhere.

"As one of the leaders in discovering the dragons' true source of magic, I was on the brink of tapping its resources when Asmond learned of our studies. He and some of his riders wanted to keep this knowledge a secret from the world, so he came after us. Thinking he was doing Kartania justice by limiting those who could discover magic to only those who bonded with dragons, creatures so noble and beloved by elves, he locked me away deep in this magical prison. Here I am now and look at all the good his decision did the world. All of the greatest power is now held in the hands of a select few. Now a single rider has used his power to control the world and he seeks to turn dragons against the other races. If non-magical creatures wish to stop the storm that's brewing, they'll need the secrets of my research to defend themselves."

Anders stood in awe, his mouth gaping at her story.

"Is that true?" Maija asked, looking to Anders.

He shrugged, "I'm just now starting to get used to the magic I was gifted. I have no idea about its history or implications."

"Asmond probably removed all documentation of us from the annals of Kartania's history," the woman said.

"How do we get her out of here?" Maija asked.

Anders was surprised by Maija's sudden change of heart about releasing the woman. He waited as Nadir called on the jail's magic. The white sphere of justice appeared in front of them, the same one that Ivan had used to free Nadir.

As the sphere hung in the air between Nadir and the cell door, he spoke, "I, King Nadir and ruler of the elven people, demand the release of Zorna from this prison."

Anders felt Maija lean in against him. Her voice was soft and breathy in his ear, "Will that work? Didn't the Council take away his…"

Anders bumped her gently with his elbow and she stopped talking. He didn't know if the Council's pronouncement had gone into effect yet, but he wasn't willing to risk their whispering to disrupt Nadir's authority.

As the sphere of light extinguished, the cell door popped open. For a moment, Anders half-expected the youthful elder to fly out of her cell, using magic to turn on them, but, to his great relief, she walked lightly across the stone floor and exited the jail cell. When the small woman started to walk past them, Nadir said, "Hold on there. You said you'd tell us what this means." He waved the piece of parchment at her.

"And I will, as soon as we're free from this prison," she said firmly.

Stuffing the paper in his pocket, Nadir started off down the hallway. Anders and Maija stepped in behind him. Anders kept an eye on the strange Norfolk woman as he held tight to Lazuran. He thought being watched by someone brandishing such a blade would put most people on edge, but the woman acted as if he was no real threat. She continued to walk alongside Nadir toward the exit.

When they reached the stairs, Nadir led them up and out the hatch. Maija followed and Anders waited for the youthful woman to go next. He stood by the stairs with his sword still trained on her. She walked a few steps up until she was standing at his height, then looked him in the eye and said, "You didn't need that sword, you know. I killed that creature last time. Oh, and by the way, you can thank me later for saving your life again when I help you with this dilemma you find yourself in."

Anders hesitated to follow, watching the strange woman continue up the prison steps. He wondered what she meant by dilemma? Was she referring to Merglan, or did she somehow know about his struggles with corrupted power? As he started up after her, Anders wondered how many more people Asmond had locked away down below for doing what they thought was the right. Shaking his head and pulling himself back to the present challenges, Anders saw the torches blow out as they left the prison.

Stopping at the courthouse door, Anders joined Nadir in assessing the square out front and the empty streets. The volatile crowd of elves was gone. All who remained were several of Nadir's most loyal soldiers, waiting for their next assignment from the King. Exiting the building while keeping the Norfolk woman closely guarded, Anders and Maija followed Nadir as he escorted Zorna toward the loyal elves.

***

Peeling away from the group, Anders and Maija walked toward their dragons. Anders caught Nadir's glance. A curt nod told Anders that they would not be stopped in carrying out their plan, even if Nadir was prevented from leaving Cedarbridge. Climbing on Zahara and Raffagaun they took flight to the north edge of the city limits. They turned right at the cliff and followed it until Maija's instruction led them to land on an expansive wooden platform built out over the cliff's edge, a feature in a home clearly designed for a dragonrider.

Dismounting on the deck, Anders examined the large cedar treehouse that had been Maija's parents' house. "This is it then," he said, walking over to her.

She nodded and pointed to the rider's shed, "That's it over there. They had all kinds of dragon tack in there, at least it was there was when I visited the house with Natalia recently."

"Alright, let's see what they have. Maybe there's something that might work for you and we can saddle you up before Nadir and the others arrive," Anders said.

He followed her to the shed where she asked, "Do you think that woman is telling us the truth?"

"She told a pretty compelling story," Anders said.

"I know. It's hard to believe someone would be imprisoned for that petty of a reason," Maija said.

"Yeah. Well, you are talking about the king who imprisoned his own son for treason."

"The whole time it was his wife," Maija said as she forced open the door to the tack room.

Grabbing a candle from the windowsill, Anders summoned a small amount of magic to light the wick, bringing the room to life with light. "Wow, you weren't kidding when you said they had some riding stuff in here," Anders said, admiring all of the dragonrider equipment. "First, you'll need a blade," he said, stepping to the wall where the weapons were stored.

"You could have one too," Maija suggested as Anders examined the swords hanging on the wall.

Anders stayed his outstretched hand before plucking down a half sword and handing it to her, "Try this one out," he said, avoiding her comment.

"I guess now that Zorna can teach you the workings of the crystals, you'll be keeping that?" she asked motioning to Lazuran.

Anders blushed and nodded, "I know how it must look, me wanting to keep this blade after what I've been through, but it's like Zahara told me; if I'm going to beat Merglan, I'll need to learn how to master my emotions. I'll need to learn to control the power before facing him again. Now that we have the key, I can practice." Anders could tell his words concerned her and he added, "Ignoring the influence his magic had over me won't help me to become who I need to be, to become what we need to be, Maija."

Her almond eyes locked with his and she nodded, "This path we're on is bigger than us and what we desire, isn't it?"

Anders handed the sword to her and said, "All we can do is our best."

Maija accepted the blade and hefted it in her palm. Focusing on the half-sword, she toyed with the grip, cutting through the air at her side with quick chopping slashes.

"Is sword fighting something you picked up in Nagano, too?" he asked surprised at her readiness with the shortened sword.

She grinned, "No. A girl picks up a few things when she lives at a dragonrider's training facility for several months."

Anders frowned and raised his brow.

"What? Did you think Natalia was only teaching me the basics?"

"I thought she was preparing you to be a rider. I didn't know she was teaching you how to fight?"

"Well, I'm not that good," Maija admitted. "We did spend more time prepping for magic."

"You look good enough," Anders said, taking the half-sword from her and handing her a longer blade. "Try this."

Maija walked out onto the deck and dropped into a fighting stance. Anders watched as she moved through a practiced routine of positions her sister had taught her.

"Not bad," he said. "You look a little rusty, but I'm impressed."

Maija bounced up, grinning at him. Anders tossed the scabbard to the blade at her and she caught it with one hand. Gently, she guided the sword back into its protective sheathing. Unraveling the belt from the decorative leather scabbard, Maija strapped the belt onto her waist and followed Anders back inside the shed. Next, they found Maija a set of riding armor; given the fit, it must've belonged to her mother. The padded leather was of the same style that Anders had been given when they'd started their training. The material moved freely and allowed dragonriders to move quickly during battle. Since this had belonged to her mother, Maija fit into the suit as if had been tailored just for her.

Together they hauled out the largest saddle in the tack room. When they fitted it on Raffa, he dwarfed the leather seat. After adding cinch straps from three other saddles, they were able to harness the seat securely onto his back. Putting up less of a fight than Zahara had initially, Raffa only commented that he didn't like it, but since the contraption would make riding safer for Maija, he was willing to put up with it.

In the shed Anders found other riding tools that he hadn't known existed, many of which he could only guess at their uses. He and Maija continued to search through the tack until Zahara notified them that Nadir and his soldiers were approaching. As Anders and Maija walked to the front of the house, he wondered how many dragons would let someone saddle them if they hadn't yet bonded.

Nadir and the Norfolk woman led a line of elves along the cliff edge. The elf king motioned for his soldiers to halt. He and the youthful elder approached.

Nadir spoke freely as he approached them. "It's brilliant!" he exclaimed looking to Anders and Maija. When Anders looked confused, Nadir continued, "The way the crystals can store power and be altered to serve a specific purpose. I've already told Natalia what to do."

"Is she in the city yet?" Anders asked.

Nadir nodded, "She's made it into the castle and is searching for Ivan."

"Is he there? Can she sense him?" Anders asked.

Nadir shook his head, "She's still searching. We walked her through the process of what she needs to do to corrupt the crystals. If she accomplishes this, the power source will be altered and when Merglan tries to use it, it won't go in his favor."

Anders stiffened, worried that Ivan had not yet been located, but refocused as he asked, "So she told you how they work?"

"Yes, it's about knowing how to tap into the crystal's chemical structure," Zorna interjected. "If you know how to identify the type of silica within the crystals, you can work a spell to alter its structure. By altering these unique crystals, one can fuel the attributes you desire into them, harnessing and storing specific magical properties."

"So, you need magic to manipulate the crystal?" Anders asked.

"Yes, identifying the crystal's properties isn't something you can see or touch, it must be felt with a different sense. In my research, I found that if I sensed the crystal's structure and found its meaning in the ancient language, the crystal would act as a vessel and take on the properties I willed into it," she said.

"How do you know it will work for Natalia, or any of us?" Maija asked.

"When I was learning the ways of magic, after I first

bonded with my dragon…"

"You're bonded?" Anders interrupted.

"You saw me use the energy from your crystal yourself," she said to Anders. "How else would I be magical?"

"Well, you said you were learning a way for the non-bonded to access the dragon's power source," he said.

"That's right. Learning, not knowing. Anyway, I spent years reading and searching through our ancestors' documents. I worked tirelessly for ways to expand our abilities into other applications. As a result of my search, I found scripts dating back to those who were first to bond. I actually read the journal of the first rider. She explained her dragon's recollection of how magic was brought to our world with the first dragons. The dragons of old spoke to the stones and injected energy into them for later use. The journal drove me and my dragon to search through the ancient language. We wanted to discover how to access the capabilities of the different crystals. That's when I came up with that diagram. Its intent was to teach other riders how to use the crystals so non-bonded races could share in the crystals' powers if need be."

Not knowing exactly where to start with the million or more questions racing through his mind, Anders decided to focus on the current dilemma for now. He turned to Nadir, "How much time do we have until the Council figures out what we're doing?"

"Before we're stuck in Cedarbridge, or the prison, for the foreseeable future?" Nadir asked.

Anders nodded.

"They could already know. I've sent most of those willing to follow me to wait for us at the riders' facility."

Walking to Zahara and climbing into his saddle, Anders said, "The sooner we're out of here, the better it will be for the cause." He directed his gaze to the Norfolk woman, "Do you share the speed of the elves?" When she shook her head, Anders offered, "You can ride with me. Our discussions about the crystals will have to wait." He lowered an arm and helped the childlike woman up onto Zahara's back.

Maija followed Anders and hoisted herself up into her new saddle, shifting to get comfortable in her new seat. Nadir nodded to them and walked swiftly back toward the line of elves waiting along the cliff. As Anders glanced over his shoulder to tell Zorna to hold on tight for takeoff, he saw the elves disappear in a flash.

Making their way swiftly to the dragonrider facilities, Zahara landed in the grassy clearing near the riders' secret city entrance. Anders saw the host of redshirt elves mixed with soldiers from the army emerging from the forest. He didn't see Nadir and his guard and knew they'd be approaching soon.

Anders jogged to the edge of the clearing and spoke the words to open the riders' entrance. As the gateway to the unprotected world opened, they could hear the gale force winds just outside the door. He watched the soldiers and armed red-shirted individuals funnel through the exit, leaving the city's protective layer. As the last of the redshirts cleared the exit, Anders saw Nadir's guard run across the open field. Nadir followed in the back with several robed elves in pursuit. They caught up to Anders in a heartbeat, Nadir nodding for them to follow the soldiers exiting into the storm.

Maija, Raffa, Zahara and Anders stepped through, the Norfolk woman close behind. Anders looked back through the door to see Nadir standing in the opening with his back to them. The Elf King faced three Council members, blades in their hands. One of them called out to him, "You step through that door and you'll never be king again!"

Nadir shouted over the howling wind, "You stop me, and this war will never end! I'm going to do what my father couldn't, bring Merglan to justice!"

The Council members' shouts were silenced when Nadir stepped through the door. Anders closed it on them behind Nadir.

"To the Bays!" Nadir shouted, rallying his soldiers.

Anders watched as Nadir's rebel army took off south around the city, heading full speed toward the trails that would lead them to the Glacial Melt Bays. He turned to see Maija staring up at the dark cloud blotting out the night sky.

"What is it?" he asked.

She shook her head, "I'm not sure. I thought I just heard something."

"Probably the muffled shouts of those elves through the barrier," Anders suggested.

He mounted Zahara and looked to the spot where Maija had been looking. He couldn't hear what she had heard, but he did feel the same strange feeling he'd felt as they entered the elven city. Chalking it up to the storm and his uneasy feeling about Zorna, the Norfolk woman, Anders helped her onto Zahara once again and bounced along on Zahara as she trotted along the forest floor. The winds were too powerful for them to fly.

***

Merglan eyed the treetops, sensing the movement of elves rushing through the forest below. He turned in his saddle as Killdoor hovered above the storm, "We'll keep our distance, but be ready to strike when I give the order," he said to the rider at his side dressed in black.

The smaller dragon struggled to maintain a hover in the strong winds. Seeing the creature in flight, Merglan cursed Killdoor for picking such whelp for his new rider. Spurring Killdoor forward and flying away from the storm cloud, Merglan could feel the presence of the dragon and rider who'd escaped his trap. He had underestimated the young rider and dragon's ability to fight back. As he moved into a position to observe the former elf king's movements, he chuckled to himself. This time he would catch them all off guard. This time Merglan would get what he wanted.

CHAPTER TWENTY-ONE

Inside the Castle

eaching into her pocket, Natalia gripped the small mirror Nadir had given her and pulled it out. As the luminous glow faded from the glass, she watched as the light extinguished into a thin strip of silver that flashed down the length of the handle, indicating she'd missed the connection. Quickly, she stuffed the mirror into an inward facing pocket inside her cloak, hoping that if Nadir called again, the light would be contained inside her jacket. Though cannon fire along Kingston's city walls boomed, the sound failed to cover the shouts of orcs and men dying inside the castle walls. The sounds had not gone unnoticed.

"What did he want?" Solomon said, reaching down and grabbing a torch from one of the dead soldier's hands.

Natalia shrugged, "I don't know, but now isn't the time or place to talk with Nadir."

"Yes, you'd better keep that thing tucked away somewhere tight. This place has a way of claiming people of importance within these walls," Solomon said, holding the torch over the bodies of the soldiers Natalia had slain and shuttered.

"That could be because humans of importance have lived here since the old capital fell at Highborn Bay."

"I'm well aware of what happened at Highborn Bay," Solomon said with a touch of anger.

"You should, you're old enough to have been there yourself," Natalia said mockingly. After she had spoken, Natalia noticed the pain in his eyes and immediately felt the need to apologize.

Before she could, though, Solomon responded, "My family has kept that tragedy close to our hearts. I wasn't alive when the dragons turned on them, but my grandfather was and I can tell you the horrors that occurred scared him deeply."

Feeling ashamed that she'd touched a sore spot in the old man's memory, Natalia placed her hand on his shoulder, "I didn't know, I'm sorry."

Solomon nodded and glanced back to the dead bodies in the hallway. He whispered, "Death takes 'em in the end. Young or old, all kings must fall."

Natalia wondered what he meant by the phrase but didn't press him further.

Solomon shuffled around Natalia and said, "I think we'd better take this route."

Following him through the castle's outer walls, Natalia wondered silently about Solomon's statement. He had revealed something of his past that allowed her to start fitting together the puzzle of how Solomon had become revered. She also began to understand why it was so important for him to be involved in the fight against Merglan.

Natalia kept her sword drawn as they walked, knowing that at any moment they could come across a soldier or an orc lurking around a corner. The hallway passed inside the thick protective walls, circumnavigating the castle. Natalia would've been lost had she not been under the guidance of the old wise man. Stopping at a turn, Solomon peered around the corner and Natalia took the opportunity to examine the view outside the walls from an archer's slotted window.

Looking through the thin slit, Natalia could see the streets below. To her surprise, the orcs who'd filled the streets outside the walls were gone. She wondered what had happened to Maylox and Inama. Had they been carried away with the orcs, possibly caught on the wrong side of the fighting? Or were they also through the castle walls, searching for a way in?

"This way," Solomon said, pulling Natalia from her reverie.

She followed away from the window, her eyes adjusting more quickly to the dark corridors now. They stopped again before a short passageway. At the end of the passage, Natalia could see the courtyard between the outer walls and the keep. Her heart skipped when she saw the space flooded with armed orcs and soldiers. She realized they were there to protect the castle while the city was under attack.

They're protecting something important, Natalia thought. *Why does Merglan want this place protected more than the city gates? Is he in the midst of conjuring powerful magic and can't break from his concentration to investigate the battle?*

"We can't get past them," Solomon whispered.

"Not even if I used magic to disguise us?" Natalia suggested.

"What are you, insane? Need I remind you that Merglan lives here?"

Natalia shifted, irritated that she'd spent so long recovering her access to magic for this operation, yet couldn't tap into it without risking being detected by the dark sorcerer. Even if he were in the middle of an incantation, he would be able to sense her if she acted carelessly with her weakened abilities.

"There's another way, a door to stairs around back. The gap between the castle and this wall is narrow and might be less well protected," Solomon said, peeling away from the passageway that led into the courtyard.

They moved quickly, hiding for a moment in different stairwells and doubling back to the last corner to avoid orcs and soldiers patrolling inside the castle walls. From the way the orcs and soldiers were positioned, Natalia gathered that they were manning the ramparts along the wall and assigning the bulk of their reserves to be at the ready should the Rollo and Lumbapi forces break through the gates. Natalia had only had a glimpse out beyond the wall since they'd entered the castle, but she didn't see Merglan or his dragon in the sky.

Why wouldn't he post his dragon in the courtyard if he was too busy or not willing to fly out? Something isn't right, she thought, wanting to reach out with her mind and sweep the castle for Ivan, Anders, Zahara, or Merglan. Restraining her instincts, she reminded herself what it was like to feel the sorcerer's mental attack bearing down on her. The image of her dragon being clawed apart as she fought Merglan flashed into her mind; in that moment, Keanu and his dragon had saved her life. If they hadn't provided a distraction, Merglan would've finished her off as he did her dragon. Perhaps he had hoped that the fall would kill her, too. Natalia shuddered at the thought and then started after Solomon again.

Stealthily, they advanced to the back of the castle. Stopping at a narrow passageway accessing the gap between wall and castle keep, Natalia wondered at their chances of getting by unseen. She could see the castle's stone exterior. The closed back door Solomon had targeted appeared simple in design and no more than a dozen yards from the edge of the outer wall. Two orcs stood with their backs against the castle's exterior, guarding the wooden door. With their limited field of view, Natalia could only see a handful of others filling the narrow gap, far fewer than those stationed in the courtyard.

"There's the door we need to get through," Solomon whispered.

"Only two orcs," Natalia said tightening her grip on her sword. "If we can get there, I can take them out."

"We'll be seen," Solomon said, shaking his head. "Even if they don't see us, among all of these eyes surrounding the keep, someone will notice us. I'm surprised they haven't sent a squad to search for us. They must've found those you slew by now."

"You're right," Natalia sighed. "Who knows, though, they might already be searching for us?"

Solomon pinched the bridge of his nose, "Think, Sol, think."

"How about this?" Natalia offered. "I'll just walk out there, quickly kill those two orcs, then you follow me, and we'll lock the door behind us."

"Did you not hear me?" Solomon asked exasperated. "We'll be seen."

"If we don't do it now, we'll run out of time. We'll be caught."

Solomon shook his head looking at the orcs, "It's a risk."

"Sol, you can do this. Just follow me," she said as she stepped around him into the narrow passage leading out into the open. Lifting the hood of her heavy cloak over her head, she walked confidently toward the exit.

Walk quickly and confidently, she told herself. *Don't look to see if anyone is looking at you; just keep walking toward the door. You are the veiled huntress.*

Keeping her head bowed and her eyes fixed on the two orcs guarding the door, Natalia walked across the opening with her sword in hand. The two orcs didn't move when they saw her, they stood motionless at the door as she approached. Natalia wondered if she might be moving faster than most humans or orcs; regardless, they didn't react until she was on them. Before the orcs could reach for their weapons, Natalia lopped off their heads in a single cross-cutting stroke. Not bothering to glance back, she grabbed the door handle and pushed in. Turning, she saw Solomon sprinting after her, the orcs and soldiers in the opening finally realizing what had happened. She closed and bolted the door behind Solomon. They managed to drop the solid beam into its iron brackets, barring further entry, just as the clan outside reached the door. The orcs would now have to break through the thick wood panels if they were going to get inside at this entrance.

Natalia half-expected Solomon to rave at her for her

decision, but to her surprise, he said coolly, "Follow me, quickly now."

They descended the stairs just inside the castle's rear entrance. The shouts and pounding dropped away as Solomon led Natalia into the dungeons under the castle keep. Taking an unlit torch from the iron holder bolted to the stone wall near the bottom of the stairs, Natalia chanced a spark of magic to set the burlap-wrapped end ablaze.

"Anders?" she said, holding the torch out in front of her and hearing the name echo into the hollow dungeon.

"Ivan?" Solomon said a little more loudly.

For a moment Natalia and Solomon paused to listen, but their words went unanswered so they stepped farther into the dingy castle basement. A weak crackling voice sounded just over the rasps of their own breathing. Natalia heard a faint, "Help." They rushed through the gaps between cells, lighting each cell with their torchlight to see who was locked inside.

Natalia and Solomon searched until they found the source of the cry. Natalia exposed a man in chains lying on the floor with an untouched bowl of water lying just out of his reach. "Ivan," she said sliding over to him and examining the prisoner. One look at his sunken features told her this wasn't the noble rider she'd known; this was a prisoner on the brink of starvation, essentially left for dead. The man's skin sagged around every bone, gravity pulling at his last waning strength. She briefly entertained breaking his chains and setting him free, but she knew he wasn't strong enough to escape. He was dead already and didn't know it. She looked to Solomon and he shook his head. Giving the prisoner his freedom, Natalia's sword ended his suffering.

"They're not down here," she said, walking briskly from the tragic scene. "We'll need to keep looking throughout the castle."

"They're coming for us now," Solomon said. "You heard the pounding against the back door. They know we're here. That door we came through, it only leads two ways, up or down. They'll figure it out quickly once inside."

"There's another way out of here, though, isn't there?" Natalia asked.

"The stairs to the main floor, but they lead right into the center of the castle. We'd likely run into guards, orcs, and possibly Merglan himself," Solomon said, shaking his head. A calm came over him, though, as he looked into Natalia's green eyes, "But it's the only way."

"Come on, Sol," Natalia said, holding his gaze. "Lead the way."

Solomon jogged across the dank room to another set of stairs. Natalia could hear his breathing become more labored as they climbed. She wanted to move faster to beat those who were searching for them. They would soon be on their way down, but she wouldn't leave Solomon behind.

Nearing the main floor, Natalia extinguished her torch and dumped it into an iron cage bolted to the wall. Daylight shone as they reached the top of the stairs. The empty hallway lined with towering rectangular windows offered them a view of orc milling in the courtyard beyond. The door to the keep burst open in the neighboring entrance hall and she could hear shouting.

"Hurry," he whispered and hustled to a hallway connecting the entrance hall and another enormous room sealed with double-wide doors. Stepping into an adjacent stairwell, she and Solomon started up more stone steps toward the second floor. Natalia looked back to see a line of orcs funneling into the dungeon. Tucking around the corner, she continued to tiptoe after Solomon as they neared the second floor.

"That was close," she whispered.

"We need to keep moving. Their search down below won't take long," Solomon said.

"But they don't know where in the castle we've gone to," Natalia said. "We could be anywhere."

"Inside," Solomon corrected. "We could be anywhere inside."

Coming to the landing, Natalia poked her head out from the stairwell and looked down the hallway. The expansive corridor was empty, lined with torches and oversized paintings of kings and other people of importance.

Stepping out into the hall, Natalia stared at a painting to her right, "Where do we go now?"

"Maybe Merglan's keeping them in a chamber room? I suggest we open doors as we go," he said starting past her and moving toward the first door to the right.

Natalia looked at a portrait of a young man with a crown on his head. He had blonde hair, blue eyes and a strong jawline etched with a trim blond beard. The black and red robes of nobility flowed across his shoulders and out of the frame. She cleared her throat and said, "Hey, Solomon, this looks like you, but younger."

"There's no time for joking around," Solomon barked as he focused on their task. "Get to searching."

Natalia knew he was right and moved quickly to the first door on the left side of the corridor. Turning latches,

Natalia continued to push through, examining furnished rooms that looked as though they'd been abandoned for years. They worked quickly, calling for Anders and Ivan as they went. As they neared the end of the hallway, she heard orcs grunting and charging their way up the stairs. The last room at the end of the hall provided their only chance to escape, all of the other rooms led nowhere. As the orcs' marching got louder, Natalia grabbed Solomon by the arm, and stepped inside the final chamber, closing the double-wide doors behind them.

Once inside the room, she looked to either side, hoping to see a brace to bar the entrance as they'd done at the castle's rear doorway, but she couldn't find one. Natalia looked up, arching her neck to see the ceiling and circling to face the expanse before them. The room was enormous. Light shone through the massive stained-glass windows lining the wall to her left, illuminating a row of columns lining each side. She ran across the width of the room, searching for an exit or somewhere to hide. Seeing that several of the pillars were broken, she and Solomon hurried toward the fragmented blocks of stone scattered on the floor. As the sound of their pursuers reached the entrance, Natalia ducked behind a large section of downed pillars. Solomon crouched next to her just as the orcs kicked open the doors and charged into the room.

Solomon tugged at her sleeve. She looked at him, following his finger as he pointed toward a small exit on the wall behind them. The narrow door wasn't far from where they hid, but once again there was nothing to hide behind if they moved in that direction. He motioned that they must go there. Natalia shifted, moving her hand to the floor.

When she placed her palm on the ground, she felt a gritty film. Charcoal marked the palm of her hand and she noticed for the first time the black burn marks along the floor. She looked at the ballooning black stain on the floor as it extended out toward the wooden door that was their destination. She quickly examined deep gouges cut into the stone floor. Four horizontal paired marks, and then four more spaced a few yards apart. She knew of only one creature that had claws that could scar stone so deeply. Dragons. Solomon tapped her shoulder and nodded, moving to a crouch and poised to run. Natalia waited for the old man to lead. When he didn't go right away, she looked at him.

He whispered, "You first!"

Natalia took that to mean she could reach and open the door much faster than he could. Once he got there, they could lock it shut before the orcs had time to react. She rolled from her seated position, getting her feet under her. A short breath later, Natalia sprang out toward the narrow doorframe.

She slipped through without hearing any reaction from the orcs and left the door cracked open for Solomon. Peeking out, she looked to see how far he was from reaching her when she heard an orc shout. She expected to see Solomon hustling toward the small doorway she'd passed through, but didn't see him at all. Natalia watched the orcs run, pointing to the far end of the room, opposite where she had gone. Natalia cursed as she saw the old man running away from her along the side wall toward the stained glass. Looking ahead of him, Natalia saw a small depression like the one she stood in just below the right window. Judging the distance, Natalia thought she could reach it before the orcs did.

Natalia made to run toward Solomon, but stopped. Along the opposite wall, orcs and soldiers began piling into the room through the main double-wide doors marking the second floor corridor she and Solomon had entered from. Natalia moved back into the shadow of the slim doorframe, knowing she couldn't cut through that many orcs in time to help Solomon. She stood with her back pressed against the wall, tears welling in her eyes. She wanted to scream and rush out with all her magic blazing, but even if she did, it wouldn't help Ivan or Anders now.

What the hell, Solomon? she shouted silently. *You fool! You stupid old fool!* Natalia felt even sadder as she realized the old man had gone the opposite direction on purpose. He'd known what he was getting into when he came with her. She cursed him for forcing himself onto her mission, then pushed off the wall and continued up the tightly winding staircase to the next floor. On the landing, Natalia hesitantly peered into the hallway. Empty to either side. She bent over, placing her hands on her knees, trying to catch her breath through her tears. She knew she couldn't wallow in the sorrow for long. She had to make Solomon's sacrifice worth something. She had to find the others.

***

Gathering her courage, Natalia stepped warily out into the open. Torches along the third floor hallway provided dim lighting. At the first door, she found a quiet bedroom, untouched with years of dust on the furniture. Quietly, she moved to the next door. Another bedroom, but his one had fresh bedding and the chairs around a decorative table appeared to have been used. She called out, "Ivan? Anders?" but heard no reply. Clothes lay in a pile next to the bed. She instantly recognized them. "Ivan," she called again, louder this time as she walked deeper into the room.

As she reached the center of the room, Natalia felt the overwhelming sense that Ivan was there, but he wasn't responding. She searched the entire royal chamber for any other signs of her friend, but his clothes were the only evidence of him having been there. As she looked around the room, Natalia knew Ivan was there, but she just couldn't see him. Suddenly Natalia saw the light from the mirror glowing within her cloak. When she pulled it from her pocket, she saw Nadir's face looking back at her.

"Natalia, we've figured it out," he said.

Confused and frustrated, she replied, "What do you mean?" She walked to the ornately decorated table in the middle of the room. A small wooden box lay on top. She glanced at it, wondering why she hadn't noticed it before. Something about it seemed different, then her attention turned back to the mirror as Nadir spoke.

"We've learned how you can alter Merglan's inhabitance crystals!" Nadir shouted over the mirror.

Natalia placed her palm over the mirror, looking to the door and half expecting it to fly open with orcs. Bringing the mirror back up to her face, she held her finger across her mouth to shush Nadir. "Be quiet for a moment," she whispered and moved toward the door. Through the crack she could hear voices in the hallway.

Natalia backed up against the wall near the door and listened to the approaching footfalls. Still holding the mirror, she pressed it against her stomach trying to snuff out its glow. She heard Nadir's muffled voice say, "Natalia, what's going on? I can't see your face."

The footsteps in the hall stopped and she knew they'd heard him. Natalia brought the mirror back up to her face and shushed him once more. She could see Nadir squinting into the mirror and moving his head around to get a look at her.

"Is that blood on your face?" he whispered.

The noise was enough to alert those in the hallway and they pushed through the door and into the room. Natalia waited until she could clearly see the first orc enter before she plunged her sword through the she-orc's throat. A second orc followed, sending Natalia backward and off balance. She blocked a swing from the male orc's blade, then stabbed hers deep into his chest before the brute collapsed on the floor. Natalia rushed to the door and looked out into the hallway. No one else was in sight, so she quickly closed it.

Lifting the mirror to her face again and seeing Nadir's shocked expression, she said, "Now, if you wouldn't mind quietly repeating what you said a moment ago. In case you couldn't tell, I'm in the middle of a rescue mission."

"Where are you?" Nadir asked.

"I'm in the castle, currently looking for Anders and Ivan. I think I found Ivan's room, but he's not here," she said.

"Oh no," Nadir said.

Natalia held the mirror closer to her face, "What does that mean?"

"I tried notifying you earlier. Anders and Zahara aren't in Southland," Nadir said.

"How do you know that?" Natalia asked.

"Because they're here with me, in Cedarbridge."

"What about Ivan? I can feel his presence here," Natalia said.

"Only Anders and Zahara escaped; Merglan had Ivan the last they saw," Nadir said.

"Then I'll find him," Natalia said.

"You have to get to the crystals," Nadir said. "We've learned how they can be altered. You can corrupt Merglan's entire supply. He's got them hidden somewhere in the castle."

"What about Ivan? I can feel him. I'm close."

"Merglan's strength grows each day. You can stop him here and now."

Natalia held the mirror to her side, thinking over her objective, "Okay. Do you know where they are?"

"They were hidden in his bed chambers last time. Try there."

Natalia snorted, "Okay, and once I find them, how do I alter them?"

Nadir had the Norfolk woman explain to Natalia the words of the ancient language that would likely work for her and how she could use them to manipulate the crystals' powers. "Find them, corrupt them, and then rescue Ivan," she repeated to Nadir. "How hard can that be?" she added sarcastically.

"Good luck, we're counting on you," Nadir said as he ended their conversation.

Natalia realized she'd forgotten to ask how Anders had escaped. Natalia's plan hinged on her escaping on Zahara's back. She didn't know if she could escape the castle now that all of the occupants were looking for her. She was on the wrong side of the battle.

She walked to the window to take in the view of the courtyard below and the city sprawling down to the ocean. The clouds clinging to the rooftops earlier that morning had lifted slightly. She actually had a clear view all of the way down to the city wall. She hadn't realized until now, but the cannon fire had stopped. She could see movement in the streets, but didn't know if people were fighting or not. Once she had a lay of the land, she looked for Merglan on his dragon. Surely he would emerge from the castle with a battle in the city.

She wondered why so many orcs were defending the castle, why Merglan would need that kind of defense if he was present. Why would the most powerful sorcerer need hundreds of orcs to defend his keep? Natalia wasn't positive, but she was confident after witnessing the relaxed way of the soldiers at the wall that they weren't expecting an attack that day. Then she realized, all in one moment, why the soldiers were so lax, why the orcs surrounded the castle, why they were searching for her and she hadn't yet been caught. Merglan was gone.

Natalia reached out with her mind, slowly at first, then she recoiled at the presence of a wealth of power. She second-guessed herself as her mind touched the brilliant wave of energy pulsing near her. Cringing as she waited for Merglan's mental presence to take over her mind, she was surprised when nothing happened. Natalia opened her mind again, the weeks of stored magic inside her dwarfed by a presence. It felt close, as if the power were right on top of her. She pressed her mind against the source of power and sensed it, raw and open.

The crystals, she thought.

Merglan's stash of crystals was somewhere in that room, she could feel them as if they were right next to her. She began searching, rifling through trunks and closets and under the bed. She turned over every possible piece of furniture to find the crystals, but didn't see them.

It doesn't make sense, she thought.

Natalia again sourced her magic and sent her senses out into the room. She could feel the crystals as well as Ivan's presence. Somehow, they were both there with her, but she couldn't see them.

Placing her hand back into her pocket, Natalia grabbed the mirror to ask Nadir what she should do. As she looked into the reflection, she saw the crystals she'd been looking for. She looked up at the ceiling and saw the brilliant white and blue display of sapphires embedded into the stone ceiling overhead. Marveling at them while simultaneously feeling slightly foolish for not having thought to glance up earlier, Natalia drew on her power. Starting the incantation, she began to speak the ancient language based on the Norfolk woman's directions. It wasn't so different from Elvish, so she had memorized the words easily.

When she said the correct word matching the crystals' essence, she felt them opening up. As their presence unraveled its protective coating, they revealed the contents within, and Natalia knew what she had to do. She focused intensely and forced her will onto the energy. The magnitude of it overwhelmed her and she lost herself in the influx of power. The energy poured into her, lifting her off the ground and causing her to glow like a beacon of magical force. Her emotions took over, the love she felt for her sister, mother, and father. The love she'd held for her dragon and the love she'd held for all things good in the world flourished inside her. She could feel the evil Merglan had poured into the crystals altering into the love she bore for her bonded and her family. She'd given herself to the crystals, letting them absorb her essence like a giant sponge. As the spell ended, she felt a part of her soul leaving with the energy as it fled from her body and back into the crystals.

Falling to the floor as the power drained from her, Natalia panted. She hadn't known how much the spell would take from her. It left her weak and aching. She knelt on the floor, trying to regain her self-awareness. Then she rose to her feet, knowing she didn't have time to rest. She had to find Ivan and get out of there. She instantly reached inward for whatever mental strength she had left. Searching the castle again, she found the same result as the last time. Ivan's presence was in the room with her.

She looked up to see if Ivan might somehow be in the ceiling like the crystals, but didn't find him. Searching through all of the places she had earlier and still unable to find him, Natalia planted her hands on her hips and scowled. Her eyes fell on the small wooden box resting on the table. Not understanding entirely why, she picked it up and put it in her cloak pocket. She walked out of the room and searched again for Ivan with her mind. Now Ivan seemed to be in the hallway with her. She lifted the wooden box from her cloak, rolling it as she examined it. *How is that possible?* she wondered.

Realizing she'd done what she had come to the castle to accomplish, she stuffed the box back in her pocket and focused on her last task, finding Solomon and escaping. Dropping down onto the second floor, Natalia let her senses guide her as she located Sol. She breathed a sigh of relief when she felt that he was alive. She looked out into the expansive room where they'd parted ways and saw that the orcs had cleared out. After finding Solomon, she guessed, the rest had returned to the courtyard, thinking they'd caught their intruder.

Natalia drew her sword and ran out into the small group of unsuspecting orcs. She cut through them with focus and precision, never allowing them a chance to defend themselves. Running to the door where she sensed Solomon, she pulled it open. Four orcs and two soldiers huddled around the old man, who was tied to a chair. The soldiers rushed her first and put up more of a fight than the orcs, but in Natalia's path of redemption, they were no match. She cut down the two soldiers before the orcs could join them. She made quick work of the four remaining and came to Solomon's side. The old man slumped, having taken a beating from the orcs.

"Sol, are you okay?" she asked.

Solomon coughed a wet wrenching sound, blood spewing from his mouth.

"I can heal you with the crystals," she said, cutting his ties.

Solomon shook as she picked him up and slung him over her shoulder. He whispered something, but she couldn't make it out. Natalia knew she didn't have enough power left over to heal the damage to his lungs, but if she could use the crystals she would.

Hustling through the open door and out into the

room, Natalia looked to the stairwell she'd descended. Orcs and soldiers funneled out into the room. Cursing, she ran with her elven speed toward the doublewide doors, exiting into the hall. More orcs waited there. She charged past them, their meaty hands ripping at her cloak as she slipped narrowly by and turned down the stairs to the main floor. Seeing all hallways crowded with orcs and soldiers, Natalia realized they hadn't just returned to the courtyard, they had spread out throughout the entire castle. She was blocked from returning to the third floor.

Sprinting to the main entrance, she kicked open the door and ran out into the courtyard. She dashed like a madwoman with Solomon slung over her shoulder as she sliced and hacked her way through to the passageway in the outer wall. Once inside, she called on her mental map to lead her the short distance to the door they'd entered. Escaping through it, she carried Solomon out into the street, running as fast as her legs could carry her.

She lost track of Solomon's breathing as she charged through the streets. She followed her memory of the city layout from the third-story window. She ran toward the sounds of fighting. Thickets of orcs and men clashed in the streets. Natalia slowed, searching for a way through them. She needed to get old Sol to safety so she could try to heal him. As she hesitated, a cluster of orcs spotted her and charged with weapons drawn. She turned and ran.

Not knowing exactly where she was going, Natalia now rushed blindly through the streets of the capital. She had to break through the fighting, it was the only way out. Holding Solomon tightly, she found the front line. Natalia clawed at the backs of orcs and men as she carved a hole to pass through. Seeing Lumbapi faces beyond the mottled orcs' heads, Natalia shouted to them. Recognizing her, the Lumbapi focused on driving through to where she boldly defended herself. In a blur of activity, she felt herself wrapped into the protection of friendly soldiers.

Clearing past them, Natalia ran. She ran far from the fighting and back to the city wall, stopping only when she had passed through the gates and found herself among the trees. She slowed, placing Solomon gently on the ground. His ragged breathing sounded of liquid. She placed her hand on his chest and summoned her magic. As she felt her energy draining trying to repair the damage to his lungs, she began to slip from consciousness. Then she felt a hand lift hers away from his body. She opened her eyes as she felt some of her strength returning.

Solomon's eyes met hers and he smiled, "My injuries are beyond your skills." He paused, coughing as blood filled his lungs.

As the wise man gasped for air, she shook her head, "I have to try."

Solomon stilled her hand, "I've lived a full life, more than most in my noble line."

Natalia thought to his comments earlier and the portrait in the castle, "You were King once, weren't you?"

He nodded, wiping the blood from his chin, "I was Kaufen's uncle. I didn't have it in me to lead the nation. My nephew was much more suited for it than I."

"You abdicated?" she asked, and Solomon nodded, coughing up more blood, bright red this time. "That's why you got involved in the war, that's why you've dedicated yourself to the cause."

"Listen, I don't have much time," Solomon said, his breathing becoming shallower. "You should know why the people here call you the," he coughed again.

"The 'veiled huntress?'" she asked.

"It was your mother," he coughed again. "You look just like her."

"But the Prophecy, it says the daughter of the veiled huntress would come on the back of a dragon," Natalia said, desperately. The old wise man's response stayed with him. Natalia stared at him, willing him to breathe again, but he didn't. She placed her hand on his chest, but there was no heartbeat. She wept for the old man she'd become fond of and the great sacrifice he had made for the countries he had once declined to lead.

CHAPTER TWENTY-TWO

The Resistance

Do you think those red streaks will ever go away?" Bo asked.

Shrugging, Kirsten answered, "Don't know. Maybe? Anders might know something we don't."

"If you do have Anders try to heal them, you should keep the marks as a tattoo," Britt suggested as she kept pace walking behind Kirsten.

Kirsten looked down at her arm, "You know I don't mind the look of it, I just wish I could take this necklace off. This heavy thing is starting to rub my neck raw."

"I don't get it," Britt said.

"What do you mean?" Kirsten asked.

"I don't know how these things work. That one just staves off magical infections and this one," she lifted the blue-hued crystal from her pocket and continued, "shoots rays, but only if you use it. When I try to use, it doesn't do anything. See?" Britt wielded the crystal as she tried to produce some kind of reaction.

"That's a good point," Max said. "Maybe it's time we hand that back over to the person who can wield it with a somewhat desired effect."

Kirsten turned to see Max walk past Britt and take the crystal from her as she stopped waving the crystal like a magic wand.

"I don't know why it works for me," Kirsten said, accepting it from Max and meeting his eyes. She held his gaze for a moment.

"But it does," he said, breaking their eye contact and looking back to Britt.

"How much farther are we going? Kirsten might need a rest," Thomas asked from behind.

"I've been telling you for days now, Thomas. I'm fine. We had more than a few days' rest at Max and Bo's," Kirsten said.

"I'm just looking out for you, Sis," Thomas said. "How long did you say?"

"Just a few more hours," Bo said, leading the group and pointing ahead.

"You said that this morning when we left," Kirsten said, playfully hitting him on the shoulder.

Turning to her, he smiled, "And I'll keep on saying that until we get there."

"Well look who's the funny brother now," Kirsten said, looking over her shoulder at Max. She saw his hand slide from Britt's as he fell in line behind her again.

"I'm flattered, truly," Bo said.

When Kirsten looked back to Bo, he avoided eye contact and spun back around to lead the way through the wooded Riverlands.

What's wrong with me? Kirsten wondered. *Why can't I just go for the one who's paying attention to me? What's changed since the Bareback Plains?* She pondered as she chewed on her lower lip.

"Rune said the Resistance had a camp near the base of the Frozentip Mountains, northeast of Brookside. My guess is that they'll find us before we find them," Max said to Thomas, but loud enough for the whole group to hear.

"So when we get there, we'll just wander around until they pick us up?" Thomas asked.

"Unless you have a better idea," Max said.

"No. I'm just looking forward to having a little downtime. Even though we really didn't do much at Solomon's or your step-folks', it's still been too stressful for me to get a good rest."

"I don't think we're going to be any safer with the Resistance," Max replied. "If anything, we'll be more of a target."

"Max," Britt said. "You don't need to point that out."

"Yeah," Bo added. "Safety in numbers, right?"

"If Bo says I'm safe, then I'm safe," Thomas called from the back of their line.

As they continued walking through the forested wetlands, Kirsten asked, "Is this where you and Max played when you were children?"

Bo answered, keeping his eyes forward, "We did our part hunting and fishing in this part of the world. Max claims this place is where he learned his sense of adventure."

"You can explore every knoll, each river and stream, and still see something new. Year after year the waters change the landscape. Nothing stays the same for very long," Max said.

"Sounds like a good place to get lost," Britt said.

"That's probably why the Resistance chose this place," Max said.

"That and it makes it difficult to track them," Bo added. "If they moved with the flow of water, tracking them would be almost impossible. There are so many different channels and canals intertwining throughout the area. It's actually pretty clever."

"Halt," a voice boomed in front of them.

Kirsten jumped, not anticipating the command. Lifting her gaze from her feet, she saw that a group of archers had surrounded them. With their arrows drawn and tips pointed at them, Kirsten instinctively raised her hands.

"Why do you seek out the lawbreakers?" the man who'd commanded them to halt asked. Kirsten's eyes fixed on him, examining his attire. The hood on his cloak successfully concealed his facial features. Kirsten eyed the others one by one, looking past their bows to see that they all wore similar brown cloaks with deep hoods.

Max and Britt pulled their broadswords from their belts, stepping forward to protect the others. As they did, Kirsten lowered her arms and felt at the crystal in her pocket, wondering if she should use it.

"We're seeking the Revolutionists," Max started. "On the trail we..." he continued until the hooded man apparently in charge shouted, "Silence!"

He stepped in closer to them, eyeing Max and Britt's swords. "If you even attempt to use those on me, my men will poke you full of holes so fast you'll be dead before you know what's happened." He pushed past them and stopped in front of Kirsten.

Kirsten stood up straight with her hand balled into a fist in her pocket, clutching the crystal. She stared forward as the man blocked most of her view. She glared at him as his head bent slightly to get a look at the streaking veins in her arm. Pulling a buck knife from his belt, the man flicked the point toward Kirsten's neck and tapped the tip of his blade on the sapphire.

"Look what we have here," he said.

"Don't," Kirsten said coldly.

"Sentimental is it?" the man asked. "You know that kind of stone could buy our army a lot of steel. Steel we'll be needing to fight the war."

"You take that sapphire and she dies," Bo said.

Kirsten eyed the man's knifepoint as he turned to look at Bo, the tip dropping down to her breast. The hooded man said, "That's not a very good threat. Usually you'd say I'd be the one to die."

"He's not threatening you," Thomas said, stepping toward the man. "He's telling the truth. See the streaks on her arm. She was bitten by a goblin. That sapphire is the only thing that's keeping the venom from reaching her heart and killing her. She took it off once already and we just about lost her."

Kirsten watched the man's shadowed face look down at her arm again.

Lifting the point of his blade slightly he tapped the sapphire again, "One little girl's sacrifice for the greater good might mean our side winning the war. I'd say that's a pretty just reason to take this from her right now." The man slipped the knife under the necklace chain and had just began to apply pressure by the time Kirsten lifted the crystal from her pocket. The light from the crystal in her hand glowed, catching his attention and he stopped. Glancing at the crystal, he asked in a low tone, "What's that?"

Kirsten gritted her teeth, "I'm much more powerful to you alive than I would be dead. What one sorceress can do with a crystal is far more than what a hundred untrained farmers can do with swords."

One of the archers said, "She's one of them," and the man turned to hear the comment. Grunting, he pulled the knife away from her throat and slid it with a practiced hand back into its leather sheath. "You're coming with us," the man said and turned to walk back to his place among the archers.

"Rune sent us to find you," Max said as he passed. "He told us we would be welcomed assets to your cause."

The man looked at Max and said, "Oh, if Rune sent you then." The man pulled his knife again and jumped toward Max. Max reacted too slowly and the man slid in close before he could lift his sword in defense. Kirsten raised her hand, pointing the crystal at the man as he held his knife to Max's throat. Kirsten made eye contact with the man and he flared his nostrils at the glowing crystal in her hand. Pushing Max away, he said, "Rune's a fool and I hope he dies on that stupid mission of his." Walking back to his men, he pointed his knife at them and commanded, "Bring them."

Several of the archers lowered their bows and approached, confiscating the group's weapons, all except Kirsten's crystal and sapphire necklace. They placed their cloaks backwards on Max and Britt, the hoods acting as blindfolds. When they came to Kirsten, two of the men warily placed the hood over her face, then quickly moved on to Bo and Thomas. Kirsten wondered how these men knew about the crystal's power. She'd only ever seen it when

Merglan and Rankstine had used them. Were there others like them in Brookside?

Under the cover of the thick cloaks, Kirsten allowed the men to lead her. Judging from the lack of noise from her friends and brother, they, too, were complying with this situation. Kirsten tripped and stumbled having to rely heavily on the man leading her for support. She thought about attacking the rogue revolutionaries with the crystal and using its powers to set her group free, but what good would that do if they were trying to locate the same group of people? She quelled her desire to obliterate the man leading them and quietly conformed. She tried to keep track of how long they'd been walking, but after the tenth time she stumbled, she shifted her focus to her feet and how to maintain her balance.

Once she heard the sounds of an encampment, she knew the cloaks would be removed soon. She felt the men force her to sit. She heard the clasping of shackles on her companions and soon felt cold steel wrapping around her ankle as well. When someone lifted the cloak off, Kirsten took a moment to observe her new surroundings. The five of them were all linked to a single chain that extended from a large wooden pole in the ground. She could hear people milling about, but a tan canvas tent provided a thin layer of separation from a look at the broader location. She saw light peeping through the tent door and tried to reach for her pocket. As she did, the man who'd removed her cloak caught her hands.

"Not so fast, witch," he said clasping irons around her wrists and latching them securely to the T in the pole over her head. Kirsten pulled, trying to lower her arms, but she winced when the shackles dug into her wrists.

"What kind of a welcome was that?" Max asked sarcastically as the man exited the tent.

"Not exactly what I was expecting from our supposed allies," Bo answered.

"I'm sure they're just taking precautions to make sure we're not spies," Britt said.

"Are you defending them?" Max asked.

"All I'm saying is I've had to do the same thing during times of war. You can never be too careful," she said.

"And if they say, Rune, your doctor sent us?" Max asked.

"I never had that happen, but I would still want to make sure we weren't a threat to my people," she said.

Kirsten was about to tell everyone to pull on the chain to try to rip the post out of the ground when she heard a familiar voice.

"Step aside," the man said.

That's the voice from my fever dreams, she thought.

The tent door parted and a man entered, visible only by his silhouette at first. Kirsten heard the others gasp when they saw him. Another man entered the tent with him. She could see them more clearly when the tent flap closed behind them. She didn't recognize the first man by appearance, but she knew his voice.

"Uncuff these people," the man ordered.

"But doc," the second man said.

"Don't 'but doc' me; do as I say. These are friends of mine and I demand they be treated with respect. Now uncuff them at once."

The man keyed open the chains around their ankles

one by one, undoing the clasps he'd previously set. As Max stood, he addressed the doctor, "Thanks, Rune. We weren't expecting to run into you again so quickly."

"I wasn't expecting you either, but I happened to run into some friends of your Captain," the doctor said.

Kirsten heard Britt gasp as two members of her crew entered through the tent door. She lunged across the tent, wrapping the two dark-skinned men into a hearty embrace. She began at once to speak to them in her native Rolloan.

Rune turned to Kirsten, "It appears you've survived the poison."

She nodded, staring blankly at the man.

"Sorry, when last we met you were unconscious. Rune is my name, as I'm sure you've gathered by now. I'm a doctor with the revolution here. Good thing your friends ran into us on the trail. I'm sure you wouldn't have made it much longer without that rapid transport to Solomon's. I am curious, what did the old wise man give you to stop the venom from spreading?"

Kirsten shook her head, "Solomon wasn't there. They tried some of his potions on me, but it's this sapphire that's keeping me alive."

Rune's eyes widened. "True enough," he said, taking her hand and examining her affected arm. "The infection's held back as long as this is on you. I figured as much, but to last this long is a miracle." He gave her command of her arm again and said, "Well, if you make it through tonight, I'll have to run some tests on you to see if we can't figure it out."

Kirsten nodded, then asked, "Why if I make it through tonight?"

"Surely you were told. The enemy army has moved

onto the Plains and they're marching this way. Soon we'll be marching to meet them," Rune said.

"No, we hadn't been told," Max answered for her as he glanced at Britt.

"Well, we have lots of work to do. The army occupying Brookside has been busy gathering recruits from the northern valleys," Rune said. "Come with me and I'll get you gear and weapons. Since you're new to our force, you'll be placed in the back of the pack. Can't have new recruits messing up the working formations we've spent so much training time on these last months. That is all except you, Rollo warriors. We'll be needing your skills at the front."

Britt hardened her expression and Kirsten saw the look she gave Max. "I'll be of more use at the front, alongside my Captain," Max said.

Rune looked to the scabbard around his waist where the sword he'd taken from the soldier had been. Nodding, he said, "Very well. The more trained fighters at the front, the better our odds." Rune waved them on out of the tent.

As they exited, Kirsten saw the sprawling village that had been used as the Resistance's base for the past several months. A sea of tents extended into the distance. She could hear men barking orders as men and women hustled to the gathering crowd at camp's edge. Bo grabbed her hand and pulled her along before the others became lost to them. They caught up as their small band walked quickly toward the rebel camp's makeshift armory.

Rune pointed to the newly constructed log building and Kirsten followed the others inside. People pushed their way in and out of the place, grabbing axes, swords, and staffs. This wasn't the kind of place that custom-fit each soldier's battle needs, but Kirsten managed to find a shirt of chainmail her size and belted on a short sword and dagger.

Britt outfitted herself with her Rolloan armor and sword her crewmen had carried for her from the ships. Max found his broadsword and slipped on a loose-fitting helmet. He also grabbed a shield. Bo already wore armor and only required a blade, while Thomas also found some chainmail he fit into. Grabbing a longbow and as many arrows as he could find, he presented himself to Kirsten.

"Aren't you going to take a blade?" she asked.

"I don't expect I'll need it. We're going to be in the back and I'm much better with this," he held up the bow.

Kirsten rolled her eyes and ran over to the barrels of blades. Pulling one she felt would suit a younger man, she handed it to him. "Take this and belt it on. You don't have to use it, but I'll feel better knowing you have something other than that bow if things get hairy."

Thomas raised an eyebrow at her, "If things get hairy? When did you become the expert on warcraft?"

"When I got us out of that mess in Grandwood," Kirsten said not giving it a moment's thought.

Thomas nodded, recalling how she'd acted in those dire circumstances. He accepted the sword, and hunted down a belt. Just as Thomas returned with the sword belted on, Rune reappeared to lead them toward the gathering army.

Kirsten rolled the crystal over in her palm as she followed the line of rebel soldiers through the wooded foothills below the Frozentip Mountains. She'd seen fighting before, even killed, but this felt different. She felt the suspense building among the larger group for a fight that wouldn't happen until sometime later. She didn't know the strategy or plan; all she knew was that her brother and Bo would be by her side in the back. Kirsten stood on her tiptoes, trying to catch a glimpse of Max's black hair alongside Britt's in the crowd of people ahead. She couldn't see them.

"Don't worry about Max," Bo said. "As long as he's beside Britt and those other Islanders, he'll be just fine."

Kirsten nodded, "Yeah. I just hope the fighting ends quickly."

"Me, too," Thomas added from her side. "I hate this part. The waiting."

As they marched to the edge of the forest, Kirsten watched the rebel army form ranks along the tree line facing toward the grassy expanse that was the Bareback Plains. Keeping close to Bo and Thomas, she followed Rune's direction to stand five ranks behind the extending file of soldiers manning the tree line.

After a moment of standing in silence, Kirsten asked, "What now?"

Rune looked to her, "Now we wait for the enemy to come to us."

She looked out at the expanding grassy fields. In the distance she saw three wide rectangular bricks of soldiers marching across the plains. Judging by their distance, they were still hours from making contact. She had to agree with her brother, she hated this part, watching the walls of death slowly march their way into view. She knew they had hours to wait before the chaos would begin.

After nearly two hours, Kirsten could see individual men in armor as they broke into smaller block formations.

Their rebel army remained still, hidden in the trees. Kirsten saw movement overhead in the gap between trees. Suddenly, she saw a burst of dragon fire lighting the sky high in the air. Leaning into Bo, she pointed to the sky, "Look!" At the same time, she heard the gasps of others who were pointing skyward now as well.

"Dragons," she heard Thomas say as she watched three dragons race across the sky.

"Is it Anders?" Bo asked, using his hand to block the afternoon sun.

"Could be," Kirsten said. "I only know of one other dragonrider."

"That's not the dark sorcerer's dragon," a girl standing on the opposite side of Rune said. "I've seen them before. His dragon is black and about the size of that red one there."

Kirsten raised an eyebrow at the girl in leather armor, not much older than she was. "When did you see Merglan and Killdoor?"

"So that's what they're called," she responded. "I saw them in Grandwood, right after you left for Solomon's. And, if I might ask you a similar question, how is it that you know the names of one of them up there?" she asked pointing to the three dragons as they flew out of view.

"My cousin is a dragonrider," Kirsten said. "Who are you?"

Reaching across Rune to extend her hand in greeting, she replied, "Ophelia. I'm the doctor's apprentice."

Kirsten took her hand, "Oh, I'm Kirsten."

"I saw you once before, but you weren't conscious. Glad to have you back now," Ophelia said.

Kirsten felt Rune's gaze on her, and she looked to him.

"You know the new rider? You know we could use him in this war," Rune started, but was interrupted by shouts from the soldiers ahead.

Kirsten's attention flashed back to the army in the field and her heart began to race. Merglan's soldiers were charging en masse.

"Get ready," Rune said. "It's about to begin."

Kirsten put her hand on the hilt of the short sword, then hesitated. Reaching her hand into her pocket, she withdrew the crystal and pulled the thin chain down over her head. The sapphire glowed a light blue and she felt a sense of comfort knowing she could defend herself with it. She didn't yet know if she was any good with a sword, but as she imagined, the battlefield wasn't anyone's first choice to find out if they were a natural.

As the screaming horde of soldiers rushed through the grass, Kirsten watched men and women from the rebel army's front rank move into block formations in front of the trees. As they lowered their spears and waited for the first wave of attackers to hit, archers filled in behind them, taking aim and firing at will. Kirsten wondered if all armies were so well trained that they didn't need commanders barking orders at them or if this group was different.

She held tight to her crystal as charging men fell under the onslaught of arrows, more charging in behind them. In a horrid clash, she could almost feel the front row colliding as they met nearly face-to-face in the open field. She watched in agony as humans killed one another to gain an upper hand. Waves of soldiers on both sides charged one another and soon the long grass was trampled flat and stained red with blood.

Unable to handle watching helplessly as these brave men and women threw themselves into harm's way, Kirsten's urge to help compelled her forward. She heard Thomas calling to her, but ignored him as she felt the need to use her gift in helping bring an end to the fighting. If she could take out the soldiers with her magic crystal and save a few lives in the process, she would.

Kirsten jumped over downed bodies as she rushed into the chaos. Before she realized what she was doing, she had expelled a blast of energy at a group of flanking soldiers, blowing them apart. Bo came into view, passing her and cutting into those among the enemy who had now turned their focus on Kirsten. Arrows pierced men scrambling for her and she knew Thomas was close behind.

Kirsten lost herself in the madness of war. She wielded the crystal in one hand and her short sword in the other. Several times she flung herself into the front lines, blasting through multiple enemy soldiers at a time, waving those behind her forward and shouting for them to fight harder. The day waned and night began to fall. The bodies piled up around them and she lost track of her friends in the fighting.

She felt a hand land on her shoulder. She turned with her sharp-edged blade raised and crystal glowing. Through the blue hue, she saw Britt. "Kirsten, we need to get out of here," she was repeating. The words didn't register until they were repeated a third time. She turned to see why Britt was beckoning her so frantically. In the distance she saw a dark line moving toward them. The sound thundered as they ran with speed. At the center of this mass, she saw a bright blue light. It swung back and forth around the neck of someone, a man riding on horseback. Even though the light of moon and stars, Kirsten knew who that man was. She knew he would be coming ever since Ophelia told her Merglan had returned to Grandwood. Rankstine and his orcs had arrived.

As she turned to flee with Britt, Kirsten heard kurr screaming their ghoulish cry in the darkness. Kirsten broke into a run, retreating with Britt as she found Max, Bo and Thomas still close by. They all retreated into the woods. Kirsten was shocked to see that she'd ventured so far out ahead of the others. Her heart pounded as the evil group moved in closer. She heard the twang of bowstrings and the whistling of arrows as they shot through the trees. Moments later orcs screamed as the rebel arrows found their targets behind her. She didn't want to turn around, but she knew they'd caught up.

Kirsten watched as a kurr passed, catching several rebel soldiers who'd lingered too far beyond the safety of the trees. As she neared the tree line, more kurr passed and she could hear the breathy huffing of one at her heels. Turning and shouting, Kirsten sent a blast of energy directly behind her. The blast blew apart the chest of a kurr just as it reached to grab her. The beast vaulted into the air and fell limply into several charging orcs. Her eyes grew wide when she saw the evil creatures had succeeded in surrounding them.

"Britt!" Kirsten shouted. When Britt looked at her, she slowed, turning to face the oncoming enemies. She then directed blow after blow of energy from the crystal into the charging force, creating a dent in their ranks. Soon Kirsten heard Britt, her warriors, Max and Bo at her side. Thomas shot arrows from the protective pocket behind them. As Kirsten formed the head of their defense, the others battled to create a buffer around her.

Their display worked exactly the way Kirsten had intended. She watched as the glowing light rode nearer. As soon as Rankstine came into view, Kirsten directed a bolt of energy at him. Deflecting it with ease, the man stepped down from his horse, orcs and kurr parting around him in the darkness. She saw an arrow zing toward him and arch around him as his protective spell cast Thomas' shot aside.

Max, Britt and her men charge through the orcs and several kurr toward him. As if orchestrating his band, Rankstine moved more kurr in on them, driving the friends aside and out of view. Kirsten sent several more blasts at the man, which he deflected as he continued to walk ever closer. While she distracted Rankstine, Bo made his move. Kirsten doubled her effort to batter the man with her crystal's energy. Rankstine moved deftly to deflect them, his eyes catching sight of Bo as he cut through orcs to get closer. When Bo was finally on him, Rankstine whipped a lashing of energy down on him. Kirsten shouted upon seeing Bo crushed under its force. She ran toward them and Rankstine whipped the lashing of energy at her. She raised the crystal and blocked it, but the force of the blow knocked her backward. A second blast landed directly behind her, the force sending her tumbling across the ground. As Kirsten rolled, she felt the sapphire necklace slide up over her head. Before she could grab the chain, it had slipped off. She stopped, instantly searching for her lifeline. The sapphire wasn't anywhere near her. At this point, Kirsten thought the poison would've taken her. Was something different? She looked down and saw the special pink-hued stone caught in the neck of her chainmail shirt.

"What's wrong girly?" Rankstine's wicked voice

sounded behind her. "Lose your crystal?"

Kirsten grinned knowing she still clutched the other sapphire in her hand. Turning and expecting to catch Rankstine off guard, Kirsten fired a shot at him. The man jumped back, surprised at her sudden move, but nothing had threatened him. Kirsten frowned. She tried the crystal again, but still nothing. She opened her hand to see that the light had gone from the stone. Tossing it to the ground, Kirsten cursed, knowing that was the only thing that could help her defeat him.

Rankstine stopped, facing her, but at a distance. As she lifted the pink sapphire's chain back around her head, Kirsten stared at the man. "Thought you would get away with it, did you?" he shouted as he raised his blue-glowing crystal over his head. "Too bad for you that I have friends in high places."

As he spoke, Kirsten saw an orange glow in the sky to his left. She smiled, her reaction confusing enough to make him pause. Before he could lash down on her with more energy, she replied, "So do I."

Jetting in from her left, a shower of flame descended on Rankstine, burning him instantly and flashing out through the enemy army at his side. Kirsten jumped back, shielding herself from the dragon fire. After the brunt of the flames had dissipated, Kirsten looked back to see a red dragon unleashing hellfire down on the orc and kurr.

CHAPTER TWENTY-THREE

Unexpected Encounter

hielding his face from the wind-driven rain, Anders blocked the pelting downpour with his arm. The darkened skies had turned midnight black while they'd been in the elven city. Using his mind to sense where Nadir and the elves had gone, Anders and Zahara led Maija and Raffa through the forest's undergrowth. Lightening momentarily brightened their path, followed immediately by a deafening clap of thunder. Skirting the city, Anders and Maija clung to their dragons. Anders could almost feel Zahara's claws digging into the soil in an attempt to brace herself against the punishing winds. They trudged through the forest at a grueling pace, not stopping until they'd reached the outer edge of the heightened storm.

Anders straightened in the saddle, feeling a tightening in his lower back from having scrunched over for so long. He could see the shadowed outline of Maija's dragon stop at their side. Maija's darkened figure loomed over them as she shifted in her new saddle. Zorna tapped Anders on the shoulder, reminding him of her presence.

"They're waiting on the path," she said in her childlike voice.

Dismounting, Anders led them toward the elven trail that headed south away from the capital. Free from the towering cloud, Anders stepped out onto the path to examine the gathering elves under the light of the half-moon and star-filled sky. Soldiers from the elven army mixed ranks with those wearing red shirts, supporters of Nadir's claim to the throne. Anders spotted Nadir in the distance, his long silver hair shining at the head of the gathering forces. The elves parted for the dragonriders as they moved toward the front of the loosely organized ranks.

When they reached Nadir, he was immersed in a conversation with an elf Anders recognized from their campaign in Southland. Bronson had remained loyal to his commander and followed the excommunicated Elf King from Cedarbridge. Capturing their attention, Anders asked, "What do we do now?"

Nadir glanced at Bronson, then replied, "With kurr roaming the area, it's best we hole up here until dawn. I don't like rushing through the forest at night when such creatures roam freely."

"Zahara and I could," Anders began, but Nadir cut him off.

"It's not necessary to push ourselves. It's late. What we need now is rest and to calm our emotions. I'll post lookouts to keep watch while we sleep. In the morning, I'll send Bronson and the redshirts to the Bays. They'll take our ships and retrieve the dwarfs. I promised Remli we'd return for them."

"What of your soldiers?" Anders asked.

"We'll bring an end to the invading kurr. With your help from above, we can locate and hunt them down. We took care of one group this afternoon. We tracked them down just outside the south gate."

"That was you?" Anders said questioningly.

"You were there?" Nadir asked.

"Maija heard them coming, when I sensed the killing. I assumed whatever was taking them out was worse than those creatures, so we flew to the rider's entrance."

Nadir cocked his head, "We missed a reunion by just that much. Funny how that worked."

Anders grinned and checked to see whether Maija had been listening to their conversation. Remembering she could probably have heard them even from the back of the pack, his gaze fell on Zorna. Nodding toward her, he asked Nadir, "And what do we do with her?"

"As far as I'm concerned, she's a free woman. She kept her word in helping us with the crystals," Nadir said.

"How do we know it worked?" Anders asked.

"The mirror," he answered, motioning to the leather pouch clasped to his belt. "Natalia tried to make contact before, but I couldn't respond. I'll try again in the morning."

Anders nodded. Eyeing Zorna, he said, "Perhaps you can teach me the ancient language, that is before you go north."

"What makes you think I'll do that?" she asked.

"You said yourself you wanted the knowledge to spread to as many willing minds as possible," Anders stated.

"What I meant to say was, what makes you think I'll go back north?"

Anders watched a grin curl the youthful elder's lips and he understood that she really did want to see them succeed. "Very well," he said turning to Nadir. "Until morning." He walked a short distance from the others, finding a cleared patch of grass near the path to lie on for the remainder of the night.

As he unpacked his bedding from Zahara's saddle, Maija and Raffa joined them. Maija helped him gather enough wood for a small fire to keep them warm while they slept. Using magic to ignite the wood, he and Maija shared a flask of water and sat close to the fire. Zorna joined them, quietly sitting down and folding her legs as she held her ankles. She stared at them through the flames.

Anders felt her gaze fix on him, "I sense something in you, boy."

"Is it greatness?" he asked somewhat sarcastically, thinking Max would've appreciated the humor.

She shrugged, "Greatness in conflict, yes. I can feel a pain in you that's subdued by your responsibility."

"What responsibility?" Maija asked.

"To fulfill a Prophecy," she said, her eyes looking over Maija momentarily as if she'd missed something, then trained again on Anders.

"How can you possibly know so much and have been held in seclusion, locked away from the outside world?"

"I can see with my mind's eye," she said, tapping her forehead. "I can see the desires and struggles that afflict you."

"And what would you recommend I do? Or do you just point out the flaws and weaknesses in people?" he asked.

Maija elbowed him and he lurched, "Anders, be respectful. She didn't point out any flaws or weaknesses and she might actually be trying to help."

"I can offer you guidance, a way to ease your suffering," Zorna said.

He narrowed his eyes, "You'll teach me how to control the sapphire?"

She nodded, spreading her hands. To his amazement, Anders saw a trail of light curl up from her palm and he thought back to when he first tapped into Lazuran's power. Anders watched intently as the growing wisps of blue-hued light rose from the Norfolk woman's skin.

In a flash, the light returned into her body. "I can show you how to control it."

Anders nodded, silently agreeing to listen to what the old woman had to say. She had already hinted that to access the crystal's power he must speak the correct word in the ancient language.

"My people believe that all riders have the ability to access the ancient dialect of dragons from the moment they're first bonded. You have this ability, Anders, and I can show you how to use it. You see, when the right combination of emotion and magical energies are directed at the true nature of an object, that object, whatever it is, will reveal its name. Speak the name of the crystal and its energy will be yours to command. As long as the magic flows within the sapphire, you can control it."

"But there isn't anything left inside the crystal," Anders said.

Zorna raised her eyebrow at him and smiled, "Are you sure about that, boy?"

Anders frowned. The crystal had whispered to him, so it had to hold energy, but how did she know? "How do I know when I've used the right amount of magic? I've tried putting energy into Lazuran's sapphire before. I wanted it to accept my energy with every ounce of my being, but it didn't work. How do I know what the right combination is?"

"Why don't you try it now, so I can see for myself," she said, motioning to his elven sword.

Anders picked up the blade in its scabbard and stared at the crystal fused to its pommel. The ornament hadn't glowed with magic since he'd used it to transport Zahara and himself away from Merglan. Focusing on the sapphire, Anders opened his mind and used his senses to probe the rough-cut crystal. He held its presence in his thoughts and attempted to search for its meaning, not sure if he would recognize the word if it came to him.

He envisioned glory, the sword helping to champion in battle. Keeping the image in his mind, he sent a steady stream of energy from his hand onto the sword's pommel. He held the flow for several deep breaths, truly wanting the sword to accept his magic and reveal its true name.

Ending his spell, Anders looked at the crystal. Its rough-cut center remained dull, without light. He slouched with a sigh.

"Don't be discouraged that easily, young one," Zorna said. "You had true emotion in your attempt. I could feel its purity from here. Whatever purpose you held for the crystal, that wasn't it. Think of something else and try again."

Straightening, Anders focused on the sapphire again, this time finding a new meaning for the crystal. He pictured Lazuran as a mighty healer, working with him to combine their magic to bring good health to the injured or ill. His palm expelled a flow of energy again and he opened his eyes. As it had done before and after all his attempts, the crystal remained dull.

"Failure can be useful in the search for success. The

points at fault in your failures can be turned into points of strength, if used correctly. Take what you know to be wrong and use it to cut away the untruths. What you have leftover will be the success you seek," she said.

Anders glanced to Maija. He tried to communicate to her through his eyes that he had no idea what the woman's cryptic message meant. Maija nodded, encouraging him to try again. He found that he missed Max's sense of humor in that moment.

Replicating what he'd done before, Anders continued to search for Lazuran's true meaning. With each attempt, he envisioned a different purpose for the sword. Each time he failed to imbue the sapphire with energy. By the end of his nineteenth attempt, Anders felt exhausted. He slumped in defeat at the fireside, the warmth of the flames lulling him to abandon his efforts.

While looking into the fire, he thought of Zorna's directive, *Look for the crystal's purpose.* He focused his attention on the sword and realized his mistake. This whole time he'd been searching for Lazuran's name and not the crystal's. The thought to view the crystal as an entity separate from the sword hadn't crossed his mind.

Struck by this thought, Anders straightened. With renewed vigor, he looked across the flames at Zorna and said, "The crystal. It's not the sword." He turned to Maija, seeing her startle at his sudden change in mood. He smiled and said again, louder this time, "The crystal is not the sword."

Maija shook her head slightly, "Anders, are you feeling okay?"

"I feel amazing," he said. "This whole time I've been

thinking of the sword, trying to find the meaning behind the blade, but, in truth, the sapphire is an entirely separate object from the blade." As Anders spoke, he recalled the times when he'd thought he'd heard something or someone speaking to him. When he first held the sword, the crystal's energy passed through him and he had spoken an ancient dialect. His words played out in light blue energy as he said them. He had felt its influence when sparring with Natalia and she grew angry with him after he allowed it to guide him. With widened eyes, he looked to the Norfolk woman, "It's been trying to tell me its name this whole time, I just never understood it."

Anders prepared for a final attempt to discover the crystal's true name. He focused on the stone and, for the first time, imagined it as an object all on its own. He envisioned the stone opening, cracking its shell to reveal a being inside. Anders could see the object clearly now, as a living thing with thoughts, feelings, and emotions of its own. Holding onto that vision, he spoke a word that he hadn't known to exist, a word from the ancient language of the dragons. Directing his focus at the crystal, he channeled energy from his palm to the stone. Anders watched intently as magic from his body transferred into the sapphire, which glowed as it began to pulse with new light. Its sudden brightness caused him to lose focus. He had to look away and shield his eyes.

Lowering his elbow as the flash subsided, Anders looked down at the sword he held across his lap. To his joy, the pommel glowed. The light blue energy from his palm had passed into the crystal and rooted itself inside. Anders gasped as he hefted the sword up and away from the fire to admire his work. The light glowed even more brightly against the night sky.

As he rolled the sword in his hands, he felt an immense sense of accomplishment. The familiar presence he'd grown attached to in Lazuran returned and Anders almost thought the sapphire was trying to speak to him. Before he pushed his mind deeper into the crystal, the old woman's clapping disrupted his concentration on the connection. Maija joined the applause and he felt the sensation from the crystal fade, replaced now with pride.

"Well done, Anders," Maija said, grabbing his arm fondly. "You did it!"

Anders smiled, then a question floated into the forefront of his mind. If he were to use the energy he had just put into Lazuran, would it have the same dangerous effect it'd had before? Relaying the question to the old woman, Anders and Maija sat in silence, awaiting her response.

"I told you I sensed a struggle in you," she began. "The struggle for control within your conscience. Only you have the power to control it. When you fueled the crystal with energy just now, you did it with intent. Magic reads the true soul of a person. When you impart your power into an inhabitance crystal, it reflects your true character. I can't tell you for certain whether the struggle you're facing within is the good trying to overcome the evil or the evil trying to overcome the good. You'll know when you call on that energy and your true self takes control." Zorna shifted her watchful eyes to Maija and said, "There is something in you as well. What that is only the future will tell. Darkness blinds me to it, but I see pain and fire."

Maija squeezed Anders' hand. "You're good. I know you are," she said with certainty. "And whatever lies ahead for us, we'll face together."

Anders smiled slightly, "I hope you're right."

During the remainder of the evening, Anders directed more and more of his energy into the crystal. Each time, he felt the crystal calling, drawing him in as he flooded it with magic. Totally exhausted and in need of sleep, Anders laid the sword at his side. Lying back on his blanket, he closed his eyes and let the fatigue take over.

***

"Anders," he heard a whisper float into his ear. He stirred, not wanting to wake from his slumber. "Anders, find me," the voice said again. This time, he opened his eyes.

"Find you where?" he asked, sitting up. He expected to see Nadir or maybe Raffa standing over him, but to his confusion, no one was nearby. He looked to Maija, still asleep wrapped in her blanket at his side.

Looking across the smoldering remnants of their fire, Anders saw Zorna, sitting in the same position as the night before. She stared blankly into the distance, which made Anders wonder if that's how the sorceress slept. He jumped slightly when she spoke to him, "Last night wasn't the first time you've spoken the ancient language."

Anders tried to recall a time that he'd spoken in the dragon's tongue. Tossing his wool blanket aside, he said, "I don't recall having spoken it before." He kept his eyes fixed on the strange woman as he stood up. "Did you say something to wake me up?" he asked, brushing the wrinkles from his pants.

Zorna shook her head, moving for the first time since

he'd opened his eyes, "I didn't say a thing, but you did."

"Talking in my sleep?" he asked. "I do that sometimes."

"You spoke in the ancient tongue. I knew you could, but when you did, I felt in you that the word you said last night wasn't the first time."

Anders recalled what Ivan had said when he first held Lazuran. "You got all that from what I said?"

"Don't you find it odd?" she asked.

Anders nodded.

"Me, too," the old woman said.

Anders shrugged, trying to focus on what he needed to do to prepare for the day. He reached down and picked up Lazuran, strapping it to his waist. He felt complete with it at his side, a comforting presence that increased his self-confidence.

As he woke Maija and packed away their bedding, Anders could hear Nadir commanding the separation of their forces. He informed them Zorna would stay on the ground with them. How she would manage to keep pace Anders did not know. Perhaps the elder knew a magic to keep in stride with the elves. *Either that or one of them will carry her on his back,* Anders thought.

With the Norfolk woman still watching, they mounted their dragons and prepared to begin their hunt for the kurr. Looking to the soldiers forming ranks to move and watching the redshirts disappear down the trail, Anders felt that he was a part of something again. After spending most of the past two weeks alone with Maija and their dragons, Anders felt as though he had some control again over the events that would happen next.

Bursting through the forest canopy, Zahara and Raffa

climbed until they were several body lengths above the trees. Anders wanted to fly low in case they needed to help the elves. As he used his senses to search the ground below, his mind wandered to Natalia. Had she found Ivan in the castle? Anders had a duty to remain with the elves and felt purpose when serving with them, but something in his gut told him he should be trying to help Ivan more directly.

Sticking to Nadir's plan, he reminded himself to inquire whether the elf had made contact with Natalia that morning as he'd planned. Zahara and Anders continued searching with their minds as the elves followed. Looking to Maija as she flew at his right, he could sense that she was trying to put into practice what Ivan and Natalia had been teaching her back at the dragonrider training facilities. The elf's capital sat camouflaged in the distance, the thunderhead still hovering over the city. Suddenly, he felt a threatening presence nearby, one dark in magic, darker than any horde of kurr could produce. Shifting in his seat, Anders prepared to use defensive battle magic as he searched for the source of the dark being. Anders looked back toward Nagano. Could the dragons have followed them? Were they behind the kurr's pointed attacks on the elven villages?

"Maija," Anders called. She broke her concentration to look at him expectantly., He said, "I can feel a dark magic nearby. We need to land and warn Nadir. I don't know if it's those dragons or something worse, but I feel certain that we're being watched."

Maija nodded and Raffa and Zahara turned, dropping down toward the trees. Spotting the elves behind them, Anders thought he saw a flash through the trees at his side. The movement couldn't have been from them since it originated far out to his right. Diverting from what he'd told Maija to do, Anders steered Zahara right, cutting under Raffa and Maija to fly toward the movement.

Zahara dropped lower, just over the trees and Anders could sense what it was that caused the movement: kurr running full speed toward the elves. Anders quickly attempted to communicate with Maija to warn the elves. Almost the instant he made the telepathic link, a sharp force cut through, stopping the message midstream. Anders retracted, putting up his mental barriers as Zahara sped toward the charging kurr.

Seeing Raffa and Maija just behind them, Anders shouted to put up their wards. He knew Ivan had been teaching her how and that she didn't need magic to protect her mind from a sorcerer. Not knowing whether she heard him, Anders looked ahead again, hoping Maija's hearing was still heightened.

"Be ready, Zahara, there's another sorcerer down there," Anders said aloud to avoid opening his mind. Anders had identified the location of the dark magic, but he could hardly believe such power could come from kurr.

Shield yourself from the flames, Zahara interjected, briefly exposing their minds as she neared the enemies' frontline.

As Zahara's chest swelled with fire, Anders conjured the shield he'd used before in Southland, hoping it would buffer the heat as it did the orc's arrows. In an explosion of red and orange flame, Zahara unleashed a deadly stream of fire down into the trees. Anders raised his arm instinctively to protect himself, though he felt the pressure pushing on him as the magic drew energy from his body. Flames billowed around them. Zahara continued to force the dragon fire down onto the kurr below. She torched a swath through the middle of the charging kurr, extinguishing only when they'd passed fully beyond the enemy ranks. Looking back, Anders saw Maija and Raffagaun making their first pass over the kurr. The dragon flew higher so Maija wouldn't be charred by flame, but the dragon's jet poured a conflagration of fire onto the kurr. As Zahara pulled up from their attack, Anders could see the forest burning below. He was shocked to see kurr continuing through the burn. Half their numbers had just been roasted by dragon fire, yet they continued to charge as if nothing could stop them.

Zahara joined Raffa in another pass at the kurr. From within the trees, Anders heard the clash as the kurr collided with the elves. Dropping low, the dragons prepared for another attack.

Anders shouted, "Careful not to touch the elves with fire!"

As they flew over, the trees flaming in their wake, Anders caught an occasional glimpse of the fighting below. Nadir and his soldiers struggled to regroup into battle formation. Their only warning about the vast number of kurr they were about to encounter was the dragon fire moments before their attack. It all happened so fast, Anders hadn't had time to warn them, especially since there appeared to be a dark sorcerer in the midst of the kurr.

Anders heard trees cracking behind them and glanced back to see Raffa using his tail as a giant club, pulverizing the creatures into the ground wherever his tail landed. Though Maija couldn't use magic, her dragon could make up for it with sheer force.

Zahara curved up as she reached the fighting, banking sharply in a sudden turn. Angling down, she plowed through the trees near the front of the battle. From the sound of crashing branches, Anders knew Raffa and Maija were close behind. The dragons touched down just beyond where elves and kurr remained tangled in a deadly struggle. Anders jumped from Zahara's back, knowing they would be twice as destructive if he could wield his sword. He charged through the forest floor, pulling Lazuran from its sheath as he passed through burning trees. The blade felt at home in his hand and he knew their pairing would bring an end to all who stood against them.

Cutting his way into the morass, Anders worked his blade to cut down three kurr who pulled away from the group to confront him. Zahara snarled while swatting and gnashing her way into the fight. Raffa and Maija soon joined the battle. At one point, Anders caught a glimpse of the red dragon devouring multiple kurr with a single bite.

As the dragons and Anders tore into the enraged kurr, Anders saw the flashing lights of magic being deployed. He'd found the sorcerer in their midst, and angled toward it. Anders found himself hampered in his pursuit, though, as he struggled to match the kurr's strength. He dodged countless strikes and continued to kill kurr after kurr, feeling it was more luck than skill. The large creatures continued to tear their way into the elves even though the two groups seemed to include equal numbers. In a final attempt to push through to the sorcerer, Anders found he was overwhelmed, so he deployed bursts of magic to clear a path back to Zahara and Raffagaun. Now on the defensive, he blocked and backed away farther from the fighting. Once he gained an opening, he climbed onto Zahara's back. She continued to gnaw and swipe at the kurr as they hounded at her from multiple directions.

Looking toward where he last saw the flashes from the sorcerer in the fighting, Anders identified their origin. Zorna was in the midst of the kurr using magic against them. From his angle on the ground, Anders couldn't see the short old woman and had assumed it to be the enemy sorcerer.

That means the enemy sorcerer is still out there watching all of this, he thought.

Spurring Zahara, Anders shouted, "The dark magic hasn't revealed itself. We must find it before it attacks."

Leaping skyward, she beat her wings through the trees and back into the sky. As she stalled in a hover, Anders searched the grounds for the dark magic's signature. Anders felt Zahara's chest swelling with fire. She was going to use their vantage point to burn more of the creatures. As Anders watched the fire's initial destruction, movement in the air nearby drew his attention. He turned to see a dragon with open jaws descending on them.

In a last-ditch effort, Anders attempted to produce a shield. It was only half-formed when the dragon hit. The dragon's open jaws bounced off the edge of the shield, knocking it to the side before the bulk of its chest rammed into Zahara. The dragon's momentum carried itself past Zahara, causing her to tumble into Raffagaun. The assaulting dragon disappeared from Anders' sight when Zahara crashed into the trees. Anders felt the blistering heat from Raffagaun's stream of fire as he rolled, sending a flash of flame through the trees and into the sky.

He gripped the handle on his saddle as they crashed. If it weren't for the magical connection active in his saddle, he would've lost this one-handed grip. He became keenly aware of Lazuran during their fall. He held the blade tightly, out away from them as they met the ground.

Lurching in his seat, Anders closed his eyes and waited to for Zahara to roll over on top of him. When he realized that they'd come to a full stop, he opened his eyes to see that Zahara had somehow righted herself and managed to land on her feet. Anders quickly searched for Raffa and Maija. Through the swaying branches, he spotted Raffagaun pressing off the forest floor with his wing in an attempt to right himself. As Raffa stood to his full height, Anders was relieved to see that Maija had stayed in her saddle and appeared uninjured.

With no sign of the dragon that had attacked them, Zahara and Raffa simultaneously launched back above the trees. Exploding through the canopy, the dragons continued to climb above the vegetation to avoid being caught hovering for a second time. With each dragon's speed increasing as they rose, Anders and Maija searched for their attacker. Anders spotted a pair of dragons hovering high above the trees over the fighting. Leveling out at the same elevation, Zahara shifted her sights to the two riders.

With his senses focused on them, Anders felt excessive power radiating from them and thought, *Merglan!*

Preparing mentally, he felt that Zahara also recognized the large black dragon. "This is it, Zahara. We're going to face them here and now," Anders said. At their side, Raffagaun unleashed a deafening roar and Anders guessed that even the wild dragon sensed this was their greatest enemy. With little time to prepare, he watched the two riders move into position, wondering briefly who the other rider with Merglan could possibly be. This would be Anders and Zahara's first rider-on-rider battle, and he hoped it wouldn't be their last. Anders prepared to use his magic.

Anders' heart raced as they came within firing range. Conjuring a shield, Anders allowed Zahara and Raffa to send streams of fire at their attackers. Anders and Maija met Merglan and his companion in a wall of flame as the dragon fire collided like two lances in a jousting arena. Fire spread rapidly in all directions and Anders momentarily lost sight of the dark sorcerer. He held Lazuran at the ready, prepared to block any physical attack that might emerge through the fire.

Zahara arched upward; Anders held on tight to his saddle during the sudden change in direction. Listing to one side, he saw the enemy dragon through the vanishing flames and latched onto Zahara. Anders struck out with his blade, stabbing at the creature as the dragons raked each other's undersides. He stabbed again at the black scales and saw the red on his blade as he withdrew it. Killdoor's massive eye turned on him and Zahara bit down on his exposed throat. Seeing Merglan, Anders reacted quickly to the man's sword. He deflected the dark sorcerer's attempts to stab Zahara and shouted for her to push away from the deadly embrace.

Merglan suddenly attacked him with his mind, bearing down on Anders and trying to distract him from his physical assault. Anders groaned as he held Merglan off. Anders continued to work with Lazuran, letting the sword guide his arm as he defended himself and Zahara on multiple fronts. The dragons snapped at each other as they kicked, trying to strike mortal blows.

In a flash, Raffagaun and Maija appeared at Killdoor's back. Raffa's enormous claws thrashed at Killdoor and Maija tried to swing at Merglan with her sword. Merglan sent a pulse of energy out in all directions causing Zahara and Raffagaun to separate from Killdoor. The dragon dropped away from them, diving back out into open skies.

"Maija, are you alright?" Anders called to her.

"Just a few scrapes, nothing looks too serious," he heard Maija shout.

"Where's the other rider?" Anders asked as Zahara set her sights on Killdoor again.

"We scared him off for now," Maija replied.

Confused, Anders panted, feeling the fatigue in his arm from the swordplay. He could hardly believe they had survived Merglan's initial attack.

Pursuing them down closer to the forest, Anders and Zahara led the charge into Killdoor and Merglan. They cut and hacked violently as Anders and Merglan each used pulses of energy to try to unseat one another. As the two dragons worked to outmaneuver Killdoor, constantly moving one dragon to his flank, Anders' confidence began to grow. Merglan's mental attacks lessened the more he used his magic to attack Anders. He was now relying more on his sword. Though his physical strength was beginning to wane, Anders felt strong mentally. He thought if they could cause Merglan to drop his sword or fall from the saddle, they would win this fight.

As they tumbled and parried closer to the burned area where the kurr and elves fought, Anders wielded his blade in an adrenaline-fueled attack on Merglan. Driving them back, Anders saw that Killdoor's wings were not reaching their full potential. He backed off and was astonished to see that Killdoor was unable to flap his wings. The dragon fell quickly toward the ground and Zahara dove after dragon and rider.

Anders forced his mind down onto Merglan's as his dragon crashed through the scorched opening in the trees. The man's wards were up, but for the first time, he didn't try to attack. Instead, Merglan sealed his mind off. Zahara landed several dragon-lengths from the grounded enemy dragon just as Zorna approached with a blue-hued crystal hanging from a chain around her neck. Anders realized she had been the one working to constrain Killdoor once they'd neared the battle again.

As if mirroring each other's actions, Anders and Merglan dismounted their dragons and dipped into fighting stances. Anders continued to send his mental strength at Merglan's, feeling Zorna's efforts working alongside his to crack into the sorcerer's mind. Merglan's mental walls remained sealed as Anders charged. Zahara and Raffagaun leapt out in front of him and met Killdoor moments before Anders and Merglan's blades connected.

Anders and Merglan fought with magically enhanced speed as neither one relented. The dragons' battle became lost to Anders as he focused wholly on breaking Merglan. Lazuran danced for Anders as he delivered a series of offensive strikes. Noticing a false step in Merglan's stance, Anders sent a pulse of magic into his limbs, delivering an inhuman sideswipe. Merglan tried to block the swing, but Lazuran sent the sorcerer's sword flying through the air. Lost in the thrill of the fight, Anders stomped at Merglan's chest, sending energy into his leg as he kicked the sorcerer off his feet. He watched as Merglan landed a short distance away on his back. Anders sprang on him, stopping Lazuran's tip just a hair's width away from Merglan's throat. The sorcerer lay dazed as Nadir and several elves rushed in to restrain him. Anders kept the point of his sword trained on Merglan as the Norfolk woman used magic to bind his arms and legs. Glancing at her, Anders could see the tendrils of energy wisping off the crystal and into her body. With Merglan magically restrained, she could focus on keeping his mind at bay.

Turning, Anders saw that Raffa and Zahara struggled to prevent Killdoor from attacking them all. Once Zorna had finished restraining Merglan, the Norfolk woman used energy from the crystal to physically restrain the dragon, leaving him to hover just inches above the ground.

Seeing the crystal's energy at work, Anders asked, "Handy, you suddenly having that crystal to help control them."

Through the lines on her face, Anders could see the woman straining to hold both Killdoor and Merglan from escaping. Through tight lips she said, "Nadir gave it to me. Said it came from his dead stepmother."

Anders looked to Merglan again, his blade still held at the man's throat, "Did you hear that? She's using your own magic against you." Anders waited for the sorcerer to respond, but he simply glared at them, struggling to break free of Zorna's control.

Anders heard elves reporting to Nadir at his back, telling him that the remaining kurr had fled after seeing the dragon fall. From the corner of his eye, Anders saw Maija rush over to them. She held a bloodied blade, pointing it at Merglan as she stopped at Anders' side.

"The other rider?" Anders asked.

"Last I saw of him, he was fleeing to the west," she said.

Anders nodded. He glanced over his shoulder and asked Nadir, "What of the kurr who escaped?"

"Taken care of," Nadir said, sheathing his sword. "My soldiers are in pursuit as we speak. Kurr are quick, but elves are faster. They'll dispatch them soon enough."

Anders looked to the Norfolk woman who held Merglan and Killdoor, "Is he fighting you hard?" he asked.

She shook her head, keeping her eyes fixed on them, "He's trying to, but he's not a match for me with the help of this crystal."

Merglan attempted to speak, the mumbled noise drawing their attention. Anders turned to him, "Let him speak. I want to hear what he has to say."

Merglan's glare turned into a snarl as Zorna allowed him to speak. His words spitting with venom, he asked, "What have you done to my crystals?"

"So, it worked; Natalia did find them," Nadir said. "I questioned it when she hadn't contacted me. But now," Nadir scoffed. "You'll never use magic again. Where you're going you won't be needing it."

Anders stepped closer to Merglan, "What did you do to my father?"

Merglan's snarl turned into a malicious grin and he started to laugh.

Frustrated with his response, Anders raised Lazuran into a striking position and repeated, "What have you done with my father?" the deadly bite in his tone stung even his ears. Anders' heart raced as he looked down at the kneeling sorcerer, trapped in a magic he could not break. The hate he held for Merglan boiled inside him and he saw the glowing light of the sapphire pommel in his hand. All he had to do was let the rage in and he could destroy his enemy.

"Do it, boy," Merglan whispered. "Let the hate in and take my head."

Anders stared at him, shaking as he envisioned Lazuran swiping cleanly through his neck.

"I know you can still feel a piece of me inside you. Let it out to play and show them all what you really are," Merglan taunted.

Anders hated the man kneeling before him. Struggling with the emotions surging through him, Anders asked through clenched teeth, "Where's Ivan?" Anders drowned out the sound of the others shouting at him to put down his sword and waited for Merglan to respond.

"What I did to Prince William, I should've done a long time ago. One day I'll do the same to you," Merglan paused, his grin fading to a scowl. In a voice only Anders could hear, he said, "I sent him straight to hell. Your pals in Brookside will be joining him soon. Too bad there's nothing you can do to stop it."

Anders fought his instinct to pass Lazuran through Merglan's neck and asked, "Who do you mean by my pals in Brookside?"

Merglan spat at Anders, hitting him in the face, mocking him for what he'd done to Merglan weeks before.

Anders shouted at Merglan as he again raised his sword, preparing to kill. Among all the cries from those behind him urging him to stop, the only voice he heard was Merglan's as he screamed, "Do it!"

Anders swung the sword, intentionally missing as it passed well over Merglan's head. Heaving, he pulled Lazuran back to his side and slid it into his scabbard. Despite his desire to kill the sorcerer right then and there, he knew deep down that if he did, he would end up just like the man at his feet. Anders turned and strode away from the sorcerer. "He's sent the other rider after my family," he said, walking over to Nadir and Maija.

"We have to stop him," Maija said.

Anders looked to the Norfolk woman, his new-found ally, "Can you restrain him as he's moved back to the prison?"

"With this amount of control," she said, nodding to the necklace. "I could control him and the dragon all of the way to Northland if you wanted."

"Let's send him back to the cells in Cedarbridge. The Council will have to let us in with a prisoner like this. We'll lock him away in a cell so deep he'll never see the light of day again," Nadir said sternly.

"Good. Maija and I will take care of the other rider," Anders said, moving toward Zahara.

After taking a moment to examine Zahara's superficial wounds, he and Maija took to their saddles and began their pursuit of the escaped rider.

CHAPTER TWENTY-FOUR

The Rider in Black

ightening his grip on the saddle, Anders lowered himself against Zahara's neck as she gained speed. The new rider who had rammed them with his dragon during the kurr attack had taken off before they could capture him. Anders pictured the stranger in his mind; he rode a green dragon and wore black leathers. As he and Zahara searched the western horizon, Anders hoped this unknown dragon wouldn't be able to out-fly them to Brookside. The last he'd heard from his friends and family, they were headed to Grandwood, but with Merglan's reach expanding to Nagano and the Everlight Kingdom, Anders feared that the evil sorcerer's control had likely reached Westland as well. All they could do now was hunt for the lone rider who'd flown toward the towering mountains that marked the boundary between human and elf nations.

There, in the distance, Zahara said, pointing out the distant dot moving against the mountainous backdrop through their telepathic link. The rider's outline was unrecognizable at such a distance, but the dark shape moved slowly as it shifted position.

"We've got a location on him!" Anders shouted to

Maija, who rode low against Raffa's neck. He pointed ahead and Maija nodded.

Locating the rider fired Anders and Zahara with renewed vigor. Increasing her speed, Zahara pulled ahead of Raffagaun. Glancing over his shoulder minutes later, Anders saw the large red dragon struggling to keep up with Zahara's more aerodynamic form. Each time Anders turned to check on them, Raffa and Maija had fallen farther behind to a point where Anders feared they wouldn't be of any use when he and Zahara caught up with the unfamiliar rider.

I still see them, Zahara's voice entered Anders' mind. *We're gaining on them.*

I want to catch them before they get to those mountains, Anders said. *It will be hard to follow their flight path if they disappear among the peaks. If that rider is smart, they will use the peaks and valleys to their advantage to lose us.*

And if they're not smart? Zahara asked.

Then we will catch them in the open skies.

As they sped over the elven forest, Anders replayed the events of their encounter with Merglan. Starting from the moment of their arrival in Cedarbridge, he worked through all that had happened to them until that moment. Anders felt a sense of unease about how the events had unfolded. Reaching out to his dragon, he said, *Zahara, did you find it odd how easily we captured Merglan and Killdoor?*

Before she responded, Anders could sense that she shared his feelings about it. *We trained hard over the months leading up to this and when last we met them, we narrowly escaped,* she said.

And that was with Ivan's help, Anders added.

It all happened so quickly, she said. *Suddenly they were there. It was like they were waiting for just the right moment to attack.*

If Merglan wanted to kill us then, why did he let that rider strike first? Why didn't he just take us out then? Anders asked.

Perhaps he knew that if he got too close to the Norfolk woman, she could beat him? Zahara suggested.

Anders frowned, staying low against her neck, *I don't know. It just felt like he was too easy to beat.*

He did mention the crystals. Maybe that was where he'd gotten all of his strength? Last time we faced him, they would've been close enough for him to access, she said.

If that were the case, why didn't he have any on him? Wouldn't he have used them if he did? Anders asked.

Do you think Merglan meant to get captured? Zahara asked.

But that doesn't make sense, Anders said, frustration clouding his thoughts.

I can read your mind, Anders. You're not convinced that we really defeated Merglan, Zahara said after a moment of silence.

It just feels like it should've been harder. Even without corrupting the stock of crystals in Southland, wouldn't he still have more experience and skill? That was our first rider-on-rider combat. Are we really good enough to take out the most powerful sorcerer in the world in a matter of minutes? Anders asked.

All I know is that we beat them and now they're going to be locked away for the rest of their days. If that isn't justice, I don't know what is. The Prophecy was right, we defeated them and now they're going to regret coming after us for the rest of their miserable lives, Zahara said.

I guess you're right. They've been captured, Anders said. *What I need to focus on now is not letting this mysterious rider get the jump on us. I don't know where Merglan found this one, but if he's going to go after my friends and family, he must have a death wish.*

Nobody even heard whispers that Merglan had an apprentice. Didn't Ivan tell us there weren't any other riders in the five nations?

Yeah, he did. Natalia and Keanu were the last ones until us. And aside from Maija and Raffa, there hasn't been another pair that any dragon or elf is aware of.

So where did he find one? she asked.

He probably forced that poor dragon to bond with one of his orcs or something, Anders suggested.

Did you see how they moved? Zahara asked. *It was with skill. That rider knows how to control a dragon, even if it was forced to bond. They've had practice.*

Anders thought about Zahara's suggestion. He had noticed that the unknown rider's control of the dragon was well executed. Raffagaun would have easily crushed a less experienced rider. A dragon of Raffa's size was dangerous even without a rider. Anders recalled the months of practice it took Zahara to gain her skill in fending off another dragon.

Looking back, Anders saw that Raffagaun and Maija had fallen even farther behind. The red dragon might be formidable in a fight, but he was no match for Zahara in speed. Turning forward again, Anders caught sight of a glowing on Lazuran's pommel. As he stared at the light, he was reminded of the voice he'd heard earlier that morning. Zorna told him he had spoken the ancient language just before waking. He tried to remember what the voice sounded like, knowing that it didn't come from anyone he knew at camp. The sound slipped from his memory and he looked ahead again.

Anders could see the rider in black more clearly now. He could easily define the dragon's shape against the mountainous backdrop. Anders reached toward them with his mind, feeling at the dragon and rider's presence. Though their signal was weak, it was enough to track even if he lost sight of them. Anders wondered whether this rider was well trained enough to conceal himself and his dragon once they dipped into the Frozentip Mountains.

Anders and Zahara had gained significant ground on the rider in black by the time they reached the foothills. The fleeing rider repeatedly looked over his padded shoulder as they struggled to stay ahead of their pursuers. From close-range, Anders could only sense the dragon's mind, not the rider's. Either the rider was very good at concealing himself or he didn't have a mind, which Anders suspected wasn't possible. Frequently, Anders glanced over his shoulder to check on the progress of Raffa and Maija. He hoped they wouldn't be too far behind when he and Zahara initiated an attack.

The rider and dragon crested the first snowcapped ridge along the Frozentip Mountain front. Diving down the opposite slope, Anders watched them disappear beyond the ridgeline. Anders focused his mind's eye on the fleeing dragon's location. It dropped quickly down in elevation as Zahara climbed the east-facing slope. Cresting the snowline, Anders caught his first glimpse of what extended beyond the mountain front. A sea of white peaks rising and falling into the distance revealed a maze of snow-covered crags. On the westward horizon, Anders saw the yellow grasslands of the Bareback Plains give way to the green Riverlands.

Gripping his handles tightly, Anders held on as Zahara dropped rapidly down the first western slope. The cold air numbed his hands and the frosty chill bit at his cheeks, causing his eyes to water. He shared the dragon's location with Zahara as he spotted it swooping out of a dive. Fighting through the chill, Anders gritted and flexed as they rocketed down toward a canyon below.

Zahara's wings vibrated, thumbing the air at her sides as she sped downslope. Lifting as she neared the canyon between mountains, Zahara's wings caught the thin mountain air and she slowed, pulling herself up. During their descent, Anders had lost sight of the green dragon again as it tucked into a gorge among the canyon walls. The rocks closed in around them as they flew deeper into the mountain range. Anders sensed the dragon's location, cutting and weaving its way ahead of them. Zahara's expert aviary skills closed the gap and Anders caught another glimpse of the black rider; they were within range of his magic. Sourcing his own energy and allowing Zahara to use her full strength in flight, Anders summoned his power.

He saw the dragon cut up and away from the canyon, escaping the narrowing walls. Knowing this could be their chance, Anders prepared a blast of energy, the glow of magic showing in his palm. He rocked forward slightly as Zahara pulled up and out of the canyon to level out. With his hand raised and a blast of energy at his fingertips, Anders was poised to release. Not finding his target, though, Anders stayed his magic, confused at where they'd gone. Cursing himself for focusing his minds eye on his magic and taking it off the other dragon, Anders realized he'd lost them. Refocusing back on the dragon, Anders searched the area.

In the canyon again, he said to Zahara, irritated that he had missed this opportunity to strike. *Stay along the rim; we'll catch them faster that way.*

Zahara doubled her speed now that she didn't have to wind through the canyon walls and Anders could feel them closing the gap again. This time he would wait to source his energy until he had a clear line of sight. He knew they were close; he could feel the dragon as it veered through the widening canyon working downslope. Suddenly, the dragon pulled up and flew out of the canyon. Anders fired a hasty blast of energy and saw it narrowly miss the pair, exploding against the canyon's rim and sending rocks scattering down the cliff walls.

Sourcing anther swell of energy, Anders reached for his magic while Zahara changed course. Pulling away now, the other rider's dragon skirted up a mountainside, hurriedly spiraling to escape. Anders wildly shot three more blasts at the dark rider and his dragon, missing with each one. Anders watched in disbelief as each one of the surges tracked toward its mark perfectly until the last moment when it then veered to the side, exploding into the snow.

His skill at evading is too good, Zahara said. *We need to get right on top of them.*

If Maija and Raffa were near, we could drive them into this pair, Anders said, looking back, but not seeing the red dragon.

I'll try to get you on top of him, Zahara said, pushing forward.

They continued to spiral up the mountain, catching fleeting glimpses of a green dragon's tail. Suddenly the dragon turned, dropping down a mountainside in a straight line. Zahara followed, gaining ground again. Anders saw his opportunity to hit the rider with another blast of energy. He felt it swell in his hand. His heart pounded. He knew that this time they were close enough to cause serious damage. As Anders reached his hand out and took aim, the green dragon pulled into a sudden climb, arching over backward. He tried to follow them with his hand and nearly released his blast, but panicked when he saw the black rider let go of his dragon and drop down onto them.

He tried to warn Zahara to move, but she'd just initiated her loop to follow. The rider hit Anders as she climbed, his outstretched arms grabbing Anders, who was too shocked to move. The dark rider's helmet slammed into Anders' chest and he felt the man's grip wrap around his torso. In an instant, Anders came unglued from his saddle and felt the air under them as they fell. He couldn't see anything as his face was tucked up into the rider's black leather jacket near his stomach. He could feel them rotate and Anders' feet roll over his head as they flipped. In that moment he tried to lift himself away from the rider, but the man's grip was too tight.

From where they'd made contact, Anders knew they weren't far above the snow-covered mountaintop. Quickly, Anders forced a pulse of energy out from all directions just as Merglan had done in their fight earlier. As they hit the ground, the momentary gap he had created between them closed again. Anders landed on the rider. Bouncing away from him after the initial impact, Anders hit the snow and began rolling. Unable to see the rider's location, Anders intentionally picked up speed as he tumbled across the hardened snowpack.

White snow and blue sky swirled together as he rolled. He then summoned some energy and pushed it in one direction, hoping to slow or stop his momentum. Launching himself into the air, Anders' rotation now slowed and he suddenly found himself looking at down at the mountainside. He saw the rider in black also slowing his downward slide, bearing all of his weight down on the handle of a blade stabbed into the snow.

Coming toward the ground, Anders used a small amount of energy to slow himself enough to land upright on the slope. Digging his feet into the snow, Anders looked to the rider as he came to a halt just downslope. Drawing Lazuran from its sheath, Anders felt the comforting weight of the blade in his hand. He twirled the sword with the flick of his wrist and watched as the rider in black sheathed his dagger and drew a long broadsword. Anders thought the rider would wait for Anders to make the first move, but he started uphill at a dead run.

Recalling Ivan's training, Anders pointed his mind at the rider's and launched a mental attack. To his surprise, his pointed attack found no mental presence to grab hold of. Anders retracted his magic and tried again, this time searching to see if he'd missed a cleverly fortified mind. As the rider plodded his way up the snowfield, Anders searched him for any mental signature. The more he searched, the more he sensed this man had no soul. There were no signs of protection around his mind, no walls or anything; he was simply a body carrying out Merglan's bidding. Having focused on his mental attack for too long, Anders lost all momentum of his potential uphill advantage.

The man in black swiped his long sword at Anders' feet. Leaping over the blade, Anders stabbed Lazuran at the rider's helmeted head. The man narrowly dodged his blade as it scraped against the faceplate. Swiping again, the rider tried to take Anders' legs out from under him. Anders reacted in time to block the low-angled strike. Quickly calling on his magic, Anders raised his left hand and shot a pulse of energy from his palm. The blast should've been enough to send them both flying, but to Anders' amazement, the magical energy bent around the rider's body and continued past him.

Thinking the blast of energy would've given them a moment's separation, Anders didn't anticipate the rider's next attack. Frantically, Anders deflected the man's continued low-angled blows, backing side hill to get away. Escaping out of reach of the rider's sword, Anders took advantage of the brief delay and poised himself for an assault. Attacking first this time in their duel, Anders fought to gain an opening on the rider. After a complicated series of blows, Anders saw an opening and took it. As Lazuran found it's mark, he expected the sword to dig into flesh, but it clanged against steel.

Anders retreated several paces, startled by the unexpected sound. He looked to the man's side as the rider felt at the hole in his leather riding jacket. Through the gap, Anders could see the light blue glow of a crystal shining from the hilt of the rider's dagger. Anders had struck the man in the side directly into the dagger's hilt, blocking his blade from the deathly blow. Seeing the rider pull aside his coat and take hold of the dagger, Anders knew his opponent now intended to strike with magic. Producing a shield, Anders was able to block the attack before the other rider could tap into his crystal. The flash from the dagger handle fragmented, breaking into slivers as it passed over Anders' shield. A split second after seeing the light, Anders felt the force pushing him down into the snow.

Once the wave had passed, he released his shield, trying to pull up out of the snow. The rider in black had been struck by a fragment of his own magic and landed on his back several yards downslope. As the man in black began to move, Anders saw his helmet slide away down the hill. Anders paused, waiting for the man to rise. With his helmet removed Anders might get his first glimpse of the stranger's face.

Sitting up in the snow with his back turned to Anders, the rider slowly rose to his feet. Seeing the man's graying hair hanging down past his shoulders, Anders' mind began to spin. He stood waist-deep in the snow looking down at the familiar way in which the man composed himself. Turning and looking back at him with dull, lifeless eyes, Anders' father stood on the snowy slope, an agent of evil. Anders shook his head in disbelief as he stared at Ivan's pale complexion glaring back at him. For a moment, he considered Ivan to be a ghost, but the sight of blood trickling down his father's face carried confirmation of life inside the shell.

Anders watched motionless and in disbelief as Ivan reached up with his hand and jumped. The green dragon passed over him and he arched as he grabbed the horn to his saddle and was carried off into the mountain air. Sheathing his sword as he sat in the snow, Anders saw his father look back at him one last time before the green dragon dipped into the canyon below.

Zahara landed on the slope next to him, her body freshly bloodied from her scrape with the green dragon. *Come on, they're getting away,* she said. When Anders didn't move or respond, she said, *Anders, get out of the snow; they're getting away!*

Anders moved his blank stare to Zahara as she stirred uneasily in the snow. He looked directly into her eyes as she extended her head toward him and sniffed, *What's wrong? You aren't injured, are you?"*

Anders searched for the right words, opening his communicative link with her but not finding anything fitting to say. He felt her confusion when she asked, *What did he tell you? You're in disbelief, but I can't feel what exactly he told you?*

Help me out of here, he managed to respond. Anders reached out and held onto her claw as she lifted him from the hole in the snow. Anders rushed to climb onto Zahara. Seating himself in the saddle, she ran down the slope, letting her wings carry them off the mountainside. As they climbed higher in the sky, Anders saw Raffa's bulky form rush over them. The large dragon roared as he passed.

Are you going to tell me what happened back there or am I going to have to read deep into your thoughts? Zahara asked again.

It's just that, I don't want to believe what I just saw, he replied.

What did you see?

The rider's helmet came off and I saw who it was, Zahara.

Ivan is Merglan's right-hand man. Anders felt her heart sink and they shared the sorrow and realization that Anders' father, the man who'd spent his whole life trying to stop Merglan, was now carrying out his bidding. The only thing that kept them going now was the knowledge that Merglan had sent Ivan to kill Kirsten, Thomas and their companions. Anders refused to let Merglan take away any more members of his family. In that moment, Anders knew what he had to do.

CHAPTER TWENTY-FIVE

King's Fall

atching Raffagaun and Maija, Zahara matched elevation with the red dragon and Anders called out to them, "Don't aim to kill! The rider in black must be captured alive!"

Maija nodded, but he could tell from her expression that she didn't fully understand why.

"The rider isn't a stranger. It's Ivan," he said. The fact that his father was working for Merglan still didn't fully register with him. His words felt hollow, void of actual meaning.

"Are you sure?" Maija shouted back, her features registering fear and concern.

Anders nodded, feeling tears welling in his eyes, "I don't know how," he started, but couldn't finish his sentence before his emotion took over, so he stopped talking. With a horrible pain growing in the pit of his stomach, he said, "We just need to stop him."

Maija nodded and they faced ahead, catching sight of Ivan and the green dragon in the distance as they climbed to altitude over the mountains.

Once we catch up with them again, how are we going to

stop him? Zahara asked.

We'll have to take out the dragon, Anders said. *Without him, Ivan won't be able to get to Kirsten and Thomas quickly. We'll have a better chance at capturing him and trying to undo whatever it is that Merglan's done to him.*

I don't like the idea of killing the dragon either. It's just as likely that it was forced into service in the same way as Ivan, she replied.

I'll do my best to avoid mortal harm, but if it comes down to protecting my family, I'll do what must be done to ensure their safety. After he finished the thought, Anders didn't hear her reply.

Zahara and Raffa pursued Ivan's dragon in tandem, tracking his path over the mountains. With Raffa and Maija close by, Anders and Zahara flew at their pace, steadily gaining on Ivan's green dragon. Anders felt hesitant to engage with Ivan again and definitely didn't feel comfortable doing it alone again.

Zahara, Anders said as she trailed Ivan's dragon by just ten lengths or so, well within striking distance if he chose to use his magic. *Can you sense any kind of consciousness from Ivan?*

No, she replied after a moment of silence. *This is the first time I've ever felt such a lack of being in something living. Usually if they're hiding it, I can still see or feel the hole in the space where they should be. Like when I know there is a fish behind a rock in a river, but I can't see it from the surface, yet I still know it's there. This is different, though. I can't feel anything from him; it's like he's not there at all.*

Like that part of him has been removed, Anders added.

Exactly. But how could Merglan remove the presence of

someone and still have that person appear to be alive and acting on his behalf?

There are so many things about Merglan's magic that we don't know.

At least his powers are limited now. He should be incarcerated by this time.

Ivan still has at least one of Merglan's crystals that we didn't know to alter. I saw it in his dagger back there. If we can separate him from the dagger, we might have a chance at bringing him back, Anders said.

That might work, unless he's doing this of his own accord? Zahara suggested.

No, Ivan would not do this! It must be the dagger controlling him. Ivan has fought his entire life; every ounce of his being has been dedicated to stopping Merglan. He wouldn't just give in and convert. He would rather die. Something else is at play here and it doesn't feel right.

As they crested the last of the ridgelines before the Frozentip Mountains gave way to the Riverlands near Brookside, a dark clustering on the landscape caught his eye. At first Anders thought it was the buildings of Brookside, but something was off. This area was miles outside of town closer to the edge of the Bareback Plains. Anders could just make out the separation of ranks formed in the grass. Focusing on them, he asked Zahara, *Do you see that?*

He felt her scrutinize the gathering of people and then she responded, *An army.*

Are they human? Anders asked, narrowing his eyes.

I can't tell from here, she responded.

Maybe Maija can hear something? Anders suggested. He waved to get Maija's attention and called to her, "See the army down there?" he pointed. "Can you hear anything from them?"

Anders watched as she leaned over so her ear was toward the soldiers in the distance. After a moment, Maija sat up and shook her head, "I can't hear anything. Sorry."

Anders kept an eye on the mass as it slowly moved closer to the forest's edge. He couldn't see or sense what they were marching toward and wondered what they were doing. Rather than letting the army below distract him for more than a moment, Anders concentrated on where Ivan appeared to be directing his dragon. Ivan's dragon dipped down, angling more directly toward the people massing near the forest.

Is he going to attack them? Anders asked Zahara. They watched as Ivan pitched down lower to the ground.

If he isn't attacking them, he's going to join up with them. We'd better intervene now, Zahara said, noting Ivan's change in direction.

Zahara dropped into action, Raffa close on her tail. A roar sounded underneath them as Maija's dragon poured forth a stream of fire aimed at Ivan. Anders' eyes widened and he felt a rage forming toward Raffa for disobeying his wishes to capture Ivan alive. Just when he was going to shout, Anders saw the intended actions of Raffa's technique. Extinguishing his anger, Anders watched as the scarlet dragon's fire soared past them, forcing Ivan to pull up from the dive.

Understanding Raffa's strategy to drive Ivan's dragon away from their assumed allies below, Anders shouted a new plan to Maija, "You two drive him from below with fire and we'll attack him from above."

He waited until he saw her nod before steering Zahara above Ivan and the green dragon. Raffa and Maija continued to tail Ivan, working to drive them farther away from the group of soldiers below. Anders reached out with his mind, trying to gain some control over Ivan, but as he found before, Ivan's body felt empty. Anders quickly revised his target and focused his assault on Ivan's dragon. As soon as he touched the dragon's mind, Anders felt the creature's walls lock down, cutting him off.

Feeling Anders' magic, the startled dragon panicked, flitting in different directions and trying to distract them. They turned back toward the mountains, the dragon trying to backtrack around them. It worked to evade Raffa; the bulky dragon was unable to turn as quickly as the petit green dragon. Ivan's dragon, however, couldn't shake Zahara. They stuck to Ivan like glue. Anders watched them carefully, realizing that the dragon's panicked state had taken control of where it flew. He could see Ivan twisting over his shoulder to see where Raffa had gone. Ivan struggled to make the dragon obey. Anders knew then that Ivan had not re-bonded with a dragon. If he had, the dragon would've worked with him. Instead, the green dragon continued to shield its mind and fly like a scared hatchling.

Anders continued to bombard the dragon with his mental attacks. The effort left him fatigued. He continually looked to the sapphire, wanting to taste its energy. He knew from Zorna that he might use it with a different result since he was the one who enriched the crystal with energy this time. Each time he contemplated tapping into it, he held back, scared by what he'd done the first time he'd used its energy. If he acted with similar hate, whether it was fueled by his magic or Merglan's, he might end up killing his father without trying to save him.

Zahara, I can keep this up, but I'm going to need some help, Anders said. *Ivan's getting frustrated. If Raffa and Maija continue to block his path and we keep forcing our way into the dragon's mind, he might lose control. He's already struggling to keep it.* Anders felt Zahara's strength seep into him and restore some of his energy. When she did, he could sense that it strained her. He realized then that she must be tiring from their sprint over and through the mountains.

We can continue to irritate them until Ivan gives up. He'll be forced to land and continue on foot. From there, we'll have him cornered, she said, reassuring Anders of her determination.

Together, Raffa and Zahara worked to drive the dragon farther from Ivan's control. Zahara chased him along the mountain front while Raffa and Maija held their position blocking him from escaping into open air. Anders continued to pester the dragon with his mind, prying open walls and letting them close again to keep the dragon in a frenzy. From his frantic movements, Anders could see that Ivan's patience was wearing thin.

After what felt like far too long, Anders saw Ivan drive the dragon sharply toward the coniferous mountainside. Reacting to the anticipated move, he and Zahara closed in on them. Without having to shout the order, Anders saw Raffa and Maija rush down with them.

As Ivan crashed his dragon into the trees, Zahara plunged into the foliage a half-second behind. Anders' vision blurred as pine needles flew in his face. He felt Zahara land in a trot and come to a halt. Anders jumped down from the saddle, whirling around as he sought evidence of the green dragon's crash. Not seeing any disturbance in their immediate area, Anders reached out with his senses, feeling for the dragon's barricaded mind. Locating it quickly, Anders motioned for Maija and their two dragons to move downslope.

This way. The dragon's not moving, so be prepared for an attack, Anders said as he pulled Lazuran from his belt and hastily moved downhill.

They rushed through the towering pines, Anders wide-eyed and ready for an attack from behind every tree. Hearing the roar of a dragon through the branches, Anders and Zahara paused for a moment to recalculate where to find Ivan and his dragon. As they burst through the branches to the source of the noise, Anders held his sword at the ready while Zahara bared her teeth in a vicious growl, the pointed scales along the back of her neck raised like hackles on a wolf, ready to fight. Anders locked his eyes on Ivan, seeing something he didn't expect.

The roar from Ivan's dragon moments before would be its last. Anders skidded to a stop as he witnessed his father's absent-minded body withdrawing the broadsword from the dragon's chest. As the dragon heaved its final breath, Ivan plunged his hand into the hole he'd created in the dragon's chest. Speaking softly, Ivan chanted words that were not of this world and Anders knew he was conjuring evil and ancient magic spawned from the dragon's ancient language.

No, Zahara roared, lunging at Ivan as he absorbed the dragon's essence, robbing it of its return to the force in all things magical.

Before Anders could stop her, Zahara had vaulted

through the air and down on top of Ivan. In an instant, Ivan went from sucking the life force from the dragon to being fully prepared for action. He faced Zahara head-on as she attacked. In a blast, Ivan clapped a shock wave of power, unlike any attack Anders had seen before. The rippling wall of energy hit Zahara, completely reversing her direction. She vanished from sight as her body soared back up and out of the forest, leaving behind only a hole in the trees.

"Zahara!" Anders shouted as he watched his dragon being expelled from sight. Turning to face Ivan, his skin now shining and rippling with blue energy taken unwillingly from the dragon's soul. "What did you do?!" Anders shouted at him.

Not speaking, the blank expression on Ivan's face remained unchanged. He stepped toward Anders at a slow and steady gait. Lifting his sword, Anders called on his magic, priming his limbs with the enhanced strength Zahara had lent him. He could kill Ivan for what he'd just done.

In a flash, Maija emerged from the trees with the speed of an elf. She struck out at Ivan with her sword and Raffa bounded in after her. Matching her inhuman speed, Ivan spun and blocked her blade from cleaving him in two. Maija's momentum continued and she dropped, sliding under Ivan's sword as she raked his blade with hers, mere inches from her face as she passed under it. Raffa bulled into Ivan with his head, smashing him with a sideways sweep as he tried to crush the rider.

Anders halted his charge, shocked at seeing Ivan somehow holding onto Raffa's snout, saving himself from being violently tossed aside. He let go and dropped to the ground in front of the scarlet dragon. With one push from his arm, Ivan directed a blast of energy into Raffagaun, sending him crashing through the thick conifers as he slid. Seeing Ivan on his feet again, Anders returned to his charge. He rushed past Maija as she struggled to her feet, engaging Ivan with the sword. Moving with more speed than he was used to, Anders fought Ivan with this newly formed power. Ivan moved much faster than he did when they'd fought in the snow and Anders struggled to keep up.

Suddenly Maija's blade swung in at Ivan's side. Before Anders could see him reaching for it, Ivan blocked the incoming sword with the crystal-hilted dagger. In a flurry of blows, Anders and Maija tried to gain an upper hand on Ivan. Even as Maija continued to stab and hack at Ivan, he somehow managed to block all of her attempts while still forcing Anders back.

Their chance at disarming Ivan appeared to be dwindling. Ivan struck Anders with surge of energy. As if in slow motion, Anders saw his blade unable to match the speed of Ivan's. Just when the tip of Ivan's broadsword moved into the open space between Anders and his sword, Maija deflected the blade away and Anders stumbled onto his back in trying to lean away from the attack. To Anders' horror, Ivan now turned his full attention on Maija. As she backed away, slashing at his two-handed attack, Anders saw Ivan launch into his signature finishing move, the way in which he used to beat Anders nearly every time they had practiced one-on-one combat.

Maija blocked the first two strikes as any novice sword-handler would, but when it came to deflect the third, her focus was on his broadsword. Launching himself off the ground with a pulse of magic, Anders sprinted to try to prevent what he knew would be Ivan's fake a stab with his broadsword so he could slip the dagger between Maija's ribs, which he did with success. Anders shouted as he dove at Ivan, seeing Maija clutching the dagger's hilt.

Anders' shoulders drove into Ivan's side, pushing him away from Maija as she fell to the forest floor. Slamming him into the ground, Anders bounced off Ivan. Using magic to drive Ivan harder into the ground, he stumbled to his feet only to find Ivan rising just as quickly. Not fully understanding why Ivan did what he was doing to them, Anders attacked before he could move toward Maija.

Hacking at him, Ivan blocked each of Anders' attempts. Seeing Ivan source magic, Anders dodged the shot that came from Ivan's hand, spinning and swinging Lazuran. His father moved much more accurately and with greater speed than he had ever seen him do before. Anders used his magic to strengthen and quicken his own attacks, forcing fatigue from his mind. Each time he faced him, Ivan matched his strength and speed. Anders sent shots of energy at Ivan trying to knock him off balance or disarm him. Without the dagger, Anders' magic could have the desired effect, but his father's body was still fueled by the dead dragon's power and he moved away from Anders' assaults each time.

Anders concentrated, letting Lazuran guide him through the attacks. He drove Ivan back for the first time and gained an opening. Punching his father in the mouth, Anders watched his dull eyes lose him for a moment when his head snapped back from the blow. Ivan's arms opened and Anders brought Lazuran down on his chest. The blade hit Ivan's energy shield, but succeeded in knocking him down. Anders chopped his blade on Ivan with relentless force, trying to break through the protective magic and bring an end to the fighting.

Ivan attempted to retaliate to the flurry of blows, battered down each time he tried to raise his sword arm. Anders panted, breathless from having worked so hard to overpower his father. Ivan managed somehow to get to his feet with an energy-fueled attempt. He tried to attack Anders, but Anders blocked the wild attempt. Ivan had used up his strength; his tremendous power was dwindling. Sending one last enhanced series of blows, Anders knocked Ivan onto his back again, dropping his broadsword as he fell. Anders stood with Lazuran outstretched, held pointedly at Ivan's chest.

He stared at Ivan's pale, expressionless face, the life seeming to have left his eyes. Anders pressed the tip of the blade against Ivan's chest. Lazuran met no resistance and he felt it cut through the leather down to skin. As he stared into his father's glassy eyes, Anders searched for any sense of Ivan's soul or personality.

"Why are you doing this?" Anders demanded.

Ivan didn't respond.

"Can't you see the hurt you're causing? Ivan, whatever he did to you, whatever happened to you, we can fix it. You don't have to keep hurting," he paused, somewhat out of breath from both the fighting and the emotional exhaustion. "Ivan, it's me, Anders, your son." As he spoke, Anders saw Ivan's eyes move to Maija and a flash of color returned to his eye. Anders moved Lazuran off Ivan's chest and turned to go to Maija's side.

The moment he turned toward Maija, Ivan attacked

Anders with a bolt of energy. The shard hit him in the back like a spear and he splayed out face down on the ground, pain shooting through his entire body. Anders tried to fight through the pain and reach for his sword, but the magic paralyzed him. He watched helplessly as Ivan stalked toward Maija, still clutching at the dagger in her side. Every hope for Ivan's redemption fled as Anders watched him stand over Maija with malice in his eyes. Anders could see her legs kicking in the dirt, trying to escape him as he bent down and grabbed the dagger's hilt.

She screamed when he pulled it from her, the sound fueling every inch of Anders' body. Forcing the pain from his mind, Anders pushed himself off the ground. He staggered toward Ivan as he raised the dagger up, intending to plunge it into Maija's chest. Anders willed the remaining magic stores held deep within his exhausted body to do the only thing he could think of. Letting the spell drain him, he placed an energy shield around Maija. As Ivan plunged the dagger down tip first, Anders keeled over, Ivan's magic still gripping him and crippling him to his knees. Though Ivan drove the dagger down with enhanced strength, Anders felt the shield pull more energy than he knew he had in him to deflect the descending blade. The dagger glanced off the sphere of protective magic, still carrying the full momentum of Ivan's thrust and buried itself hilt-deep in the center of Ivan's own chest. He stepped back, realizing the result, then turned slightly and tipped over backward, thudding onto the forest floor.

Seconds later, the intense pain left Anders' body and his vision blurred with stress and fatigue. Stumbling like a drunkard unable to fully stand, Anders fell at Maija's side, dropping his sword in the dirt. Looking at her body, he saw the blood soaking her shirt and starting to pool under her. It was too much blood loss. Anders knew she was dying.

Her pale face quivered and her body shivered as she looked back at him with her beautiful amber eyes. She whispered softly, "Anders, I love you, too."

As this final sentence left her lips, shock set in and she slipped into darkness. Anders saw the light fading from her eyes and shook her, trying to keep her alive, shouting for her to stay with him. Tears and exhaustion further clouded Anders' mind and he knew what he had to do. Acting without considering the consequences, Anders accessed the energy within his sword's inhabitance crystal.

The blue-hued light wisped silently from his pommel on the ground at his side and into his extended palm. The energy brought strength into his body and his heart began to pulse harder and faster than before. An awakening that he'd been craving surged into him, but this time it was different. Whether it was the seriousness of what he must do or whether his reaction was different, Anders was able to maintain control of himself. He began speaking the words to heal Maija, not caring if he had enough energy to keep himself alive. Anders was prepared to give his life to save Maija's. This was his fight and he had dragged her into it.

Anders felt the magic draining into Maija's body, the blue light stitching closed the hole Ivan had created in her ribcage. As the energy worked to mend the base of her lung and restore the blood loss, Anders began to waver. He did not end the spell before he fell down at Maija's side, the energy from his body still pouring into Maija's. As he lay on the ground becoming more chilled, he saw the form of two dragons come into view. Their muffled voices didn't register in his thoughts, but he felt the chilling grip of energy loss end and he blinked. A glow formed over him and he felt warmth re-entering his body.

For a moment Anders thought the sudden reversal of sensation was his healing attempt gone awry. Fearing that Maija was being robbed of his healing power, Anders cried out and bolted upright, now sitting at her side. As the light that consumed him vanished, Anders saw Zahara, beaten and bloodied, standing in front of him. His eyes widened and he turned to his right, calling Maija's name.

To his surprise, Anders saw Maija also sitting up, her arms wrapped around Raffagaun's massive snout. Immense relief came over him as he realized that she wasn't dead. He sighed and turned to face Zahara. Before he could do anything but look at her, a wave of light flashed over them. Anders put his arm over his face to shield the blinding light as the air rushed around them, continuing in a ripple out through the trees causing them to bend and sway.

Anders held his breath in fear that Merglan had just attacked them. When the light vanished and he realized he hadn't been blown to bits, he turned to check on Maija. She grinned back at him with the same realization. They'd survived yet again. Anders shook his head, not understanding what had just happened. Maija threw herself at him, now wrapping her arms around him and hugging him tight. Anders fell back with Maija gripping him snugly and thanking him over and over again.

"Are you alright?" he managed to stammer as she pulled him back up to sit at her side. Her smile beamed and he felt a glowing about her that he hadn't known she possessed.

Maija rose to her feet and lifted her shirt to examine the area where the dagger had penetrated her ribs. The hole where blood had seeped out was gone, replaced with healthy, smooth skin. "I feel amazing," she said, helping Anders to his feet.

"But what was that brilliant flash of light?" Anders asked. Maija continued to smile and took a step back to stand near Raffa's enormous face. Anders looked at them for a moment, trying to understand why they stared at him and Zahara in silence.

A voice came into his mind, *They've bonded.*

"You bonded?" Anders asked, wavering in his stance. His head felt light and the energy Zahara had pumped into his body to keep him from slipping over the edge was only just enough to keep him from passing out.

Maija nodded eagerly and Anders looked to Zahara, *But how did you know they'd bonded?* Zahara tilted her head at him. From her reaction, Anders added, *Didn't you just tell me they had bonded?*

No, Zahara said. *I came back in time to see you giving away your life to heal her. I had enough extra energy to bring you back. Raffa was there, too, and he used his magic to bring Maija out of her shock. After that, I was focused on you. That light was just as alarming to me as it was to you.*

But who just told me that they had bonded? Anders asked her.

I did, the voice came again and this time Anders could hear the distinct male attributes of the mental vibrato.

Anders spun around, looking in all directions for whoever was speaking to them. He didn't recognize the voice, yet somehow it felt familiar to him.

"Who said that?" Maija asked, suddenly more anxious.

"You heard it too?" Anders asked.

She nodded, as did Raffa and Zahara.

"Who are you!?" Anders shouted, reaching a shaking hand down and picking up Lazuran. "Show yourself!"

I'm afraid I cannot do that, the sturdy voice replied, reminding Anders of the noble way in which the late King Asmond used to speak.

"And why is that?" Anders asked, still searching for the source of the voice.

Why, because I'm stuffed into this stone, of course. You wouldn't ask a dragon to become a dwarf, would you? Besides, none of you possess the power required for me to be revealed, especially in your current state.

Anders frowned, looking at his sword. He looked down to the pommel in the hilt and saw it was glowing brighter than it had before. Dropping it, he backed away, saying, "What the?"

That was rude, the voice said. *Here I thought you would've been surprised to have such a key asset at your fingertips, pardon the pun.*

When Maija stepped closer to Lazuran Anders warned, "Maija, be careful! We don't know what kind of magic is possessing that thing."

She hesitated and the blade spoke to them again, *Let me introduce myself. I am Tarron Pintler, chair of the Alliance of Independent Riders, son of Orrian Pintler, creator of the High Council of Elves, and right hand to the leader of our order. I assume you've heard of me. How can I be of assistance?*

Anders looked to Zahara. She shook her head, indicating she had never heard of him before. Anders slowly bent down and picked up Lazuran. Holding it between his thumb and forefingers like a dead mouse, Anders responded to the crystal, *None of us knows what any of that means. I don't know how you came to be in that stone, but we don't have much time to deal with this right now. We are in the middle of a war.*

Tarron sighed, *I thought this might be happening. All those years being shut away without use.*

"What's that?" Anders asked.

I first felt life after someone layered magic in over the top of me. I was trying to make my presence known, but before I could, the magic ran out, indicating the crystal wasn't in use, but I still tried to reach out to anyone nearby. Then a short while ago I felt the magic again and I knew someone had found me again. I called out, this time knowing I was heard. But that's strange that you didn't know, because you figured out that only the power of a bonding in my crystal's presence can summon me.

"Wait, so you're the voice I've been hearing?" Anders asked. "That wasn't some part of Merglan that was calling to me, it was you?"

Well I don't know who this Merglan fellow is, but essentially yes. If you have had my crystal with you as of late, you would have been the one to hear my calls.

Anders gripped the blade again, no longer fearing the mind inside the sapphire. He slid the sword into its scabbard and said to the others, "We should get moving. I didn't like how the army gathering in the plains looked to be marching to battle."

"You're right. We should make sure Kirsten and the others are safe before we do anything else. Who knows what other assassins Merglan has sent after them," Maija said.

Might I ask who you are at war with? Tarron said, inserting himself into their conversation.

"Look, Tarron, unless you can tell us how to wipe out a nation of orcs or show us how to use corrupted magic to our benefit, I would appreciate it if you let us alone until we can figure this mess out," Anders said. He saw the look Zahara gave him and knew the comment was blunt, but after what Anders had just dealt with and done, he couldn't help but feel on edge.

Well, I don't know any one sure way to kill thousands upon thousands of orcs, but I do know quite a bit about magic and altering its properties.

Anders walked the short distance to where Ivan's body had fallen. He stared down at the man who he had known to be the embodiment of honor and what was right in this world. He looked at the fallen king as he lay dead with a dagger in his chest.

What happened to him? Tarron asked.

"Tarron, a little privacy. That was his father." Maija said, irritated at his indecency.

When he didn't respond, Anders knelt down and grabbed the hilt of the dagger. Quickly he pulled the blade from Ivan's chest and turned away from him, walking back to Maija, Raffa and Zahara. Tossing it to the ground before them, Anders said, "Alright then, Tarron Pintler. Show us how to safely harvest this crystal's energy and transfer it into yours."

For some reason, I sense that you have some knowledge of how to do this already, Tarron said. *But as I can tell that you four are exhausted and in desperate need of healing, I will oblige. It will take some time. Not many sorcerers are able to alter the property of magic. It takes a toll on your emotions as well.*

"Just do it," Anders said, drawing Lazuran and thrusting it tip fist into the dirt next to the dagger. He then walked several paces away from them.

As Anders waited for Tarron to alter the energy in Ivan's dagger to a substance safe for them to use, he stared into the evening light in the forest. He replayed Ivan's death in his mind, searching for anything that he could've done differently to prevent it from happening. Zahara came to his side and lay down next to him. She didn't speak, feeling his sorrow and knowing his pain. She hadn't witnessed what had occurred between them, but she shared an emotional connection with Anders and could feel everything that was happening as it played out.

Maija came to his side next. Anders felt her hand taking his and she wrapped her other arm around his, bringing her head to rest on his shoulder. Whispering, she said, "You had to do it, Anders. He was going to kill me."

Anders looked over his shoulder at Ivan's body sprawled out on the ground. With a quivering voice, he said, "It doesn't matter now. He's gone and we're alive."

Maija tightened her grip on his hand and said, "Whoever that was that attacked us, it wasn't Ivan."

Anders shook his head, "That was my father."

"No, Anders. Your father was the man who devoted his life to protecting you from evil like this. He was the man who took you under his wing and showed you how to use your magic for good. He knew that we are the only ones in this world who could stop Merglan. And in the end,

Merglan took his soul long before whatever he did to his body. I know Ivan and there's no way he would ever let himself do something like this to us. Merglan took him, separated his mind from his body and used dark magic to send his likeness after us," Maija said resolutely.

"How do you know that's what really happened? What if Merglan broke him and he did this of his own free will?" Anders asked.

"I don't know how I know, I just do. That wasn't Ivan, Anders. That wasn't your father," Maija said again with certainty.

She's right, Anders heard Zahara say. *Ivan's mind was not present in his body. Merglan created this dark magic to drive fear into our hearts. He might've forced us to act in a way we never wished, but in the end he did not win. We beat him and his magic. You beat him.*

Anders looked out into the forest as darkness fell. He knew what they were telling him was true, but he still felt that he had killed Ivan's body. He'd still caused his father to stab himself in the chest with his own blade. Trying to come to terms with the fact that his father was gone from this world, Anders said, "Zahara, will you help me show Maija how dragonriders perform a funeral?'

She nodded, rising to all fours as Anders led Maija over to Ivan's body. In the same way he and Ivan had released Keanu's soul into the magical force that flowed within their world, Anders and Zahara lit his body and the dragon's he'd flown on fire and spoke the ancient words. Raffa joined them as they watched what little of the green dragon's spirit remained dance in the flames, returning to the force surrounding them.

No such spirit rose from Ivan's body so Anders knew his presence really had been removed from his body before Merglan turned his body against them. While Anders waited for the energy from Merglan's crystal to be safely converted into Lazuran's pommel, he paid his respects to Ivan's corpse. The fire quickly consumed their flesh. Anders felt more at peace with himself for having sent Ivan's body off the right way. He only hoped Ivan's soul wasn't being held in some kind of prison somewhere, hidden away by Merglan. With the evil sorcerer imprisoned in the most secure place in the five nations, Anders hoped that once he found his family, they might finally stay together for good.

CHAPTER TWENTY-SIX

Cedarbridge

s he working harder against the restraints now that Anders is gone?" Nadir asked as he eyed the Norfolk woman's focused demeanor.

"He's not so much the one I'm trying to keep still," Zorna said in her adolescent voice. "It's the dragon who's putting up the fight."

"Why didn't you have Anders stay? He could've helped," Nadir said.

"He was needed elsewhere. I could feel it between them," she nodded to Merglan. "He had a plan for that other rider and, as it sits right now, I'd say the other rider is more of a threat. I wasn't sure at first, but feeling his potential now, I'd say those crystals were what gave him such dominant control over other riders."

Nadir nodded, "I'll have a runner send word to Cedarbridge and the High Council. Perhaps we can summon any elder riders who've outlived their dragons to help with the transfer."

"Not necessary. I'll need a different kind of assistance," her voice strained slightly as Killdoor struggled to move against her restricting magic. Keeping the giant dragon pinned, she continued, "I'll need carrying. All my energy and that of the crystal you gave me must be focused on keeping these two in check. Circumstances might be different if my bonded was here. She should already be on her way."

Nadir gave her a sideways glance, "Your dragon is coming?"

"Should be, I said," Zorna corrected. "The moment I left that elven city, the shield barricading the Norfolk from finding the passage south was lifted."

Nadir snapped his fingers and waved several nearby soldiers to his side. After commanding one of them to carry the message of Merglan's capture to the High Council, he asked Zorna, "Your people were intentionally kept separate from the rest of the world?"

"This isn't common knowledge?" the youthful-looking elder asked.

Nadir shook his head, turning his attention to the remaining elves he'd summoned. He issued orders for them to carry Zorna as they walked back to the city.

"I assumed it would be," she said, her voice straining slightly again as she quelled a sputum of flame from Killdoor's innards, the glow in his chest dying before it swelled to full strength. "As part of my punishment, your father had his order of elven riders seal my people off from the rest of the world. Only non-bonded dragons could come and go as they liked. At least they had that much sense," she said.

"Why would that make a difference?" Nadir asked.

"Northland is primary habitat and hunting grounds for dragons. The prey are much larger for them there and it's not too far across the water from their homeland in Nagano. The dragon population would likely dwindle if they were forced to live in such a limited area."

"When I freed you, the magic restraining your dragon and your people lifted?" Nadir asked.

She nodded, keeping her eyes on the prisoners as they waited for the elves to begin their march.

"How will they know the passage has been lifted?" Nadir asked.

The elf soldier appointed to carrying the woman, lifted her as she responded, "They'll know, youngling; they always know."

Nadir frowned in confusion. He didn't know whether he should expect the arrival of just one dragon, bonded to Zorna, or her entire people. He focused on their current task before diverting too much of his attention to this new development. The Norfolk woman shifted their captives' hovering bodies into place among the elven ranks. Even though the restraints on Merglan were bound in magic and continually held in bondage by the sorceress, Nadir still wanted as many armed soldiers on hand with their weapons trained on Merglan in case of an accident.

With a group of his most highly trained soldiers fixing their swords and spears on Merglan, Nadir signaled for them to begin their march. Nadir sent one scout ahead to inform Cedarbridge of their expected arrival and the prisoners in their company. He didn't want to waste any time in the transport. He knew how powerful Merglan could be, regardless of how many inhabitance crystals were at his disposal.

Nadir held his gaze on Merglan and Killdoor as the

soldiers in the lead began to move. He thought it strange to watch such a huge creature as the black dragon being held against its will in such a contorted and unnatural position. Zorna had splayed the dragon's limbs out to either side and curled his head back so his enormous jaws pointed directly toward the sky. Nadir guessed this was to ensure that should the dragon manage to unleash a blast of flames, the flames would pass into the air overhead instead of into the soldiers marching in front.

The remaining numbers of Nadir's force followed behind their king as he walked alongside the soldier carrying their sorceress. His elven sword in hand, the Elf King would be ready if any kurr had remained in the area. Half of his soldiers ran in pursuit of the creatures who'd survived the attack. Nadir just hoped they would execute them quickly and continue to the Glacial Melt Bays as commanded. Their orders, as he gave them, were to wait for the redshirts' return with the ships. He didn't know how he would be received by the High Council. If it went poorly, he planned to have Bronson take command of his remaining forces.

Nadir now focused on Merglan, his hands bound behind his back with magic and pressed out away from his body. His legs were likewise bound, but stretched out in front of him, straight as if he were sitting on the ground. Nadir noticed that unlike Killdoor, Merglan seemed calm, as if willing to accept his capture. The Elf King wasn't sure if this calm was due to the fact that he hadn't helped in Merglan's capture. Nadir felt immense dissatisfaction in the dragonrider's capture. While he contemplated what he could have done differently to help Anders and Zahara, Nadir would have to be pleased enough with having played a role in communicating to Natalia how the crystals could be changed.

The walk back to Cedarbridge always seemed to drag on forever when he couldn't run. He hadn't had to walk anywhere since he'd gone with Anders and Ivan to Eastland. He could tell the soldiers felt the same in the way that they continually bumped into one another. Occasionally, Nadir heard hushed grunts and groans in frustration. Nadir didn't want to take chances here, though. If the pace was what the Norfolk woman needed to haul Merglan and Killdoor to jail while remaining in control, then they would continue at this horribly slow pace.

Covering the distance that only took them a few hours to run continued for most of the day. Each time Nadir looked to his left, Zorna appeared to him to be slightly more fatigued. Nadir saw her glance skyward whenever they passed under an open patch in the canopy. He wondered if she was hoping to see Anders return or looking for her dragon from Northland. As they neared the capital, Nadir took note that the storm cloud that had billowed high over the forest city for days had vanished. Instead, they enjoyed blue skies and a calm breeze. Soon Nadir could see robed elves standing in front of Cedarbridge's gates.

The soldiers in Nadir's troop parted to allow Killdoor and Merglan to be wrangled closer to the city's outer wall. Walking in stride with the soldier carrying Zorna, Nadir saw the glint of helmeted elves peering over the top of the living barrier that surrounded the capital. Only a trained elven eye could know where to look to see the top of the wall disguised in greenery. Naturally, Nadir knew where to find the wall and now took note of the soldiers watching curiously.

Outside the gates, Nadir glanced to see Killdoor struggling to break free. The Council members leapt back in fear as the dragon thrashed yet remained in his magically held bonds. Merglan continued to sit in his uncomfortable position, silent and motionless. The gates to the city cracked open and Nadir moved to walk around Merglan and his dragon. As he stepped around the sorcerer, Nadir stared at Merglan who continued to look straight ahead. Nadir nearly jumped when the man's eyes snapped onto him and held his gaze. While their stares lingered, Nadir continued past, the first to break the look. Instead, he shifted his gaze toward the elves standing closer to the gate.

As he approached them, Nadir walked with his chin up and chest out, full of confidence. The robed acolytes to the throne had been his father's most trusted advisors for over a century. They wore bright green robes trimmed with embroidered floral patterns and a cedar tree running the length of each sleeve. Nadir noticed that their usually smug faces were twitchy and fearful.

Stopping midway between his prisoners and the Councilmen at the gates, Nadir gripped his blade tightly in one hand and said, "Do not fear me, I come in peace."

"Sheath your weapon and walk slowly toward us," a Councilman in the middle of the group responded.

Nadir did as requested, placing the elven blade back in its scabbard. He walked slowly toward them with his hands held up to show he wasn't hiding anything.

"Halt there."

Stopping, Nadir said, "I've brought evidence of the end of this war."

Neither of the three Council members responded.

Nadir eyed them, then asked, "What, you don't trust me? What did I say to you yesterday?"

The Councilman to his left closed his eyes and was about to speak, when Nadir cut him off, "I remember. I told you I was going to bring an end to this war once and for all, something we should've been actively participating in before it got out of hand. And your reply was?" This time Nadir listened for a response.

"If you ever wished to be welcomed back into this city again, you would have to defeat Merglan himself," the elf said, looking past Nadir at the sorcerer.

"I've managed to do just that," Nadir stepped closer to the members of the High Council and said in a hushed tone, "I am the King of the Everlight Kingdom. The next time I say we're going to bring a stop to something that could destroy the entire world, you're going to damn well listen." He pulled back and inhaled deeply, letting his chest rise as he straightened. "I assume you've assembled these heavily armed soldiers to escort the prisoners to their cells?" Nadir asked, pointing toward the elves lining the rim of the wall.

The robed elves scowled, knowing they'd been beaten at their game. Waving them forward, Nadir led his soldiers and their captives through the city gates. Nadir grinned as he walked past the tunnel of elves lining their path, those who had gathered to see their King return victorious and vindicated. Cheers drowned their stamping as the armored soldiers made their way toward the elven courthouse. His arrival just a day prior had been starkly different. Cedarbridge's population had been in a volatile state just hours earlier; opposition to Nadir's claim had run rampant through the civilian crowds. Their King's arrival with

Kartania's most feared enemy bound and restrained, converted even his most staunch opponents to cheering supporters.

As he walked up the courthouse steps, Nadir swelled with pride. The full High Council now stood just inside the entrance to the elven court. When Nadir entered, they bowed, showing their respect for his authority. He turned and watched as the Norfolk sorceress maneuvered the prisoners through the enormous doors. Even the Council members gasped and then hushed when Merglan floated in, a sly grin across his face. Killdoor barely fit through the entrance designed for dragons, truly telling of his enormous size.

Once inside, Nadir addressed the members of the High Council, "Do we even need to discuss his punishment?"

Collectively they shook their heads, "The honor is yours, your Grace."

Nadir nodded, "Merglan, I sentence you to eternal imprisonment in our deepest cell."

"Not to death?" Merglan asked, speaking for the first time since he'd been taken from Anders.

"Death would be too kind," Nadir replied. "The punishment where you're going will fit the crimes you've committed. The magic in these cells is stronger than you could ever imagine." Nadir nodded to Zorna, "Take him down."

The door to the prison opened and a dragon-sized extension that Nadir knew was there but had never before seen formed at the entrance. His jaw tightened as he watched his soldiers haul Merglan and Killdoor into the chamber where the magic would contain them indefinitely.

As they drifted into the shadowed entrance, Merglan called back to Nadir, "Not killing me now is a mistake, elf."

The doors to the prison closed. Nadir knew that the magic woven into the prison was stronger than Merglan ever could be. Nadir held his gaze on the spot in the floor where the trap door had just closed. He felt a hand hit him on the back, snapping him from his stare. He turned to see a member of the High Council at his side.

Shaking his hand, the elf said, "Well done, my King. You've righted a wrong that has plagued our world for decades."

Nadir nodded blankly at the elf. He couldn't believe it. Merglan had finally been incarcerated, no longer free to wreak chaos as he wished. All of Kartania was free from his oppression.

Nodding to the crowd who'd followed them to the court building, the Councilman said with a wink, "You'd better address your people. They'll want to know what they can expect from their King."

As Nadir walked toward the entrance, one of his soldiers rushed ahead to open the door for him so he could address the gathering outside. The mass of elves looked up at him expectantly, anxious to hear what he might say. This gathering felt different from the one just a day earlier.

A green-robed elf standing atop the steps near Nadir announced him to his people, "All hail your monarch and rigorous ruler, King Nadir!" The crowd erupted in cheers. Nadir raised his hands and the cheers grew louder. He reveled in their praise, basking in his hard-won recognition. When they finally quieted, Nadir spoke of the leadership he vowed to uphold as their king.

***

The door clanked closed behind them. Zorna maintained her magical spell on Merglan and his dragon, Killdoor. The prison's admittance chamber felt full to the brim with the bulk of the dragon. Merglan sat in the air, legs still outstretched and arms pulled back. The soldiers who had accompanied them down into the prison held their blades pointed at the sorcerer, not trusting that he would remain still. Sweat beaded on Zorna's forehead as she began to shake from her efforts. Zorna saw the crystal's glow dimming as its additional strength began to run dry. Resorting to her iron willpower, the Norfolk woman trembled as the magical bonds became too much to bear. The dragon's struggles continued, causing most of her fatigue. As far as she could tell, Merglan appeared to be accepting the punishment.

"To the bottom then?" Merglan asked.

"You're less worried about this than I would've expected," Zorna replied, trying hard to sound relaxed, masking her struggle against Killdoor.

"You want me to be angry or upset that I've been bested?" Merglan said.

The woman eyed him as she held her spell on him, "Now that the door is closed, you're subject to the prison's powers. The magic here is so strong not even you and your dragon could escape it."

"Then why are you still restraining me?" Merglan asked.

The woman didn't respond, she wasn't going to tell him anything about how the magic in the prison worked. She watched as the soldier she'd spoken to mentally did as she instructed. He tapped on a stone in the wall, opening a panel. Placing his finger on the panel, he traced the symbol just as she instructed. As the elf removed his finger from the panel, the room's walls started to glow. With a jolt, the entire chamber began to move down.

"Once you're tucked neatly into your cell, I'll lift these restraints," she said, hoping he wouldn't hear the quiver in her voice.

Merglan started to laugh.

"I don't know what you think is so funny about this. You're past the point of return now. It's all over," Zorna said.

As she spoke the last word, she felt the sorcerer beginning to push against her. It started slowly at first but increased rapidly. The dragon thrashed, loosening its bondage. She willed for the strength to hold him still, but the creature began to move more with each attempt. The soldiers in the confined space started shouting at the dragon, telling it to hold still. They moved uneasily with their blades turning away from Merglan and onto the dragon.

The old woman shook as she tried to restrain both the dragon and Merglan simultaneously. Slowly tucking his feet in, Merglan moved his legs under himself. The woman in white struggled frantically, beginning to panic as Killdoor fell to the ground and Merglan came to stand.

Seeing the dragon gaining more control, the elf soldiers in the space tried to restrain it. At first they used their bodies, but as the dragon regained more control of his abilities, they began to use their swords. Doing everything in her power to stop the dragon from going wild and killing them all, Zorna also watched as Merglan pushed his hands apart and struggled to bring them in front of himself.

The elf who held Zorna on his shoulders let go of her legs and drew his blade. Holding the point toward the sorcerer, he ordered, "You stop moving now, or I'll be forced to run you through."

Merglan offered him a slight smile, then in a burst of energy, broke through his magically bound restraints. The soldier lunged forward attempting to stab the sorcerer in the chest, but Merglan was too quick. With his magic, he pulled the sword from the soldier's hand and flipped the point around. Before the elf knew what had happened, Merglan had stabbed him in the heart with his own sword. Twisting the blade sideways, Merglan pulled the sword out to the side, spilling the elf's chest apart and dropping him to the floor.

Letting go her grip from the dragon, Zorna concentrated all of her powers and directed them at Merglan. She met him in force, their magic energy clashing as they struggled to gain control over one another. The room thundered with the roaring and screaming of elves being killed in a confined space by an enraged dragon. The floor ran red with their blood as Killdoor clawed and bit into the elves.

The Norfolk woman shied away, watching the evil duo command control over their bodies. She just needed to last until they reached the bottom. Once the chamber opened and sensed the woman's truths, the jail's magic would take over. She lay in the corner of the room, clutching the tapped crystal and chanting in the ancient language, turning her magic inward in an attempt to ward off Merglan and Killdoor, who were trying to claw their way through.

Merglan's frantic push to break through her protective

spell increased; he doubled his efforts to kill her. Holding them back until she'd used every ounce of available energy, Merglan finally peeled away the last of the barriers between them. Holding out his arm, Merglan pulled her neck into his open grip and held her off the ground.

Her body went limp as his hand tightened around her throat. Taking the sword he'd used to kill the elf, Merglan pressed the point against her chest. She gasped and gurgled as the blade slid into her body, filling her lungs with blood. Merglan held her in his hand as she kicked and said, "I would thank you for making this so easy for me, but I will admit, you were harder to kill than the others."

He dropped her lifeless body to the floor as the moving room slowed to a halt. When the light from the prison's magic began to seep into the room, Merglan was ready. He captured it, pulling it into himself and bending its ancient design to his will. With the newly harvested power, Merglan held the entire prison from the bottom up under his control. He laughed as he ordered the prison's magic to release every prisoner through the courthouse entrance.

***

Nadir stepped back, the roar of the crowd welling in his ears. For the first time since he'd become king, he felt good about it. Stepping inside the elven court, he addressed the members of the High Council, "I will take a patrol of elves out into the forests to root out any kurr still wandering in the kingdom."

"How many elves will you require?" one of the members asked.

Nadir started to answer but stopped. He thought he felt the ground trembling under his feet. He turned to see if the cheers had grown louder, but the crowd appeared to be dispersing. They were returning to their shops and homes, yet the rumbling continued to grow. Now Nadir could feel the ground trembling for certain.

"What's happening?" he shouted, looking to the High Council.

He could tell from their expressions that the sudden shaking was as much a surprise to them as it was to him. The trap door in the corner cracked and began to open. Those in the entrance hall could hear the roar of a stampede headed their way. Nadir could now see into the prison chamber. His best-trained soldiers had been destroyed. Nadir gaped at their bodies. The floor below was littered with elves shredded to pieces by the dragon. The Norfolk woman named Zorna lay in the center of the crimson floor, her mouth open in a silent scream.

Nadir's eyes widened as a stream of creatures long locked away now poured through the opening. Pulling his sword from its scabbard, he squatted, ready to face the brunt of the attack. Fairnheir, kurr, goblins, and some monsters that he hadn't known existed rushed out of the prison. Nadir met them with the swing of his sword, cutting and hewing as they came. The screams and shouts faded with the exploding force of Killdoor bursting through the court's marble floor. The last thing Nadir saw was the giant beast crawling out from the hole he'd created in the door before the entire building caved in.

When he opened his eyes again, Nadir found himself in the forest in the dark of night. The only light he could see was the glow of burning through the trees. As he regained consciousness and became self-aware, Nadir realized he was being dragged, his bottom half being pulled through the dirt. Calling out to whoever was dragging him, the movement stopped. He stood, seeing wounded elves and soldiers walking with shocked expressions through the forest. The glow of Cedarbridge burned through the trees. Nadir reached for his sword, but it wasn't there. He moved to begin heading back toward the city. The elf who'd been dragging him grabbed his shoulder, stopping him.

"If you're going back there, you'll need this," he said, handing Nadir his sword. "Found it in the rubble where you were lying. But If I were you, I'd lead these survivors far from there. Cedarbridge has fallen, my King, that dragon made sure of it."

At that moment Nadir looked up to see a flight of dragons fleeing to the west and away from the city. He looked at the line of people moving down the road. The soldier was right, these people were going to need leadership. He was their king and would lead as best he could.

Running to the front of the line, Nadir rounded up several soldiers, telling them to bring everyone to the Glacial Melt Bays. Nadir ran back toward the inferno and, for a time, waited near the gates to show any and all the direction where he'd sent the others, south to the Glacial Melt Bays. As the number of civilians seeking to escape began to dwindle, Nadir forced himself away, knowing that he wouldn't live to bring his people justice if he remained through the evening. As he rallied his people toward the Bays, he hoped the ships had returned.

CHAPTER TWENTY-SEVEN

Alive

rystal blue light streamed from the dagger handle as Anders allowed it to transfer into his stores. Like a dried well replenished by spring rains, he felt the intensity of pure magic surge into him, restoring his aura. Closing his eyes, Anders told himself to close the connection before the power consumed him. As he ended the transference of energy, he felt completely in control. The desire to keep fueling himself, that uncontrollable urge he'd felt the first time he'd tapped the crystal's power was gone.

Anders opened his eyes to see Zahara standing before him. Her chest and legs were thrashed with claw marks from having fought two dragons. He could feel her pain burning in the back of his mind. The blast of energy Ivan had delivered at her had sent her backward through the trees where she'd landed on her back. She'd made her way back to Anders, tattered and bruised. With his newly found energy, Anders knew that he could heal her. With Tarron's help, Anders had converted the dagger's energy into pure magic. He knew he now had enough energy to heal both dragons and also breathe restored energy directly into Maija's reserves. Lifting his hand, he began conducting the spells necessary to close their wounds and restore their flesh.

As he worked his magic on Zahara, Raffa and Maija, Anders wished he knew how to heal their minds. Zahara and Maija's thoughts pressed hard on him as he tapped into their beings. The loss of Anders' father traumatized them, scarring their minds in a way he couldn't repair with magic alone. Now having bonded, Raffa shared in Maija's grief for the former dragonrider in the same way Anders and Maija mourned the death of the green dragon. After seeing its struggle to free itself from the monster that Ivan's body had become, they knew for certain the green dragon had been forced to carry out Merglan's bidding. Finishing the last of the healing, Anders admired the green dragon's survival instincts. In its fearful state, its will had been strong enough to break free from Ivan's control. Anders felt a pang of regret at having tormented the dragon's mind in his effort to stop them from reaching his cousins and friends.

After closing the last of Raffagaun's wounds, Anders walked silently to the dagger Merglan had used to control Ivan's body. Picking it up from the dirt where he'd left it for Tarron, Anders wiped the blade clean of the blood from both his father and his true love. Walking to Maija, he flipped the dagger over in his hand, holding it out to her hilt first. He nodded as her eyes moved between the dagger and his face.

Wrapping her hand around the dagger's handle, she took it from him, "Are you sure?"

Nodding, Anders said, "You know best how its bite stings. It only seems fitting that you should wield it."

Maija smiled slightly, the grin fading from her lips almost as soon as it showed.

"I want to see my cousins," Anders said, moving toward Zahara. "They could still be in danger. Who knows what enemies Merglan has sent their way."

He's the kind of man who would have multiple fail-safe solutions set up in the event his primary plan didn't work, Maija's mind sounded into Anders' thoughts.

That's right, and I don't want to take chances when we're dealing with such a monster, he replied.

Maija jolted when he spoke. "What is it?" Anders asked, worried that the crystal still had some residual energy trying to take hold of her.

Maija shook her head, "I'm sorry. I didn't mean to make that thought known."

Anders relaxed, "It takes some getting used to, controlling who can listen in on your thoughts. We'll have to practice more tomorrow. Once we know that the others are safe, we could use a solid night's sleep. Then we'll practice."

Maija smiled, "The only thing is, after receiving that energy, I'm not tired. I feel like I could run from here to Nagano and back and still be ready for more."

"You might need to use that energy if we come across any more assassins," Anders said, hauling himself into his saddle.

Maija mirrored his action and he nodded to her, indicating they were ready to take flight. As Raffagaun and Maija led Zahara up from the forested mountainside, Anders glanced over his shoulder, looking down one last time at the place where his father, once the King of all human nations, had fallen. Riding out into the night sky, a troubling thought entered his mind. Now that Merglan had been incarcerated in the elven prison, Anders was the next in line to be king. With all of his immediate family members dead and gone, he was the heir to the throne and would have the right to rule the three nations of humankind. As Anders returned his focus to the rolling foothills of the Riverlands and the swaying grass of the Bareback Plains, he knew that he didn't have what it took to be king. All he wanted was for his family and friends to be rid of the threat of dark magic. He wanted to be able to return to their home on Highborn Bay. He doubted his desires would matter if anyone in politics discovered his true heritage.

As Anders' eyes trained on the space where he'd last seen soldiers gathering in the plains, all thoughts of the future fled from his mind. Lit by partially clouded stars and a rising moon, Anders could see horror had struck along the tree line below. Dead bodies extended out into the plains. He also saw a cluster of giant human-like forms moving quickly across the darkened battleground. He shared his concerns with Zahara, so she angled down toward them. He then saw a man on horseback carrying a glowing light high over his head. Realizing what it was, he forced Zahara into a dive. Suddenly a crystal flashed, but its source wasn't from the man on horseback; it originated closer to the tree line. Reaching out with his mind, Anders felt the overwhelming presence of kurr as they broke into the retreating ranks of humans. Moments later he felt the minds of his cousins and their companions. Recognizing where to look for them, he could see that Kirsten was wielding a crystal while the others banded around to protect her.

Drawing near, Anders tapped into Maija's mind, *Kurr are attacking them. See the flashes of energy?* Anders felt her eyes move to their friends and the man attacking them. They broke apart, several being swept away by kurr, leaving only two to protect the crystal bearer. *It's Kirsten using a crystal against the man on horseback. Thomas is with her,* he broke off, watching one of their companions charge forward, cutting his way through the kurr to reach the man. Anders couldn't tell if it was Bo or Max, but the effort with which he powered through the giant beasts was impressive. Seeing the man attack with a whip of energy as it crashed into their friend, Anders began to panic. Zahara and Raffa flew in just over the trees, and Anders saw that his cousins had been separated. Thomas was being overwhelmed with nothing but his bow and a dwindling supply of arrows. Kirsten was then blasted backward by a powerful wave of energy hurled by the enemy crystal bearer.

Anders shouted into Maija and Raffa's minds as Zahara ducked in just behind them, *Burn the crystal bearer!* He felt their recognition while Zahara dropped from the trees and raked her claws into kurr heads as she flew. Passing over where Thomas appeared to be trapped, Anders leapt from the saddle, pulling out his elven blade. Using the surplus of magic at his fingertips, he pushed energy to absorb the brunt of his landing and met the ground near his cousin at a run. With Tarron guiding his hands, Anders swung at the kurr surrounding around his cousin. Lazuran cleaved through the first of the kurr's horned heads and Anders saw the sky ignite with flames. From beyond the flying heads of kurr, he could see Raffagaun and Zahara demolishing the encroaching kurr. With no opposing dragons to stop them, Raffa and Zahara would burn through all of the kurr who tried to advance any farther.

Clearing a wide space around them, Anders turned to Thomas. His cousin stared at him. Anders shouted, "With me! Thomas, stay with me!"

Anders saw recognition dawn on his face and his cousin moved to follow. Anders charged toward the place he'd last seen Kirsten being thrown. Spotting her while she watched the dragons burn the enemy, Anders could see three kurr charging her from behind. Knowing he couldn't reach her in time to protect her with his sword, Anders unleashed a well-placed shot of energy. The light brushed past Kirsten, pushing her forward and nearly causing her to trip, but the pulse broke across the middle kurr, sending all three soaring high into the air. Kirsten looked to Anders and he saw the fury in her eyes as she readied to attack another sorcerer. Anders watched her expression turn to relief when she realized the burst of energy had come from him and not another attacker.

"Bo!" Kirsten shouted as soon as Anders arrived at her side.

He arched his trajectory to match hers while she ran toward the charred ground and then crawled through the grass where Raffa had torched the crystal bearer. Kirsten fell to her knees at Bo's side, his armored protection cut through by the enemy's energy. Anders doused the burning grass around Bo's downward-facing body while Kirsten keened with worry, her sobbing ringing over the battlefield. Kirsten rolled Bo onto his side and held his limp body. Anders knelt beside them to examine the extent of his injuries. The force of the hurled magic had burned through Bo's metal armor, cutting and burning into his flesh along the length of his entire backside, ending along his neck. Kirsten wept while holding him. Then Anders witnessed something he couldn't explain. Bo's lethal injuries began to steam and the exposed flesh began to heal. He sensed Tarron in his sword, but the magical being wasn't the one healing Bo. Some other presence had stopped the wound from taking Bo's life.

Anders looked to Kirsten, noticing for the first time a pinkish sapphire hanging around her neck on a gold chain. Red veins swelled in her left hand as she cupped Bo's face. When she looked at Bo, Anders recognized the look in her eyes. She felt deeply for Bo and was realizing it in that moment. He had seen the same look in Maija's eyes when he let it slip that he loved her.

Not knowing how or what was keeping Bo alive, Anders told her, "Stay with him and he'll live." Anders rose, looking at Thomas' horrified face. Grabbing him by the shoulder, Anders pinched down hard enough to get his attention. "Protect them," he said, hoping his words got through to his cousin.

Anders now turned his attention to the kurr still attacking into the forest. He connected with Zahara's mental link, *Zahara, have Raffa and Maija continue to burn back the kurr. I need to keep an eye on Kirsten and Thomas while I help out in the forest.* Anders felt her agree and turned his mind to finding Max and Britt.

Locating them, still alive and fighting, Anders moved toward them, felling the kurr that had been blocking them from their fellow soldiers. Anders saw a look of hope flash over their faces, and couldn't help but smile, even in this dire situation. Standing several dead kurr lengths from them, he shouted, "Don't just stand there, we have a battle to win!"

Max and Britt smiled at each other, then rushed

forward, following Anders as he moved to take on more kurr. Gathering survivors in their effort, Anders used a combination of magic and his sword to gain ground against the enemies who'd been cut off between the dragon fire and the rebel army. The army had retreated into the forest. With their numbers growing and the enemy's dwindling, Anders led the rebels to victory while Maija and her red dragon forced the enemy army to flee across the Bareback Plains. Dawn brought a grim visual of the devastation that had occurred on the plain's edge. Anders returned to Zahara, who stood guard with Thomas.

Bo's eyes were open as he rested in Kirsten's arms. Once the kurr had gone, they had removed his armor. In a glance at Zahara, Anders felt her recollection of events. He saw as she had, Thomas and Kirsten removing Bo's armor and Zahara using her remaining magic to bring Bo's wound to a close. It would require more mending, but with the help of whatever presence had stayed his death, Bo appeared to have survived the injury. As Zahara's memory came to an end, Anders saw a fleeting glimpse of Kirsten and Bo locking lips. Zahara had then looked away, giving the humans their privacy. Anders came to their side, a shared grin of hope on all of their faces.

Max ran to the group and wrapped his arms around his brother. At the same time, Thomas grabbed Anders in a heartfelt hug. Anders returned his cousin's embrace, and then saw Kirsten move in toward them. Now in a group hug, the three held onto one another for a minute while laughing with the joy of having survived a battle.

Pulling away, Thomas said, "We should never split up again."

Rubbing his cousin's head in a brotherly way, Anders said, "Letting you go off on your own was the most irrational mistake I've ever made. We're a family and we are better together."

"I can't believe we made it this far without you," Kirsten said, pushing her left hand through her battle-grimed blonde hair.

Anders caught sight of the red veins in her hand and asked, "What happened to your hand?"

Kirsten looked to her hand, examining it as though she didn't even see the red streaks scarring her body. After checking the backside and the palm, she nodded, "Oh, you mean the venom."

"Venom? What venom? Are you alright?" he asked, taking her arm.

He pulled back her chainmail sleeve to see the red lines continue up her forearm and out of sight. Pulling her arm from his grip, she said, "I'm fine now. It would be better if I showed you." Kirsten removed her chainmail shirt and Anders noticed she was insistent that the sapphire necklace didn't lift over her head with the shirt, holding it fast against her chest. As she pulled up the short-sleeved shirt underneath, he could see the white oval where the goblin had taken her flesh. While Anders looked closely, she said, "I was bitten by a goblin when we were fleeing Grandwood. Luckily, we bumped into a surgeon on the road who took us to Solomon's. Once there, these guys found a potion to pull me from my coma. Since then, as long as I have this necklace on, I'm fine."

"A goblin did this?" he asked, ignoring the other points of her story and focusing on what he knew about goblin venom.

"Yeah. Rune said everyone he knows who's been bitten has died if the infected limb isn't removed within the hour," Thomas interjected.

Anders' forehead creased and he considered this development. He wanted to learn more about what drove them from Grandwood and how the old wise man had fared after the battle and how he had returned to Westland so quickly, but he forced the questions from his mind. In all his studying and training to be a dragonrider, he had learned nothing about treating goblin bites. Racking his brain, Anders searched for the answer but didn't know what solution was right. Before he made his decision, he asked, "How did you manage to survive long enough to make it to Solomon's?"

"It was this sapphire necklace," Kirsten said, pointing to the special stone. She pulled back her collar to reveal where the red faded near her heart. "It stopped the venom from reaching my heart and kept me alive while they carried me to Brookside." Anders suddenly identified the presence he had felt, the one that had stopped Bo from being killed by the energy thrashing.

As he thought, Thomas asked, "Can you heal her? So she won't die if the necklace comes off?"

"I have an idea of something that might work," Anders answered, looking at Kirsten. "But it's going to hurt."

Meeting his gaze, Kirsten nodded, "Do it."

Anders withdrew the knife from the backside of his belt. Quickly passing his hand over the knife's edge, he purified the steel of any external contamination. Grabbing Kirsten's left arm, he pulled her close to him. Raising the blade to the white patch of skin where she had been bitten, he asked her, "Ready?" She nodded and Anders cut his knife into her arm, tracing the white flesh.

Kirsten groaned and clenched against the pain, while Anders used his magic to remove the patch of dead skin that had filled the goblin's bite. When he did, Kirsten screamed and passed out, Thomas catching her so Anders could continue without hesitation. Anders focused on his thoughts and used his powers to separate the goblin venom from her blood. Pulling the poison out at its point of entry, Anders drew the venom from Kirsten's veins. As the red liquid floated in the air, Anders saw all those around them take a step back. He lowered the poison to the ground and, with a single word, set the venom on fire. Once the poison was taken care of, Anders turned his magic on restoring Kirsten's flesh. With his magic once again draining from his body, he used his energy to heal his cousin's shoulder.

Stepping back to catch himself from fainting, Anders sourced enough energy from Lazuran's crystal to replace that lost to him in his act of healing. Feeling his lightheadedness subside, he saw Kirsten open her eyes. She looked from Anders to her arm, turning it over to see that the red streaking was gone. She felt at her shoulder and pushed it forward to examine her healed scar. The white patch of dead flesh was gone; as if to verify that what she saw was real, she poked herself with her finger where the bite had been.

Laughing, she said, "I can feel that."

"Go ahead," Anders said, motioning to her necklace. "Take it off."

Kirsten looked to Thomas, then to Bo and the others. They all stood by nervously. Kirsten slowly lifted the sapphire necklace, holding the chain open and hovering over her head. She paused for a moment; when nothing happened, she held the sapphire in her hand at her side.

Kirsten tossed the necklace to Thomas and said, "It's all yours now," then rushed to Anders, hugging him again.

As she thanked him, Anders saw Raffagaun circle in and land near Zahara. As Maija's dragon captured the attention of all those around them, Anders said to Kirsten, "You're welcome. I know you would do the same for me." Anders followed Kirsten's eyes, seeing them train on Maija. The others swarmed around her and her newly bonded dragon. The small group bombarded Maija with questions. Still standing apart from the others, Anders noticed Kirsten's gaze staying on Bo as he leaned against his brother for support. Nudging her with his elbow, he said, "I saw the look when you chose him."

Pulled from her stare by his words, Kirsten asked, "How did you know I was choosing him?"

Anders raised an eyebrow and scoffed, "Really? You think I don't know when one of my own realizes she should be with someone?"

Kirsten shook her head, "That's right, you have that mind-reading gift now."

"It wasn't that," Anders said. "I saw the same look Maija gave me when I told her," Anders paused, "When I told her that I wanted to be with her."

"You approve then?" she asked. "Not that I need it or anything," she quickly added.

Anders nudged her with his elbow again, "I think you picked a good one."

He stepped away from Kirsten and joined the others gathered around Maija. Taking her aside, he said, "We'll need to use our magic to help as many of the wounded as we can. I can teach you the magic to heal superficial injuries, but believe me, you don't want to overdo it. Giving too much of your energy to heal others can kill you. I almost did it to save you, but Zahara came just in time."

There's another way to generate more energy, you know, Tarron's voice sounded into both of their minds.

And how's that achieved? Anders asked, curious as to what else this ancient being could teach them.

I have a feeling you won't like it, but in this particular scenario, you have a surplus of dying energies going to waste.

You're suggesting we steal energy from the dying? Maija asked.

"Stealing" is not the right word, Tarron replied. *You already take the lives of your enemies so willingly. Why not harvest their fleeting energies before they're gone?*

To be clear, Anders said. *You're talking about the kurr and any soldiers operating under Merglan's command?*

That is correct. I can show you how to take the energies of those dying and store them in the crystals. It's actually quite humane, you know. Taking the energy from them will end their suffering quickly and painlessly.

Anders looked to Maija and shrugged, "If it will help save the lives of those fighting for our cause and bring a swift death to the kurr who are already too seriously injured to survive, I don't see the harm in it." From Maija's responding look, he could tell she wasn't quite as eager to harvest the essence of dying kurr. He thought of the way in which Ivan had taken the soul from the green dragon and absorbed its powers and asked, *We won't have to physically remove it, will we? This can be done with magic, like when we use the crystal's energy?*

Precisely, we will do this with magic only. I won't let your hands get dirty, as some would say.

"Okay," Maija said aloud.

Anders nodded and agreed, *Alright Tarron, show us how it's done.*

Riding their dragons to as many of the dying enemy as possible, Anders and Maija filled the sapphires in each of their weapons with life's pure energy, a power source they could use to fuel the healing required by their injured allies. When the sapphires were rich with power, Anders and Tarron instructed Maija in the healing ways as they moved across the battlefield. They were able to save countless more lives than Anders could have the last time he'd used his magic to heal the Rollo warriors in Eastland.

While Anders and Maija finished their work, Anders saw the rebel army forming into ranks. With those in charge leading them to pack up their camp and return to Brookside, Anders could sense the overwhelming satisfaction in knowing that their fighting had been for the preservation of their homeland. The people of Brookside and the surrounding area could return to their homes, no longer fearing an attack from an occupying army. Any survivors among the opposition had fled into the Bareback Plains. If the elements didn't claim them, perhaps the riders of Equine would.

Kirsten and the others searched the battlefield for the two tapped crystals and scavenged any weapons that could be useful in case more of Merglan's forces arrived in the future. Suddenly, a movement in the sky caught Anders' attention. He looked out over the Frozentip Mountains to see a flight of dragons. Anders called to Maija and pointed toward them. Staring at the mass of dragons as they flew northwest over the mountaintops, Anders wondered what could cause such a migration.

He thought perhaps they were taking advantage of the freedom from potential oppression now that Merglan had been subdued. The more he thought about this theory, though, the more he knew it was wrong. Anders felt a pit in his stomach again. His instincts told him something had gone horribly awry in Cedarbridge. In his heart he knew this meant evil would follow. What kind of evil, he did not know.

***

Standing at the bow of his elven ship, Nadir watched as the densely forested coastline of the Glacial Melt Bays faded into the darkness. With their ships weighed down by the extra dwarfs, the elf fleet sailed away from the fallen Everlight Kingdom. He felt a firm hand pat him on the small of his back and saw the dwarf leader at his side. Unable to see over the ship's stern railing, Remli leaned his back against it and crossed his burly arms over his chest.

With the base of the dwarf's thick beard pinned between his arms and chest, he said, "I know exactly how you're feeling."

Nadir glanced down as the dwarf king raised his eyes up at him. "I doubt it," Nadir said with a sigh.

"You weren't the only kingdom to fall," Remli said. "Had it not been for your ships, my people would have been at the mercy of the long-legged beasts that roam the Eastland territories."

Nadir scowled, "Hardstone has fallen? But how?" he asked.

"Dragons," Remli replied.

"But your kingdom has survived hundreds of years of living alongside the wilderness of dragons. How did this come to be?" Nadir asked.

"How is it that Merglan flipped the most secure prison in the five nations on its head?" Remli asked in response.

Shaking his head, Nadir said, "It was planned. That's the only way I see that it could've come to pass. So you think he orchestrated the dragon attack?"

"Why didn't he come burn your ships as we sailed away from Southland? The evil slug had this takeover planned far in advance," Remli responded.

"What happened?" Nadir asked.

"We were all set to meet your ships to carry our army to Southland. My army was marching out the front doors in full, the entire dwarf force. That's when they struck. Dragons by the tens came swooping in, burning and crashing into the entrance. I lost a quarter of my army before they could clear out. I just hope there were survivors to lead those who remained inside through the mines and to safety," Remli said.

"From what I've heard, the way out from the mines isn't exactly safe," Nadir said.

"We haven't had a goblin attack in quite some time," Remli said.

"What of the dragons?" Nadir asked.

Remli shook his head, "They broke through, swarmed the entrance of the city like wasps to a beehive. They covered the entire base of the mountain as we fled, making sneaking into the cave exits impossible. The dragons had to have been given detailed instructions as to what to do. There isn't any other way to explain why wild dragons would band together to attack us, especially with such perfect timing. This was Merglan's doing; I know it and I know he's turned your kingdom inside out."

"All who were able to escape the city are aboard these ships," Nadir said. "A fraction of my army and a host of angry elves and injured citizens."

"Truthfully, I had hoped your army would be greeting us with the ships. With your speed, we might have been able to infiltrate the caves and lead an escape," Remli said. "But now, we are more helpless than if we had stayed in Southland."

"If Anders returns to the city, Merglan will kill him," Nadir said, rubbing his face with worry.

"The boy and his dragon live?" Remli asked.

Nadir nodded, "But for how long depends on his absence from the Everlight Kingdom. He flew after Merglan's apprentice and did not return."

"Hopefully he's realized the events and is purposefully distancing himself from the elf capital," Remli said.

A light emanating from behind him forced Nadir to look over his shoulder. An elf carried his family's pocket mirror, the one he used to communicate with Natalia. Thanking the elf, Nadir looked to see Natalia's war-weary face staring back at him. "Natalia, I've been trying to reach you. Merglan has taken over our capital."

Natalia shook her head, "No, that's not possible! There were thousands of orcs that came from the east, but Merglan wasn't with them."

Nadir frowned, not understanding her explanation.

Remli stood on his toes trying to see Natalia in the

mirror. With a strained voice, he said, "Maylox, is she there? Does my daughter live?"

"Remli?" Natalia asked, raising in the mirror to try to look down on him as if she were looking through a window. Nadir was about to tell her it didn't work like that when he decided to hold the mirror out so she could see them both.

"She's on another ship," Natalia said. "Your daughter lives but has suffered an injury."

"What kind? Was she wearing her armor?" Remli asked, fear in his voice.

"Broken leg," Natalia said. "I was able to set the bone before we were forced to leave Kingston."

"You said there were orcs?" Nadir asked, realizing what she meant earlier.

"We weren't expecting them," Natalia said. "After we were forced from the castle, they swarmed the city through the east entrance. The Lumbapi and Rollo Islanders didn't see them coming until they were at the front lines."

"The Rollo Islanders?" Nadir asked.

"A number of them must have listened to Anders' plea and sailed to the Ramhorn. There the Lumbapi and Rollo warriors launched an attack while we infiltrated the castle," Natalia said.

"Did you find Ivan?" Nadir asked, knowing they needed his guidance now more than ever.

Nadir saw Natalia lower her eyes and chew at the inside of her lip before responding. "Sort of," she replied.

"What does that mean?" Remli asked.

Nadir looked more closely into the mirror as she explained, "I found his presence, his mind or possibly his soul." She reached out of the frame for a moment and returned with a wooden box that just covered her palm. "It's in here," she said pointing to the box. "I haven't figured out how to make contact, but Ivan's body was not inside the castle. I saw his clothes, but only his mind or soul was present. I searched every inch of the place once I realized Merglan wasn't there." Suddenly, she looked concerned, "What did you mean, Merglan has taken over the capital?"

Nadir explained the events of Merglan's faked capture and his control over the evils in the prison. He informed her of Remli's kingdom falling to the dragons and of Anders and Maija chasing the black rider.

"Maija was on the scarlet dragon?" she asked.

Nadir nodded, "She hadn't bonded, but they rode together and fought the kurr and drove away the rider in black."

Natalia nodded more to herself, and said, "It's coming to pass."

"What is?" Nadir asked.

"'A son of a King and the daughter of the veiled huntress will come on the backs of dragons,'" she quoted the Prophecy. "Anders is Ivan's son, the true King of the human nations, and Maija, she's the daughter of the veiled huntress."

Nadir furrowed his brow, "But wouldn't you also be a daughter of the veiled huntress then?"

Natalia nodded, "We both are, but my opportunity passed with the death of my dragon. As I have come to learn from the passing of a dear friend, our mother is known in Southland as the 'veiled huntress.'"

"Who died?" Nadir asked.

"Many, I'm afraid, but the death I speak of is that of a

former King in Southland. Solomon the wise has died," she said sadly.

Nadir stared into the mirror as her explanation of the events washed over him. He had known that the king before Kaufen had abdicated, but he didn't know it was Solomon, the human who'd been so helpful to those in need during The War of the Magicians.

"Nadir," he heard Natalia say to regain his attention. "What should we do? Cedarbridge was the one place where Merglan couldn't touch us."

"We need to retreat, to an island or somewhere where we can see him coming from a long way off," Nadir said.

"The Rollo Islands are the most remote," Natalia suggested.

Nadir nodded, "I agree. Now we just need to convince Red to house us for the betterment of humanity."

"I believe Red has lost some of his control over his clans," Natalia said. "Otherwise they would've stayed in Argon and not come to our aid."

Nadir nodded, "Let's hope our arrival doesn't start another war."

"What about my sister and Anders?" Natalia asked. "They need to know what's happening."

"We don't have a way to contact them," Nadir said. Natalia searched the corner of the mirror and Nadir could tell she was struggling to find an answer. "We must have faith in the Prophecy," he said, breaking their silence. "If Anders and Maija are meant to destroy Merglan, we must trust in their ability to survive."

"You mentioned the rider in black was headed for Brookside?" Natalia asked.

Nadir nodded, seeing where she was going, "And we'll be passing by on our way to the Islands."

"Stop and see if they're there. If you don't find them quickly, spread the word that Merglan is in the elf capital and hope that they don't go searching for him. Perhaps they'll think as we have and seek us out in the Islands," Natalia said.

"I can leave a message with a reliable source if they're not there. I trust there are more humans on our side now that this war has reached other nations," Nadir said.

"As you said, we must trust in the Prophecy now. It's all we have left," Natalia said.

Nadir nodded, "Keep me updated on your status each morning. If I don't hear from you, I'll know something has happened and I'll turn our ships to the Kewian Islands. They are within reach of Southland, but they'll be better than landing on Southland itself."

"Good luck," Natalia said, and Nadir saw the light fade from the mirror, the reflection returning to that of a looking glass.

As Nadir pocketed the mirror and looked out to the evening sea, he felt a sense of purpose again. Keeping his gaze on the Marauder's Sea at their bow, Nadir said, "We may be fallen kings, unseated from our thrones and leaving our kingdoms in ruin, but at least we are together in this struggle."

"It would seem the fall of Kartania's kings has driven us together now more than ever. In this I have faith that our peoples will survive," Remli said, his thoughts resonating with Nadir's as they sailed toward an uncertain future.

GET THE BOND OF A DRAGON PREQUEL NOVELLA FREE AND A HANDCRAFTED MAP OF KARTANIA!

The best thing about being a writer in today's world is being able to connect with my readers. I want to build lasting relationships with anyone who enjoys the fantastical world I've created. If you sign up with my mailing list, I'll occasionally send out updates about new releases, special offers and giveaways and other pieces of news about the characters from Bond of a Dragon series, as well as what's going on in my writing life.

If you choose to sign up for my mailing list, I'll send you these free items:

- An eBook copy of the Bond of a Dragon series' prequel novella, Dragon Wars: War of the Magicians.
- A hand-crafted map of Kartania, the fantasy world I've created for my stories!

You can get the prequel, a novella of +30,000 words, and map, for free, by signing up here:
https://www.subscribepage.com/w9t1m7

Enjoy this book? You can make a big difference by leaving a review…

Reviews by readers like you are by far the most powerful tool in my cache when it comes down to receiving attention for my books. Where as New York publishers have the budget to take out full page ads in the newspaper or entire posters on the subway, I unfortunately don't have that kind of budget for advertising; not yet at least.

What I do have, that is without a doubt more powerful and effective than paid ads and something that those big-time publishers would kill to get their hands on, is **a group of loyal and committed readers like you.**

Valued and honest reviews by my readers will help see my books into the hands of other readers who'd enjoy discovering these stories.

If you've enjoyed this book, I would greatly appreciate it if you could spend just a few minutes of your time and leave a review (it can be as short as you want) on whichever platform you purchased my book.

Thank you very much.

ACKNOWLEDGMENTS

I want to thank all those who've helped me in creating the Bond of a Dragon series. This idea started when I was a young man and has grown into this magnificent story it is because of the help and inspiration of many people. Thanks to my parents, family and friends for their support and encouragement along the way. Many of you might find it hard to believe that reading and writing didn't come naturally to me, as I am severely dyslexic. I wouldn't have developed the skills necessary to create these works without the support from my family. Thanks to Susan, the brilliant woman who spent long hours combing through my many mistake-ridden drafts. Your help has been instrumental in creating these stories. Thank you to my loving wife who's always inspired me to chase my dreams and desires no matter how ridiculous or far-fetched they may seem. And Thanks to you, the reader, for allowing me to express my creativity on these pages.

Special thanks to:
Susan Penner – copy and developmental editor
Mark Reid at authorpackages.com – cover design
Lorna Reid at authorpackages.com – book formatting
Maggie Walker – Kartania Map, watercolor
Team Kartania – Members of my Advanced Reader Team

ABOUT THE AUTHOR

A J Walker is a Montana author and creator of the Bond of a Dragon series. If you would like to find out more him or the fantasy world he's created you can check out his website ajwalkerauthor.com. You can connect with A J on the Bond of a Dragon Facebook group here or you can send him an email at ajwalker@ajwalkerauthor.com.

Follow A J Walker on:

Facebook
https://www.facebook.com/ajwalkerauthor/

Instagram
https://www.instagram.com/ajwalkerauthor/

Amazon
http://amazon.com/author/ajwalkerauthor.com

Bookbub
https://www.bookbub.com/authors/a-j-walker-561f93ab-fe88-41c0-a6a2-e5df95ab08f8

Goodreads
https://www.goodreads.com/author/show/17915073.A_J_Walker

characters, then you'll love A J Walker's prequel-novella.

Pick up Dragon Wars: War of the Magicians for free and embark on the adventure of a lifetime today!

Free Download
https://dl.bookfunnel.com/lom634bvx4

Bond of a Dragon Book One
Bond of a Dragon: Zahara's Gift

A young man forced into action. A juvenile dragon alone in a new world. Whispers of a terrible evil returning to power.

Nineteen-year-old Anders lived a fairly normal life until the only family he had was taken away from him. When he finds himself forced to embark on an action packed adventure, he discovers there is more to the world than he was told. The magical force that flows within everything around him becomes revealed. Dragons, elves, orcs, and goblins lurk around nearly every turn along the path as he pursues his two kidnapped cousins.

As Anders discovers more about his family's past, he learns of their involvement in The War of The Magicians and the circumstances leading up to the attack of his hometown. When Anders is told about his potential involvement in a prophecy involving dragons and their powerful magic, he will need to make a difficult decision. Will he continue to follow the path that is laid out for him or can he make his own destiny? Will he ever be reunited with his family again? And if he succeeds, will he ever be able to return to the life he once knew?

Bond of a Dragon: Zahara's Gift is the first book in an adventure fantasy series.

If you like fast-paced adventure novels, fierce dragons, powerful magic, and a hero fighting for justice, then you'll love the fantastic starter in A. J. Walker's new page turning series.

Unlock Bond of a Dragon: Zahara's Gift to embark on this great adventure today!

Bond of a Dragon Book Two
Bond of a Dragon: Secrets of the Sapphire Soul

A dragon and her rider put to the test. Betrayal among allies. With Kartania's fate in the balance, who will take control?

Anders knows the war to stop Merglan from reclaiming his grip on the world is just beginning. With no certainty about where or when Merglan will attack next, Anders and his companions must take action to stay one step ahead of the cruel sorcerer and his evil dragon.

As he searches for ways to stop Merglan's domination of their world, Anders discovers more than he expected. With several nations of Kartania on the brink of collapse, he must make a difficult decision. Is the young rider ready to deal with the consequences he's facing? Can Anders overcome the odds and unravel the secrets of the sapphire soul?

Bond of a Dragon: Secrets of the Sapphire Soul is the second novel in an adventure fantasy series.

If you like gripping suspense, bold dragonriders, and page-turning action, then you'll love A J Walker's latest installment in the Bond of a Dragon series.

Discover Secrets of the Sapphire Soul by picking up a copy today!

Bond of a Dragon Book Three
Bond of a Dragon: Fall of the Kings

Anders is lost and without guidance. Merglan's imperial grip tightens on the free nations. A Resistance movement arises to combat venomous magic, but is it too late? In the end, all kings must fall.

When Anders awakens in a foreign land, he finds himself far from the campaign in Southland and anxious to get back. The sapphire's intoxicating grip has given him more than just a craving for power. Its tainted magic pushes him closer to the precipice of becoming more like the evil that he is foretold to destroy. In his attempts to resist the darkness, Anders must work through his pain before he can return to the fight he abandoned so suddenly.

After the allied armies are forced to disband, the five nations begin to feel the effects of the dark sorcerer's imperial rule. Foreign invaders occupy Westland. Southland is flooded with orcs. Humans and dwarfs must band together in resistance. Unlike the elves, who can hide behind their magically protected walls, the other races in Kartania's kingdoms are drastically affected by the absence of an allied dragonrider. With the fate of Kartania hanging in the balance, will these various allegiances unite to combat Merglan's expansion? Can Anders work with his dragon, Zahara, gain back what advantage they once had? Will Kirsten survive long enough to see Westland's revolt? What has become of Ivan and those left behind in Southland?

Bond of a Dragon: Fall of the Kings is the third

installment in the Bond of a Dragon series. This highly suspenseful and emotional tale builds to a crescendo in the final chapters; don't miss out on this epic by A J Walker.

Get your copy of Fall of the Kings to continue your dragonrider experience!

For news and updates joining my mailing list!
ajwalkerauthor.com

DEDICATION
To the reader. Cheers to you and yours.